Dirty Candy

Zane Menzy

He's drunk he tastes like candy he's so beautiful.

He's so deep like dirty water. God, he's awful.

PROLOGUE

Six months earlier

The dingy motel room reeked of nasty sex and regret. And the sex wasn't even over yet. Shay's feet dangled in the air while the old man gripped him by the ankles, nailing his arse at a heart-hammering pace. With a clenched jaw, and praying to Jesus for the first time in years, Shay rode the pain as his sphincter caught vicious fuck-punch after vicious fuck-punch.

"That's it," the old man huffed. "Your pussy loves my big dick, doesn't it?"

"Yes, Dave," Shay panted. "I love it. Really love it."

He had lost track of how many minutes his rectum had been getting pummelled but he knew they'd been fucking for quite some time. The pain was diabolical but he just stared up at the ceiling and let the grey-haired geezer fuck him like his life depended on it. But that's because Shay's life did depend on it. If he didn't leave this room pleasing the two men taking turns to fuck his arse then Shay's days were numbered. It was only a matter of time before one of Shay's dealer's henchmen caught up with him and when they did Shay knew his life would be ended in ways much more painful than taking a dick up his blurter.

The other man, a fat Samoan dude called Sione, stood beside the much older Dave and watched Shay's tormented face with intrigue. Sione had already lost his lollies—right down Shay's throat. It had tasted fucking horrible but Shay had swallowed every drop like it was fizzy drink, desperate to impress his potential employers.

Now I just need this old white bastard to bust his nut.

At least there was less talking now that Sione had cum. Before the fat fuck had blown his load over Shay's tongue, the pair had been much chattier together while they had taken turns fucking Shay's arse and mouth, flipping him around the bed to use and abuse both ends of his body. While doing so, they had spoken casually to one another other about how tight his "boy pussy" was while passing judgement about different parts of his body.

"His arse ain't perfect but I'd still give it a solid eight out of ten," one of them had grunted.

"Yep. I'd agree with that," the other had replied. "What about the upper body?"

"He's in pretty good shape but you can tell the drugs have dragged him down a bit. Nothing a healthy diet and a few weeks in the gym won't fix though."

The most mortifying part of the ordeal had been when Dave had ordered Shay to get his cock hard. It hadn't been easy with a dick in his mouth and one fucking his arse but Shay had tugged his pecker for all he was worth until finally he was rock-hard. When he had removed his hand from his shaft to reveal his six-and-a-bit inches he was horrified to hear Sione say, "Do you think his dick will be a problem?"

A contemplative sigh had followed from Dave.

"Probably not. We already have our resident top so he doesn't need to be a big boy."

Such callous comments about his manhood should have been mortifying but Shay had been too horrified by the echo of Dave's wrinkly ballbags slapping his arse cheeks to be offended at the time.

Shay was brought back to the current moment when Dave suddenly unwedged his cock from his anus and leaned forward, rubbing his sweaty palms up and down Shay's torso. The man's wandering hands felt gross, numerous rough callouses scraping Shay's skin.

Shay stilled, bunching the sheet in his fists while Dave's gnarled fingers caressed his torso, exploring his armpits and belly, making Shay want to writhe from the ticklish contrails. He did his best to hold still and just sweated into the bed and prayed his *audition* would be over soon.

As Dave's hands scraped up and down Shay's body, the older man's drooling knob knocked at Shay's balls and taint, leaving dabs of precum to dry on his skin. Dave gripped Shay's nipples, pinched and rubbed them, making Shay hiss out loud.

"Someone's got sensitive titties," Dave said, smirking.

Shay tried to settle his breathing. Thank God he was still high. If it wasn't for the drugs there was no way he'd have been able to remain so calm at having some old git use him like a blow-up doll.

"I need you to get hard again for me, son," Dave said. "But this time I need to see you cum as well. We gotta know what your cumshots are like."

Shay nodded and wrapped his fingers around his deflated dick, tugging it back to life. He closed his eyes to conjure up sexy fantasies, praying that his dick could deliver a respectable eruption. He was pretty confident it would, provided he could actually get turned on enough to blow.

The whole time he masturbated he could feel the two men scrutinizing his squirming body, no doubt sizing him up to see if he was worthy. With his eyes still closed, he fantasized about his ex-girlfriend Casey, imagining her wet cunt sliding up and down his pole. It helped. Helped a lot. After several minutes, he began to leak little moans as he felt the orgasm brewing in his balls. "I-I'm close," he stuttered.

"Show us what you got, boy," Dave ordered.

Shay cupped his balls and pressed a finger against his taint, just hard enough to pull the trigger. He let out an exhausted cry that was half-shriek, half-moan. His muscles locked and his toes curled as he shook and shuddered with the power of release. He opened his eyes just in time to watch the first white ribbon fire from his prick, it splattered over his abdomen, followed by another four more powerful shots that wet his chest and collarbone.

The peak of pleasure and intensity ebbed, and then he relaxed, the complete physical release of climax accomplished. The shudders passed, and the calm bliss of post ejaculation came in soothing waves. He watched as the last dregs of sperm dribbled out of his prick and wet his pubes. He panted loudly, trying to enjoy the usual afterglow that accompanied an orgasm but it was short-lived. He was too fucking nervous and felt far too embarrassed.

"Not bad," Sione said. "Not bad at all."

"But now for the real test," Dave said. He swiped a finger through the pearly mess on Shay's chest and slipped the soiled digit in his mouth. He mashed his lips together, a contemplative look on his face before declaring, "Typical half-breed. You boys nearly always fall into the sweet category."

Ignoring the pompous prick's casual racism, Shay hoped like hell that was a good category to be in.

Dave reached down and scooped up more cum and Sione followed suit. When they'd both finished with the taste test, they nodded at one another before Dave rammed his fuck-meat right back inside Shay's shitter.

"Oh fuck!" Shay cried out, immediately overcome with the same burning pain as before. He swore it hurt more now that he'd cum.

Dave didn't start slow like he had the first time he'd inserted his cock. Every lunge was long and deep, his crusty old balls making sweaty slaps against Shay's arse. The way his thick cock withdrew nearly all the way out and slammed back in with brutal aggression told Shay this was not going to be a marathon. It was going to be a sprint. A fast and furious fuck that would leave his arsehole stretched and sore.

Shay's head bobbed around while Dave raped his hole, skewering him like kebab meat, again and again. The man's fucking was different to before. It was darker, more primal somehow, as if he were teaching Shay obedience and humility through terrifying, hate-filled ruts.

"That's it, bitch," Dave grunted. "Take that cock."

Shay's head bobbed around while Dave raped his hole, skewering him like kebab meat, again and again. This wasn't how he'd imagined the audition to go. He had been expecting pain, and maybe some embarrassment, but what he hadn't counted on was being made feel less than human. To Shay's relief though, he could hear Dave's pants getting more urgent, more desperate, the older man's body tensing like he was close.

"Here it comes, sunshine," Dave damn near shouted. "Here. It. Fucking. Cooomes!"

Shay choked on a gasp when he felt Dave's dick twitch

inside him, spewing hot liquid deep inside his cavity. The force behind the powerful jets took him by surprise and the volume of Dave's semen was overwhelming.

Dave chuckled when he saw the shocked look on Shay's face. "That's my jizz, son. Take it. Take it all. You earnt it." When his cock had stopped twitching and spurting, Dave said, "Can you feel how special this moment is? You just received a blessing in your new cunt."

Oh my God…

Absolute shame throbbed in Shay's heart. Its trembling grew violent, stabbing deep into his bones. He lay frozen in place, overcome from the sensation of knowing Dave had just emptied his balls inside him. He felt broken and small, and way too fucking vulnerable. After such destructive intimacy, Shay had the weird yearning for a hug, or at least an affectionate rub. But all he got was a slap on the thigh before Dave ungraciously yanked his cock out of Shay's ravaged pit and wiped it clean on Shay's lower leg.

Dave crouched down to inspect the damage he'd caused. "Would you look at that," he said, his breath stroking Shay's gaping slit. "Look how pink and puffy his pussy lips are."

The old man's sidekick knelt down beside him, staring at Shay's wrecked shitter with absolute wonder. "It's a beautiful sight when they get broken in like this."

"It sure fucking is," Dave agreed, stabbing a finger inside Shay's cum-filled orifice. He sawed it in and out a few times, filling the room with lurid squelching noises.

Shay groaned in embarrassment. He couldn't believe he'd just let himself get fucked in the arse, something he never thought he would do. His love of pussy was too strong to ever resort to cock and he'd certainly never been short of female admirers, yet here he was, laid naked on a crumby motel bed with a baby boomer's spunk dripping out of his now-gaping arsehole.

But it had to be done, he told himself. *There was no other way.*

Dave rose to his feet and stared down at Shay's defiled body. "Cheers for that, sunshine." He tugged on Shay's dick. "Now go take a shower while me and Sione talk in private for a moment."

Shay lifted his head and saw Sione nodding in the direction of the bathroom. He slowly stood up, grimacing at the feel of semen slipping out of his butthole. He bundled up his clothes and staggered into the bathroom and closed the door behind him.

Underneath the hot water of the shower, he closed his eyes and desperately tried to wash away the stench of man sweat that clung to his body. It was everywhere. Both men had perspired heavily atop of him, soaking him in a strong stench of male pheromones. When he was finally showered and dressed, Shay entered the bedroom again and found that Sione had gone. Dave was now fully-dressed and sat alone at a small table by the window. He motioned for Shay to come and join him at the table.

Shay wandered over and sat down. In front of him was an open folder with a bunch of papers. *It's a contract!* This looked promising. "Have I got the job?" he asked excitedly.

"Hold your horses, sunshine." Dave raised an eyebrow. "Are you sure this is something you want to do?"

"I'm sure." The words left Shay's mouth at lightning speed. Of course he was sure. He didn't have a choice in the matter. If he didn't get this job then he was fucking dead.

"But are you *absolutely* sure?"

Shay was surprised by Dave's questioning. He would have thought Dave would have wanted him to sign immediately. After all, it was Dave who had approached him about the job, not the other way around.

"Yeah, bro. Absolutely sure."

Dave shot him a deadpan look. "I'm not your *bro*, sunshine, so don't ever call me that."

"Sorry, man."

"Or man. My name is Dave."

Someone's a bit fucking precious. "Sorry, Dave."

"Now the reason I want to make sure you are positive you want this job is because it isn't an easy job, which is why it is so well-paid."

"I understand."

"And you understand that you will be getting paid to do exactly the kind of thing me and Sione just did to you on the bed, right?"

Shay nodded. "I do."

"And you're fine with that? You don't care if men ram their cock up that cute Māori boy arse of yours or make you lick their sweaty balls? Every day for the next twelve months?"

"It's fine by me. I-I don't care."

"Really? But you're straight, aren't you?" Dave's eyes narrowed to suspicious slits. "I would have thought you might care just a little bit?"

Shay tugged on his earlobe, worrying if he'd given a wrong answer. "Uh, I can be gay if you need me to be."

Dave laughed. "What I need you to be is honest, son."

"Then, yeah, I'd say I'm straight. But I'm really openminded."

"Even so. Does it bother you at all? And remember. Be honest."

Shay chewed his lip, nearly drawing blood. He couldn't lie. "Yes. It bothers me but I really, really need this job, Dave. My life literally depends on it."

"I understand your situation, sunshine. You have told us numerous times," Dave said in an impassive tone, sounding like he didn't give a shit if Shay lived or died. "What I want to know is do you think you can give up pussy for a whole year? Because that is how long this contract is for?"

"I've been to prison before. Not for a year but I've done two six-month stints and my hand got me through just fine."

"And how will you cope with the day in and day out of having sex with my male clients? Unless you were the cellblock bitch then I am assuming sucking dick and being fucked anally is not something you are accustomed to."

"I was never touched in prison," Shay said firmly. "But I will cope with it just fine."

"How?" Dave challenged him with a firm gaze.

"Money," Shay replied, returning an equally hard glare. "I will think of the money."

Dave grinned. "Perfect. That's the spirit we are looking for." He pulled a sheet of paper out of the folder in front of him and slid it across the table.

"Does this mean I have the job?"

Dave took a deep breath and exhaled slowly as he admired Shay's face. "You are a handsome lad but you're not what we normally go for. However, there is something about you that caught my eye and…" he left the sentence hanging like a dream without an ending. It was becoming unbearable until finally he said, "I think you are worth taking a gamble on."

Shay leapt up from his chair and gave Dave a hug. "Thank you. Thank you. Thank you."

"Alright, alright." Dave pushed him away. "Settle the fuck down, son."

"Sorry." Shay sat back down, grinning ear to ear. "I'm just so grateful. You've just saved my arse so much."

"Fucked it and saved it one day, huh?"

Shay laughed edgily. "Yeah. I guess you could say that." He began tapping his foot, unbound energy rushing through his body.

"Now I need to run through the contract with you before I get you to sign, okay?"

Shay glanced down and the first thing he noticed was the word *Pet* in black bold writing. "Pet?"

"That's your job title. Maybe I am a sentimental old fool but I consider the boys who work for me as my pets. I love you all and make sure I take good care of you."

"Awesome," Shay said, despite thinking it was rather creepy.

"Usually I sign a lad up for two years but you're a bit older than what we normally go for so we are just going to hire you for the one year on $120,000 so I hope that is fine with you?"

"That's more than fine." Shay couldn't believe his luck. This felt like winning the lotto.

Dave reached down beside his chair and picked up another folder which he retrieved a sheet of paper from. His eyes skimmed over the paper just briefly before focusing again on Shay. "I see here that your blood tests came back all clear which is great. You will continue to have medical check-ups but they will be carried out on site once a month from a member of my team. In this industry it is essential that you remain fit and healthy to protect yourself and the client. Another part of being healthy is keeping fit which is why we have a gym in the building for the pets to use and we expect you boys to work out regurlarly. When you arrive, Sione will write up a personalised fitness plan for you and you will be expected to follow it. Is that understood?"

Shay nodded, secretly finding it funny that a man as fat as Sione would come up with fitness plans for other people.

"Now I want you to know that while being a pet can be hard work and challenging at times, we also have your best interests at heart and will make sure you are taken care of. That means we provide you with accommodation and food for the entirety of your stay. And no, it does not come out of your payment. But in return for our generosity we expect the pets to follow the rules."

Shay sat there nodding as an avalanche of words continued to pour out of the older man's mouth as he explained the ins and outs of the business and what was expected of him. Shay took little notice. He just needed his name on that piece of paper ASAP. He let Dave ramble on while he daydreamed how he would spend all that money when he had finished his year's work.

Shay flinched and snapped out of his daydream when Dave jabbed the table with his thick finger. He looked down and saw that Dave was pointing at a particular line of the contract. "You will see here that I have put you on what is called a *tier one* contract."

"What's that mean?" Shay asked, scratching at the noticeable tic in his jaw.

"A tier one means you will only be working with our upstairs clients. If you were on a tier two then you would be expected to work downstairs as well."

"It sounds so Downton Abbey," Shay joked. "What's the difference?"

"Our upstairs clients are the men who are more what you would call vanilla. The work is far less demanding and doesn't pay as much. The pets who work downstairs are dealing with men who have more *creative tastes* and so they get rewarded for the added effort."

"How much more do they get rewarded?"

"A substantial amount," Dave said cryptically. "I'm not

promising anything but if you work hard and impress me I may consider upgrading your contract at some point down the line."

Shay nodded again. To be honest he wasn't sure what he thought about this tier two business, he was just grateful to be getting a contract at all. Not only did this contract save his life but it meant he would be able to live in a proper house again. Eat decent food. No more having to get washed in public toilets. To avoid being killed the past two months, he'd taken to living in an old burnt-out bus on the edge of Brixton, living off whatever he could steal from houses and cars and shops.

"And one last thing," Dave said.

"Yeah?"

Dave's finger went to a line in tiny font near the bottom. "This here explains how I have the right to be serviced by you whenever and however I please."

"Oh…" Shay looked warily at his new employer. He already knew working for Dave would be dodgy on some level—the man just had that sort of vibe about him—but that line confirmed it. Still, it was a lot less dodgy than owing money to drug dealers who had threatened to chop his cock off before slitting his throat.

"Is that going to be a problem for you?"

"Nope." Shay shook his head. "You're the boss."

"Good." Dave handed Shay the pen. "Now all I need is your signature and we can officially welcome you to the family."

Instead of scanning the contract with due caution, Shay quickly flipped to the last page and scribbled his name on the dotted line. He just wanted to get the money and save his life from the constant threat of danger. He handed Dave back the pen and signed contract, and sat there bouncing his leg.

Dave checked his signature then put the contract back inside the folder. "This contract gives me a lot of power over you but I can assure you I won't abuse it. For starters I am not actually at The Castle all that often. Maybe two or three days a week. So you don't have to worry about me pestering you the whole time."

"The Castle?" Shay frowned. "What's that?"

"That, sunshine, is where you will be living. It's the name of our establishment. You'll see why it's called that when you get there."

"Coolies."

"And I hope you play well with others because you'll be living with three other pets; Twitch, Ace and Jock."

Shay snorted. "What's with the weird names?"

"Those are their pet names. When you arrive at The Castle you won't be Shay anymore. You'll have a pet name too. Now what you boys call each other in your downtime is your business but in my presence I expect only to hear pet names used."

You really are a weird fucker, old man. Shay hid his derision at the idea of pet names behind a curious smile. "What will my pet name be?"

Dave thumbed his chin, taking his time to respond. "Considering how pink and puffy my cock made your pussy lips then I think the name Pinky is quite fitting."

"What the fuck?" Shay blurted. "Pinky?"

Dave glowered. "Do you have a problem with that name?"

Shay had a huge problem with the name but he was too scared of Dave ripping up the contract to voice his opinion. "No problem. It's just that..." his voice faded.

"Just that?"

"It'll take a bit of getting used to," Shay answered with a slight catch in his voice. "That's all."

Dave's annoyance receded and he smiled. "Don't worry, Pinky, you will get used to it soon enough."

Shay cringed inwardly, hating the name and hating even more the story behind why he'd been christened it.

"Speaking of names," Dave added. "I expect my pets to either address me as sir or daddy. Call me old-fashioned but I like there to be respect between an employer and his subordinates."

"Okay… *sir*?" Shay's voice came out more like a question than an actual response.

"If I'm being honest I actually prefer it when my pets call me Daddy but sir is fine."

There is no fucking way I am calling you daddy, bro. No fucking way.

"I think you will be very happy at The Castle, Pinky," Dave said, leaning over the table and stroking the side of Shay's face. "I can't wait for the other pets to meet you."

Shay smiled, his skin crawling where Dave's calloused hand had touched him. "So what happens now?" he asked.

"You have 24 hours to do whatever you want before coming back and meeting us here at the motel tomorrow. Once you're here Sione will go with you to pay this drug debt of yours. Consider than an advance. Then we will drive you straight to a rehab facility where you will stay for the next thirty days before we come and get you to start work." Dave stared at Shay's trembling leg. "I won't tolerate drugs or alcohol in my business so I expect my pets to be drug free… which you clearly are not."

Shay wasn't looking forward to rehab and giving up the one thing he'd used as an escape the past seven years but the decision was out of his hands. "Is there anything I need to do before I come back here tomorrow?"

"I suggest you go get high one last time and fuck as much pussy as you can because it will be a while before you taste any." Dave laughed.

Shay laughed too, even though it wasn't a laughing matter. He slowly stood up and thanked his new boss once again for saving his life.

Just before he made it to the door, Dave called out. "Pinky…?"

Shay turned around. "Yes, sir?"

"How about giving me a quick blowie before you go? All this talk about business has got me horny again." Dave pulled his cock out of his pants then rose from his chair and walked over to where Shay was standing. "It'll do you good to get used to the taste of Daddy's dick."

Heartbeat.

Blink.

Heartbeat.

Blink. Blink.

Blink.

Shay gazed down at the old man's ugly pecker that had already been buried deep inside his tortured arsehole. It didn't look dirty but it didn't look entirely clean either and he knew it would probably taste like his own shit. He swallowed the lump in his throat and for just a split-second he wondered if he'd made a mistake signing the contract.

"Daddy's waiting, Pinky?" Dave's sour breath wafted over his face. "Get down on your knees where you belong."

With a sigh of defeat, Shay slowly dropped to his knees and opened his mouth for *Daddy*.

CHAPTER 1

This is pretty fucking crazy, Levi thought.

But he didn't stop driving.

Navigating along the bumpy terrain, Levi white-knuckled the steering wheel and swallowed his rising trepidation. The peaceful countryside with its patches of forest blurred past him as he motored along the lonely dusty road towards a meeting with a man he didn't really know. The little he did know about Demon Dave was that he was a hardcore kinkster, lived in the middle of nowhere, and had some sort of connection to Shay Jacobs.

The video Demon Dave had sent of Shay was disturbing to say the least. Like Shay, the video was hot as hell, but that didn't make it any less ominous. Something about the way Shay hung from a scaffolding-like contraption while his cock was hooked to a pumping tube milking him of all his cum reeked of nasty darkness. Levi's former babysitter did not look like he was hanging there willingly, and the sounds he had made—peaking moans and wallowing wails—fluctuated in a limbo of agonizing pleasure.

Yep. This is definitely crazy.

Crazy or not, Levi didn't have much choice about today's meeting. His father's body was missing and he needed to find out from Shay what the hell he'd done with the corpse. Just thinking about Shay digging up the body sent a shiver down Levi's spine. Barry Buttwell had looked gross enough freshly dead so Levi dreaded to think how bad the man would have looked decomposing.

Why the hell would you dig him up you bloody idiot?

The answer to that wasn't overly important, all that mattered now was finding out where his father's remains were. If the body had been buried in another part of Wairua Valley then it ran the risk of being dug up when the housing development went ahead, and there was no fucking way Levi could let that happen since he'd foolishly forgotten to empty his father's pockets that night and had let his mother and Shay bury the man with his cell phone still on him. Not only would the phone easily reveal Barry Buttwell's identity but it would also expose a house of horrors and would lead to the three of them being arrested.

Ridding himself of visions of being in prison, Levi took a sip on the can of coke sitting in the drink holder beside him. The cool fizz eased his parched tongue and slid down his throat in a cooling manner until it bubbled in his belly. He put the drink back down and looked out the window at the countryside he was passing through. Aside from Ureweras, you'd be hard pressed to find an area more remote than this in the North Island, he thought.

According to the map on his phone, the road he was travelling on was called the Forgotten Highway. The word forgotten seemed about right but it was less a highway and more a shitty skinny path that bumped his car all over the road, the journey filled with narrow tunnels cut through the grey clay of cliffs blocking the path. More than once he'd had to slam his brakes on to avoid hitting roaming cattle. The big black beasts would just stare at him like he was the one where he shouldn't be.

After forty minutes of driving along the Forgotten Highway, he turned onto an even more isolated road, one that felt like it would never end. The paddocks were beginning to give way to more and more forest and he hadn't seen a house for miles. The trees grew tall with branches reaching over the road like they were trying to shake hands with their counterparts on the other side. The darkness created by this natural tunnel was ominous, like he was driving into the unknown. Which in a way Levi supposed he was.

Although he was coming here to speak with Shay about his father's missing body, that wasn't the reason he'd been invited. He was driving to meet Demon Dave under the pretence of discussing with him the offer of financial help.

Demon Dave's short message offering financial assistance had been abundantly vague, as had been all the follow-up messages that had included an address and a preferred day and time for Levi to visit so they could discuss "an arrangement." What the arrangement was Levi did not know but he was pretty damn sure it would be sexual in nature.

Levi had inflicted the shame of whoredom on others in the past so he knew to tread carefully when it came to any deal that was presented. Easy money was never easy money. He also knew there was a fine line between profiting from one's beauty and becoming a prostitute. He'd spent the past couple of days wondering where that line was and how far he could push things before crossing it. The guys he'd paid for sex in the past were always pushed past the line, their bodies and morals corrupted past the point of saving. Some of the guys were just grateful for the money, oblivious to what they'd just become, but most left the room with regret etched onto their flustered faces. They knew that till the day they died they would walk around with a price tag. It seemed contradictory but the truth was that in this instance to know your worth was to feel worthless.

"But desperate times call for desperate measures," he muttered to himself.

Driving three hours south through remote backroads to a house in the arse-end of nowhere to meet a man he didn't know to talk about a deal he knew nothing about seemed to meet the definition of desperate measures. So yep, he probably would consider blurring the lines a little today if Demon Dave made the right kind of offer. He certainly would not let Demon Dave fuck him, but if the guy wanted to suck his toes or give him a full body massage then Levi could have his arm twisted for the right price.

It seemed ridiculous that someone from the wealthiest family in Fitzroy was giving serious thought to exchanging sexual favours for cash but this was the situation Levi had found himself in thanks to his stepfather confiscating his credit card. With access to his stepfather's bank account gone, Levi only had his Candy Boy money to live on and the small allowance Danny had gifted him.

Just thinking about Danny reminded Levi how full his arsehole felt. Danny had given him two loads in quick succession earlier that morning, filling Levi with an abundance of teen cream that was slowly seeping out of his arsehole. Danny's dick may not have been huge but the kid ejaculated sperm by the gallon, producing cumshots worthy enough to be in a porno.

To safeguard against any leakage, Levi had made sure to wear two pairs of underwear beneath the outfit Danny had chosen for him to wear. Telling Levi what to wear had somehow become one of Danny's privileges in their fucked-up power dynamic. Levi wasn't sure exactly how he'd allowed that to happen but for the past four days Danny had dictated what clothes Levi wear before leaving the house. Each day Danny had picked out a similar ensemble to what Levi had on right now; a plain t-shirt and shorts. Levi didn't wear shorts often but Danny said he liked seeing Levi's legs on display and that he liked how it gave him easy access to Levi's arse.

Can't accuse him of not being practical.

With the amount of times Danny dropped the words "bongo drums" it made sense for Levi to wear something that was easy to pull down so Danny could stick his dick in him.

In a weird way, Danny's cock now held a special significance for Levi because of how many times it had entered his body. No other man had been inside him that many times and Levi knew every detail of his stepbrother's manhood. The vein that throbbed underneath its length. The balls hanging loose beneath. The foreskin just letting the rim of its head be known under it.

Danny had been a late developer, having entered puberty a good year or two later than other boys his age. Because Danny was so new to his masculine traits he was still positively fizzing with hormones. Levi figured that's what was adding to the boy's insatiable appetite. The boy was fucking him six or seven times a day, treating Levi's arse like a drink for his thirsty young cock. Levi had a high sex drive too but it was no match to a newly deflowered sex machine. It was just as well his kid brother was only five inches because otherwise Levi's arsehole would be getting wrecked to ruin with the amount of pumping it had had.

Levi was still struggling to wrap his head around the

power he'd bestowed upon his younger stepbrother who until very recently Levi had treated with pity instead of respect.

For years Danny had been the typical geek found hiding in libraries at schools all around the world; skinny, pale-skinned, kinky hair, a few pimples and the start of a fuzzy beard. And don't forget the eyeglasses... boys like that always wore eyeglasses to add to their overall look of wimpiness.

But Danny looked different now. He hadn't bulked out or anything like that but courtesy of a pair contacts, a clear face, new clothes and a sexually active cock—which had gifted him a tonne of confidence—he'd been transformed into a man. He even walked differently now, swaggering around the house like he had a ten-inch cock dangling between his scrawny legs.

Despite Danny's sudden transformation, he was still a skinny runt and quite frankly the most unlikely candidate to be an alpha male. But that's exactly what Levi had christened Danny as the moment he let Danny fuck him. Since that drunken night Danny shafted him on his bed, Levi had been under a knee-weakening spell of submission and had come to view Danny as the more dominant male.

In the blink of an eye, Levi had gone from being man about town to being his stepbrother's bitch. The craziest part of all was how much Levi enjoyed it. He genuinely got off on submitting to the teen's horny demands, only too happy to swallow his pride and Danny's cum. That's not to say he didn't regret it. He regretted it so much. Not because it was wrong, or that he hated being submissive—clearly he didn't—but because it had opened his eyes to an attraction he never knew he had. An attraction that was sick and fucking twisted.

Lusting after his stepfather.

He tried to reason why he'd suddenly started thinking of Mark in a sexual way. Was it purely from having sex with Danny? Was it because Dwight had tricked him into sniffing Mark's sweat-stained briefs? Levi wasn't sure. And he wasn't sure he wanted to know the answer.

Although Levi had never acknowledged it out loud, he had always known Mark was a handsome man but he'd never once in his life had sexual fantasies about him. But now they wouldn't stop popping into his head. It was unnerving to find himself thinking about what Mark would look like naked—naked and standing over him and…

Just the thought of his arse riding his stepfather's cock made his own dick twitch to life while his stomach rolled with slime. How the hell could he be attracted to Mark? It made no fucking sense! The dude was a numbnuts of the highest order and had been a royal pain in Levi's backside for years.

But I still wanna suck all the cum out of his balls.

"Gross," Levi muttered in response to his filthy mind while his cock twitched again.

No matter how much his dick liked the idea of getting down and dirty with his stepdad it was never going to happen. Even if Levi agreed with what his body wanted there was no way he could shag his mother's husband.

I just have to keep out of Mark's way until this fucked-up crush passes. And it will pass!

Since discovering how attracted he was to Mark, Levi had been avoiding him like the plague. Every time he heard Mark's voice he would scarper to the other end of the house, not wanting to lay eyes on the man whose ball sweat turned him on so much.

In a bid to try and keep Mark out of his thoughts the past five days, Levi had concentrated on Josh's impending return from Bali. He couldn't wait to submit to Josh's kinky curiosities and have another taste of the guy's sexy cock. Levi needed his best mate to use him, and use him good, so he could forget all about Mark and the sexy smell of the older man's underwear.

Unfortunately Levi had not received any messages or video calls from Josh for a few days. He figured Josh must have run out of data over there. In the meantime, he was still feeding Josh's cat and using the trips as an excuse to jack off in Josh's bed—a place he hoped Josh would soon be fucking him.

Josh's dick is way bigger than Danny's. And I'm sure he can fuck a hell of a lot better.

Levi was so distracted with his sexy thoughts about his best mate that he hadn't realised the narrow dusty road he was on was petering to an end. He slammed his brakes on and skidded to a halt just in front of a large metal gate with a sign above it that read **The Castle**.

He looked beyond the ominous gate that blocked off a gravel driveway that fed halfway up a forested hill before circling its way out of sight to the other side of the hill. This was the place. Demon Dave had said in his messages that he lived in a remote area up the end of Te Henui Road and that his house was up a long driveway tucked behind a hill covered in native bush. He'd advised Levi to park his car here and walk the rest of the way unless he had a 4wd vehicle.

Levi had always thought where Dwight lived was remote but this made Dwight's place look like Times Square. Everything about this location reeked of creepy and dangerous. Shit, it was the kind of place you imagine a serial killer to live, the perfect place to peel people like an orange and bury their dismembered bodies beneath the bloodstained dirt.

Maybe I should turn around and go back home?

Sirens full of warning went off in Levi's head but he squashed his fear when he reminded himself that the only murderer here was him—and a certain childhood hero who he had hoped to never lay eyes on again in his life. He still hated Shay for pulling a gun on him and pissing all over his face but the issue of his father's missing body was too great to ignore.

As he climbed out of his vehicle, adrenaline flooded his system, his senses firing on high alert. It went without saying that he had to be careful today. Not just with his actions but with his words too. He quickly rehearsed in his head how to play the visit. *I act hard up for cash. Which isn't a lie. I make it seem like the main reason I'm here is a chance to make money, and pretend like any chance to see Shay is just a bonus. Once I've spoken with Shay, I can turn around and never have to speak to the cunt again.*

The plan seemed good enough. The sooner Barry Buttwell's corpse was found and reburied somewhere no one would find him the sooner Levi could go back to forgetting that part of his life had ever happened. Including ever knowing Shay Jacobs; a piece of shit lowlife he'd once thought of as a rebel with a heart of gold.

CHAPTER 2

The *click* of the padlock coming off his chastity cage was the most beautiful sound Shay had ever heard. For the past five days his cock had felt like a lonely little creature in some sketchy foreign zoo, pathetically squishing its hairless, malnourished flanks against the bars of a teeny-tiny cage. The experience had been a lesson in pain and patience, inflicting him with a serious case of blue balls.

The extra weight had taken a bit of getting used to, as had pissing through gaps of the metal cage while sitting down on the toilet. Brayden, the apartment's resident fuck-tard and Dave's favourite pet, had taken great delight in mocking Shay for "pissing like a bitch." If Brayden dared speak like that to Shay in the outside world, Shay would have had no qualms in fucking the blond twink up but unfortunately in the walls of The Castle Brayden reigned supreme amongst the pets.

Anger and humiliation aside, the worse part of the chastity experience had been going to bed each night and waking up in pain from his cock's raging nocturnal boners. The device was already pretty tight around his flaccid member so when his luckless schlong tried to do its nightly stretches under lock and key, the pain would wake him up immediately. And because men's dicks are slow learners, Shay was woken up several times each night.

Shay gazed down at Dave who was now removing the actual device. *Be gentle you bastard. Be very fucking gentle!* Thankfully the older man's meaty mitts were surprisingly tender as they slid the metal sheath away before carefully popping Shay's nads through the scrotal ring.

Dave gave Shay's cock a playful tug. "How's it feel to be free again, Pinky?"

"Fucking amazing." Shay sighed in relief. "So fucking amazing."

Dave gave him another playful tug. "That little pecker of yours positively stinks." He wasn't wrong. Shay had only been allowed one wash since the device went on and that had been three days ago, he now had an obscene amount of dried precum and piss stuck to his cock. "Can I trust you not to play with yourself while you go get clean in the shower?'

"Yes, sir."

"Because if I see you playing with it when I watch the security footage later, I'll put you back in this cock-trap for a month."

Shay's pulse rocketed but his voice was steady. "I promise, sir. I won't play with myself."

"Good boy, Pinky. Good boy."

Shay took a step back, needing some space between himself and the older man. "Why did this client request I not cum for five days, sir?" he asked, enjoying the air swirling around his dick and balls.

"I don't think that's important but what I can tell you is that this person is less of a client and more of a special guest."

"A special guest?"

Dave ignored the obvious question attached to Shay's response and just pointed in the direction of the bathroom. "Go get that dirty brown cock of yours washed. Nobody likes a stinky Māori ." He laughed like he'd just told the best joke in the world. Dave was quite the racist piece of shit when he wanted to be but like most rich white dudes Shay had ever met Dave tried—and failed—to mask his racism as humour.

Dave gave him a friendly slap on the arse and sent Shay off in the direction of the bathroom—the larger one.

There were three bathrooms inside the apartment used to house the pets. Two were quite modest, each with a run-of-the-mill shower box, basin and toilet. Not bad but not overly flash, the sort of bathrooms found in most family homes. The third bathroom though—the one Shay was heading towards—was much larger and much grander and was most certainly not found in family homes.

The larger bathroom was decorated with expensive furnishings from a deep bath tub encased behind glass walls, three porcelain hand basins beneath a giant wall-length mirror, two toilets in open view of the entire bathroom, and at the far end was four showerheads jutting out from the tiled wall. At waist-level, beneath each shower head, was a row of enema machines the pets were expected to use before and after a session with a client.

Of course there was no shower curtain or wall to provide some form of modesty. Shay suspected the bathroom had been designed especially for everything to be witnessed. If Dave wanted to, he could walk inside and stand in the centre of the room and watch them shower, shit and shave on all angles. Thankfully he didn't tend to do that but Shay assumed it was safe to say Dave and Sione probably watched them on the security cameras that were constantly filming their every move inside the apartment. Aside from the rooftop garden, there was no such thing as privacy inside the pets living quarters.

After taking a dump, Shay made his way towards the showerhead closest to the corner of the shower wall. He chose this one specifically each time because this particular shower had the enema machine with the smallest nozzle, only three inches.

He reached for the enema machine and removed the nozzle from the hook. He also squirted some clear water-based gel into his hand from the dispenser and rubbed it all over the nozzle. With a slight grimace, he inserted the nozzle and proceeded to fill himself with warm water.

He still hadn't got use to the sensation of having water rush up his rectum but it hurt a lot less than the other things he'd had shoved up his arse since he'd begun working here. His severe case of blue balls flared up when he found himself getting erect from the nozzle being inside him. He closed his eyes and thought about smelly sneakers and then maggot-covered dog bones, anything gross to kill off the threat of an erection. Five days locked up was bad enough, there was no way he was risking going an entire month without being able to cum.

The gross images worked and the threat passed, allowing him to concentrate on the task of getting clean. After a few minutes of clenching and holding, he released, sending dirty arse water swirling in circles down the shower drain. Shay had never really had much shame, totally at ease with being naked, but knowing he was being filmed while douching made him feel a tad self-conscious. But like every other time he felt embarrassed, he reminded himself about the money he was earning here.

Now that his life was safe thanks to Dave paying off his drug debt, every cent Shay earned was his to keep.

Unfortunately he wouldn't have access to the money until his contract was up but it was good knowing that in six months' time he would be leaving The Castle with over six figures in his bank account.

He turned the shower on and began lathering his body up with liquid soap, paying careful attention to cleaning his cock and balls. He was desperate to play with himself and cum but he wasn't about to risk the punishment he would get for doing so.

At twenty-six, Shay wasn't anywhere near the walking hard-on he had been as a constantly horny teenager but he still liked to bust a nut on the daily, so this past five days had been difficult. Perhaps the only good thing about it was he was almost looking forward to having sex with the client just so he could empty his balls. He was that horny he wouldn't even need any pills to help him stay hard like he sometimes did.

Ideally he'd be topping some rich businessman, filling their arse with the five days' worth of seed trapped inside his balls. However, Shay suspected his dick wouldn't be going inside a hole today since the "special guest" booked in to see him was a downstairs client. The sick fucks who frequented the downstairs rooms very rarely wanted anal and if they did it usually came after a long round of sadistic foreplay.

He wasn't happy about working with downstairs clients but Shay felt like he only had himself to blame. After all, it was his signature on the dotted line of his revised contract. That wasn't to say he he'd signed it entirely willingly. He hadn't.

Dave always gets what he wants.

That is what the other pets had said to Shay three months earlier when Dave first requested Shay start working downstairs in the basement. At the time Shay had scoffed at the suggestion, telling them all he would never sign the contract.

It hadn't taken him long after arriving at The Castle to know that Dave putting him on the lesser pay of a tier one contract had actually been a blessing in disguise. The money was considerably less than what the other pets were on but so were the expectations. Upstairs clients were just after regular cock-in-hole sex. Sure, it had been tough at first for a pussy-mad straight boy to get used to the taste of dick and being fucked up the arse but after a while you sort of got used to it—unlike the world of pain down in the basement.

The little bits of information the other pets had let slip after his arrival about what went on in the basement had made Shay adamant he didn't want to work down there. But like the other pets said, Dave always got what he wanted.

For nearly three weeks Shay stubbornly held out, withstanding some major cuntiness from Dave until finally the bastard made his sinister move—a night of wicked humiliation that had involved Shay being forced to submit to Dave in front of the other pets. It had been fucking mortifying and had left him with a sore arse, a foul-tasting mouth and severely wounded pride. When Dave threated to pull the same stunt the very next night, but with the added threat of allowing the pets to join in and take turns using him, Shay knew he had to accept the new contract.

Thankfully by accepting the new contract Shay had avoided a repeat performance and had also earned him a promise from Dave that he would never force Shay to submit to the other pets again. Unfortunately Dave's promise didn't stop fuckface Brayden reminding Shay every God damn day how he'd added "Pinky's pussy" to his list of conquests.

At least I got a raise out of it, I suppose.

The extra sixty grand the new contract scored him would come in handy but the twisted demands of the downstairs clients meant that he earned every fucking penny. You weren't treated like a person in the basement, you were treated like a prop in someone's dark fantasies. These clients were all incredibly wealthy men but when they had a pet in front of them to use how they pleased they ceased being well-to-do business men and became dangerous animals as their primal urges took over.

The only saving grace about the work downstairs was it was very in-frequent. Maybe once or twice a week. Shay figured the reason for that was the customers must have had to pay a fuck tonne of money to act out their fantasies downstairs. So far Shay had been lucky to avoid anything terrible happening to him but "accidents" did happen as Dave liked to say.

Dion and Kane had both suffered instances that had left them injured and unable to work for a few days; usually a case of someone getting carried away with flogging or overestimating a rectum's capacity. To Dave's credit though, he did step in if he deemed a client had gone too far. The last guy who'd gone too far with Dion, leaving the boy with permanent scarring on one of his arse cheeks, had been banned for life—right after Dave ordered Sione to beat the shit out of the guy. Dave of course would say he did this because he cared for them all but Shay suspected the truth had more to do with the old man not liking his clients damaging his stock.

Turning off the water, Shay stepped out of the shower and grabbed a towel. Just as he began to dry himself off, he heard Dion's trademark sunny voice say, "Hey, Shay."

Shay turned around and smiled at the lanky boy. Dion was all sweaty and in just a pair of silk boxers, looking freshly fucked. "Hey, bro. You just finished a session?"

"Yup." Dion checked himself out in the mirror, carefully scanning his chest and neck for any signs of love bites. It was part of the routine. Dave hated them having hickeys unless the client had specifically paid to do so. Dion raked a hand through his sandy-coloured locks, pulling a tough guy face. It looked more dorky than tough guy though and nearly made Shay laugh.

Somewhat boyish in his attractiveness, Dion's appeal was most notable in his lively green eyes and pouty lips. His lean physique was a tad on the runty side though. A runner's build, slim on muscle, but his long legs and six-three height gave him the illusion of strength.

"I can't believe how long my hair is now," Dion said, more to himself than to Shay.

"Do you like it being long?"

"It's okay, I guess. But I sort of wish it was short now that it's the summer."

Shay nodded, sympathising.

Dion's hair had certainly grown a lot in recent months and was now down to his shoulders, long enough for him to tie up into a man bun. The kid hadn't started rocking a hipster look by choice, it was Dave's suggestion to try and cater to clients looking for hipster trade. Dion certainly had the hair and outfits to pull the look off but his personality was more redneck farm boy than urban woke warrior.

When he was done checking himself out in the mirror, Dion removed his boxers and sat down on one of the toilets. "I'm telling you now this is gonna be noisy," he warned with a smirk. "I just got double teamed by these two crusty old dudes." He pulled a revolted face as his arse erupted with hissing splutters. "I was hoping they'd be too old to get it up but nope, both the old coots managed to give me two loads each." He giggled as his arse hissed some more, shitting out the remains of his session.

Shay laughed at the noises Dion's arse was making. That's really all you could do. Laugh.

"Oh wow, your cage is gone," Dion said.

"Yep. My little man is finally free." Shay gentle stroked his dick. "It makes me appreciate him all the more."

"Just be grateful you weren't locked up for as long as Kane has been."

"Fuck that for a joke," Shay said loudly. After the past five days Shay had a new appreciation for their fellow pet Kane—aka Jock—who had been in chastity his entire time here at the castle—a whopping eighteen months. Kane was washed daily by either Dave or Sione but he was never allowed to climax, which probably went a long way to explain why the guy had a permanent scowl on his face.

Shay had no idea why Kane's dick had been in lockdown for so long but he knew better than to ask. He'd been warned by Dion that Kane didn't like to talk about it and had actually decked two former pets who had dared enquire about his imprisoned cock. The only reason Shay even knew about Kane being in chastity was because he'd asked Sione once why Kane never showered with the other pets. Sione had refused to go into too much detail though, just saying that it was part of Kane's contract.

"Have you got a session soon?" Dion asked as he stood up and flushed the toilet.

"Yep. He better fucking let me bust a nut too. There's so much cum in my balls I reckon they're about to explode."

Dion chuckled. He walked over to the shower Shay had used and proceeded to lube up the enema machine that had just been inside Shay's arse.

"You might wanna use one of the others," Shay said. "I just used that one and haven't cleaned it yet."

"I don't care," Dion said like it was no big deal. "It's not like you haven't put your dick in me before."

The comparison didn't make a lot of sense but Shay sniggered and nodded anyway. "That's true."

It hadn't happened often but occasionally the pets would be booked in pairs. So far Shay had only ever worked with Dion, thank God, because he loathed the idea of ever being partnered with Brayden. If he was allowed to pick who he could work with then it would have been Kane. Although the sneering stud barely spoke to him Shay did find Kane quite captivating, like there was a story there waiting to be told.

Shay watched as Dion raised one leg and insert the enema nozzle. The boy smirked a little as the water turned on and began to fill his anal passage. It seemed crazy but he looked so innocent despite doing a very un-innocent thing.

"What will you do if you don't get to cum with the client?" Dion asked.

"Come back to the apartment and have the quickest wank in history."

"If you wanted to you can chuck a load in me," Dion said without an ounce of shame.

"Thanks for the offer, bro, but I think I'll be quite alright with Mrs Palmer and her five daughters."

"Let me know if you change your mind." Dion raised his eyebrows a little. "The offer is there if you want it."

There was a time Shay would have laughed at such an offer, maybe even react violently, but now he found it more than a little appealing as he stole a glimpse at Dion's firm buttocks.

Tempting. Very fucking tempting.

When he had started working at The Castle, Sione had told Shay that during the course of his employment he would learn things about himself and his sexuality, strongly insinuating Shay may find out he wasn't as straight as he thought. Shay had dismissed the suggestion at the time but Sione had been right. As much as he despised what had been done to him by the numerous clients, there had been tantalizing moments amid the misery.

He now knew that with the right guy, and under the right circumstances, he could quite happily fuck another bloke and not get paid for it. But it wouldn't be with Dion. If Shay were to resort to such measures then it would have to be with a man more masculine than himself.

The other reason he couldn't take Dion up on his offer was he didn't want to be a hypocrite. Shay had lectured Brayden more than once about using Dion for sex, telling the twinky blond that it was wrong to take advantage of Dion's good nature. Brayden didn't listen though and would usually respond with something like, "Why wank when you can fuck a faggot?" Maybe Brayden had a point but Shay didn't like it much. Mind you, there wasn't much he did like about Brayden.

In the outside world, someone like Brayden wouldn't be an alpha of fuck all but here in the castle strength wasn't about muscle or mana, it was about youth, sex appeal and how big your cock was, which meant as an attractive teen with a whopper cock Brayden was king.

The bathroom door opened again just as Shay was finishing drying himself off. "Pinky, I need you to get a wriggle on." It was Sione.

"I'm nearly ready."

"Your client will be here shortly and I need to help get you set up."

Shay nodded. "Do they want me wearing anything in particular?"

"Your birthday suit will do just fine."

Even though nudity was the order of the day, Shay

slipped his briefs on anyway. He liked to have them nearby when a client had finished with him. It might have seemed silly to want to wear them immediately after a fuck but he didn't like these men seeing his dick a second longer than he had to allow it.

"Let's rock n roll," Shay said as he draped his towel over the towel rail. He waved goodbye to Dion and followed Sione into the living room where they caught the elevator down to the basement. The fastest route to the basement was to take one of the numerous slides that fed from their apartment down to the ground floor and then take the lift just one floor down, but Sione's days of tumbling his lard arse down a yellow tube were well behind him.

Shay was glad it was Sione who was helping to get him ready and not Dave. Sione was better to deal with. The large Samoan man was a former pet himself who now worked for Dave as a sort of live-in caretaker and personal assistant. The best thing about Sione though was how he never demanded sexual favours like Dave did.

If Dave was the one walking a pet to one of their jobs, he would nearly always demand they give him a quick suck before the client arrives. It was disgusting, not just because the dude was damn near sixty but because his dick was an ugly fucker. The fleshy rod was curved and had a weird brown birthmark along the side. A right mutant dick.

Mind you, it was better to suck the cunt off than be fucked by him, which he'd only done to Shay a total of three times—four including Shay's initial *audition.* One of the things Shay had learned in his six months working here was that most men's dicks were about five or six inches when hard. It was only a small handful of times he'd encountered a client with a cock bigger than seven inches, so the few times Dave—the owner of a brutal seven-and-a-half-inch spike—had demanded Shay bend over it hurt like buggery taking every inch of the old fart's ugly dick.

Thankfully it was usually Dion or Kane who got the dubious honour of being Dave's fuckhole. For the most part he left Shay's derriere alone, and he never ever fucked Brayden—despite Shay wishing Dave would. Brayden got treated so much better than the other pets and he had no idea why.

Shay had asked the other two pets why that was and Kane, a man of few words, had replied cryptically, "If you want the answer to that then you gotta earn yourself a night in Dave's apartment."

Shay had pressed for more details but Kane wouldn't say anymore and left Shay wondering what the hell he was on about. As much as Shay wanted to know what Kane was referring to, he wasn't about to go out of his way to earn a night with Dave just to find out why Brayden was so fucking special.

On account of Dave only staying at The Castle two or three days a week, invites to his apartment weren't given out that often, but when they were, the chosen pet would follow after him grinning ear to ear. They weren't smiling because they craved the old man's todger, they were happy because it gave them a chance to sleep on a proper bed and not on some crumby mattress inside a giant Perspex box—nicknamed *the bitches box*—suspended four floors above a bloody dance floor.

The other benefit to spending the night with Dave was that the chosen pet got to eat any meal they wanted, watch shows on Netflix and Neon, and he'd even let the pet use his laptop to look up any porn they wanted—a big deal to pussy-deprived straight boys. As appealing as all that was Shay wasn't quite at the point he was desperate enough to let Dave fuck his arse for a whole night just to catch up on

The Walking Dead.

The elevator made a *ding* sound when they got to the basement. The doors opened and they were greeted with the dark hallways lit with ghoulish red lighting. With Sione leading the way, they made their way down the darkened maze-like hallway, passing room after room.

Shay was wondering which kinky den he would be a prisoner in today. There were a lot to choose from. If he had a preference then it would be the room called *the lagoon* which was just a room with a paddling pool. He'd been in there once and it was the best session ever. He'd had to dress up as a merman and splash about while some dude sat on the side and masturbated. Not only was it easy but it had been sort of fun.

Bugger, Shay thought when they passed the lagoon room. *No splashing around for me today.* Just before they reached the end of the hallway, Sione stopped at the door of one of Shay's least favourite rooms—Hell's Kitchen.

Fuck my life. He rolled his eyes in annoyance and followed Sione inside. The oblong room was almost bare, aside from a large mirror at one end and a sling at the other. Pretty mundane stuff compared to some of the other rooms but the room's purpose was far from mundane. What gave the room its cheesy name was the large heat lamp that burned down above the sling with a sickening heat, cruelly designed to make whoever was locked in the sling bare the full brunt of the heated light and sweat up a storm.

Shay had only been in here twice before, both times with clients who had a kink for licking sweaty feet and armpits. Compared to some of the other shit that happened in this building, having a man lick the sweat off your body was pretty tame but he still wasn't a fan of the intense heat, or how it managed to intensify the funk of sweaty balls and crack.

"Great. I go five days without cumming to then be made sweat like the inside of a fat bitch's thighs."

Sione chuckled. "You'll be fine, Pinky."

"Easy for you to say," Shay grumbled as he pulled his briefs down. He flicked them away with his foot then heaved his naked body onto the sling, looping his arms and legs into place so that Sione could then lock him in.

Thanks to the mirror on the wall, Shay had a perfect view of what he looked like. Naked and spread-eagle. The position of his raised legs stretched wide apart meant that his arse cheeks were parted just enough to expose his arsehole, pink and vulnerable.

On a pleasing note though, he could see how defined his abs were. He was in the best shape of his life thanks to the rigorous workout regime he was forced to keep. One of the few advantages of living in this fucked-up asylum.

Sione walked over to the heat dial that controlled the temperature of the lights, cranking it up high until the light shone orange like a sunset. As he returned to Shay's spread-eagled body he pulled something out of his pocket.

"What's that?" Shay asked casually. As Sione lifted the blue object attached to a red strap, Shay began to panic. "Oi, nar, nar, bro. No one said anything about me being gagged."

Instead of answering, Sione's hand flew towards Shay's mouth and rammed the ball between his lips like a ruthless dentist. He then pulled the red elastic behind Shay's head, setting the gag in place.

Shay writhed and squirmed, hating how full his mouth was from the large blue ball filling his gob. He wasn't a fan of being restrained at the best of times but the gag made it so much worse, reminding him of the time he'd almost been murdered at the hands of a sick and evil man.

"I'm sorry, Pinky. I know you don't like being gagged but this is what Dave ordered."

Shay tried to respond but his stuffed mouth only made muffled noises as drool dribbled down his chin.

What the fuck do you mean Dave ordered this? I thought I had a client.

He wasn't sure what the fuck was going on but he had a bad, bad feeling about this. A sickly shudder ran through his body, reinforcing the sense that a major turning point in the storyline of his life was about to happen.

CHAPTER 3

The sun beat down ruthlessly as Levi trudged his way up the steep driveway, the arduous climb causing him to perspire and his calf muscles to burn. It was sticky-humid, and his shorts felt like they were glued to the sweaty crack of his arse, which wasn't helped by the wetness of Danny's sperm.

From where he'd parked his car, he'd assumed the bumpy driveway—nothing more than a dirt path—climbed a sizable hill but now that he was nearing the top of said hill, he was pretty sure he'd just scaled a fucking mountain. The whole way he cursed his smoking habit and promised himself to join a gym when he got home so he could be fitter in the future. Once he reached the top, his knackered state was rewarded with a panoramic view of what was on the other side.

Shit… that's actually quite beautiful.

The hill gave way to a dramatic cliff edge that dropped off to a wide, dark green river below. Levi couldn't be sure how far down it was—fifty, maybe sixty metres—but he knew it was death material. The water was perfectly still and had a haunting quality to it. With a hand above his eyes, shielding the sting of the sun, he peered into the distance and followed the rivers winding path through the forested ranges. The ranges went for miles and miles, and on the horizon he could make out the hazy outline of a snow-capped mountain. *Fuck living here*, he thought. The isolation was bad enough but the climate would be a cunt. With no sea breeze nearby you'd bake in the summer and freeze your nuts off in the winter.

He was so busy taking in the wider view that he'd missed the most obvious part of his surroundings. A humungous house about one hundred yards to his left at the end of the worst driveway in New Zealand. The odd-looking structure carried a super creepy vibe about it and had Levi questioning if he should turn around and go back to his car.

At first glance Demon Dave's abode was a simple country cottage with a large A-frame triple garage built close by. The doors to the garage were closed but two large Utes were parked out the front; one black, one a burnt orange colour. This struck Levi as being pretty normal for a hick living in the middle of nowhere to have a garage twice the size of his home and to own two monster-sized vehicles to navigate the driveway—and probably compensate for a small cock. But what wasn't normal was the rest of the house.

Towering above the rear of the cottage was another four floors of house that were circular and built of concrete. This rear section of the house looked like it had once been a gigantic water tank. But it wasn't a water tank anymore because there were small tinted windows dotted around the different levels of the tower, and most creepy were the curly yellow slides that penetrated the walls of each of the four floors like a McDonald's playground.

It's official. Dave is definitely a fucking nutter.

The windows were all too tiny and dark to make out any movement behind them but Levi could feel eyes on him as he approached the creepy building. The hair on his arms rose at the unnerving feeling of being watched.

Reaching the house, Levi climbed the front steps and was surprised to find the front door wide open. He was about to knock but as he poked his head inside, he saw that the door opened up to what looked like a waiting room with a reception desk and small office.

What the flying fuck? Is this a business?

Levi stepped inside and noticed that above the reception desk was a sign that said: **Please press the buzzer if unattended.** He looked along the counter of the desk and saw the button for the buzzer and pushed it. A faint *dinging* noise sounded in a room behind the reception area. While he waited for someone to come forward, he took a moment to peruse the strange waiting room.

There were seats along the walls, magazines on a stylish coffee table and a large black-framed fish tank filled with chubby orange goldfish. That stuff was all pretty normal as far as reception areas went but what wasn't normal was what was plastered to the walls.

Rows and rows of dicks.

The walls were covered in flesh-coloured dildos, all shapes and sizes, hung like a hunter would hang the heads of dead animals. He probably should have found the scene alarming but mostly he found it funny, especially when he saw that beneath each cock was a name; Gripper, Bowie, Pinky, Chester, Cherry Pie.

Levi was openly chuckling when the door at the rear of the office finally opened. He wiped the smirk off his face and turned around to introduce himself to his host.

A large Samoan man, probably in his late-thirties,

waddled towards the desk. He was tall, bald and his body was made up of more fat than muscle but he looked staunch as fuck. However, when he smiled a lot of the staunchness slipped away. "You must be Candy Boy."

"The one and only." Levi smiled in return. "Demon Dave?"

"No, I'm Sione, Dave's assistant. Dave's outside in the garden waiting for you. Come with me and I'll take you to him."

Sione waddled out from behind the desk and walked to the corner of the waiting room and unlocked a door with a swipe card he had in his hand. He held the door open and ushered Levi inside, locking it behind them.

Sione stepped past him and led the way down a long, narrow passageway. A yellow bulb drenched the wooden floor of the passageway in a dirty glow, each door along the dimly lit gauntlet was closed which only served to add to the depressingly claustrophobic vibe.

Just before the end of the hallway, which came to an abrupt stop in the form of something that looked like a bright red bank vault, Sione took a sharp right turn into another hallway. At the end of this much shorter passage was another locked door. Sione used his swipe card to unlock the door and held it open for Levi to walk through. Levi stepped through and saw that he was back outside in what appeared to be the back garden. There was a curved patio that followed the base of the turret section of the house, which now Levi realised was much larger than he had first thought. There would be some serious living space inside this part of the home, he thought.

Size-wise, Demon Dave's house reminded him a lot of the Candy mansion, both homes were huge by New Zealand standards, as were their sections, but where they differed was style. The Candy mansion was grand and plush whereas Demon Dave's abode was a Frankenstein project of creepy architecture. Levi doubted Demon Dave was worth as much as his stepfather but there was no denying that the man was affluent on a serious level.

"Dave is over there," Sione said, pointing past the patio and across the large stretch of lawn towards a small garden table beneath an oak tree.

Levi could vaguely see the figure of a man but he was too far away to make out any real detail. Just as he was about to say thank you, Sione promptly shut him outside and he heard the door get locked again.

You fuckers are rather tight on security around here.

Levi didn't care if they locked him outside, it was being locked inside that concerned him more. Wiping his hands down the front of his shorts, he strolled across the large lawn, admiring the fruit trees that dotted the grassy field.

As Levi got closer to his host—who was sat dressed in a ghastly Hawaiian shirt and cargo shorts—he was able to get a better picture of what Demon Dave looked like. The man was tanned, had short grey hair and dark, dark eyes. Age wise, he appeared to be about sixty but in no way did he look what you would consider withered or past it, if anything he was probably considered quite fit for his age. He was solid without being fat, weathered but not broken. Thick wiry hair coated his forearms and legs—and probably the rest of his body covered by his clothes.

Demon Dave stood up and spoke with the masculine drawl of a Kiwi farmer. "Gidday, Levi. How's it going, mate?" He grabbed Levi's reluctant hand, shaking it with an iron-like grip

Levi resisted the instinct to flinch at a stranger saying his name but he'd been expecting this. If Shay and Demon Dave knew each other then there was every chance Shay had told the guy what his real name was.

"It's going good, thanks..."—*what the fuck do I call him?*— "Demon Dave."

"Just call me Dave. I'm only a Demon when I'm online or in the sack." The older man flashed a wolfish grin while his eyes made a leisurely sweep of Levi's body before landing back on his face. He motioned for Levi to sit down. "Take a seat."

Levi sat down, resting into the back of the chair, trying to appear as relaxed as possible.

"I can't believe I am finally meeting the infamous Candy Boy," Dave said, his eyes gleaming like steak knives. "I have been a fan of your blog for years, mate. You're a bloody legend with them spicy stories you write."

"Cheers."

"I can't count the amount of smiles you've put on my face." Dave lowered his voice and added, "Or the number of sore wrists I've had."

Levi feigned a polite laugh then commented, "It's a nice place you have up here."

"That's kind of you to say but even I know the house looks a bit strange but nonetheless it's fit for purpose." Dave pointed to a jug of juice in the centre of the table and two glasses. "Fancy a drink? It's feijoa juice. Best flavour in the world if you ask me. Feijoa." Dave grinned. "Well, maybe the second-best flavour. A nice clean cock would probably be my favourite thing to wet my lips with."

Levi coughed up a laugh to be polite but was reluctant to accept a drink.

Dave sensed his hesitation. "If ya worried about it being laced with poison then I can assure you ya worrying about nuffin. I plan on having a glass myself from the same jug."

"Sure... a drink would be nice."

Dave filled the two glasses and slid one across to Levi. "So how was the drive here? It's quite a long way from

Fitzroy, ain't it?"

"Took me just over three hours."

Dave slurped back his drink then nodded. "I thought it would have taken you more like four but I guess a young fella like you drives the whole way with his foot to the floor."

"Guilty as charged." Noticing that Dave had not dropped dead from the feijoa juice, Levi braved a sip. Damn it tasted nice. Cool and sweet and refreshing. It tasted so good he swallowed back a second more generous mouthful.

"Mmm. Someone looks like a thirsty boy," Dave said, sounding overly sexual.

"Yeah, well, it's pretty hot out here."

"It is that."

Neither spoke and silence dropped over them like a wet blanket, stodgy and uncomfortable. After nearly thirty seconds of Dave continuing to stare intensely at him, the older man said, "You really are quite a beautiful creature, aren't ya?"

"Ha. Thanks."

"But you really are." The older man continued to drink up Levi's appearance, craning his neck to the side to scope Levi out from head to toe. "Now I've been on this shitty planet long enough to learn that every young person is attractive. Doesn't matter if they have a bushy pussy or sweaty bollocks dangling between their legs. Youth is youth and youth is attractive but very few people of any age are what you'd call beautiful, but you matey… you are fucking stunning."

Levi chewed the inside of his mouth, not sure what to say back to the flattery that was being laid on thicker than a fat man putting jam on a sandwich.

"This is why I was so keen to meet ya," Dave added.

"Because even though I had never seen your face I could tell by the pictures on your blog that you would have a face as beautiful as your body."

Levi suddenly felt embarrassed as he realised the amount of nude pictures he had shared of himself on his blog. He may have been sat there fully-clothed but Dave would have had a very good idea about what lay beneath his clothes. Shit, the old man probably knew how many hairs grew around his arsehole.

"Don't be embarrassed," Dave said smarmily. "If I was your age again I would be posting pictures of my willy all the time too."

"I'm not embarrassed. I'm proud of my body."

"And so you should be. Not many lads can claim to own such desirable real estate as you do."

Before Dave could flatter him anymore, Levi changed the topic. "What is this place? Is it your home or is it a business?"

"It's both."

"Both?" Levi echoed, trying to get Dave to elaborate.

"I divide my time between here and Auckland." Dave inhaled as he took in the surroundings of the garden. "I like Auckland for certain things but I'm a country boy at heart so I always try and come down here as much as I can so I can try and get some peace and quiet."

"I imagine you'd get a lot of that down here."

"I do to a point but the business takes up a lot of my time when I am here."

"And what is the business?"

"A private endeavour." Dave smirked, purposely playing coy.

"Is it to do with all those cock trophies on the wall?"

"Right you are. It is to do with *all those cock trophies*." Dave chuckled. "I run what you would call a boutique bed and breakfast. I hire rooms out for people who like to come and have a kinky getaway for a weekend. I supply the room, the toys, and the boys."

"You mean a brothel," Levi said flatly.

"I like to think what I'm running is a bit classier than that, but yeah, I guess you could say I am running a brothel of sorts."

Is Shay one of his rent boys? That can't be right. Levi couldn't imagine the same man who'd pulled a gun on him for trying to make him go gay for pay would ever consider living and working in a gay brothel but how else would Dave have video footage of Shay hooked up to a milking machine.

"Does that sort of business bother you, sunshine?" Dave asked, filling the quiet air.

"No. Why would it? It's legal."

"Exactly."

"Even if it was illegal I wouldn't care."

"Oh really?"

"As long as you're not hurting anyone then what's the big deal, right?"

Dave smiled, nodding. "We agree on that."

Levi began putting pieces of what Dave had said together and jumped to a conclusion. "Look, if you've invited me here because you think I could be one of your rent boys then I better tell you now that you're wasting your time. I would never sell myself like that."

"I would never dream of offering you a position here. I can tell you're not the kind of boy to do that line of work. You're far too classy."

"So what is it that you were thinking could help me out financially?" Levi asked, getting straight to the point.

Dave ignored the question by asking one of his own. "I'm guessin' Forbidden Candy has not solved your money woes then?"

"Not exactly." Levi sighed. "It did okay but it's not given me the kind of money I was hoping for."

"That's a shame because I must say it was certainly a scandalous story. Definitely one of your hottest. And that kid… is he really your stepbrother?"

"Of course. Candy Boy always tells the truth," Levi said, defending his brand.

"Mmm. I wish I'd had a cute stepbrother like that."

"You think Danny's cute?"

"Danny," Dave said slowly, "Nice name. And yes, the parts I saw of him in the pics and video lead me to believe that your brother is quite a sexy little boy."

Levi could have punched himself for being so stupid for letting Danny's name slip out so easily. He could have also punched Dave for sounding so turned on from the gross way he said *little boy.*

Dave leaned forward over the table, a horny grin spreading over his thick lips. "Did your brother really produce the most precum you've ever seen?"

Levi nodded.

"I bet he tastes delicious."

"Uh…" Levi didn't know what to say.

"I've read the story four times already. It sounds like you really gave his iddy biddy hole quite the thrashing."

Levi's stomach tightened, not enjoying Demon Dave's descent into blatant smut talk. "Yep. I definitely popped his cherry for him."

"Have you two fooled around again since?"

Levi took a sip on his drink, an excuse to think over his response. He decided that while his alter ego might tell the truth, Levi himself wasn't obliged to. "We haven't actually seen each other since that night. I woke up the next morning and he was gone. He's down in the South Island with his dad for his birthday."

"Well, maybe when he gets back you two boys could share a bit more brotherly love. I for one would love to see more pictures of Danny. Especially his face."

Levi waited for Dave to continue talking but he just kept staring like he was examining an art exhibit. The silence stretched beyond awkward.

Dave's voice finally broke the air. "May I ask you what sort of money you were hoping to make with Forbidden Candy and how much you actually made?"

Levi found the man's nosiness beyond fucking rude. But if he wanted to meet up with Shay while he was here then he knew he'd have to play along. "I was hoping Forbidden Candy would make me over two grand but I'll be lucky if it brings in twelve hundred for the month."

"I see." Dave's creepy gaze intensified. "Twelve hundred dollars isn't to be sneezed at."

"It is when you come from the family I do."

Dave smiled. "Your sense of entitlement is adorable."

Levi rolled his eyes.

"That's not me being rude, sunshine. I actually admire your determination and your lack of morals to make money. So many people of your generation want something for nothing but what makes you stand out from your peers is you are doing whatever you can to get your share of the pie and you don't care who you shit on to get it."

Levi may have been guilty of those things but he didn't appreciate being insulted by some fucking arsehole he didn't even know who lived in the middle of nowhere in a house that was a cross between a hippy commune and Pee-Wee Herman's Playhouse. If he wasn't so desperate to speak with Shay then he would have flipped the dude off already.

"Well, Levi, today is your lucky day because I have a proposition for you that I think you might like."

Levi nodded, just going along with it. He doubted this man was going to make an offer that would interest him. "And what would that be?"

Dave shot him a smile so filthy it could have doubled as a sewer. "Instead of twelve hundred dollars, how do you feel about making thirty thousand dollars?"

What. The. Fuck?

Levi darted his tongue out and wet the edge of his lip as his nerves skittered into overdrive. That was not the sort of money he thought they'd be talking about today. Far from it. He remained silent, thinking it over. Was he about to do something he swore he would never do?

CHAPTER 4

Levi began to pay more attention to Dave's appearance. His stomach turned as he imagined the feeling of being pinned beneath the old man's beastly body and being rammed by such mature meat. He'd always said he would never have sex for money, but maybe, just maybe, thirty-grand was enough to make an exception.

"So, um…" Levi cleared his throat, staring at the grey hairs of Dave's chest that were visible through the top of his shirt. "How would this work?"

"Let me put you out of your misery, Candy Boy. I'm not offering you thirty thousand dollars to fuck you. Don't get me wrong, I would love to have my wicked way with a sexy lad like you but there is no way I am willing to pay that sort of money for one fuck to any boy, even one as gorgeous as you."

"Oh…" Levi was relieved, and felt a little foolish for jumping to a conclusion.

"But you are more than welcome to stay the night with me out of the goodness of your own heart." Dave winked.

"I think I'll pass, thanks."

Dave chuckled. "I thought you might."

"So what would I have to do to make thirty grand?"

"By supplying me with a new 'cock trophy' as you so elegantly called them."

"Huh?"

"Those cocks on the wall in the reception are actually replicas of each boy I have had work here. On their first day I get a mould of their dick and *erect* it on the wall." Dave snorted at the innuendo.

"So you want me to help you find a new rent boy?"

"I would prefer it if we used the term employee," Dave said in an acidic tone and wiped the back of his hand across his lips. "Consider it for yourself a move into the world of HR." Dave drank from his glass of juice leisurely before adding, "One of the boys who works here is coming to the end of his contract and I need a replacement. Someone who is keen to make some good money while living here on site for at least a year."

"You want me to find you a guy who would live here for a year? Having sex with men?"

"That's correct."

As much as Levi liked the idea of making thirty grand, this was out of his jurisdiction. "I would love to help, Dave, but I think you are asking the wrong person. I don't know anyone who would be into that sort of thing."

"I think you will find you do. After all, you helped me find Pinky."

"Who the fuck's Pinky?"

"Sorry. I mean Shay. I'm so used to calling the boys by their pet names I sometimes forget their real ones."

"Pet names?"

"That's what I call the boys who work here. My pets. You know how a cat or dog can be a pain in the arse with how needy they can be? How you gotta house and feed them and clean up after them? but you still love 'em anyway? That's how I feel about my boys. They're my pets. They can be a lot of bother sometimes, and naughty little fuckers, but I adore them."

"Okay," Levi said with a straight face despite feeling like he was entering the twilight zone.

"When I 'hire someone,'" Dave said, using air quotes, "I don't just give them a job where they turn up and do a shift. They move in and live here for up to a year—sometimes longer. They get paid a generous salary and in return I expect them to help make my clients fantasies come true." He pointed towards the creepy house. "That's what this is… a place where men can come and fulfil their desires."

Levi had lots of questions but the most pressing one was, "How did I help Shay get a job working here?"

"Because of Candy Boy," Dave returned. "Of all your stories, my absolute favourite is Twisted Candy. Even though fuck all happened in it, I couldn't stop wanking over those pictures of Shay. Mmm. A Māori boy with sexy baby blues like that… fucking adorable."

"That still doesn't explain how Shay a job here. Did you already know him or something?"

"Nope. Never seen the bloke in my life but one of the pictures in your blog post included a photo of him in his work shirt which happened to have his name and the name of his employer on it. I simply rang the company up and asked to speak to a Shay and arranged to meet him to discuss a deal… sort of like what you and me are doing now."

"And what? You just said 'fancy being a gay hooker full time?' and he said yes?"

Dave chuckled. "Not quite that boldly but along those lines."

Levi was stunned. He knew Shay had a connection with Demon Dave, and it may have been sexual in nature, but he'd never assumed it involved Shay living on site at a gay brothel. That just seemed a step too far for a guy like Shay. It was so unbelievable that Levi found himself asking for clarification. "Does Shay really work here? For real?"

"You've seen the video of him being milked."

"Yeah but there's a big difference between one video and a guy living full time at a gay brothel."

"I have no reason to lie, Levi." Dave's voice became strained with annoyance. "What the hell is so hard to accept that Shay is one of my employees?"

"Because he's straight."

"Most boys who work for me are."

"Yeah but…" Levi shook his head. "Shay's *really* straight."

"If that's the case how did he end up on your blog?"

"Because I paid him."

"Exactly. And Shay is paid to work here." Dave shook his head, smiling. "Are you sure you're not touched with a case of mild retardation, kid? 'Cos you seem awfully fucking slow at times."

"It's not that I'm thick it's just that…" Levi debated if he should tell Demon Dave the whole story behind the Twisted Candy saga.

"That Candy Boy, the infamous truth teller, may have penned a story with a few lies?" A wicked smile crossed Dave's face. The bastard obviously knew the full story already.

"I never lied," Levi said adamantly. "I just didn't share every detail."

"Is that what you call it."

Levi felt the need to protect his blog's honour. "Candy Boy is honest. I tell the truth. That is what sets me apart from everyone else on—"

"Cool your jets, sunshine. I know you tell the truth. You're an honest egg compared to the rest of us on that site. But I have heard the story from Shay himself so I know there's a lot you didn't share about what happened."

"So you know what he did to me?"

"How he pissed all over your face?" Dave laughed hysterically, only stopping when he spotted Levi scowling at him. "Sorry. I shouldn't laugh. But it is quite funny, you gotta admit?"

"Since you obviously know the full story then you will be aware that the arsehole pulled a fucking gun on me just to get out of sucking me off, which is why I am struggling to see how the hell you convinced someone that homophobic to agree to fulfil men's fantasies for a whole year, fantasies which I can only assume go way past oral sex." Levi took a breath to calm himself down. He knew he was sounding jealous. He was feeling jealous. He also realised that his bitter outburst had probably just made it harder for him to speak with Shay under the guise of catching up with an old friend.

"A couple points here, mate. Firstly; I don't think Shay is as homophobic as you might think. And secondly; I pay him a fuck tonne more than the pittance you paid him."

"How much more?"

Dave paused. "I don't like to air my pets' private business but what I can say is it is a very generous six figure contract he is on."

"Holy shit," Levi whispered. "That... that's a lot of cash."

"It is, which is why I can assure you that Shay is one of my pets."

Levi turned around and looked towards the bizarre building. "So Shay is in there right now?"

"He sure is."

Levi's mind was like an overloaded tumble dryer, a tonne of questions threatening to spill out uncensored. And then one did. "Why do you need me to help find you someone to work here?"

"Because you have easier access to a demographic that I don't. You can find me another Shay."

Levi was weary. "Don't get me wrong. I like the sound of earning thirty grand. I more than like it. I fucking love it, but why do you need me to find you another guy like Shay when you found Shay yourself?"

"It was an absolute fluke that I managed to find Shay in the first place. Had it not been for your blog and the photo with him wearing his work shirt then I'd never have been able to locate him." Dave paused to take another sip on his drink. "Sure, I can find guys on my own, I have done for years, but as I get older it's getting harder and harder."

"How come?"

"I'm fifty-seven, Levi, and although I don't consider myself an old man I know that to young fellas like you and Shay I'm the bloody crypt keeper. Unless I have a heads up that a guy is open to going gay for pay, I just don't stand much of a chance when I try and strike up a conversation. Lads like Shay are much more open to letting their guard down to another young guy like yourself. You're good-looking and non-threatening, I imagine you're the type of person who makes them feel at ease and who can get them considering doing things they may not normally consider doing. That's what I need. A talent scout if you will."

Levi frowned. "And you specifically want a guy like Shay?"

"Before you start thinking I am asking you to go out and find me some drug-fucked Māori hood rat, that's not what I mean. I couldn't give a toss about a boy's ethnicity, what I am looking for are *real* guys."

"Okay," Levi said slowly, taken aback by the heat in Dave's tone.

"I want you to find me a new pet who is an everyday sort of guy. That's what makes me money. Not some hairless little twink or some gym-obsessed faggot who's ripped with a huge cock and an arsehole shaved within an inch of its life. Now, personally, I'm quite partial to a twinky slut with a tidy man-minge but the majority of my customers prefer real guys. They like the kind of guys you blog about. Your hookups tend to be masculine, cocky and a bit rough around the edges. Some might even call them trashy. Boys like Shay have a certain spunk about them, don't they? And I ain't talking about the kind that comes out the end of their cocks." Dave sniggered to himself. "My customers, all very wealthy men, enjoy those rougher types because they don't have access to those sorts of boys in their everyday lives."

"So if I were to agree to this, how long would I have to find you someone?"

"Ideally I would like a new pet within a few weeks but I don't want you to rush this. I would rather you find me the perfect pet than a mediocre one. I'm not in the business of handing over money for the sake of it, so be warned that if you supply me with an unsuitable candidate then I will straight up say they are not fit for the role and you won't get paid."

"Fair enough," Levi said as his gaze locked with Dave's dark eyes. "And what would make someone unsuitable?"

"Being ugly," Dave said bluntly. "I'm not expecting you to find me a younger version of Brad Pitt but they do need to have a face that is pleasing enough that my clients don't feel the need to constantly fuck them doggy style."

Levi snorted. "Gotcha."

"And they can't be too old. To be honest, Shay is actually a few years older than I normally go for but them baby blues of his convinced me to take a chance on him, which I am glad I did, but he is definitely the exception. I am looking for someone in their teens or early twenties. And ideally I am looking for a lad with a decent sized dick. I'm talking an eight incher. A seven-and-a-half at the very least. My resident top, Twitch, is near the end of his contract and none of the others here have anything over seven."

Levi could have taken many things from Dave's list of demands but the only thing he thought of was *So Shay's dick is less than seven inches.*

"Actually that's a lie," Dave added. "Jock is a pretty big boy but he's been in chastity the past eighteen months so his wee fella is really fucking wee now."

"You've had a guy in chastity for nearly two years?" Levi asked in a shocked whisper.

Dave nodded. "Jock was keen to make as much as possible so I told him if he wanted extra then that was the role he would have to take."

"And the chastity has made his dick go smaller?" A squirmy feeling ran down Levi's own dick just thinking about it.

"Fucking oath. It takes a while to happen but once a man's been locked up for a while, and provided you've been progressively downsizing the cage, then their todger shrinks along with it."

Levi was horrified. "Do they go back to normal?"

"Sometimes, sometimes not. Some men just stay small."

"So this guy might have a permanently shrunk cock?"

"That's the risk the boys take when they sign a contract with that particular clause." Dave must have mistaken Levi's shock as disapproval because his voice became defensive "That's why they get paid extra, sunshine. I don't expect a man to take that sort of risk with his wiener without adequate compensation. Jock may very well walk away from his time here with nothing more than a clit between his legs but he will only have himself to blame."

"Fuck," Levi muttered.

"I wouldn't let your pretty head get too hung up on shrinking penises. I'm not asking you to find me a chastity slave. I'm after a top, remember? A handsome face with a big dick. Understand?"

"Handsome. Big dick." Levi nodded. "Got it."

"It's not like I am asking you to trick some youngin into going to prison." Dave laughed like the notion was ludicrous. "You would actually be gifting a young man a golden opportunity. What other job do you know of where someone like Shay could make this sort of money?"

Dave had a good point. There wasn't any. The only way someone like Shay would ever make big money was if they won the lottery.

"So, Candy Boy?" Dave's feijoa-flavoured breath wafted across the table. "Can I can count on you to find me a new pet?"

Levi cast a sweeping gaze around the peaceful gardens then up at the house. *The house is kinda loopy but it can't be that bad living here for a year? And the guy would know what he was signing up for. And he gets good fucking money. As will I. And Like Dave says, I'd actually be helping someone.* Levi's internal voice was whirring with all the positives, suppressing the nagging feeling in his gut that told him something about this felt terribly wrong. He turned back and nodded. "I'm in."

"Glad to hear it, sunshine. I think you and me will make a wonderful team."

"So what do I do when I think I have found you a suitable candidate?"

"Contact me online. You have my email address. Under no circumstances are you to bring a potential candidate here or tell them where my business is. I'm not running a secret society or anything but I have to respect our clients' privacy."

"Not a problem."

It went quiet for a moment and Levi knew this was the time he had to ask about seeing Shay. "So, uh, would it be okay if I spoke with Shay while I'm here?"

Dave eyed him warily for a moment before nodding. "Of course. He's actually inside waiting for you right now. I arranged for you two to have a room to yourselves in case you wanted some privacy."

That sounded creepier than it ought to but Levi didn't let his unease show. "Thanks, Dave."

"You're most welcome, Candy Boy." Slowly, Dave tilted his head. His lashes lowered and lifted through a long blink. "I must ask though, why would you want to see the person who pulled a gun on you and pissed on your face?"

Because I have to ask him where he's put my father's body. Levi's hazel eyes glazed over with a faraway look; one he wore whenever he fell into the haunted black hole of his past. "I just want to know he's okay."

"I can assure you Shay is perfectly fine."

"I know but I guess it's just that because he disappeared without telling anyone where he was going that it's got people worried."

"You do know why he couldn't tell people, right? And why you can't tell anyone about him being here?"

"Your clients' privacy?"

"Not just theirs. It's for Shay's privacy as well. Shay doesn't want his friends and family knowing what he is doing. A young man like that would be mortified if it got out the kind of job he was doing here… his reputation as a lad about town would be ruined."

"You don't have to worry about me saying anything."

"I know you won't say anything." Dave bared his teeth with a feral smile. "That's why I trust you to be my new talent scout."

"Yep. I'm very good at keeping secrets. I have enough of my own."

"Don't we all." Dave polished off the last of his drink and put the glass down with a *thud*. "I guess I better take you to Pinky."

"I'm sorry but I have to ask… why is Shay called Pinky?"

Dave grinned a knowing smile. "Rather than tell you it might be best if I show you."

CHAPTER 5

Masking his unease, Levi followed Dave back towards the odd-shaped building where the older man led them to the door Sione had let Levi out of earlier, unlocking it with a similar swipe card. This time, instead of heading back to the reception area, Dave took Levi farther down the main hallway right to the end, pushing in a code on the red door that resembled the front of a bank vault.

The large metal door slowly opened to reveal darkness and the soft sound of music. To the right was a curved stairwell but they walked past it and headed towards another chunky red door which Dave unlocked with another swipe of his key card. As Dave pushed the door open, it unveiled the most outrageous indoor space Levi had ever seen.

The room—which appeared to be a bar or nightclub of some kind—was huge, absolutely fucking huge. Adding to its impressive size was the highest ceiling Levi had ever seen. It was open space all the way up to the roof of the building. On one side of the nightclub was a curved wall, and on the other side was a giant mirrored wall slicing through the middle of the building. The mirrored wall reflected the vast array of colourful kinky apparatus hanging from the opposite wall. It was like walking inside a kaleidoscope.

As they threaded their way through the club, Levi's head spun around as he checked out the private booths, the dance floor, the sex toys glued to the walls, the stage equipped with a catwalk, stripper poles and two metal cages. There was a long narrow bar that ran around one part of the curved wall. The fridges behind the bar were fully-stocked with an array of colourful liquors, framed chains and whips hung from the wall like artefacts in a museum. The place was a fucking trip.

"I totally didn't expect to see a nightclub in here," Levi said.

"It's more just an entertainment area," Dave said like it was no big deal. "We don't use it all that often but a few times a year we put on events and sometimes our clients might hire it out for birthdays or special occasions."

Levi glanced up and was again blown away by what he saw. Dangling high, high, high above the dance floor was a large box comprised of bright red and yellow transparent cubes. It was hard to tell but he was pretty sure he could see someone moving around inside the giant box. "What the hell is that?" he asked as he pointed heavenward.

Dave didn't even look up. "The bitches' box."

"What's the bitches' box?"

"If you decide you and Shay can play nice together then maybe we can let him give you a tour later and he can show you."

Levi was curious as hell to know what was up there but he wasn't curious enough to find out if it meant spending more time with Shay than he had to. All he needed from Shay was the location of his father's body, not a tour.

As they walked across the dance floor Levi spotted the yellow tubing he'd seen on the outside of the house. It was a slide like he had thought, ending in a pit of colourful rubber balls beside the stage. The fact it was decorated like some sort of children's playground made it feel wrong, especially when there was so much sex paraphernalia about.

Dave led them to the side of the stage where there was an elevator. Just as Dave was about to push the button, there was a light sound of laughter coming from near the bar.

Dave motioned with his hand for Levi to follow him towards the source of the noise. They walked to the end of the bar and rounded a small corner to a private booth where they found Sione sat down talking to a spectacled man with curly brown hair.

Both men promptly stood up as soon as they saw Dave, like they were showing respect to a senior officer.

The curly-haired man looked much the same age as Sione. Mid to late thirties. Unlike the ancient Dave and obese Sione, he was arguably quite a handsome man who looked like he was in good shape. He was dressed in black dress pants, black leather shoes, a white-collar shirt and was wearing a gold wristwatch. His image was one that oozed moneyed professional but he also had a distinct whiff of try-hard about him.

"How did Twitch and Jock's check-ups go?" Dave asked the curly-haired man. "Are they squeaky clean?"

"They most certainly are. There's nothing at all to be worried about." Curly Sue spoke with a pompous accent that seemed about as authentic as a Big Brother house showmance. His voice took on an air of disdain as he pointed at Levi and asked Dave, "Is this Twitch's replacement?"

"We should be so lucky," Dave said with a throaty

chuckle. "This is Levi. He's agreed to help me find a replacement for Twitch."

"Nice to meet you, Levi," said the curly-haired man, stepping forward and holding out his hand for Levi to take.

Levi accepted his hand and grasped it warmly. "You too …" Levi left the sentence dangling, waiting for the man to give his name.

"Doctor Harten." The doctor quickly released Levi's hand and returned his attention to Dave. "How long before Twitch leaves us? He insisted that today was his last physical but I told him I'm pretty sure I have to see him one last time before his contract is up."

"He has three weeks to go," Dave began, "then he's back into the big wide world and no doubt will be running dick-first into the first twenty wet, willing cunts he comes across."

"Like they all do," Sione added cheekily.

"I hope Twitch is a bit wiser than that," Dr Harten said, sounding very prim and proper. "If he had thought less with his penis then he wouldn't have been here in the first place."

"What did this Twitch person do?" Levi asked nosily.

The doctor shot Levi a poisonous look but Dave appeared all too happy to answer the question. "Young Twitch got himself into a spot of bother back in his hometown after getting not just one but five girls at his school pregnant." The old man sniggered. "Talk about having fertile balls."

"Crikey," Levi said before the word *school* fully registered with his brain. "Wait… how old is Twitch?"

"Old enough to know better," Dave said sternly. "After causing such a scandal, he needed a change of scenery and the chance to earn some money to help the girls with the cost of raising *his* children. I forced him to split the advance I paid him between the five girls but I severely doubt if any of them will see a cent of the money he gets paid when he leaves."

"I'd agree with that," Dr Harten mumbled. "Twitch doesn't strike me as a young man with much honour."

"No unfortunately," Dave agreed with a forlorn smile. "But he is a special little rascal and I'll miss him like crazy. I just hope the rules and discipline he's learned while here will stand him in good stead for his future endeavours."

Levi was beginning to wonder if he was in a brothel or Demon Dave's school for wayward boys. He was soon brought back to the reality of standing inside a brothel though when Dave and Doctor Harten started discussing how it had been over a year since any of the pets had caught an STD.

While the doctor and Dave spoke between themselves, Sione asked Levi if he would like a drink from the bar. Levi politely declined, still not entirely comfortable with accepting hospitality from what felt like a twisted establishment.

The entire time Dave and the doctor spoke, Levi could feel the doctor's gaze slipping towards him—most noticeably towards his crotch. *Definitely a mo*, Levi thought. He wondered if the doctor got paid with freebies. A shag on the house in exchange for his services. Even though Levi didn't know the man he wouldn't put it past him. Something about the guy just felt off, like a chicken salad left out of the fridge overnight. It might look alright but one bite would be bad for your health.

Dave abruptly ended his conversation with the doctor by asking Sione, "Is Pinky ready for us? I'm about to take Levi down to see him."

Sione nodded. "Yes. He's set up as you requested."

Set up?

Dave turned to Levi. "Well, sunshine, shall we go say hello to your pal?" Dave didn't wait for a response, he started walking back towards the elevator beside the stage.

Levi hurried after him and watched as Dave swiped his card before pressing a button labelled **B**. The basement he assumed. When the doors opened and they stepped inside, Levi clenched his fists, fighting the galloping thud inside his fearful heart. He gulped when the elevator jerked to life and slowly descended, taking him below the ground to a reunion he had never wanted.

CHAPTER 6

It was a short ride to the bottom of the building but when the doors opened Levi saw that the basement was completely different to the party of colour upstairs. Down here it was dark and dim, the only light coming from sinister red lights that hung above them like carnivorous monster eyes. They passed numerous doors as they walked down a passageway that curved and zigged and zagged. Levi wondered what was behind each of the closed doors but it was left to his imagination as he followed behind his briskly walking host.

Dave came to a hasty stop and Levi nearly walked into him. "We're here," Dave said. He swiped his card and opened the door.

Levi was blinded by the light inside the room and immediately felt a wave of heat. As he blinked to regain his vision, Levi lost a breath, his heart coming to an abrupt halt before slamming against his rib cage.

There he was in all his glory. Shay motherfucking Jacobs.

Unruly black hair. Creamy coffee skin. Piercing blue

eyes. The rebel with a heart of gold looked as gorgeous as he ever did. But what he didn't look was comfortable. He lay helpless and naked in a sling, his limbs secured, his mouth gagged. Shay's electric blue eyes were wild with adrenalin and when they caught sight of Levi, his entire body shook at the restraints holding him prisoner.

Levi felt dizzy. Not from the immense heat or the bright light but from the fact he was laying eyes on a sight he'd fantasised about countless times. A sight he'd wanted to see for so many years was blatantly on display and his eyes drank in the debauchery. It was like laying eyes on a foreign land you'd always wanted to visit. Despite the insidious nature of what he was witnessing, Levi could not deny the raw beauty of Shay's naked form.

Shay's body was slim and muscular, toned like it used to be before the drugs had fucked him. His pubes were black and his flaccid cock a soft brown colour. Below that were Shay's moderate-sized balls—two perfect, egg-shaped testicles covered in soft, wrinkly skin and long, thick black pubes.

Dave walked right over to where Shay was and ran a hand down Shay's leg. "Isn't he beautiful?"

Levi scuttled over, his gaze still focused on Shay's boy bits. Up close he could see that Shay was covered in sweat. He could smell him too. A strong musky smell that filled his nostrils with a powerful male stench. Levi knew this smell. It was Shay's natural odour intensified a thousand times. He'd smelled it a lot growing up when Shay would hug him. He'd always liked the smell for how safe it made him feel. But today it didn't make him feel safe. It just made him horny.

Dave tugged on Shay's balls. "I was gonna get him shaved for you but I decided you might wanna see him au naturel."

Shay tried saying something as he shook in his restraints but his words came out as mumbles. Levi glanced up into the eyes of his childhood hero. They were wide and flickering with anger. Or was it fear? Levi couldn't be sure. He saw that the gag was making Shay dribble, puddles of drool wet his chin.

When Shay rocked the sling again, Dave slapped his thigh, hard. "Enough of that, Pinky. Your little prince is here to see you so I want you to be on your best behaviour."

Shay groaned, his chest deflating. Levi didn't need subtitles to decipher the colossal amount of shame seeping through Shay's muffled voice. It was understandable though. He couldn't run or hide from this moment, his vulnerable body's secrets were all there waiting to be explored by someone he never wanted to discover them.

"You wanted to know why I called him Pinky?" Dave smiled at Levi. "Here's why." He lifted Shay's balls to expose his arsehole more clearly. Still gripping Shay's balls, Dave licked a finger on his other hand then used it to stroke the length of Shay's hair-lined crack, prodding his arsehole. Dave jabbed the tip of his finger inside, causing Shay to whimper. "Settle down, Pinky. You've had bigger things than a finger up there." Dave chuckled then returned his attention to Levi while he kept fingering Shay with his thick finger. "See how pink his pussy lips are? That's how he got his name." Dave rammed his finger deeper, going as far as his first knuckle. "You'll see how pink they really are when you've finished fucking him."

Tension gripped Levi's insides, but he kept his expression relaxed and voice calm. "You want me to fuck him?"

"You can fuck him, blow him, spank him. Hell, you can even piss and shit all over him if that's your thing."

Levi was speechless and more than a little grossed out. He glanced up at Shay who had a furious look of *don't you fucking dare!* in his eyes.

"There's a funnel gag over there on the toy rack if you want to put it in his mouth to force him to drink your piss." Dave pointed with his free hand towards a shelving unit filled with sex toys. "I figure you might want to give Pinky here a taste of his own medicine since I understand he forced you to drink his."

Shay closed his eyes, no doubt regretting ever sharing that story with his employer.

Dave retrieved his probing finger and gave Shay's balls a hearty tug. "When you're finished having your fun just undo him and he can give you a tour of The Castle if you like."

Levi hadn't come here for sex but that didn't stop his dick from hardening inside his shorts.

"Just so you know, Pinky has gone five days now without so much as a wank," Dave said.

"Oh…" That seemed odd and completely irrelevant.

"When I got your email to let me know you were visiting, I made sure to put Pinky in chastity for you."

"Why?"

"Because I thought you'd appreciate fucking him while his balls are full as fuck. This way you can get several loads out of him." Dave waggled his eyebrows. "It also means that it won't take much to get him hard. Just fiddle with his diddle for a minute and you'll finally get to see what Pinky's been hiding from you all this time."

"Er, thanks," Levi said, mostly out of obligation rather than any real sense of gratitude.

"But just between you and me, sunshine, I wouldn't get your hopes up. Pinky's not exactly the biggest boy in the world." Dave sniggered before speaking directly to Shay in a patronizing baby voice, "But you do have a vewy pwiddy widdle dicky, don't you, Pinky winky?"

Another embarrassed groan came from Shay as the older man tickled him beneath his balls.

"Right," Dave said snappily. "Remember that the dildos and paddles are over there if you need them. As are condoms and lube." He pointed once more to the rack on the wall. "But if you're like me, you'll just give it to the bitch raw." Dave blew Shay a condescending kiss then left the room.

Levi found himself blushing even though Dave's spiteful remarks hadn't been aimed at him. He looked over at the rack of sex toys with its colourful selection of silicone dildos. On the floor beneath the rack, he spotted some green material which he realised were a pair of boxer briefs. He turned back to look at Shay who had stopped struggling and now just hung suspended with a judgemental gaze on his scowling face.

"Don't look at me like that," Levi snapped. "This wasn't my idea."

He waited for Shay to respond but of course he couldn't. Shay's gagged mouth continued to leak little rivers of spit, the saliva glistening his chin, as he somehow managed to inflict copious amounts of guilt without saying a word.

"If you want to be angry at anyone then be angry at yourself for putting yourself in this situation. I never told you to run away to join a fucking brothel." Levi shook his head, flicking Shay a scathing glare. "I know you went off the rails and were doing some crazy shit but a gay brothel? Seriously? I thought you were better than this." Levi's voice was loaded with derision.

Despite the heat pouring down from above, Levi found himself shivering, fighting the intense want running through his veins. He'd never have another opportunity like this again. Once Shay was unlocked from the sling he'd soon put his briefs back on and Levi would never see the hot Māori 's dick again.

Ignoring the voice in his head telling him to undo the straps around Shay's wrists, Levi traced the outline of Shay's foot, paying close attention to the high arch and his long, skinny toes. *Size twelve* Levi whispered internally, remembering Shay telling him his shoe size the day he'd tried to add him to Candy Boy's list of conquests. That day hadn't gone to plan but right now he could touch these feet as much as he liked and there was not a damn thing Shay could do about it.

Shay squirmed and grunted when Levi began to tickle the sole of his foot. When Shay jolted particularly violently, Levi stopped. He wanted to explore, not harm, even if that harm was just from the idiot being ticklish.

He studied the hair on Shay's legs that were soaked with perspiration. They weren't the hairiest legs in the world but they definitely had a decent covering of fuzz. He let his hand glide up Shay's calf muscle, past his knee, and towards the inside of his thighs where the skin was smoother.

He took a moment to admire how muscular Shay had become, a definite improvement on what he'd seen the last time they had met. He loved how Shay's pecs were dusted with just the right amount of hair. It narrowed and tapered down the centre of his chest, briefly widening over his toned stomach, before narrowing again and feeding down to his pubes.

Levi's dick was making its presence known, stiffening at the realisation that Shay Jacobs, his childhood hero, was here for his pleasure. Whatever happened in this room today wasn't about revenge, it was about learning the physical secrets of a sad sack of shit Levi had once thought of as a living legend.

Lowering to a crouching position, Levi gazed longingly at Shay's arse—the body part that Shay used to joke was his best feature on account of how good his butt looked in a pair of jeans. Shay's bare arse was every bit as gorgeous as Levi had expected, had hoped. More so. The flesh was flawlessly formed, pale brown, sprinkled with a light amount of hair.

Levi stroked Shay's butt, his palm gliding over the sexy skin. He gently parted the cheeks, exposing the crack hairy with dark fur, the hole pink and relaxed, gateway to some eternal secret. As silly as it was to call someone Pinky, Levi could see clearly why Shay had been given the nickname. His arsehole was just so pink and pretty, a beautiful contrast to the light brown skin surrounding it.

With his index finger, Levi rubbed between Shay's sweaty arse cheeks and teased his hole, not breaching him, just pressing against it, making little circles around the edge. He began to wonder how many dicks had been inside here and how many had filled the Māori stud with cum. The thought of random strangers fucking and filling Shay was intensely erotic and Levi wished he could spend a day watching them defile this once proud straight man. But at the same time it pissed Levi off knowing so many men had got here before him, claiming this sexy hole as their own. He gave Shay's damp trench one final stroke then rose to his full height again.

Shay's grim, sweaty visage and haunted eyes were there waiting for him, still judging him.

"I told you this is all on you so quit looking at me like I'm some sort of creep." Levi almost wished Shay wasn't gagged so he didn't have to have an imaginary argument with himself. "You're the one whose bright idea it was to work here."

Casting a sweeping gaze over the length of Shay's naked body, Levi tried to memorize all the pieces that made such a beautiful work of art. He surveyed the landscape of Shay's muscled chest and his nipples that looked oh so suckable. His brown skin was positively glowing under the light, and was even sweatier than his legs. Levi admired the dark tangle of hair in Shay's armpits and considered licking them clean. He leaned forward and stroked the hairs on Shay's chest, groaning lightly as he did so. He thought back to when he was thirteen and how he used to enjoy staring at this patch of masculinity, often wondering what it would feel like to touch Shay here. Now he had.

Shay sucked in his stomach as Levi's bent index finger skimmed down over his left pectoral muscle to his nipple, then down the centre line of his abdomen, across his six-pack and on down to his pubes.

Levi raked his fingers through the wiry black hair then gently stroked Shay's cock. Shay visibly shuddered as Levi's fingers closed around his sensitive skin, squeezing the fleshy tube gently in his warm, slightly sweaty palm.

I can't believe I have shay's dick in my hand! A sense of awe came over him to know he was touching a once forbidden piece of flesh. He suddenly felt Shay's cock twitch in his grasp. Then it twitched again. And again. And again. *Fucking hell!* He was barely even playing with it but Shay's body was reacting to his touch and his dick seemed determined to grow and swell to its full size.

"You really are horny, aren't you?"

Shay sort of nodded, his eyes shuddering.

Levi began to tug harder, determined to see how much of a man Shay Jacobs really was. Shay's cock throbbed in his palm, extending and thickening another inch. His nuts rolled up in their sack as he breathed noisily through his nose. Levi continued staring at Shay's growing cock, his face dipping ever so slightly toward it.

He was going to lick it, kiss it, maybe even suck it, but he pulled away at the last second and looked into Shay's eyes as he gripped Shay's cock a little tighter and slid his hand up and down.

A jolt passed through Shay. His eyes squinted, then bulged open. He stared down at Levi's hand pumping his steel-hard cock. He suddenly looked shocked, disgusted, as if he was seeing what was happening for the first time. He exhaled sharply out his nose then made a whimpering grunt.

Levi's thumb squished over Shay's exposed tip and trailed a slippery mess of pre-cum down the rock-solid underside of his shaft. The precum kept drizzling, leaking out Shay's piss-slit like a glass of spilt milk.

Shay whimpered again, his legs quaking as his fingers furled into fists. He was either on the verge of an orgasm or hating every second of this. *Probably both.*

Levi opened his fingers and Shay's cock rose mightily out of his hand, jutting up toward his face as if in invitation. Levi inhaled deeply through his nose and experienced a powerful waft of ball sweat: the heady testosterone aroma that permeated Shay's virile crotch.

At its full hardness, Shay's cock was about six and a half inches, pretty similar to Levi's in length but Shay's was a bit thicker. Definitely nothing to be ashamed of like Dave had insinuated.

Rather than go straight back to jerking him, Levi took a moment to admire the beauty of Shay's manhood. He memorized every veiny inch and the slight upward curve, like it was designed especially to be held onto. For years he'd wondered what it looked like, how big it was. Growing up, Shay had often shared dirty sex stories with

Levi, telling him all the lurid details about the girls he had fucked. But there was one detail he'd always leave out—the size of his dick.

But now Levi knew.

"So this is Shay Jacob's famous cock," Levi said with a smirk. "I've wanted to see your dick longer than you'd believe."

Shay's pretty blue eyes stared back, blinking wildly.

"Six and a half inches," Levi whispered. "That's what you are."

In some way it was surprising to find out that the guy he'd once thought of as the closest thing to a real-life superman only had an average dick. A bit like being told Santa Claus isn't real. But it didn't make this moment any less powerful. Levi felt like he finally possessed carnal knowledge he'd been searching years for.

And that's all he needed.

He was done.

Stepping out of the 'V' of Shay's spread legs, Levi made his way to the other end of the sling and removed the gag from Shay's mouth. He braced himself for a torrent of abuse.

Shay sucked in a lungful of air and stared up at Levi with a huge smile. "It's so fucking good to see you, LP."

Levi was shocked. He'd expected a "fuck you" at the very least, maybe even a ball of spit fired at his face, but Shay looked genuinely pleased to see him. He quickly undid the restraints around Shay's wrists and ankles before helping him out of the sling.

Shay wobbled on his feet, like he was learning to stand again. Finally, when his body was straightened he lunged at Levi, wrapping him into a hug. "Thank you for coming to see me. Thank you so much!"

This is fucking awkward.

Once upon a time Shay hugging him would have felt like the most natural thing in the world. Not anymore. Now it felt like being wrapped up in a muddy blanket.

When the hug kept going and going with no sign of letting up, Levi gently pushed Shay away. "We need to talk."

"Yeah, man. We can talk." Shay nodded deliriously before a more serious expression came over him. "But can I ask a favour first, bro?"

"And what favour would that be?"

"Can you finish what you started?" Shay tugged on his dick. "I was really fucking close before."

Levi smiled. Then chuckled. Then laughed.

"It's not funny, bro. You heard what Dave said. I ain't bust a nut in five fucking days."

Levi kept laughing. Shay Jacobs was still dead to him but at least he could still make Levi laugh.

Shay didn't look impressed and gave his dick a stroppy tug that spilled drops of precum onto the concrete floor. He must have sensed Levi had no intention of jerking him off because he walked over to the discarded green briefs on the floor and put them on.

When Levi controlled his giggles, he lowered his voice and said, "We need to talk about Dad."

Shay acted like he hadn't heard the comment and instead said in an even tone, "It'll be good to catch up." His eyes widened, a silent command telling Levi to shut up.

Levi got the hint immediately and nodded, only now realising that Dave was probably hidden somewhere still watching and listening.

CHAPTER 7

After leaving the basement, Shay took Levi upstairs to the apartment he had been calling home for the past six months. Thankfully none of the other pets were around to force Levi into unwanted chit-chat but that didn't save him from having to talk with Shay like they still got along. Now and then Shay would give him a knowing look, letting him know it still wasn't safe to speak openly.

After giving Levi a full tour of the lounge, living area, kitchen, bathrooms, and even a games room stocked with nearly as many video games as Danny owned, Levi decided that what Dave provided here was pretty decent. Actually, it was *very* decent. It was certainly a lot nicer than any place Shay had lived in and had it been situated in the centre of a city its rent would command a hefty price tag.

"Where do you sleep though?" Levi asked after Shay had finished showing him the last bathroom.

"I've saved the best for last," Shay replied with a healthy dose of sarcasm. He led them back into the lounge and climbed inside one of the large holes in the wall. These holes were dotted around the apartment and Shay had explained they were used by the pets to get downstairs instead of using the elevator.

"Come in, LP," Shay called out from inside the hole. "This is the way to my bedroom."

"You have to be fucking kidding me."

"For real. It's this way."

"Fucking hell," Levi half-laughed. He climbed inside and followed behind Shay in a shuffle-like crawl. Unlike the other holes Shay had talked about this one didn't appear to go down, it went up. And up and up in a series of tubes and ladders until finally Levi found himself crawling out into the giant Perspex box he'd seen dangling above the dancefloor. *The bitches' box.*

As he stood up, the first thing he noticed about the bitches' box was how badly it smelt. It was fucking rank. The air was clogged with the stench of sweaty socks, unwashed clothes and just the general funk that came when you had too many men perspiring in one place.

The second thing he noticed was how it looked like the place Piñatas came to die. The large space was overloaded with colour, a lot like the dance floor area but the colour hair was even more garish because it came from furniture that looked more suited to a child's bedroom. There was bright pink and yellow shelves, solar system models hanging from the ceiling, and rainbow trimmed mirrors. It felt like it had been decorated to mock the grown men who slept here.

"So this is where you sleep?" Levi said with a raised eyebrow. "I feel like I've just walked into an acid trip."

Shay laughed. "It's pretty crazy, aye?"

"You can say that again." Levi looked down at the transparent floor, able to see the dance floor down below. "You wouldn't want to sleep in here if you were afraid of heights."

"Yeah," Shay agreed. "She's pretty high up."

Levi suddenly realised he couldn't see any beds. "Where do you sleep? There's no beds."

Shay pointed to a corner of the room. "We have mattresses and blankets we lay down at night."

Levi looked over and saw the skinny mattresses leaned against the wall. A ruffled pile of sheets and blankets lay on the floor in front of them. "That can't be very comfortable."

"It's not too bad. You get used to it after a while."

"I suppose it would be a bit like staying at the marae."

Shay snicker-snorted. "What marae's do you know that look like this?"

"Good point."

"You don't mind if I get changed?" Shay asked. "Or would you rather I just stay in these?" He waggled his eyebrows.

Levi rolled his eyes. "Get dressed," he said dryly as he stole one last glance at Shay's bulge.

Shay chuckled and stepped his way through the mess of shoes and scattered clothes until he came to a bright pink box with the name **Pinky** on it. There were three other boxes; one blue, one green and one yellow. They each had silly names on them: **Twitch, Ace and Jock**.

Levi sympathised with his former childhood hero for a brief moment. It must have been infuriating to be treated like a child and have a patronizing nickname rammed down your throat.

Shay pulled out a bundle of clothes that he dropped to the floor then whipped his underwear down his legs. Levi turned around to give him some privacy.

"You don't have to turn away, LP." Shay chuckled. "It ain't like you haven't seen it before."

Levi didn't respond, just kept his back turned and

scoped out the rest of the bitches' box. On the far wall there was a lime-green shelving filled with pristinely-kept skater shoes. "Whose are the cool shoes?"

"Brayden's."

Levi turned around to see Shay tucking a packet of cigarettes into the pocket of the navy blue trackpants he'd put on. He was shirtless, his feet still bare.

"This Brayden fella must really like shoes," Levi said.

"He sure does," Shay replied with frostily. He silently mouthed the word *wanker* as he made a tossing gesture with his hand.

"Not a friend of yours I take it?"

"Not at all." Shay came over and stood beside Levi. "But what home is complete without its token wanker, right?"

"What about the other guys? Do you get on with them?"

"Yes and no. I'm a bit older than the others so it's a bit challenging. Dion's pretty cool though. Thick as pig shit but he's a sweet kid."

"Is that the one in chastity?"

Shay looked surprised Levi knew that. "Nar, not him. That's the other guy. Kane. He's closest to my age but he isn't much of a talker."

"Would you be if your dick didn't work," Levi joked.

"It's not funny," Shay said flatly. "It's actually quite sad."

Levi didn't like being scolded, even if it was only mildly. "Where to now?" he huffed.

"Follow me, LP," Shay said brightly and led the way to yet another tube, not the one they came up in. He gripped the top of the open hole then tucked his legs up and flung his body inside, disappearing from sight.

This place is majorly fucked up, Levi thought to himself then followed suit, flinging himself down the yellow tube which turned out to be a curly slide that took him all the way down into the apartment's lounge. He came out of the slide in an ungraceful crashlanding that saw him skid across the carpet on his arse. He unfolded his body and brushed the seat of his shorts.

"It takes a bit of mastering that one," Shay said, grinning beside the couch.

"Thankfully I'm not the one selling my arse so I don't have to learn how to master it," Levi said spitefully.

Shay nodded glumly. "Guess not."

Levi felt bad until he reminded himself why they no longer talked. Belittling Shay for his current occupation was nothing compared to the shame and hurt he'd inflicted on Levi the last time they met.

In an icy silence they made their towards a flight of stairs that took them up one final level. And what a level it was. *Talk about saving the best for last.* "Wow... a rooftop garden," Levi said with genuine awe. "This is really nice."

Shay immediately responded with, "It's safe to talk now."

Levi sighed, like he'd been holding his breath the entire time. "I take it there are cameras inside?"

"They're throughout the apartment."

"And what about in the basement?"

"Dave says there aren't any down there but I wouldn't trust anything that pakeha says." Shay lowered his voice to a snarly whisper. "Especially with what it is you want to talk about." He matched his surly tone with an equally surly strop over towards the ledge of the building, peering out into the distance.

Levi followed, blown away by the stunning view of wilderness that stretched for miles behind The Castle. He could see rolling ranges and in the far distance snow-capped peaks. *That must be Mt Ruapehu and Mount Ngauruhoe.* He wasn't an expert on geography by any means but they were the only mountains they could be in this part of the North Island. His eyes then skimmed to the fence line acting as a barrier to the sixty-foot cliff that dropped off into the fast-moving river that ran behind the property. He then looked to his right and saw the large oak tree he'd sat under with Dave earlier. From up here he got a better appreciation for just how much land this section was on. Easily two or three acres of mowed lawns, scrappy orchards, vegetable gardens and several garden sheds.

Shay pulled the packet of cigarettes from his pocket, plopped one in his mouth then held the open packet in front of Levi. "Want one?"

"No thanks."

Shay sparked his fag up and took a quick drag, exhaling a heavy plume of white smoke. "So why do you want to talk about your dad?"

"I need to know where you moved the body?"

Confusion mapped Shay's face and raised his voice higher. "Say what?"

"Where did you move his body. It's gone."

"I never moved the fat bastard's body." Shay looked at Levi like he was crazy. "That's just fucking grim."

Levi let out an irritated sigh. "Just tell me where it is, Shay. Me and Mum need to know just in case it has to be moved again."

"Bro, I'm telling you the truth. Why the hell would I want to dig up a dead person." He grimaced and shivered. "That's just creepy."

"Are you sure you didn't do it while you were high?"

"I'm the first to admit I did a tonne of stupid shit when high but nothing that fucking twisted."

"Well his body's gone, Shay, and someone must have

moved it."

"How do you know that?"

"Because Mum and me went to dig him up and he wasn't there."

Shay looked horrified. "Why would you want to dig him up, LP?"

"Because a housing development is about to go up in Wairua Valley and we need to move him before one of the diggers unearth the body."

Shay looked worried for a moment before confidently saying, "Maybe youse didn't dig in the right place. He's buried under the tree with—"

"Yeah, we know where he's buried… or where he's supposed to be buried."

"Honest, LP, I haven't moved him. I've never gone back to Wairua Valley since that night." With his shoulders slumped forward and a dull sheen over his eyes, Shay appeared to be drowning in a violent ocean of memories. "Just the thought of going there makes me think of things I'd rather forget."

"Then who would have dug him up? We're the only ones who know where he was buried."

"Beats me," Shay said. "But if no one has said anything then I don't think it matters where he is. Besides, the fat fuck will be nothing but a pile of bones by now."

Levi nodded despite wanting to shake his head. "But it does matter."

"Why?"

Levi cringed as he confessed the mistake he had made that could send them all to prison. "I didn't empty his pockets." Shay looked confused so Levi said it again. "I didn't empty his pockets before we buried him like you told me to."

Shay's jaw ticked.

"I-I didn't empty his pockets properly and we buried him with his phone still on him. His phone that has all those pictures."

"Oh fuck," Shay muttered under his breath. "Fuck. Fuck. Fuck."

"I'm sorry," Levi snapped. "I know it's my fault and I'm really fucking sorry. If it'll make you feel better then feel free to give me a bollocking for being such a scared little idiot."

Shay turned to him. "I'm not going to give you a bollocking, bro."

"I deserve it."

"No you don't. You were just a kid."

"A kid who was a fucking coward and who has now got us all in the shit."

"You're not a coward, LP," Shay said soothingly. "We were all scared that night."

"Yeah right," Levi muttered. "Mum might have been scared but you weren't. You were cool as. Like you always were."

"I might have acted like I was fine but on the inside I was shitting bricks." He looked desperate for Levi to believe him. "Honest. You were probably the bravest one there."

"Don't take the piss."

"It's true. The only coward from that evening is me. I wasn't man enough to handle what I'd seen so I ended up spending the next seven years fucked off my face on anything I could smoke or snort up my nose."

It went quiet and Levi knew this was the moment he was supposed to tell Shay he was wrong. That he wasn't a coward for turning to drugs. But Shay didn't deserve that. He didn't deserve sympathy, pity, nothing.

When Shay must have realised Levi wasn't coming to

his pity party, he returned his lips to his cigarette before adding. "I've no idea who would have dug him up."

Levi had a *Eureka!* moment. "Wait a minute. Remember that car?"

Shay raised an eyebrow. "What car?"

"The car that came down while we were digging. You spoke to the guy who was driving. Someone with his girlfriend."

Shay nodded slowly, like he was trying to fight the fog of time to remember clearly. "Yeah. That's right. Someone turned up, didn't they."

"Yep. And you knew them. You talked to him. Youse both joked around."

"Fuck. I did know them too, didn't I?" Shay patted himself on the head, trying to jog his memory. "Who the hell was it?"

Please remember. Please remember. Levi prayed that Shay's drug habit hadn't killed the part of his brain capable of storing memories. "You must remember. It's not like we went around burying bodies everyday."

"Nar, bro. I-I remember. The problem is I can't remember the dude's name. It was someone I knew but didn't consider a mate. Like, we weren't super close or nuffin." Shay closed his eyes and slapped his head again. "Think Shay. Think," he ordered himself. "Definitely not a mate but a mate of a mate I think."

For fuck's sake! Just remember already.

It went quiet for a moment before Shay cautiously uttered, "If I remember rightly then it's a dude who used to fuck around on his missus a lot."

Levi rolled his eyes. "That's half of Brixton's male population."

"He had quite a few kids to different women… tall dude… a real hard fucker… shaved head."

As soon as Levi heard the last detail, he blurted out the answer. "Fergus!"

"That's it!" Shay said excitedly, opening his eyes again. "It was definitely Fergus." His excitement waned though when he added, "But do you really think Fergus would have done that? Dig your father up?"

"Who else could it be? He's the only one who came across us that night."

"But he didn't actually see where we buried him though. He didn't even know what we were doing down there."

Shay had a point but Levi couldn't think of who else it could be. "It's gotta be him. Just has to be."

"If it helps, I don't think Fergus is the type to nark on a fellow Brixton-ite."

"Yeah but he doesn't consider me one of those."

"But you are though," Shay said earnestly. "From Brixton."

"Fergus doesn't think so. He just thinks I'm a spoilt little rich prick."

Shay thought that over for a moment. "Even if that's the case I don't think he'd drop me in the shit. Which means he won't drop you or your mum in it either."

"You're probably right, but we still need to know where the body is, or at the very least Dad's phone."

"I wish I could help LP but I can't do much from here. There's really strict rules regarding us contacting people on the outside."

Levi didn't find that remotely surprising. "That's okay. I will speak with him."

"Can you handle him? I know he can be quite a fiery fucker."

"I'll be fine," Levi said, sounding much more sure than he actually felt.

They stood in silence for a while and watched the river

below. Shay eventually dropped his cigarette over the side, letting it fall to the hard patio below. He then surprised Levi by wrapping an arm around his shoulders, trying to reel him in closer. "It's so good to see my little prince again. Fuck I've missed you."

"Don't do that," Levi said, shrugging Shay's arm away.

"What's wrong?"

"You don't get to hug me, or call me your little prince anymore."

Shay looked puzzled. "Why?"

"I only came here to talk about finding Dad's body. You and me… we're dead to each other."

"Don't say that, LP." Shay looked hurt. "Is this about what happened at your house last time I saw you?"

"That *and* the fact you then went onto blackmail me for money."

"Bro, I was off my fucking face. I-I didn't mean to be a dick. I had a problem. You know that. I'm forever sorry that I hurt you. But I promise you I am clean now. Dave sent me to rehab before coming here and I swear I will never go back to drugs again. Never. You have my word."

"I don't give a fuck about your word. What you did was unforgivable."

"I know I took things too far but that wasn't me. Not really. That was a different person than the Shay you know. The one who considers you *whanau*?" Shay's baby blues pleaded for forgiveness. "I've always thought of you like my little brother, LP. We're family you and I. That will never change."

"We're not family, Shay. We're not friends. We're not even associates."

"You don't mean that," Shay said in a croaky whisper.

"I do mean it. Just the same way you meant everything you told me that day."

"Wh-What did I tell you?"

"That my mother was a slut."

Shay's mouth dropped open. "If I said that I didn't mean it."

"Don't act like you can't remember. You know what you said."

Shay nibbled his bottom lip and nodded. "I know I said lots of things I shouldn't have. Lots of things I didn't mean."

"But you and Mum did have an affair, right?" Levi glowered.

Shay hesitated. "I-I don't think that's important."

"Just answer the fucking question, Shay."

He nodded again. "Your mum and I were close for a while. Real close. But I never meant any of the bad things I said about her. That was the drugs, bro."

"But you did have an affair?"

"We did." His gaze fell to the ground. "I'm sorry."

"You don't have to be sorry for that. You were both adults."

"I know but… I feel like I betrayed you."

"You didn't betray me."

"Maybe not, but I feel like I have betrayed your mother by telling you about it. That wasn't cool."

"I wouldn't worry about that. It turns out Mum is quite the expert at dropping her knickers for dropkicks." Levi felt like a prick for saying that, but he was still mad with his mother for cheating on Mark and risking their cushy lives.

"You shouldn't talk about your mum like that, bro. Jenny's a top lady. And she loves you so much."

"If you can call her a slut why can't I?"

Shay looked like a stunned cat, unsure what to say.

Levi took advantage of Shay's stunned silence to go off on a random tirade. "The drugs made you admit to having an affair with my mum so from where I'm standing it makes me think the drugs made you more capable of telling the truth that day, in which case it's safe to assume you really did mean what you told me."

"What did I tell you?"

"That I'm just like *him*… an evil cunt who molested children and murdered people. So yeah, it's fucking great to know that's what you really think of me."

"It was the drugs," Shay insisted.

"So you keep fucking saying."

"I only said that to hurt you, LP. You are nothing like him. Fuck no. That man was scum and there isn't an ounce of him in you."

"Then why would you say it?"

"Because you broke my heart," Shay said without a moment's hesitation.

"How on earth did I break your heart?"

"Because you only invited me to the house to pay me for sex. And don't act like you didn't."

"How is that breaking your heart?" Levi scoffed. "Especially now considering you've decided to make sucking dick your full-time fucking job."

Shay puffed out a heated breath but he didn't raise his fists like Levi had expected. "Because it told me you didn't respect me enough to not try and turn me into something you despise."

Shay hit a kink in Levi's armour. "I don't know what you're talking about."

"Yes you do, Levi." Shay calling him Levi was the equivalent of a parent saying a child's full name. His anger was real and extreme. "You forget I know you better than you think. You might have been living the high life for the past seven years but I'm the one who knows the *real* you. I know the boy who could climb trees higher than anyone else in the neighbourhood. The boy who had monsters living in his closet. The boy who used to think I was the coolest dude in the world." Shay's anger began to slip away, replaced with raw emotion. "The same boy who had the shit beaten out of him nearly every day. The boy I looked out for because he was the sweetest, kindest little prince I'd ever met. The one who with just one hug would make me smile even if I'd had the shittiest day. I know this boy's good points, his bad points, and I can name his demons."

Levi looked away. His chest was constricted and his eyes throbbed with tears that he refused to let loose.

"Don't look away from me," Shay growled. "You look me in the eyes while I tell you this."

Levi sucked in a deep breath, then turned to meet Shay's eyes.

"I know why you were paying those guys for sex. It's not because you are like your dad. It's the complete opposite of that. It's your way of trying to undo the shit he put you through. It's a way for you to feel better about it all. But the problem is you do it at the expense of others, Levi. You were willing to do it at the expense of me."

"You're wrong." Levi's voice warbled. "I do it because I like sex. Simple as that."

"It's more than that. You do it to try and patch up old wounds. But that won't fix it, Levi. It never will. Just like the drugs didn't fix my problems. All you're doing by paying those guys for sex is turning them into the thing you despise most in this world... *yourself*."

"That's not true." Levi shook his head and bit the inside of his cheek. Shay's words were sucking away his control, his breath, his ability to fight a welling of tears. He reached up to dash the dampness away from his cheeks.

"It is true. You hate yourself and it's time you put a stop to it." Shay stepped forward and placed a hand to Levi's chest. "Beneath this hard shell of yours is a good person. You're strong. You're kind. And you're still my little prince." He wrapped Levi into a hug and squeezed him tight.

"Don't hug me," Levi pleaded as he fought to hold back the tears.

"You're a good person," Shay whispered in his ear as Levi squirmed in his arms.

"Please don't hug me," Levi snivelled.

"You're a good person," Shay whispered again and kissed Levi on the cheek. "And I still love you."

That did it. That pure, kind, caring kiss.

For the first time in years Levi lost control of all his emotions. His back heaved with a sob and he erupted with tears that rolled down his cheeks, wetting Shay's neck.

"You're a good person," Shay whispered again, rubbing his back. "Such a good person."

The tears kept flowing and Levi's armour melted away as he found safety in the arms of the one person who'd always protected him.

His rebel with a heart of gold.

CHAPTER 8

As Levi drove away from The Castle he felt lighter, his spirit less weighed down than before. He was still embarrassed about bawling his eyes out on Shay's shoulder but he knew he was better for having done so. It hadn't fixed anything, but how do you fix someone who is so broken they don't even know where all their pieces are anymore?

Maybe it did fix one thing.

Shay had been restored as the hero Levi used to envision him as. The cool big kid who was tough as fuck and would kick anyone's arse who dared laid a finger on Levi. Even though Levi wasn't a child anymore it felt good to know he had a superhero in his world again. It helped balance out the numerous villains he had in his life.

None of them are as bad as Dad though.

Shay had unearthed some ugly truths Levi liked to keep locked away. Things about himself he'd rather forget and let die in a time capsule buried deep inside his brain. The problem with this time capsule though was it had stuff inside even Shay didn't know about, and no matter how many times Shay told Levi none of it was his fault, it didn't make Levi feel any less responsible for ruining so many lives.

I was such a fucking moron back then!

Although he was only thirteen when it had started happening, Levi couldn't help but feel a fool for not picking up on the signs as to what sort of man his father was. After all, it wasn't like he hadn't been warned.

Lucky, Levi's closet-dwelling imaginary friend (or whatever the hell he was) had taken great delight in telling scary stories about Levi's father. Night after night the naked sticker-covered deviant would wander around Levi's bedroom, sticking his tongue out and tugging on his dick, while he polluted Levi's young ears with lewd details no child should have to hear.

Unfortunately, as soon as Shay's grandmother had blessed the house and rid it of Lucky and the others living in Levi's closet, Levi chose to forget all about the foul-breathed Lucky and his ominous warnings.

And for a while it had been fine. Perfectly fine. But that all started to change the day Levi's father did the unthinkable… he begun to be nice to Levi.

Seven years earlier

Much to Levi's delight, the very first day of his school holidays had gone amazingly well. He'd wandered to the Brixton shops with Scott to help Scott find a birthday present for his mother. The boy had a grand total of twelve dollars to buy his mother a gift but rather than spend it on a present, Scott shouted them both hot chips and a bottle of coke from the bakery.

This was partly done out of their selfish hunger for the tasty chips doused with chicken salt but it was also a *fuck you* from Scott to his mother for buying him tennis balls for his fourteenth birthday the week before.

When they had devoured their meal, washed down with the shared bottle of coke, Scott said, "I feel a bit guilty now."

"Don't feel guilty," Levi said. "Just think of the tennis balls she got you."

"They were nice tennis balls though," Scott countered.

"But they were still tennis balls, bro. That's shit."

"Yeah." Scott nodded. "It is shit. But I still need to get her something."

"You could pick her flowers?"

Scott looked like he was about to agree to that idea until he eyed the pharmacy gift shop across the street. "Or what if we grabbed her something with a five-finger discount?"

Levi grinned. "I thought you were already trespassed for stealing from there?"

"Nar. That was Dobson's chemist up the other end of town."

Scott had been stealing from stores since they were eleven. For the most part it was just candy bars from dairies but occasionally he'd have a go at other stores. He had been trespassed from several shops in Brixton already and a couple of the malls in Fitzroy so it wasn't like Scott was perfect at the art of thievery but nine times out of ten he didn't get caught. Levi didn't mind helping his pal out though. Provided he wasn't the one busted with the goods there wasn't shit all the shopkeepers could do.

Five minutes later, they were inside the pharmacy gift store so Scott could score his mother some birthday presents. Levi distracted the girl behind the counter by asking her for suggestions as to what ointment worked best for athlete's foot. It was a random ailment to choose and he just hoped she didn't ask him to take his shoes and socks off to show her the non-existent infection.

Levi surprised himself by being able to talk absolute rubbish about athlete's foot for nearly five minutes while Scott roamed the gifts on display behind him. Just as Levi was running out of stuff to say about his supposedly sore toes, he heard the distant sound of a snotty nose being sniffed—Scott's que to let Levi know he was done.

Levi told the girl he'd be back later in the afternoon and promptly walked outside where he found Scott walking along the footpath like he was in desperate need of a shit.

Levi laughed at his friend's awkward walk, knowing it was because of whatever he'd shoved down his pants. "Did you get anything good?"

"Yeah, bro. If we go over to the domain I'll show you."

Once they were at the domain, Scott sat down on the park bench and adjusted the obvious bulge in his pants caused by the stolen goods.

"I got Mum some earrings," Scott said excitedly. "Look how pretty they are." He held them up to show Levi. "Nice, aye?"

"Those are for little girls you dick."

"You reckon?"

"When was the last time you saw someone your mum's age wear stars with rainbow unicorns on them?"

Scott studied the earrings in his hand and nodded. "Maybe I can give them to my sister."

"What else did you get?"

Scott's hand disappeared back inside his pants, digging around in his briefs before coming out holding a purple candle. "Mum loves candles." He sniffed it. "And it's scented."

"Yeah, scented with your sweaty balls."

Scott laughed. "The best smell in the world." He jokingly waved the candle in front of Levi's face. "Have a sniff, bro."

Levi laughed, moving his head away. "Fuck off, homo."

Scott's hand made one last descent into his pants and he pulled out a silver ashtray. "I know for sure Mum will love this."

"That's pretty cool," Levi said, admiring the ashtray that was decorated with patterns of marijuana leaves.

"I like it too but it's making me desperate for a smoke."

"Same," Levi fibbed. He didn't really smoke, just bum puffed on them when Scott would share one with him. Scott though had been smoking for nearly two years and was always getting into trouble for stealing them from his mother's packet.

"I tried to take us a couple from Mum's pouch this morning but she busted me."

"Bummer."

"Tell me about it." Scott sighed loudly. "I don't suppose you got any?"

"I got nada."

"Do you think we could nick some off your dad?"

"Only if you want a trip to the hospital. He'd kill me if I tried touching his smokes."

"True dat." Scott nodded solemnly before his eyes lit up with an idea. "I do know one way we could get some."

"What's that?"

"Hemi was telling me last week that there's a guy who lives down at the motor camp who will give young guys cigarettes if they show him their cock."

Levi sniggered. "Gross."

"It's not like he touches it. Hemi reckons he just likes to look."

"And how the fuck does Hemi know? He doesn't even

smoke."

"His older brother told him."

Maybe the story had some merit then. While Hemi was the sensible bookworm in the Retimana family his older brother Rawiri was the problem child.

"Would you actually show someone your dick just to get a smoke?" Levi leered at his friend.

Scott hesitated. "Maybe… Yeah."

Levi sniggered. "Bro, you need to quit if this is what smoking does to you."

"Come on. It'll be a laugh."

"I ain't showing some crusty peado my cock."

"Go on," Scott whined. "That way we will get one each."

"Sorry, but you're on your own with that one."

Scott frowned with disappointment. "Will you at least come with me while I do it?"

"What are you gonna do? Walk around the motor camp asking every dude you see if he's the one that hands smokes out to dick flashers?"

Scott shrugged. He obviously hadn't thought that far ahead.

Before Levi could tell his friend it was a numbskull idea, he heard a girl say his name. Whipping his head around, he saw the one and only Tina Barr. She looked stunning, her body stretched tight inside of a red tank top and painted-on jean shorts. Her legs looked satiny-smooth and coated with some type of shimmer oil. Walking with the confidence of a supermodel, Tina bowled right on up to where they were sitting and smiled at Levi.

"H-Hi Tina," Levi said, his tongue tripping over itself. "It's really hot today, isn't it?" *Good one idiot. Talk to her about the weather why don't you. Lame.*

Tina nodded. "I guess so."

"So, uh, what are you doing?" Levi asked.

"I just got back from Fitzroy with my sister. We went shopping for some clothes." She motioned at her denim shorts. "I bought these."

"They're nice." Levi swallowed, his dick inflating in his shorts.

"What have youse been up to?" she asked.

"We just pinched all this from the pharmacy," Scott said proudly.

Fuck up you moron. Levi wanted to hit him.

Scott held up the earrings. "You can have these if you like?"

Tina stared at the earrings like they were cat vomit. "Er, no thanks. Those are for kids."

Scott studied the earrings again. "That's what Levi said."

Tina ignored Levi's dopey sidekick and said to Levi, "What are you doing after you leave here?"

"We're going to the motor camp," Scott replied.

"I wasn't talking to you," Tina said coolly.

Levi's dick hardened some more. "Uh, I, uh, I'm not doing anything."

"Good. Then maybe you'd like to meet me at the swimming hole in Wairua Valley. I reckon it's the perfect day for a swim."

"Absolutely," he returned, smiling. "What time?"

"Meet me down there in an hour." She shot him a flirty wink. "And don't forget your togs."

When she walked away, Levi turned to Scott, grinning like a loon. "Oh, man I think I'm in there. And you know about those rumours, aye?"

"What rumours"

"You know… that she sucks guys off down by the creek."

Rather than be happy for him, Scott looked sour. "I

can't believe you'll let that stuck up bitch suck your dick but you won't help score me an extra ciggy by flashing your dick."

Levi laughed. "I'll tell you what. If Tina sucks me off then I will steal some tobacco from my father's pouch for you."

That cheered Scott up and they left the domain with a smile on both their faces.

∞

As soon as Levi got back to his house, he raced to his bedroom and got changed into his togs. Once he had them on he figured they were probably a bit pointless considering it was unlikely they were going for a swim. *Maybe she likes to suck dick under water?* That seemed unlikely but the more Levi thought about it the more he wondered what that would feel like.

After cramming a beach towel into his school bag, he made his way shirtless to the kitchen to have a glass of milk before he left. That was the wrong fucking thing to do.

"Boy wonder is finally home," said his father who was sat at the kitchen table smoking a fag.

"Hi, Dad," Levi grunted before opening the fridge and proceeding to pour himself a glass of milk.

"Where did you fuck off to this morning? I woke up and found your bed empty."

"I went to the shops with Scott to help him buy a present for his mum's birthday."

"And what did you little pricks pinch?"

"Nothing," Levi hurled back. "I'm not a thief."

His father took a drag on his cigarette. "The whole

town knows little snotty Scotty is light fingered. Max who owns the dairy on Chatty's Corner told me he calls the kid *'the rat'* because his sticky little mitts are faster than a rat up a drainpipe." His father laughed so hard he coughed.

Levi rolled his eyes then dished out the lie he'd already prepared. "I'm about to go hang out with Scott again. Did you want me home for dinner or can I stay and have dinner there?"

"I don't give a fuck what time you come home but before you go anywhere I need you to mow the lawns."

"I can't. Scott's waiting for me."

"Well, Scott will just have to wait until you've mowed those lawns. They're way too fucking long and need a mow."

"Why don't you mow them then," Levi dared to fling back.

"Because I am the man of the house who goes to work every fucking day to put a roof over you and ya mother's head, so I don't think it's un-fucking-reasonable for me to expect your lazy arse to pull its weight now and then."

Levi sizzled with anger. The bastard was such a hypocrite. The man worked part-time as a bus driver, not exactly manual labour. He also did fucking nothing around the house. Levi's mother did everything while his father usually pissed off to the pub in the evenings before coming home to sit his fat arse in front of the television—and that was if he even came home from the pub.

"Can I mow them tomorrow?" Levi asked, hoping to reach a compromise.

"No. I want them done today."

"But Dad!" he protested, cringing at the whine he heard in his voice. "Scott's expecting me *really* soon."

"Tough titties for you because you have lawns to mow."

Levi wanted to scream out "There's a girl waiting for me

who wants to suck my dick!" but of course he knew that wasn't the best thing to say. Or maybe it was? He tried a watered-down version. "What if I told you I actually have a date with a girl? That's why I'm in a hurry to leave."

"I would still say get ya lazy fucking arse outside and mow them fucking lawns unless you fancy getting a hiding?"

"But Dad."

"No *but dad.* Just get outside and do as your fucking told."

Levi pleaded with his eyes, desperate for his father to give him a break.

"The way I see it," his father said in an eerily calm voice, "You can go meet this girl and not mow the lawns, but if you do that then you won't have a bed to sleep in tonight. Or you can do what ya fucking told and not find your ungrateful arse living on the street."

Levi was shaking with a mixture of rage and pent-up hormones. "Fine," he huffed, dropping his empty glass in the sink. "I'll go mow these fucking lawns then." He threw his arms up in the air and stomped his way out of the kitchen.

I fucking hate you, he thought to himself. Just as his bare feet left the clammy linoleum floor of the kitchen and stepped on the manky carpet in the hallway, his father's voice boomed behind him. "Get back here."

Levi hesitated. Frozen in place. His heart squeezed, worried that his father was gonna give him the belt for swearing at him.

"I said. Come. Here." His father's voice was low and intimidating as hell

Levi slowly pivoted and wandered back towards the kitchen table. "Yeah?"

His father hauled himself to his feet and stepped

towards him. Levi's heart thudded as he watched his father's hand slowly raise. He closed his eyes, expecting a fist to crash into his face. But no fist arrived. Instead, his father's hand reached for Levi's arm and he held it up, inspecting his armpit. "When did you start growing hair under there?"

Levi shrugged. "Dunno. A while ago." That wasn't true. Levi knew exactly when. He'd spotted his first strand of pit hair two days after turning thirteen. Six months ago.

His father smiled. "Fuck me. I had no idea you were turning into a man already." His gaze strayed down to Levi's crotch. "You sprouting them down there too?"

"Dad," Levi whispered in embarrassment.

"Well… are ya?"

Levi laughed nervously. "Yeah. I've had them longer."

"Show me."

"I'm not showing you my dick." Levi grimaced. *This is as bad as Scott's mystery motorcamp man.*

"Stop being a fucking wuss and show your old man what you're sprouting."

Levi went to say no again but when he saw his father's eyes flash with fiery impatience, he tugged the front of his shorts down and showed his dad the small forest of hair down there. He didn't drop them low enough to show his bits, just enough to prove that he did in fact have hair down there.

His father looked utterly mesmerized, not saying a word until finally he nodded his approval. "Well done, son. You really are becoming a man."

Levi blushed and pulled his shorts back up.

His father began staring into his eyes, like he was looking at Levi for the very first time. "You're actually growing into quite a pretty little fucker, ain't ya?"

Levi laughed, more out of nerves than humour. "Boys

can't be pretty. Boys are handsome."

"Handsome. Pretty. It's the same thing when lad's are your age."

A brief silence lingered as his father's gaze flicked between Levi's crotch and face. A smile then appeared on the man's thick lips. "You got a date with a girl you say?"

"Yeah. Her name's Tina. She's in my math class and she just saw me in town and invited me to go swimming with her."

"I suppose I can let you mow the lawns tomorrow then if it's a date ya going on."

"Really? Thanks, Dad. You're the best!"

"But just so you know, I'll expect a favour from you in return."

"Sure, Dad. Anything you want."

His father chuckled and clapped Levi on the shoulder. "Alright, son. Go get ya girl."

Levi sped off before his father changed his mind, too excited about meeting up with Tina to give much thought to the weirdness of what had just happened between them.

He had just missed the first sign.

CHAPTER 9

"It's time you start looking harder for a new job," Gerald's patronizing tone found Lucas over the blaring television on in the background. "You can't rely on others to hand you opportunities. You have to find them for yourself."

Lucas nodded and smiled like he always did when Sophie's father started lecturing him about how much of a screw-up he was. Lucas didn't need reminding. He was well aware about his failure to provide for his family.

Sophie's father had never been his biggest fan which was probably understandable considering Lucas had got Sophie pregnant at just seventeen. He had hoped that after four years Sophie's father would have grown to like him at least a little but that had never happened.

"I don't know why you can't find something full-time," Gerald continued. "Pushing lawnmowers around for fun is not what I would call a real job."

Lucas sniggered.

"What's so funny?" Gerald demanded.

"You thinking I mow lawns for fun. It's actually really hard work."

"Real hard work would be you working forty hours a week to keep a roof over my daughter and granddaughter's head. Working part-time as you are just means you have more time to fluff about."

Would you just shut the fuck up, Lucas wanted to tell him. But he had no place talking to Gerald like that. Certainly not in the man's own home. Every Tuesday evening Lucas and Sophie came here for dinner and every evening was the same; Sophie's mum would cook them all a nice meal and after dinner Mia would watch a movie in the den while Sophie and her mum would do the dishes and let the men talk in the lounge. If Lucas had a choice in the matter he would have swapped places with Sophie and cleaned up in the kitchen rather than sit with Gerald while the older man busted Lucas's balls for not taking good enough care of his darling daughter and precious grandchild.

"Lucas doesn't fluff about, Dad" Sophie said as she came in from the kitchen. "If he's not working then he is at home helping me take care of Mia." She sat beside Lucas on the couch and gave his knee a reassuring squeeze.

"If you say so," Gerald muttered under his breath.

"Are you being rude again, Gerald," Sophie's mother said as she joined them in the lounge. She shot Lucas a sympathetic look. "Just ignore him, Lucas. Gerald can't help being a grumpy old man."

"Forgive me for caring, Beverly," Gerald said to his wife. "These two worry me. They're raising Mia while they haven't got two pennies to rub together."

"We're fine, Dad," Sophie said with a smile. "Things are tough at the moment but we will come right."

Lucas hoped so because despite what Sophie was telling her father they weren't fine. Not even close. They had bills coming out their ears, a kid who was constantly outgrowing her clothes and a car that sounded like it was shitting blood and guts out its exhaust pipe.

"You'll come right when one of you starts working full-time," Gerald said. "And you both know my views on who that should be."

"Lucas is trying his best, Dad," Sophie countered. "There's just no work going at the moment."

"What are you talking about?" Her father scoffed. "Your brother just started a new role last week. He had to turn down three other jobs that wanted him."

"To be fair, Dad, Brent is a software developer with ten years experience. It's not like him and Lucas are applying for the same sort of work."

"Which is why an education is so important," Gerald said to his daughter. "Neither of you seem to realise that."

While Sophie tried to placate her father, Lucas sat quietly and kept out of it. The worst part of Gerald's constant snipes wasn't that the man was being cunty and rude it was that Lucas totally agreed with him. He knew he had a responsibility to take care of his family and at the moment he wasn't meeting that responsibility. Instead of worrying about having enough money for food and rent each week they should have been saving up for a house deposit or towards having enough money to finally get married. It killed Lucas that after fours years of being together he still didn't have enough money to buy the girl of his dreams an engagement ring.

Maybe Uncle Dwight will increase my hours soon?

Lucas wasn't counting on that happening though. He would work sixty-hour weeks if Uncle Dwight asked him to. It didn't matter how physically demanding the job was at times, Lucas would gladly do the work. He got a real sense of satisfaction from mowing lawns that he had never gotten from working at his last job, and he enjoyed spending time with his father's best mate. Uncle Dwight was a cool cunt with a crass sense of humour that had Lucas cracking up most days. The only thing he wasn't so keen on was the funny looks Uncle Dwight would sometimes give him. On a couple occasions he could have sworn he'd caught Dwight checking out his arse. But he must have imagined it because there was no way Uncle Dwight was a poofter. The guy scored more pussy than any man Lucas knew.

"Who feels like some ice cream and jelly?" Sophie's mother asked interrupting her husband still going on about the importance of education.

"Yes please, Mum," Sophie answered before turning to Lucas. "What about you, babe? Ice cream and jelly?"

Lucas hesitated, still lost in his thoughts. "Er, none for me, thanks."

"Are you sure?" Sophie's mother asked.

"I'm already sweet enough," Lucas joked with a half-smile.

"You can give me Lucas's share," Gerald said cheekily to his wife. "I think we all know I could do with some sweetening up."

You ain't wrong there, arsehole.

"Then you better come help," Beverly replied. "You can take a bowl down for Mia."

Gerald grinned and shot up out of his chair, not because he was particularly inclined to do what his wife told him but because he always jumped at any chance to treat his granddaughter who he made no secret of being his favourite person in the world. This is what Lucas always found odd. How could Gerald hate him so much when if it wasn't for him (and a drunken four minutes in the back of his old Toyota Corolla when he forgot to use a condom) then Gerald wouldn't have Mia in his life.

Lucas jolted when he felt Sophie's hand grope his

package. "Why hello," he said, glancing at her with raised eyebrows.

"Hello you," Sophie said in a sexy whisper as she gave him another grope.

"I wouldn't advise you do that too much or I'll end up pitching a tent in front of your parents."

"It wouldn't be the first time." Sophie's delicate fingers stroked him through his jeans. "I was wondering if we ask Mum and Dad to let Mia stay here tonight so we could have some alone time."

Lucas grinned. "I like the sound of that but I don't think we have enough gas to come get her tomorrow for school."

"That doesn't matter. Mum will drop her off in the morning if I ask her too." Lucas swallowed, watching Sophie's hand get friskier with his package. "We haven't made love in over a week," she added softly. "I miss pleasing my big, strong man."

Lucas missed it too but the truth was he hadn't been in the mood since finding out Sameer had died. Any time he began to get hard his brain would inconveniently remind him that he had killed a man, and just like that his dick would shrivel.

Sophie gripped his balls tightly through the denim, causing that little bit of pain he always enjoyed. "Okay. If you're sure your mum won't mind."

"Good." Sophie squeezed his nuts one more time then removed her hand.

He patted his hardening crotch, hoping his dick would rise to the challenge when they got home.

"Maybe we can stop off for a bottle of wine on the way home," Sophie suggested.

"I would love to, babe, but I haven't got a bean."

Sophie nodded. "What if I asked Dad to lend us some

money? He won't mind."

"But I'll mind," Lucas grumbled. "You know I hate asking your dad for money."

"That's why I will ask him."

"But then he'll just come lecture me when you leave the room about how I ain't taking good enough care of you and Mia."

"And I will come back and tell him you take care of me and Mia perfectly."

"Is that true though? I haven't even got enough money to buy you a bottle of wine."

"There's more to taking care of someone than money, babe." She placed a hand to his cheek and turned his head for a kiss. "Love you."

"Love you too."

The kiss and "love you" only added to the stiffness in his pants and Lucas found himself wanting to skip on desert and take Sophie home right this minute so they could make love all night.

Sophie's mother entered the lounge holding two bowls of ice cream and jelly and handed one to Sophie before sitting down on the other couch. A minute later, Gerald returned carrying his own bowl of desert which was stacked ridiculously high with red jelly.

While the others sat devouring their desert, Lucas excused himself to go use the toilet. After relieving his bladder, he poked his head into the den to check on Mia. He smiled at the sight of her pretty face smeared with chocolate sauce and jelly chunks.

"What cha doing, monster?" he asked.

"Watching The Wiggles," she replied with her mouth full. "Come watch."

"Daddy would love to but he has to go talk with the adults."

"Watch one song with me." She giggled "I like it when you do the dances."

Levi sighed, pretending to think it over despite knowing he'd already given in. "Okay… but just one song."

"Yay!" Mia dropped her spoon and clapped excitedly.

He went and sat down beside his daughter and suffered through a ear-grating rendition of the ABC song, clapping along like an toddler superfan. But one song became two songs and then three. Once Mia had finished her desert, she began pestering him to get up and dance with her. Lucas got to his feet and began waving his long limbs about as he hopped around in circles looking like an utter tool. Mia hopped around with him and together they looked like dying flies buzzing about on a window sill. His unco daddy dance was interrupted though when he saw Gerald standing in the doorway trying not to laugh.

Lucas grinned bashfully at Sophie's father. "Someone asked for a dance."

"Daddy's a good dancer," Mia squealed.

"I can see that." Gerald smirked. "Lucas… can we have a word in private."

Mia tugged on his arm. "Don't go."

"Daddy's got to go talk with granddad. I'll be back soon."

"Huwwy up," she said then got back to bopping about.

Lucas followed Gerald into the hallway where the older man pulled out his wallet. "What are you doing?" Lucas asked.

"Giving you this." Gerald pulled two fifty dollar notes out of his wallet.

Lucas shook his head. "I don't want your money, Gerald."

"Don't be a proud fool. Just take it."

"I don't need it."

Gerald sighed. "Look, I wasn't eavesdropping but I overheard Sophie before asking you to buy her some wine for a romantic evening at home."

Oh God… Lucas felt a blush roast his cheeks. "You weren't supposed to hear that."

"I gather that," Gerald said dryly. "But I want you to take this money and buy her some wine and whatever else she wants."

"Gerald, we're fine. We don't need your money."

"Evidently you do, Lucas, or you wouldn't be telling my daughter you can't afford to buy her a bottle of wine." He grabbed Lucas's wrist and placed the money in Lucas's reluctant hand. "If it makes you feel better then you can pay me back. But only when you can afford to do so."

Lucas bit his lower lip, nodding in shame. "Thank you, Gerald."

"You can thank me by finding a better job," Sophie's father replied before disappearing back to the lounge.

Lucas hated feeling so damn helpless and emasculated. As he slipped the money in his pocket, he promised himself this would be the last time he ever got a handout from Sophie's father.

It'll be the last handout from anyone!

Luckily for Lucas financial freedom was just about within reach. The answer to all his problems was in the back of a badly-dented Ute hidden on Uncle Dwight's property. Unfortunately it was the same Ute every cop in Fitzroy was looking for.

He'd beat himself up over those blasted cigarettes hidden in that Ute for weeks now, wondering if he should tell Uncle Dwight he wanted no part of selling goods stained with the blood of an innocent man. But as he stood in Sophie's parents' hallway, feeling utterly emasculated, Lucas decided he didn't have a choice.

He needed to step up and be the man Sophie needed, and God help anyone who got in his way.

CHAPTER 10

With a mind full of happy daydreams, Shay sat at the dining table sketching a picture of the river and hills that ran behind the property. Since arriving at the castle he'd found himself drawing more and more, finding it a good way to cope with the boredom. It sure as shit beat sitting with the others in the lounge and talking pointless crap like they were right now. Shay wasn't against talking crap with mates but that was the problem; the other pets weren't his mates. Even after living here for six months he still felt like he was on the outer with them.

Things had improved a lot since he had swallowed his pride and submitted to the hierarchy of the group but he still hadn't made a genuine connection with any of them. Dion was a sweet kid and definitely the friendliest towards him but that wasn't saying much considering Kane pretty much ignored him and Brayden was always gunning for an argument.

Despite the lack of comradery, Shay still found the boys entertaining to watch, which he tended to do most evenings. The dining table gave him a perfect view of the lounge and he was able to watch them interact as if he were spying on monkeys in their natural habitat. Monkeys that grunted, squabbled, and scratched their nuts a lot.

One of the intriguing things about the pets after-dinner ritual was how they would go to the lounge and sit in the same places every night. You didn't need a psychology degree to know the seating arrangement was a visual representation of the pecking order.

Naturally, Brayden had the best seat in the house; the left-hand side of the couch which gave him a direct view of the television and easy access to the coffee table. Kane had the next best spot; sat beside Brayden. Then, like a raft drifting into the distance, Dion was always sat further back in one of the armchairs closer to the dining area, confirming his status as the lowest-ranked of them all. Technically that was wrong, Shay was probably at the bottom of the pecking order, but on account of not giving a flying fuck he figured that made Dion the weakest link.

He found it strange how the other two bowed down to the tough-talking, fist-shaking Brayden. The kid wasn't physically intimidating; he was average height with a slim build and was more of a pretty boy than a fighter. Back in Brixton, boys like Brayden usually got the shit kicked out of them until they learned to shut their arrogant mouths. Shay could understand why Dion backed down; it wasn't in the boy's nature to fight back. But Kane? Muscular, tatted, surly-looking Kane? He could have easily beat the shit out of Brayden but never once had Levi seen Kane challenge him.

When he'd finished drawing the river and hills, he started on a new picture. One of Levi. Seeing a familiar face had put a huge smile on Shay's face for the rest of the afternoon. It had been good for his soul to catch up with his little prince and heal old wounds. They'd talked for nearly two hours, exchanging apologies and reminiscing about days gone by before Levi announced he would have to start making tracks. Shay had given his little prince one last lingering hug, wrapping him up in his arms and holding him tight, grateful to have some genuine, honest affection. Secretly though, he wouldn't have minded if the affection had delved to less innocent places.

Other than the unfinished handjob, Levi hadn't made any moves of a sexual nature. That was probably for the best but a part of Shay—most notably his balls—wished Levi had finished what he'd started down in the basement and gifted him a much-needed orgasm.

The quickest and easiest solution to deal to his blue balls would have been to go have a wank but he didn't want to use his hand if he could avoid it. He wanted sex. Correction: he *needed* sex. Going five days without ejaculating made him feel that the only cure for the painful desire constantly licking his taint and balls was a fuck. He didn't care that his only options were of the male variety, he was past caring at this point.

He tapped his foot nervously under the table, knowing he was planning on doing something tonight he swore he'd never do—fuck another man just for fun. Dion was the easy option but if Shay was going to go gay without pay then it had to be someone bigger and more rugged than himself… someone a lot like Kane.

Out the corner of his eye, Shay watched Kane lean into the back of the couch. Kane's fingers were laced together resting on his stomach, and his legs were outstretched, with his bare feet crossed at the ankles resting on the coffee table. He looked casual, manly and sexy, the sort of guy who in the outside world would kick Shay's arse for having lewd thoughts about him. But they weren't in the outside world, they were in The Castle where straight men did things they wouldn't normally do.

Which means he might just say yes.

Aside from being the most physically appealing of Shay's housemates, the added benefit of Kane was Shay knew the tatted-up bad boy would keep his mouth shut. The last thing he wanted was for Brayden to find out he'd started dicking guys for pleasure. He'd never hear the fucking end of it.

With a six-two frame and bulging inked biceps, Kane had the sort of physique found on a kickboxing champion, strength and testosterone oozing from every pore of his rugged body. He was also the only pet Shay had not seen naked, probably due to Kane's unspoken embarrassment about his caged cock and how tiny it had become. But it wasn't Kane's dick Shay was interested in, it was his firm arse and the manly grunts Shay imagined he would make while being shafted.

When Shay had first arrived here, he had wrongly assumed Kane was a piece of shit skinhead. It was an easy mistake to make considering the guy's shaved head and white power tattoos on his chest and thighs. But it was all a mirage. Just another case of Dave dressing one of his pets up to cater to his clients' bizarre fantasies. Every few weeks Kane's brown hair would be shaved and the henna tattoos redone.

The little Shay did know about Kane was that he had once been a rowing champion who worked as a bartender. How he came to be employed here was a mystery which Kane refused to talk about it. Whatever the reason it was probably safe to say it was shameful in nature. All their stories were to some degree.

"Hey, Dion," Brayden suddenly hollered. "Fetch me a coke from the fridge."

Shay looked over and saw that Dion was so engrossed

in the show they were watching he didn't appear to have heard Brayden.

"Oi, deaf cunt! Get me a can of coke," Brayden shouted, causing Dion to flinch.

"Sorry. What?" Dion blinked back.

Brayden pinched the bridge of his nose and sighed impatiently. "I said… get me a can of coke."

Dion stood up like the dutiful slave he was and made his way towards the kitchen.

"Grab me one too," Kane said expectantly.

On his way to the fridge, Dion stopped at the dining table to ask Shay who he was drawing.

"It's my friend Levi," Shay replied, shading in a patch of Levi's hair. "I've known him for years. He's pretty much family."

"Are you drawing him cos you miss him?" the boy asked in his simple tone.

"I do." Shay nodded. "A lot more than I thought."

"I miss my friends too," Dion said. "When I get back home I am gonna have the biggest party with them all. I'll be able to shout all the drinks and—"

"Stop fucking yakking, Dion, and bring us our drinks," Brayden screeched. "I'm fucking thirsty."

Seeing the way Dion rushed to the fridge like he'd just had an electric shock annoyed the hell out of Shay so he broke his rule of not getting involved with their drama and decided to say something. "You know, Brayden, you have two perfectly good legs of your own that you can use to get up and get your own drink if you're that thirsty."

"I wasn't talking to you, faggot," Brayden flung back.

Shay laughed. "That might be the wrong word to use around here, don't cha think?"

Brayden heaved out another sigh. "What the fuck are you on about, Pinky?"

"Considering what we do for a job you might want to reconsider using the word faggot as an insult… you're only insulting yourself."

"A man's only a faggot if he takes it up the arse," Brayden returned. "And unlike you three homos, I don't do that."

"You might not get fucked by the clients but we all know you take Dave's dick every night he invites you to stay at his apartment." Shay knew that was a lie but he wanted to rattle the young prick.

"Dave doesn't fuck me," Brayden hissed. "You're just jealous he never invites you to stay the night in his room."

"I ain't jealous cos unlike you I'm not a fan of pensioner penis going up my arse."

"Fuck up, dick," Brayden muttered.

Dion rushed into the lounge and quickly handed Kane and Brayden their drinks. "Pinky's only joking, Bray," Dion said, trying to play peacemaker.

"No I'm not," Shat said. "I'm being absolutely serious. Why else do you think Dave buys him so many pairs of shoes."

Brayden shot him the evils. "Maybe you'd like me to tell Dave what you're saying? I bet he won't like hearing that you're spreading lies again."

"And maybe you should try not being a narking little bitch all your life." Shay stared back just as evilly.

"Could you two knock it off," Kane said gruffly. "I'm trying to watch the television."

"Don't tell me to knock it off when it's Pinky who started it," Brayden snapped. "He's always the one starting shit."

Kane didn't say anymore. The fact he'd even interjected in the first place was surprising.

Shay wanted to keep winding Brayden up but he didn't

want to upset Kane and ruin his chances for a hookup, so to avoid the escalating argument he decided to go to the toilet and take a slash.

When he returned from the bathroom, Shay found that the sketch he'd been drawing of Levi was ruined; drenched in puddles of cola. He looked towards the lounge where he saw Brayden sniggering. "Cheers for that, arsehole."

"You're welcome, Pinky," Brayden replied. "It was a shit drawing anyway."

Shay composed himself with a series of deep breaths, knowing it wasn't worth losing his shit over. He went and grabbed a tea towel and wiped up the mess and started a new sketch.

For the next hour, he carried on drawing while watching Kane out the corner of his eye, waiting for a chance to speak with him alone. Because Kane was dressed in a jumper and trackpants not a lot of his body was on show but Shay admired the flesh he could see; Kane's handsome face, his manly hands and big feet. Shay found himself particularly engrossed by the dark hairs that were visible just above Kane's ankles, and his dick twitched like crazy when he saw Kane lift up his pants leg and scratch at his hairy calf. It was crazy to think that Kane's feet and a sneak peek of his leg were the reason Shay's briefs were turning into a piece of precum soaked cloth, but he wasn't ashamed. He was going to fuck Kane with pride and give the sexy fucker five days' worth of cum.

I need you two to fuck off already, Shay screamed inside his head at Brayden and Dion. *Go to the games room and play table tennis or go fuck each other in the bitches box like you usually do. Just go away so me and Kane can talk!*

Five minutes later, Levi's prayers were answered when Brayden suggested to Dion that they go hang out in the games room. The young pair toddled off, leaving Shay alone with the scowling stud. He only waited a minute before going over and sitting beside Kane on the couch.

"What are you watching?" Shay asked.

"Episodes."

"Episodes of what?"

"No, dork." Kane sniggered. "Episodes is the name of the show."

"Oh… is it any good?"

"It's okay. Quite funny in places." Kane looked at where Levi was sitting. "You're taking your life in your hands to be sitting there, aren't you?"

"Did you want me to sit somewhere else?"

"I don't care where you sit but Brayden will have a fucking hernia if he catches you in his spot."

"Anyone would think he's sprayed it and claimed it as his," Shay joked.

"He might not have pissed on it but its definitely got his jizz all over it."

Shay laughed, assuming Kane was joking.

"No shit," Kane said flatly. "Dion's sucked him off there plenty of times and he nearly always coughs some of it up."

Shay's arse suddenly felt grossly uncomfortable but he didn't want to move away before he'd asked Kane for the rather big favour of bending over. "Hey, um, there was something I—"

"Shh," Kane hissed. "I'm trying to watch the fucking show."

Shay pretended to zip his mouth shut and looked ahead at the television. He wouldn't usually tolerate a guy being so rude and dismissive towards him but Kane had something he wanted so he remained quiet. As he sat there pretending to watch the television show, he kept looking over at Kane's lap, trying to imagine what his padlocked dick might look like. He didn't have any sexual interest in the bloke's todger but that didn't mean he wasn't curious to see it. Kane's dick was a bit like the loch ness monster. Often discussed but never really witnessed.

What Shay had seen however was the mould of Kane's cock on display in the reception area. Like the rest of the pets, Kane too had been forced to let Dave take a mould of his dick on his first day here. Shay had no idea how big or small Kane's dick was now but what Shay did know was that upon Kane's arrival to The Castle the athletic jock was sporting the kind of cock any man would be proud of. It wasn't as large as Brayden's—few were—but it still belonged in the category of the well-endowed.

For Shay, the reception was an embarrassing place. He hated seeing his cock on the wall with every other pet who had ever worked at The Castle. His dick, with the embarrassing nickname *Pinky* below it, was one of the less impressive on display. It was pretty obvious Dave preferred his boys to be well-hung, which probably explained why the old bastard had seemed a tad hesitant to let him sign a contract after his audition. Luckily for Shay, his good-looks were probably what scored him the job. And in spite of all the sexual suffering he'd endured while working here, Shay really did consider himself lucky. The alternative of being "taken care of" as they said in Brixton had never been the better option.

When the ads came on, Shay swallowed heavily, urging himself to ask Kane for sex. *Just say it. It's the only way you'll know if he's keen.* Just as he opened his mouth to utter the words, Dave's voice blared over the intercom. "Pinky and Brayden. I would like you both to come down and see me in the classroom. If you have heard me wave at the cameras."

Shay waved at the camera installed above the television.

"I can hear you."

In the distance he heard Brayden respond similarly.

"Good boys. Now make it down here snappily."

Shay let out a frustrated sigh and got to his feet. "I guess I better go see what dear old Dave wants."

"Have fun," Kane replied, gaze focused on the gogglebox.

Brayden suddenly came sprinting into the lounge. "You better not have been sitting in my fucking seat, Pinky," he muttered as he rushed past them both towards the kitchen and hurled himself down the slide beside the fridge. The slide was one of many in the apartment but it was the only one with a direct route to the first floor, two levels below. Shay waited a few seconds before making his way towards the slide. He dangled his legs into the yellow tube and flung himself forwards, sliding down the sloping loop until his body was spat out two floors below, greeted by Brayden mooning him.

Shay narrowly avoided crashing face-first into the boy's bare arse. "Put it away, dick."

Brayden laughed. "Aw, doesn't Pinky like my bum?"

"What do you think?"

"You know you love it." Brayden smirked like an arsehole.

"Keep dreaming."

They made their way along the wide hallway of the first floor, bickering the whole way until they entered the classroom and waited for their dark master to come see them.

The classroom with its multiple posters of nude men, rectum diagrams, and various-sized dildos attached to the wall was certainly one of the weirder places in The Castle. The pets came here to attend weekly lessons covering all sorts of topics ranging from the kinky to the downright bizarre. Yesterday they'd been given a refresher course in how to rim like a pro, the week before it had been a lecture on the mating rituals of cuttlefish.

"I wonder what he wants to see us about," Brayden commented as he looked towards the whiteboard. "He might wanna watch me screw you."

"Sometimes I think that is your dying wish in life."

"It ain't my dying wish. I've already done it once."

"And you ain't ever doing it again."

"Don't be such a cocktease, Pinky." Brayden licked his lips as he groped himself. "You fucking loved having my big dick inside you."

Shay rolled his eyes. "I think you'll find that's Dion's domain."

"Boys," said Dave's gravelly voice. They both turned their heads towards the door and watched Dave come and stand in front of their desks. "Firstly, I wanted to commend you both on the essays you wrote last week. You two were by far the star pupils of that class."

"Is this the essay about licking arse?" Brayden returned cheekily.

"Yes, Twitch. The essay on rimming." Dave leaned forward and ruffled Brayden's blond locks. "You really are a cheeky rascal."

"I do my best, daddy." Brayden looked up at Dave with puppy dog eyes.

Brayden's blatant greasing was nauseating. *No wonder you did so well on writing an essay about rimming. You're constantly kissing this prick's arse.*

"But that's not why I have asked to meet you both."

"Are we here because you want to watch me fuck Pinky?" Brayden said, probably only half-joking.

Dave chuckled. "Not tonight, Twitch." He turned his attention to Shay. "Unless of course that is something

Pinky would like daddy to watch?"

Shay bristled. "Not really, sir."

"Moving right along," Dave said, completely unfazed before switching his attention back to Brayden. "I wanted to speak with you both about your leaving party. It's only a few short weeks away and I wanted to go over the farewell and inking ceremony."

Brayden coughed nervously. "You mean when I have to get the tattoo?"

"That's the one."

"Is the tattoo an absolute must do?" Brayden asked, clearly not keen.

"Of course it is, sunshine. It's what links you to all the pets that have come before you and all the ones who will come after you. It will hurt a little bit but you will be able to leave here and wear it with pride."

Shay loved seeing Brayden squirm for once. The only stink part was knowing that he too would one day be marked for life with the same hideous design. This would be his first time witnessing a pet's farewell ceremony but he'd heard about it from the others, and he had seen what the tattoo looked like on Sione who was a former pet himself. The tattoo wasn't huge or particularly eye-catching; just the word pet scribbled in black ink. To future lovers the random word wouldn't mean a lot but to each man with the letters carved into his flesh it would carry a tonne of meaning, none of it pleasant.

"Have you given any thought as to where you want it written?" Dave asked Brayden. "As you know, it's completely up to you."

"I was thinking maybe my chest?"

"You do have a lovely chest." Dave smiled at his favourite. "It would look very nice there just above one of those sexy little nipples of yours."

"Thank you, Daddy," Brayden whispered bashfully.

"I don't mean to be rude," Shay began, "but if this chat is about Brayden's leaving doo, why am I here?"

"That's a very good question, Pinky," Dave replied. "I'll let Twitch explain it to you. He's attended three leaving ceremonies now so he knows the answer."

Brayden shifted uneasily in his seat. "The newest pet and the one who is leaving have to be naked for the entire ceremony." His voice was about as enthusiastic as a man being told he had to scrub his balls clean with a cactus, and considering Brayden had never been afraid to get naked Shay suspected the worst was yet to be said. "We will have to do stuff on stage together while everyone watches."

"Be more specific, Twitch," Dave said in his domineering tone. "Pinky isn't a mind reader."

"We will have to suck each off. Sixty-niner styles. Then…" Brayden gulped. "We drink a glass of each other's piss."

"What?" Shay squawked and glared at Dave. "Why the fuck do we have to do that?"

"Because it's how it has always been done, Pinky," Dave replied. "It's tradition."

Shay shook his head. "No way am I drinking that window licker's piss."

Brayden's eyes narrowed and Shay could see the tiny wheels turning inside the pea where smarter men had brains. "What the fuck's a window licker?"

Dave sighed. "He's calling you a retard, sunshine."

With a delayed reaction that almost proved Shay's point, Brayden fired back, "Fuck you too, Pinky. I'm not a fucking retard. You're the fucking retard."

"Enough," Dave snapped. "I don't need you two fighting right now. Not when I need you to get along for such an important ceremony."

"It sounds like one seriously fucked up ceremony, sir," Shay muttered.

Dave's eyes narrowed to nasty slits. "If you don't feel you can participate, Pinky, then you are free to terminate your employment and I can ask Dion or Kane to step in and do it for you."

"I-I don't wanna quit," Shay spluttered. "I'm just a little shocked. That's all."

"How do you think poor Twitch feels? It will be much harder for him."

"How?"

"Unlike you, Twitch isn't the kind of pet who is accustomed to sucking dick, so his leaving ceremony will see him doing two things he's not used to. Not just the one." Dave's lips curved into a vindictive smile. "Unless of course you've already enjoyed the taste of a man's golden juice?"

Shay shook his head. He'd had a few clients piss on him but none so far had been gross enough to demand he drink it.

"Do either of you boys have a full bladder at the moment?" Dave hitched an inquisitive eyebrow. "It would be wise for you both to start practising. I won't tolerate any spitting out on the day."

Shay and Brayden exchanged worried looks before they both shook their heads.

Dave sighed like he was disappointed. "I haven't told the other pets yet but Sione and I are leaving for Auckland tomorrow morning and we will be gone for about a week. I have asked Dr Harten to stay on and supervise you all until we get back."

Not that prick! Dr Harten was almost as bad as Dave. Actually, he was worse. At least Dave had a sense of humour and was down to earth. Dr Harten was just a pretentious wanker.

"I have told him I expect you boys to have made a start at getting acquainted with the taste of each other's piss before I get back," Dave continued. "This means that until further notice you two are only allowed to drink water. That means no hot drinks and no fizzy."

"But Daddy," Brayden whined. "Water's gross."

"Trust me, Twitch, you'll thank me when it comes time to drinking Pinky's juice. I find it goes down a lot easier if the pet has only been drinking water. You don't want to be downing anything too strong." Dave placed his hands behind his head and leaned back in his chair, eyeing them both with a wolfish grin. "I don't think I have been so excited for a leaving ceremony pairing in quite a long time. I think you boys will put on a memorable show for all our guests."

"Exactly how many people will be watching?" Shay asked nervously.

"It depends on how busy our members are but we usually get close to a hundred attending."

Fuck my life. It was bad enough knowing he had to drink Brayden's piss but to have such a degrading act witnessed by a large crowd was fucking mortifying.

"Now I want you boys to promise me that you will behave and do what Dr Harten says while I am gone."

"Yes, Daddy."

"Yes, sir."

"As for the rest of the ceremony I'll go over the finer details closer to the time but for now I think the most important thing is for you to both embrace your inner piss pig." Dave couldn't hide the hint of a smirk. The dirty fucker was totally getting off on this. "Now, do either of you have any questions?"

Shay had many but he didn't want to hang around a

second longer than he had to.

"Do you know who my replacement is yet?" Brayden asked.

"Not yet but I have someone working on it as we speak. I just hope whoever they find is half the man you are, sunshine." Dave's eyes glowed with parental pride, like he had convinced himself Brayden was his son. "You have been an absolute joy to have here the past two years and I can't say I won't shed a tear on the day."

"Aw, I'll miss you too, Daddy."

"I hope so, sunshine. You've really wormed your way into my heart."

Get me a fucking bucket. Rather than sit and listen to the creepy sweet talk between the pair, Shay asked if he could leave.

"Not just yet, Pinky. I need you to get naked for me first."

"Why?"

Dave tsked. "You would do better if you just did as you were told, Pinky."

"Can I stay and watch?" Brayden asked.

"By all means. Pinky doesn't mind one of his brothers seeing him without his clothes on."

Pinky does fucking mind, actually.

Rather than voice his displeasure at Brayden watching, Shay rose from his chair and proceeded to get undressed. When he was fully naked, he let his arms rest at his, his overly horny dick sporting a semi.

"You've got a boner!" Brayden said loudly, pointing at Shay's cock.

"I don't have a boner," Shay grumbled.

"Yes you fucking do." Brayden reached over and tugged on his dick. "That's fucker's more hard than it is soft."

"Keep your hands to yourself, Twitch," Dave said. "I

don't want Pinky erect. I need him soft."

Brayden glared at Shay with a grimace. "Did you get turned on thinking about drinking my piss?"

"Fuck off," Shay snapped. "I don't want to drink your piss any more than you wanna drink mine."

"Then why are you sporting a woody, faggot?"

"You're the faggot ya little prick."

Dave clapped his hands. "Boys, boys, settle down. I don't like it when youse fight in front of me."

"Sorry, Daddy,"

"Sorry, sir."

Dave reached into the black bag he'd brought with him and pulled out the cock cage Shay had only been freed from earlier that day.

"W-Why do you have that?" Shay asked nervously.

"Because it's going back on your pecker, son."

"But I haven't done anything wrong!"

"I know you haven't, Pinky, but I just had an email from our dear friend the milk man and he's booked a session with you for this Saturday. I thought we could treat him to an extra big load if we kept that pretty penis of yours locked up until then."

"But that's four days away!" Shay's voice came out all whiny and pouty.

"And?" Dave stared at him blankly.

"And I just spent five days in that fucking thing." Shay grabbed his dick, giving it a sympathy tug. "I haven't even had a chance to cum yet."

"Whose fault is that?" Dave's tone was void of sympathy. "I unlocked you hours ago. You've had ample opportunity to take care of your needs."

"Can I go and have a quick wank right now? It won't even take a minute."

"No," Dave replied sternly. "It's going on right this

moment."

"Please, sir. I really, really need to cum first."

"What a desperate, bitch," Brayden muttered.

"Fuck up, cunt." Shay waved a fist in Brayden's direction.

"Settle down, Pinky, or you'll be eating a knuckle sandwich made by yours truly," Dave warned.

Shay began to sweat, his balls screaming for release. *I should have had a wank hours ago.* He was that fucking desperate to cum he lowered himself to begging. "Please, sir. I'll suck you off if you let me cum."

"All I have to do is give the order and you'll be on your knees sucking me off if I let you cum or not. That's what being a pet is all about." Dave bared his yellow teeth with a savage smile. "But I can see you are very keen to strike a deal so maybe we could come to some sort of arrangement."

"I'm keen, sir. Really keen."

"How about this… I was planning on letting Twitch stay the night in my apartment but perhaps I could let you join us."

"Okaaay," Shay said warily, waiting for the catch.

"If you accept my invitation then I will let you masturbate to your heart's content on the condition I get to watch Twitch fuck you during the night as many times as he likes." Dave grabbed hold of Shay's balls, plumping them in his hand. "I think that's a compromise we could all be happy with."

"That sounds like a great idea, Daddy." Brayden licked his lips. "I'll fuck the cum right out of Pinky's little dick for him. More than once."

Shay glowered at Brayden's smirking mug. "Fuck that." He stared down at Dave's gnarled hand still groping his balls. "Just lock my cock up already."

CHAPTER 11

The first thing Levi did upon arriving back in Fitzroy was drive to Josh's house to feed Phoebe. Actually, that was the second thing. The first was to stop off at a supermarket to buy Phoebe some ridiculously expensive tinned food. Paying six dollars for a tiny tin of gourmet cat food was absurd but the most annoying part about the purchase was the fact Levi was legitimately worried if his card would decline. That was not a feeling he was used to and he didn't like it. Thankfully the eftpos screen flashed with the glorious word **Accepted** and he raced to Josh's place to give the fussy feline her tasty treat.

Phoebe, in true cat style, turned her nose up at the food Levi had bought especially for her and meowed at him until he gave her some cat biscuits stored in the pantry. *Fussy bitch.*

After filling Phoebe's water bowl, Levi decided to give his childhood friend Scott a call to see if he and Fergus would be home tomorrow. He wasn't overly thrilled at the prospect of visiting the dropkick stoners. Scott would no doubt be ripped and Fergus no doubt would be an arsehole, but it had to be done if it really had been Fergus who'd seen them at Wairua Valley the night they buried Barry Buttwell.

Levi wasn't sure how likely it was that Fergus had seen enough to go back and dig up the body. It had been dark and the actual burial site was not out in the open, not to mention why the fuck would Fergus wanna dig up a body only to then bury it somewhere else? It didn't make any sense.

After eight rings, the call went to Scott's voice mail: *If you're hearing this message then my phone's either dead or I'm too busy getting shitfaced. Leave a message.*

Levi rolled his eyes and quickly adopted a sunny tone after the beep. "Hey Scott, I just wanted to see if you and Fergus will be home tomorrow. If you think you will be then flick me a text and I'll pop round to catch up. Ciao, bro."

Slipping his phone back into his pocket, Levi glanced down and saw Phoebe staring up at him, meowing yet again. "You're worse than bloody, Danny, you are. Always after something." He was beginning to wonder if he'd have to go buy her something else to eat but just at the last second Phoebe marched back to the bowl filled with meat and began to scoff it like it was the tastiest thing she'd ever been fed.

"Why the hell didn't you just eat that in the first place?" He shook his head, glad he didn't own a cat.

While Phoebe continued scoffing, Levi hunted around for a pen and paper so he could leave Josh a note. Josh was due home from Bali in the next day or two and he wanted Josh to find a sexy little something waiting for him. After scribbling down a few lines about how much he couldn't wait for Josh to use his body, Levi signed off using the shameful name *Cum Bucket.* He hated that fucking term but he knew how much Josh liked it so he figured it was worth swallowing a bit of pride.

He took the dirty note down to Josh's bedroom and placed it on Josh's pillow. *He's gonna love this. He'll be calling me to come over the second he reads it!*

Aside from the fact Josh was sex on legs, Levi got off on the idea of fooling around with his best friend because he knew it would be a secret "fuck you" to Dwight. Josh's father had been livid to find out Levi and Josh had already done stuff together and Levi knew that if he and Josh were to go all the way—Josh's cock buried balls-deep inside Levi's arse, or better yet, Levi's dick buried balls-deep inside Josh's arse—the trashy older Stephenson would have a serious bitch fit.

Imagine his face when I tell him I bitched his son out and made him a faggot.

The war of wills he'd been locked in with Dwight had been intense. It was like some sort of lethal collision between fiery passion and dark hatred. For the briefest of moments, Levi had foolishly thought that there might have been something between them, that maybe that volatile desire they shared could have led somewhere.

It had certainly opened his eyes to a desire he had never known he had. A submissive need to have a daddy. It was cringy as fuck but the arousal he'd felt while being pumped with Dwight's thick meat and calling the man daddy had been very, very real. But so had the pain when Dwight did the unthinkable by leaving him tied to the bed before texting Josh on Levi's phone to come untie him.

Levi felt his body trembling with anger just thinking about that day. As far as Levi was concerned it had been rape. He had not given permission for Dwight to invite another person into the room to fuck him. And to top it off, Dwight the nasty fucker had stolen over fifteen grand from Levi's credit card to fly himself and Josh to Bali. It was so low. So very fucking low.

But you got yours Dwighty. You definitely got yours.

Dwight had played a dirty game but it was Levi who had played the ultimate dirty move; burning the trashy prick's house down so he would have nowhere to live. *I probably did him a favour. It was such a piece of shit.* Dwight probably wouldn't feel that way but Levi didn't care. He just wanted Dwight to know that he had fucked with the wrong person.

You didn't cross Candy Boy and get away with it.

Dwight knew it was Levi who'd burned down the house but Levi wasn't the least bit concerned. It wasn't like Dwight could prove it and if he even tried to cause trouble with the police then Levi could just as easily press charges for the money stolen from his credit card.

Which means you are shit out of luck old man. There ain't nothing you can do.

Levi had a tonne of problems at the moment: his lack of funds, his sordid arrangement with Danny, his mother's affair, his father's missing body. As stressful as all that was, Levi still felt better knowing that Dwight Stephenson was no longer on that list. He'd taken care of that.

I don't have to worry about you ever again.

∞

The sun was fighting a losing battle to stay relevant in the darkening sky as Levi pulled into the driveway of his family's sprawling home. He dipped the car lights, not wanting to notify Danny of his return. The last thing he needed was his stepbrother to come rushing out and say the magic words "bongo drums" and whisk Levi away for sex. Of course he would take care of Danny's needs tonight but first he had to speak with his mother in private.

To add to his stealthy return, he switched the car engine off and rolled quietly down the curving ramp into the rarely used basement garage. One half of the Candy mansion was built into a hill, allowing two floors below the main entrance of the house. One floor of the basement housed extra bedrooms, a bathroom, and a large locked lair that Mark referred to as his "man cave." The bottom floor though was used as an extra garage. It was rarely used and was more a showroom to house Mark's non-work vehicles—shiny hunks of metal that cost more than the average Kiwi family earned in a year.

As Levi stepped out of his vehicle, he glanced towards the elevator. He'd always thought it was quite cool how their home had a lift but after what he'd seen today at The Castle he wasn't so sure.

Avoiding the elevator, Levi made his way instead to the internal stairwell, deciding it would be the quieter option to make his way up the two floors to the ground level. He damn near shit himself one floor up when he heard the door to Mark's man cave open and shut. Levi flung his back to the wall, hiding in the shadows just in case Mark emerged again into the stairwell.

Levi breathed a sigh of relief when a minute later, he heard Mark put on his stereo and started blasting some old school rock. *He must be mad about something*, Levi thought. Mark went to his man cave a few nights a week but he only ever blasted music when he was annoyed about something—usually if Levi had fucked him off.

It can't be me that's upset him. I haven't been here all day.

Levi just prayed it wasn't anything to do with his mother and her affair with Johan. He figured that probably wasn't the case though, or else there would have been bags of clothes being thrown out the windows.

After about thirty seconds to make sure the music didn't abruptly stop, Levi continued his way up the stairs, grateful to avoid running into the person who'd been plaguing him with taboo fantasies.

Once up on the ground floor, Levi slunk through the hallway like a stealthy spy, slipping from room to room with deft footsteps to try and find his mother. When he reached the front door and the main stairwell of the home, he could hear the faint sound of classical music coming from one of the upstairs bedrooms. *Danny's.* The dorky teen often listened to classical sounds while taking a break from study. Levi assumed that probably meant Danny was up in his room. He relaxed his rigid posture and searched the rest of the ground floor with more ease.

It was at the other end of the house, near the games room, where he found his mother. She was sat in her reading room on a loveseat with a book on her lap. Yellow tendrils of light coming from a small antique lamp gave the room a soft glow, painting her pretty feature with an angelic-like quality.

"Mum," Levi whispered.

She glanced up and smiled then got up and walked over to where he was standing. "What happened? Did Shay tell you where it is?"

Levi nodded and proceeded to tell her the entire story at whisper volume.

"Oh dear," she sighed when he had finished explaining what Shay had said. "What are we going to do?"

"I've already called Scott, that's who Fergus practically lives with, and left a message saying I'll pop by tomorrow to see them. And don't worry, I won't just outright ask him, I'll bring it up subtly… as subtle as one can be when asking about a missing dead body."

"Maybe it would be best if I speak with Fergus."

"Do you know him?"

"Yes, darling. Every woman who has ever lived in Brixton knows who Fergus Liggett is." She giggled softly. "Fergus would wolf whistle or poke his tongue out when he drove by anything in a skirt."

When his mother said *poke his tongue out* Levi figured it was not done in the way a child would. Hardly surprising though. Fergus was like a chunk of boiled ham with all the sophistication of a hand job in a carpark.

"I always found that sort of behaviour rather juvenile," she continued. "But some of the ladies must have liked it because he certainly had a lot of girlfriends… and a lot of children."

"He certainly has a lot of kids," Levi agreed.

"If you give me Scott's address where you think Fergus is staying then I don't mind talking with him. Fergus always quite liked me."

That's because all the men like you, stupid.

The thought of his mother alone with grubby Fergus who oozed major rapey vibes turned Levi's stomach. "If it's alright with you Mum, I'd rather you let me handle this."

She smiled at the protective heat in his gaze. "I appreciate your concern, darling, but I am more than capable of looking after myself."

"I know, Mum, but I put us in this mess so I want to be the one to get us out of it."

"This is not your mess, it's your father's mess. If anyone should be cleaning it up then it's him."

"Trust me, Mum. I can take care of it. By this time next week we will never have to worry about Dad ever again."

His mother reached forward, stretching out one of her hands to place over his left forearm. "Are you absolutely sure?"

He lifted his gaze from her hand to her warm hazel eyes. "I'm sure. I've got this."

She slowly removed her hand. "Just be sure to let me know if there is anything I can do to help. I don't want you to feel like you have to do everything."

Levi nodded. He was about to leave the room but couldn't leave before asking her one last question. "Mum…?"

"Yes?"

"Have you decided what you're doing about Mark and Johan?" He saw the displeased look in her gaze so he quickly added, "I'm not asking to be nosy. I just want to know if I need to be packing my bags anytime soon."

She let out a long exhale. "There has been a development to the situation but I didn't want to burden you with it while all this is going on."

"What's the development?"

Without any pause, no imaginary drum roll, she said softly, "I'm pregnant."

"You're fucking what?" Levi shrieked.

"Keep your voice down," she scolded.

Levi looked at his mother's tummy, no signs of a bump. "H-How far along are you?"

"Not far. But it's certainly made me see things a lot clearer." She nodded like she was reinforcing her own belief. "I need to be with the father of the baby."

Levi gulped. "And is that Johan?"

Please don't say it is. Please don't say it is.

"Yes," she answered. "Of that we can be absolutely sure."

Fuck. Fuck. Fuck!

This was the last thing he'd expected. His mother being pregnant! To Johan! An aging crystal-worshipping, anti-vaxxer, berry-eating, yoga-obsessed nutbar. It was like the world was taking a giant dump all over him and laughing at his expense. He forced himself to remain calm despite feeling like his world was about to implode. "How long until you tell Mark you're leaving?"

"It won't happen right away and I'll let you know before I say anything."

"That's good because I'm gonna need as much time as possible to plan where to put my cardboard box."

"What are you talking about?"

"The cardboard box I'll be living in after Mark throws my arse out of the house."

"Mark won't throw you out."

Levi threw her a deadpan look. "I wouldn't be so sure about that. We don't exactly get along. The only reason he tolerates me is because of you and if you're not here then I'll be the first thing he hiffs out the door."

"I think you are underestimating Mark's good nature."

"So you're guaranteeing me that Mark will let me stay living here?"

She hesitated, just like Levi knew she would. "You know I can't guarantee that."

"I didn't think so," Levi muttered.

A tense silence fell between them as they avoided each other's gaze.

His mother eventually replied. "I am sorry if any of this causes upheaval for you, darling, I really am, but have you thought maybe now is the time for you to be out living your own life. It could be the start of an exciting new adventure."

"An adventure where I have no money and no job." Levi scoffed. "That's sounds really exciting, Mum. Not."

"You can find a job. I know it will take a bit of getting used to but work can be a lot of fun. I used to enjoy working at the supermarket when I was with your father."

Not as much as you have enjoyed spending Mark's money the past seven years.

"I'm not going to find a job that pays me the money I am used to though," Levi whined. "I'll be lucky if I'm paid anything more than minimum wage."

"To be fair, Levi, you haven't had any money for the past two weeks and you've coped just fine."

"Because I am living rent free in the nicest house in Fitzroy. What happens when I have to try and find a shitty little apartment in town? Or worse, finding a shitpit in Brixton!"

"If the worst comes to the worst then I am sure Johan won't mind letting you stay with us at the community for a while."

A while. Those were the magic words. After years of living in the nest it felt like his mother was ready to spread her wings and knock him out of it.

She must have sensed his fear because she stroked his hair, smiling with her eyes. "I will always be around, Levi. That's never going to change."

"Then why does it sound like it is?"

"I know you might be living at home right now but I suspect that has more to do with the house than you being a mummy's boy." She chuckled softly. "You're much more independent than you think and I know you would go crazy staying with me and Johan in his cabin."

"The dude lives in a cabin?"

She nodded. "It's on site at the community. Lovely little place but it is very small."

"Oh God," Levi groaned.

"Which is why I know you would much rather find a place of your own."

"So being homeless it is then," he muttered.

"Don't be so dramatic," she said in a stern voice, a tone she rarely used. "You are much stronger than you give yourself credit for. If you want to succeed and live a wonderful life like the one you've become accustomed to then I know you are more than capable of achieving that."

He wanted to believe that but he also knew that he'd spent his entire time living in the Candy mansion specialising in the art of being a spoilt brat who didn't lift a finger to get what he wanted.

"What did Johan say when you told him you were pregnant?" Levi asked.

"I haven't told him yet."

"Are you worried he'll tell you to get rid of it?" The words slipped out of Levi's mouth, and he wished he could pull them back inside.

"Excuse me?"

He tried a softer approach. "Are you worried he won't want to stay with you when he finds out you're pregnant?"

"Don't be absurd! Johan is a good man who loves me." She looked at Levi with concern. "I can't believe I raised a boy with such a chauvinistic outlook."

"I'm not being chauvinistic I am just being practical. What is the point of leaving Mark unless you know for sure Johan wants to stay with you? The dude might not want a kid at his age. Shit, he's practically at death's door."

"Johan's not that bloody old."

"The man looks old enough to have grey hair on his balls so I'm picking he's not a spring chicken."

She shook her head, scowling. "You know, Levi, I had hoped you might actually be excited about this. You always used to want a little brother or sister."

"I'm sorry, Mum." He shot her an apologetic look. "I-I'm just a bit shocked is all."

"Why? Because you think I'm so old as well."

"Yeah," he said with a playful smirk.

"Gee, thanks," she huffed and folded her arms.

"I'm only joking." He reached over and rubbed her shoulder. "Honestly, Mum. If this is what you want and you are happy then I am happy for you."

"Do you mean it?"

No. "Yes. I mean it."

They hugged and she squealed excitedly. "You are going to be such a good big brother."

"I don't know about that but I'll give it my best shot."

"What will you give your best shot?" sounded an accusing voice.

Levi tensed. How long had that voice been standing behind them?

CHAPTER 12

Levi spun around and saw his stepbrother standing in the doorway, arms crossed over his chest as if he'd been there a while. His heart crawled up his throat, convinced Danny had been eavesdropping the entire time. *He's going to go tell Mark she's pregnant with another man's baby!*

As Levi began to have visions of his stepfather throwing their clothes out the window, his mother very calmly said, "Levi was just telling me he was going to give his best shot with his studies." She spoke with so much ease it was unnerving how convincing her lie was. "I've been worried he might not pass his papers this semester."

When Danny smiled at him, Levi realised his stepbrother had only heard the tail end of their talk. His heart slid back into place and he immediately calmed down.

Danny walked over and patted Levi on the back. "I can help you with your studies," he said. "I know it isn't the same subjects I take but if you have any essays due I could definitely help with that."

"Thank you, Danny," Levi's mother said. "I think your *brother* would appreciate all the help he can get."

Levi gave her a subtle eyeroll. Here she was treating Danny like he was Levi's sibling right after excitedly telling Levi he was about to become a brother for the first time. It made the maternal affection she had shown Danny all these years feel so phony.

"What's the time?" Danny asked Levi's mother. He pointed to the clock on the wall and added, "I haven't got my contacts in so I can't see what it says."

Levi's mother turned to look at the clock for him. "It's just after eight o'clock."

The liar in the room had just been lied to. Danny could see perfectly fine. The boy used the two seconds his stepmother's head was turned to grope Levi's arse and whisper in his ear "*Bongo drums.*"

Levi's hole twitched, knowing it would soon be getting invaded.

"Thank you, Jenny," Danny said with the innocence of an altar boy. "Shall we go upstairs?" he said to Levi.

"Uh, yeah." Levi nodded, looking back at his mum for confirmation it was okay to leave.

"We can talk more about *studies* tomorrow," she said.

"Okay, Mum." Levi nodded, his heart still somersaulting in his chest from what he'd just learned.

"Come on, Levi," Danny said. "There's something I wanna show you."

Let me guess…. Your penis.

Levi gave his mother a fierce *I-love-you-Mum* look that only a son could give then followed his stepbrother out of the room.

The whole way to Danny's bedroom felt like walking through quicksand. Levi's legs felt heavy, his feet almost dragging themselves up the stairs. Danny on the other hand was walking with swagger, a confident strut that had only come about in the past two weeks since they'd begun their incestuous arrangement. Danny may still have been a nerdy teen at the bottom of his high school's pecking order but at home he was top dog. A top dog who had a willing slut to use in place of a cum sock. Of course their arrangement was wrong and unhealthy but Levi craved the depravity of it all. Something about being just a hole for his stepbrother filled a savage, bitter place inside his heart. And he needed it filled more than ever right now just to try and zone out.

While Danny hummed a happy tune like he was whistling from his balls, Levi's mind whirled with the heaviness of what his mother's pregnancy meant for him. *Mark is going to boot my arse out that door so fast I'll break the sound barrier.* As soon as his mother broke the news to Mark, all the wealth and all the luxury Levi had become so accustomed to would be gone. Gone forever.

And it wouldn't just be the money that would be gone. It would be his social standing that had come with it. There was no way on this earth he could remain a Fitzroy Flyer let alone the most popular one when he didn't have a cent to his name. His good looks had always helped, as had his charm and charisma he could turn on like a tap, but neither of those things were what had made him king of the social scene.

When they reached Danny's bedroom, Levi left his worries at the door and switched into fuck-hole mode, the submissive mindset he reverted to whenever Danny required his body. It was only now in the privacy of Danny's bedroom that he began to take notice of his stepbrother's appearance.

Danny wasn't wearing any of the trendy outfits Levi had bought him for his birthday, instead he had on a pair of khaki pants, a black polo shirt and black leather shoes. It wasn't as bad as some of the shit Danny used to wear but the clothes still looked too mature for an eighteen-year-old boy.

Walking as if on autopilot to the foot of Danny's bed, Levi lowered his shorts and placed his palms down on the mattress, serving his arse up for Danny to take it.

Do what you gotta do buddy so I can go back to freaking the fuck out.

Danny walked up behind him and groped his arse. "I want to kiss you first."

"Just fuck me, buddy." Levi wriggled his arse wantonly. "Stick it in me."

"No," Danny said sternly, sounding more like a sulky kid than the dominant man Levi wished he was. "You know I like to kiss you before we make love."

Make love… two words that never failed to make Levi's skin crawl.

Leaving his shorts snagged at his knees, Levi straightened his body and turned around so they were standing face to face, his flaccid dick and smooth balls openly on display.

"What's wrong?" Danny asked as soon as their gazes met. "You look worried about something."

"I'm not worried." Levi faked a smile. "I just missed you. That's all."

"Aww, I missed you too, baby." Danny kissed Levi on the lips, slipping his squirmy tongue inside. He was still a far cry from being an expert kisser but he'd improved a lot since the lizard-like kiss he'd given Levi the first night they had fucked. As their kiss fell into a choppy rhythm, Danny hugged Levi closer to him, force-feeding him his tongue and unwanted affection.

Reluctantly, Levi raised his arms and hugged Danny in return, trying to mimic the passion his stepbrother was obviously feeling.

Finally, Danny broke the kiss and stared at Levi like he was staring into the face of an angel. "Where were you today? You've been gone for hours."

"I had to help Peach with planning the Flyer's ball," Levi lied.

"You should have text me. I could have come and helped when I'd finished at school."

"I didn't want to bother you."

"Helping you is not a bother, baby." Danny grabbed hold of Levi's cock and began tugging it, trying to bring it to life. His light strokes did the trick and within a minute Levi was sporting a full-on erection. Danny squeezed Levi's length possessively, staring down at Levi's member with envy. "You have such a nice penis."

"Cheers."

"I never knew I liked dicks until I saw yours." Danny wiped the pad of his thumb over Levi's piss slit. "Now I spend most of the day thinking about yours. Isn't that funny?"

Levi didn't think so but he nodded anyway. "Pretty funny, alright."

"And I think about your bum too." Danny blushed. "It's hard to stay focused in class because I sit there really horny just counting down the minutes until I can come home and fuck it again."

"That's what my arse is here for," Levi said in a seductive whisper. "For you to fuck it."

"While you were out I was looking online about anal sex," Danny said as he rubbed his hand down Levi's prick and gave a shivery-nice caress to his balls.

Levi sucked in an unsteady breath. "Were you looking up new positions to try?"

"No," Danny said flatly. "I wanted to know if I would damage your sphincter if I fucked it too much."

I don't think we will have that problem with what your packing, Danny.

Danny reached around and patted Levi's butt. "And apparently you can damage the rectum if it is overused. Usually from too much fisting."

"You're not going to try fisting me..."—Levi gulped— "are you?"

The little shit had the audacity to pause and think about it before finally shaking his head. "No. I wouldn't want to hurt you."

"Good."

"But it did get me wondering if maybe you should start doing the exercises they recommend to make sure your sphincter maintains its elasticity." Danny's words tangled together at the end of the sentence. He cleared his throat. "You don't want to start suffering from anal leakage."

Levi suppressed the urge to rip Danny's tongue out so he wouldn't say such stupid shit again.

Danny continued to waffle on about what he'd learned online after his deep dive into the horrors of anal destruction. He took it upon himself to try and educate Levi about the exercises he could do if he ever felt his arse muscles slackening and the surgery options available to him.

"How about we save the sweet talk for another time, buddy?" Levi joked. "You're kind of killing the vibe."

"Sorry. I just want you to know that if you ever needed surgery then I would pay for it."

Levi chuckled. "Good to know."

Danny returned to playing with Levi's balls, stroking the smooth surface of his scrotum. When the dorky teen's baby blues twinkled mischievously, Levi could tell Danny was about to throw out some random order. It had taken Danny several days to realise how far-reaching his power was but after asking Levi for clarity about their arrangement he had begun to use his authority to make Levi do pointless shit. So far it hadn't been anything too outrageous, that wasn't the sort of person Danny was, but he did seem to get a kick out of seeing Levi obey him.

Danny let go of Levi's genitals. "I want you to take all your clothes off and do twenty press-ups."

Levi ditched every article of clothing he had on then dropped to the floor to begin the push-ups, his erection stabbing the carpet with each downward movement. When he was finished, he rose back to his full-height and awaited his next order.

Danny giggled. "I can't get over how you will do whatever I say. It's so cool!"

"I'm glad you enjoy it."

"I do enjoy it," Danny said earnestly. "But I still don't understand why?"

"It's my way of showing you respect."

Danny nodded like he knew what Levi meant despite the clueless look on his face. Levi didn't blame the kid for not understanding his twisted need to honour him in humiliating ways. Hell. Levi barely understood it himself.

"Maybe you can show me respect by sucking my dick," Danny said, trying to sound sexy but failing miserably.

Levi sank to his knees and ran one hand lightly over the modest bulge between Danny's legs and felt him tense. He then unbuckled Danny's belt, unbuttoned the top of his khakis and slid the zipper down, revealing a pair of light blue boxer shorts. He reached into the fly, took Danny's cock in his hand and carefully lifted it out.

Danny gasped as it flopped out, finally free of the confines of his pants. The curved five-incher was proud and hard, emanating heat and hormones. A whiff of stale crotch accompanied its reveal, hitting Levi like a drug.

Someone still hasn't got around to having his shower today.

Danny was usually a very clean specimen but Levi knew the boy had run out of time to shower this morning after spending too long fucking Levi before school. It didn't matter though. The smell of Danny's crotch was one of Levi's favourite things about his stepbrother's body because it was faintly reminiscent of the smell Levi had inhaled when gagged with Mark's sweaty briefs—the most humiliating yet most erotic moment of his life.

Slowly, gently, Levi licked along his stepbrother's shaft. As his tongue traced the throbbing veins along Danny's length, he picked up a weird taste: sweet, earthy, sort of funky. It suddenly dawned on him that this was the same skin that had been inside him that morning; from piss slit to pendulous balls, this unwashed flesh had been lodged deep inside his arsehole.

The hunger burning in Levi's balls warred with the awareness of what Danny's dick was flavoured with, and he was ripped from the haze of lust. He started to rise but was enraptured by Danny's glittering eyes staring into his own as Danny rubbed his cock against Levi's face. Levi leaned away, but Danny gripped the back of his head, and the sticky tip of his dick smeared Levi's lips.

"Suck it," Danny commanded.

Levi opened wide, deciding submission was more important than the grossness of sucking his stepbrother's dick clean.

"That feels so good, baby." Danny guided Levi's head forward as Levi moaned around his shaft. "So good."

A spurt of pre-cum drenched Levi's tonsils as Danny palmed the back of his head. The room became filled with Danny's muffled grunts and the wet sloppy sound of his dick sliding in and out of Levi's mouth.

Danny exerted his authority, fucking Levi's mouth

roughly. Rather than be bothered by his stepbrother's brutal approach, Levi was grateful. This is what he wanted: to be treated like a disposable slut for a superior man's dick. How on earth Danny was superior was still a mystery to him but Levi gave into the fantasy as he sucked his stepbrother's leaky prick.

While Danny fucked his face, Levi slipped a hand inside Danny's boxers and explored the boy's sizable balls. The scrotum was sticky and clung to Levi's fingers as he gently rolled the nuts around inside the hairy sack. While Danny's dick was a permanent resident in depressingly average territory his balls were manly beasts that put Levi's nuts to shame.

"I love how big your balls are," Levi slobbered over Danny's cock. "So big and full of cum."

"You should give them a suck," Danny panted. "I like it when you do that."

Levi didn't have to be told twice. He dragged Danny's pants and underwear down until they pooled at the boy's feet and immediately pressed his face into the unwashed heat of Danny's nether-regions. He inhaled deeply the scent of Danny's sweaty-pink balls, his taint, his ass. Danny's heavy nuts were the most fragrant, their potent testosterone-laced aroma filling the air between them. "You smell so manly," Levi mumbled. "So fucking manly."

Danny sniggered. "That's because I am a man, silly."

Yes and no, Levi thought privately. Legally, yes, Danny was an adult but it was only the lower-half of his body that exuded manliness. Danny's upper-half radiated juvenile youth courtesy of his smooth face and hairless torso.

Levi sucked on his stepbrother's balls, sucking the sweat off their skin. While he slurped loudly on Danny's boy bits, Levi gripped his own cock and began running it up and down the forest of hairs on Danny's lower legs. The virile sensation was so sexy and it made him start leaking jizz on Danny's shin.

He reached up and started jerking Danny off while he still had a mouth full of sac. His own prick bounced between his spread legs where he squatted, fully firm with arousal. Levi didn't know if it was Danny, the taboo act of sucking clean sweaty balls, or knowing how much joy he was gifting that made him so damn hard. Whatever the reason was it made him feel needed and safe.

This is who I am. Danny's slut.

Pure, unadulterated acceptance of himself sluiced through Levi's veins and turned his sucking, licking, and foraging more voracious than ever. He whipped his hand up and down Danny's prick with rough speed, causing Danny to whimper and moan so much that the boy whacked Levi's hand away.

"Suck my dick some more," Danny panted.

Levi reluctantly released the feast of Danny's balls from his mouth. He batted his tongue against the swinging weight of Danny's nuts one last time and then stuck his nose into the crease of his groin and thigh, inhaling the pungent, heady male fragrance of sex and sweat. He licked his way through the dark pubes to the root of Danny's cock and followed a raised vein to the leaking tip. Murmuring an appreciative sound, Levi ran his tongue around the crown and across the slit to savour all the pre-cum he could get. A hint of bitter whispered across his taste buds and revved him up for more. He took hold of Danny's length, opened wide as he moved in, and sucked down half the teen's scorching-hot cock again.

"Yeah, baby." Danny stroked Levi's hair. "You're so good at that."

The compliment spurred Levi on, proud to have his cocksucking skills acknowledged. He slid his hands round the back of Danny's thighs, stroking up to gently cup Danny's taut buttocks, enjoying the feel of the boy's firm arse. He slurped up and down the length of Danny's prick with tight wet lips, hitting the base and bobbing his head back up with a slight twist each time. He was now humming "mmmmmmm" as he blew him, adding a little vibration to the suck-off.

Like it always did, Danny's dick begun leaking copious amounts of ball juice onto Levi's tongue. *You could sell this stuff by the bottle if you wanted to.*

A dull and dreamy euphoria closed in. Nothing existed except the cock in Levi's mouth and the one between his legs. He reached down to rub myself, moaning around Danny's dick as it fucked his mouth, as it took control and used Levi for its own pleasure.

Urged on by his need to worship, Levi pulled his mouth free and lay on the floor then asked Danny to sit on his face.

"But I haven't had a shower today," the boy confessed.

"It doesn't matter." Levi gulped, scared of his own desires. "I'm going to lick it clean for you."

Danny's eyes widened in shock but he relented with a nod. He stepped out of his pants and slowly lowered his arse, his pendulous balls swinging between his legs, until his bum was dangling only mere inches above Levi's face.

The damp heat of unwashed arse emanated from Danny's crack. For a split-second, Levi regretted making the offer but he quickly reminded himself of his place—beneath Danny. Also, if he wanted to clear his mind then the best thing to do was to sully it with filth.

Here goes nothing…

He licked Danny's crack which was a jungle of dark curls, probably hairier than Levi's. He forced his tongue to ring the lips of Danny's hole, sampling the bitter funkiness a day's worth of sweat. It had a nasty taste; sour but compelling, so putrid but the perfect flavour for Levi's submissive mood. He pressed against the opening, probed it with the tip of his tongue, and Danny gasped, pushed out so his hole widened, granting him deeper entrance. Levi spread his cheeks further, so he could dig deep, deeper still.

"Oh golly. Oh, golly. Oh, golly," Danny said on repeat as he squirmed his dainty anus over Levi's suckling lips.

It tasted foul but so what? This was part of a lesser man's job. Danny was the alpha male now and had to be serviced like one. It wasn't lost on Levi that outside of this house he was the big man in the scene but here, in the privacy of their own home, he was a geeky teenager's personal fuck-hole and arse cleaner, and man that was a turn on.

As he licked and nibbled on Danny's tight slit, Levi thought back to the night they'd first had sex and how he'd devirginized this tasty hole. *Pity I won't be doing that again.* Never again would he be fucking this tight little hole. It was off-limits for good.

While he licked out Danny's shitter, he reached around and stroked Danny's throbbing prick, masturbating him in time with his thrashing tongue.

"Hold on a second, baby," Danny rasped, sliding free of Levi's tongue. He knelt on the floor beside Levi's laid out form, panting as he held his dick in his hand.

Levi lifted his head and looked at him, concerned that he'd done something wrong in the act of honouring his stepbrother. It was a needless worry. Danny's expression wasn't disappointed, but mirthful. "That was amazing. So, so, so amazing, but I don't wanna finish like this before I have a chance to fuck you," he said, grinning. Levi smiled back at him reflexively and cleared his throat of saliva with a soft cough.

"What position do you want me in?" Levi asked.

"Doggy style."

While Danny fetched a bottle of lube from his bedside drawer, Levi crawled up onto the bed and spread his legs wide in eager anticipation of a good doggy style buggering. Slowly, he reached back, grabbed both his buttcheeks, and spread himself open for his young master.

He felt the bed move as Danny shuffled up behind him, settling between his legs. Danny stroked a finger down Levi's crack, his gaze burning into the centre. "I still can't get over the fact I put my penis in here every day." His hushed words whispered over Levi's hole. "Every. Single. Day."

Shame throbbed in Levi's heart but it was pale in comparison to his need to fulfil his role as Danny's bitch. "Give it to me." Ragged desperation filled Levi's voice. "Please."

Danny chuckled arrogantly. "It's coming, baby. Just be patient." He didn't rush to apply the lube, instead he continued to stare at Levi's arsehole to the point it got embarrassing.

"Is something wrong?" Levi asked.

"I was just thinking it might be a good idea of you shave back here." Danny stroked Levi's hair-lined crack. "I'd like it if it was smooth like your balls are."

"Oh..."

"You can do that tomorrow for me," Danny said expectantly. "I'll probably enjoy the sex more if it was smooth."

Levi wanted to tell Danny not to be an ungrateful brat, that he should consider himself lucky to be fucking his arse at all, but Levi reminded himself of his place. *He's the boss. Not me.* If Danny wanted him to shave his arse then unfortunately he would have to shave his arse. "Okay. I'll see what I can do."

"Don't just see. Do."

Levi bit back his resentment and nodded into the mattress. "Yes, Danny."

Danny uncapped the bottle and dribbled lube over his dick and the seam of Levi's arse. "Remember to make those noises I like," Danny said, pressing the tip of his finger inside Levi's hole, delving partially inside. "Those sexy girly ones."

Levi hated making those noises but Danny fucking adored them and insisted on hearing them every time they fucked. It was one thing to be fucked like a bitch but to be made sound like one was humiliating. But of course, Levi would do it.

A horny breath visited his ear, followed by the press of Danny's erection against the back of his balls, flesh on flesh, heat on heat. Danny rubbed up and down Levi's back with one hand as he fit his member to Levi's entrance with the other. Levi's ring pulsed a fast beat against the tip of Danny's slick cock, and vibrations from the rest of Levi's body shimmered between them.

Like the amateur he still was, Danny bucked his hips with no warning or care, ramming half his length inside Levi's rectum.

"Fuck," Levi heaved, gritting his teeth. His arse was certainly used to Danny being inside it but that initial breach still managed to hurt. Not screaming pain, but a sharp pinch that lingered.

Danny grunted and bucked again, this time fully claiming Levi's arse. He slowly retreated until just the head of his cock was pulling at Levi's taut anal lips then he slammed back home, balls deep.

"Oh," Levi moaned, forcing his arse back, into the moist, wiry nest of Danny's pubic hair. "Give it to me,

Danny. Give it to me like the bitch I am."

Danny grunted affirmatively and ignited a hectic arse-fucking rhythm, treating Levi's anus like it was a hole in a wall. The boy was definitely in the mood to fuck.

While Danny annihilated his sphincter with savage fuck-punches, Levi groaned and gasped for breath, air coming in short bursts to his lungs. Once he settled his breathing, he set about delivering the vocal performance Danny liked, moaning and whining like some slutty little girl. It was humiliating but the fucked up part was that the humiliation only served to amplify the lust in his balls which in turn upped his volume and desperation.

Not all the noises he made were fake though. Danny had got a lot better at fucking in a very short time and had already learnt to stab his cock on side angles if he wanted to make Levi give him a very real squeal.

The only other men to have fucked Levi were Dwight and Kaleb, both of whom sported more size, girth and experience than his young stepbrother but what Danny had was a natural curve to his cock that somehow managed to brush Levi's p-spot and milk trembling moans from his body. This fuck was proving no exception.

"That's it," Levi grizzled. He bumped his hips back in a circling motion and worked himself off on Danny's cock. "Fuck yeah. Do it." His eyes fell closed and he bared his clenched teeth as he took another full hit to his arse. "Fuck me." His channel squeezed in a suffocating hold around Danny's length. "Take me hard."

"I'm going to, baby," Danny breathed in response.

"Unngh . . . unghh . . . unghh . . ." Levi winced. "Fuck my arse. Fuck me like a bitch. Oooo."

"You sound like a bitch," Danny said snidely.

Levi's body spasmed as the humiliation rippled through him, but he let it roll out, focusing on the bliss tickling his balls as he continued to moan and leak faggy whimpers.

Chants of gratitude flew from Levi's mouth, paying homage to his unlikely superior. He gripped the bedsheet hard in each hand, not even bothering to try and touch his cock. This wasn't about his pleasure; this was all about Danny's.

Not only had Danny's fuck skills grown tremendously but so had his ability to swear and talk dirty. When the boy was in the heat of the moment his wimpy mushiness disappeared, replaced with dirty talk that involved f bombs and referring to his cock in the third-person.

"You love Danny's dick, don't you, baby?" Danny puffed. "Danny's dick drives you fucking wild."

"Yeah, man. I love it. Love Danny's dick so much."

"Danny's dick likes you too." The teen's comment was followed by a stinging slap to Levi's butt cheek. "It especially likes to fuck you."

"Thank you, Danny's dick. Thank you for fucking me."

"And you want Danny's cum in you too, don't you?"

"Yes, Danny. I want it so bad. So, so, so bad."

Danny pumped Levi's accommodating hole, thrusting from the tip to the hilt each time. Levi rocked his body back and forth to meet Danny's thrusts. He could feel his stepbrother's balls swinging against his own each time the horny teen slammed home. Again and again, filling him, stretching him, owning him.

Levi lost track of time as his world narrowed to the sensation of being filled and the sounds of his feminine wailing and flesh grinding on lube-coated flesh.

Faster now. He could hear Danny breathing heavily. He was stimulating Levi's prostate every second, as he slammed, slammed, slammed his cock all the way in, causing Levi's own cock to leak jizz in response.

As close as Levi was to losing his lollies, he knew Danny

was closer. They had fucked enough times now for Levi to know the boy's warning signs of impending orgasm. And he knew it was close when Danny's breath became choppy and his hands gripped Levi's hips tighter.

And then, just as Levi had suspected, came a whiny, "It's coming, baby."

Danny latched onto Levi's waist with a painfully tight grip and began positively slamming his hips into him. The boy's thrusts grew slower and more sporadic as his cock fired squirt after squirt after squirt of teenage ball juice.

Levi moaned as torrents of hot jism flooded his arsehole, his anal walls spasming uncontrollably as Danny pumped him full with his hot, creamy sperm.

"Oh, baby," Danny cried out as he collapsed on top of him, forcing Levi to lay flat on the bed with the boy's full weight above him. Their chests heaved in unison, shallow panting breaths that defined this forbidden passion between them. He didn't ask Danny to roll off him right away, preferring to let him finish the job of emptying his balls.

When Danny's dick had finally twitched its last twitch, Levi quietly said, "You're kind of crushing me, bud."

"Sorry." Danny flopped off of him and lay on his back, wiping sweat from his brow. "That was amazing."

Levi carefully rolled over to lay on his side, clenching his arse to try and keep Danny's cum inside him, but as soon as he relaxed his sphincter rivulets of hot jism oozed from his ruptured arsehole. "Fuck." He put a hand between his cheeks. "I think I'm getting cum on your sheets."

"That's okay." Danny smiled warmly. "You can't help it."

"I guess not."

"What's it feel like?" Danny asked. "Having semen

inside you?"

"Wet… warm… and very stodgy."

"Do you suffer from anal leakage?"

Levi couldn't help but snort at the way Danny spoke like he was reading from a brochure. "Anal leakage?"

"Yeah… does it ever leak out?"

"My briefs are on the floor if you want to have a look," Levi didn't expect Danny to investigate but that's exactly what the teen did; climbing down off the bed and sifting through Levi's shorts.

"You had on two pairs of undies today?" Danny frowned with confusion before coughing out a gasping squeal. "Oh my gosh! There's stains!"

Levi chuckled at Danny's horror. "You sound surprised?"

"I am a bit." Danny stared at the cum-stained gruts in his hand. "I didn't expect it to be so messy."

"Really? You must shoot the biggest cum shots in town. Not to mention you put five or six of them inside me every day so what do you expect?"

"I'm sorry."

"You don't have to be sorry. You can't control how much you ejaculate. If anything you should be proud to brew so much jizz. Those are proper porno loads coming out of your dick."

"It must get annoying though walking around with dirty undies on."

The truth was Levi didn't mind that much. Sometimes it even felt quite sexy. Especially when he would imagine it was Mark's load and not Danny's that was making his strides moist.

Danny climbed back on the bed and lay beside him. He grabbed Levi's erection, giving it a gentle tug. "Did you want me to finish you off?"

"You don't have to do that. This arrangement is all for your pleasure. I'm just here to catch the fun."

"I know. But I still feel like I should help you out."

"Don't worry about it." Levi patted Danny's chest and slowly sat up. "I'll just go finish myself off in the shower." He began to swing his legs off the bed when Danny suddenly yanked him back. "What?" Levi asked, pretending he didn't know what was coming next.

"We haven't kissed yet," Danny said.

"Yeah we have."

"But I want to kiss you some more."

"Do we have to?" Levi groaned. "I kind of need to go take a shit. You just pumped me with an army's worth of your kids."

"Just a kiss. One little kiss." Danny smiled mischievously, knowing damn well it wasn't going to be *one little kiss*.

Reluctantly, Levi lay his leaky arse back down and merged his lips with Danny's as they started what predictably became a pashing marathon. As the kiss stretched out like the horizon, Danny rubbed up against him, grinding his softening prick against Levi's thigh.

Finally, Danny retrieved his tongue and stared into Levi's hazel eyes adoringly. "You're so special," he said.

"Ditto, buddy."

"No one has ever made me feel the way you do." Danny playfully tweaked one of Levi's nipples. Rather than go down the pointless path of reminding Danny he was confusing emotions with sex, Levi just nodded and closed his eyes, feigning tiredness. "You make me feel so good that I actually did something a little crazy today."

"Like what?" Levi mumbled.

"Like telling Dad I'm gay."

Levi's eyes snapped open. "You what?!"

CHAPTER 13

Danny smiled contritely. "I told Dad today that I've met a guy I like and that I think I might be gay."

"Oh my God!"

"Before you get mad, I didn't tell him the guy was you was but he did say he wants to meet who it is."

"But you're not gay, Danny."

Danny glared at him like he was an idiot. "We just had sex, Levi, for like the thirtieth time. I think you'll find that makes me pretty gay."

"It's called experimenting with your sexuality. That's all."

"This is way more than experimenting. That's why I talked with Dad in the first place."

"What do you mean?"

"I went to ask him for advice on what to do if you're in love with someone." Danny's cheeks reddened. "You know… because I'm in love with you."

Levi knew he was supposed to say something back to that but he couldn't. Just couldn't.

Unfazed by Levi's silence, Danny continued. "Dad

asked me the name of the girl I was in love with and that's when I told him it wasn't a her, it was a *him*."

Levi's throat ran dry. "What did your dad say?"

"He told me I need to find out if this person feels the same way. That I should find out if we have a future together."

"I mean, what did he say when you told him it was a guy?"

"Not much. I think he was a bit surprised but he didn't get mad if that's what you think."

Mark might not have reacted poorly to Danny's face but Levi figured it was a pretty safe bet that Danny's conservative father was having kittens in private about discovering his own flesh and blood was fond of cock. *That's probably why he's hiding out in the man cave tonight.*

Levi was at a loss for what to say. He knew Danny had been reading too much into their arrangement but he never thought Danny would be stupid enough to come out to his father.

"Do you think we have a future together?" Danny asked hopefully.

"Of course we have a future together. We're brothers."

"I know but I was hoping we could have something more than that."

"What do you call this?" Levi raised a brow. "How many guys do you know get to fuck their older brother whenever and however they like?"

"I know I am lucky. So lucky. And I love, love, love the sex but I can't stop thinking about you. Whenever you're not with me I just wish we were here in bed together. And I am worried it will come to an end."

"Our arrangement isn't coming to an end anytime soon." *Actually, it probably is but that's because you and your father will hate me and Mum very soon.*

"Are you sure?"

"I'm sure."

"So you like this?" Danny's gaze pointed at both their dicks. "You like the way I make love to you?"

"I love the way you *fuck* me," Levi said, emphasising the f word. "Look at my dick. See how hard it is? That's all because of you and the way you fuck me." That was actually very true. Despite the boy's sugary pillow talk and amateur thrusts, he did somehow manage to rev Levi's engines.

"Seriously?" Danny's face glowed with pride.

"I have grown very fond of that dick of yours. And I feel proud to walk around the house with your cum in my arse."

Danny snorted. "I do shoot pretty big loads."

"You sure do. Those big, hairy Candy balls were made for filling sluts with cum."

"You're not a slut."

"I am when you fuck me. As soon as your dick is inside me then I belong to you and am at your mercy. That's what this is all about."

"I suppose that is pretty hot."

Levi nodded, encouraging the boy to buy into the fantasy. "That's right. So don't get hung up on this love stuff, just enjoy the fun we are having."

"But don't you think it would be more fun if we were boyfriends?"

"We can't be boyfriends. We're brothers."

"We're brothers who fuck," Danny snapped in a pissy tone. He quickly softened his expression and added sweetly, "So I don't see how us dating would be a problem."

Levi didn't know what to say. It seemed the more he tried to talk sense into Danny the less Danny listened. The room went quiet and Levi could tell his kid brother was annoyed with him.

Danny broke the quiet first. "Part of the reason I spoke with Dad was to ask him to raise my allowance so I could start supporting my lover."

"You asked Mark for more money… to give to me?"

"Yes. I want you to know that I can take care of you. And you deserve way more than the piddly thousand dollars I gave you."

"I'm not a whore, Danny," Levi said icily. "You can't buy someone who isn't for sale."

"I know you're not for sale but I want the person I love to be taken care of. That's what a man is supposed to do." Danny bit down on his bottom lip, smirking slightly. "And it seems pretty obvious that I am the man in the relationship."

"Arrangement," Levi clarified. "And just in case you have forgotten, we are both men."

"Yeah but I'm more like the *real* man, wouldn't you agree?"

Levi was speechless, but he wasn't surprised. Danny had always had an oddly chauvinistic vibe about him. Not in the beer-guzzling, ball-scratching, slap your lady about sort of way but more like some immature git who didn't realise he was living in the twenty-first century. Levi blamed Mark's influence of endless lectures about men behaving with honour and doing their duty. Whatever the fuck that meant.

"And because I am the *real* man," Danny continued arrogantly, "that means I have a responsibility to take care of you and provide a home for us."

"Oh my God," Levi groaned. "You're talking like we're about to get married."

"We could do one day. Gay marriage is legal."

Levi reeled himself back from lashing out with anger and instead humoured Danny with a smile. "Why do I get the impression you've been thinking a lot about this?"

"Because I knew the first night we made love you were the one for me. I can't believe I never realised it sooner. I love you Levi and I know you love me too."

Danny's blue eyes shone with a sincerity that made Levi's chest tighten. *I've created a monster.* Had he known fucking the kid would have opened up such a tidal wave of problematic feelings, he would never have stuck his dick in the boy's virgin hole.

What the hell do I do now?

The sensible option was to probably let Danny down gently and tell him that everything sexual between them had to stop. But Levi didn't have the strength to do that. He didn't want to deal with the inevitable tantrum and tears. But there was more to his reluctance than just that. He still felt under some sort of submissive spell, a desperate need to remain the boy's bitch.

I have to introduce him to a pretty girl who will fuck him and shift his affection elsewhere. Levi knew that a drop of pussy juice would not only cure Danny of his obsession but would probably cause the boy to look back at their arrangement with shame and regret.

Out of sheer curiosity, Levi asked. "What did your dad say when you asked him to increase your allowance?"

"He told me I shouldn't try and buy peoples affection. That if you loved me then you would love me for me."

"Your dad's right about that."

"But he still agreed to increase my allowance," Danny replied smugly.

"He did?" Levi furrowed his brow. "How much of an increase?"

"He doubled it."

Mark you wanker! It fucked Levi off knowing his stepfather had doubled Danny's allowance but had cut Levi's off after giving Levi a lecture that to be a man he had to learn to support himself. *Double standards much.*

"I guess if you're sure we can't date officially then I can tell him to drop my allowance back down," Danny said, playing the victim.

Levi hated himself for what he asked next. "Just out of interest, how much of your new allowance were you planning to use to *take care of me*?"

"If you had checked your bank balance today you'd know the answer to that." Danny smiled and gave Levi's still-hard cock a gentle tug.

Levi's erection bucked. "Have you put more money in that credit card you gave me last week?"

Danny nodded. "I put across an extra five grand. I know that's not as much as you are used to but I thought if I could give you that much each month it would be a start until I can make more money of my own."

Five grand wasn't as much as Levi had once been bleeding out of Mark's wallet per month but it was a fuck-tonne more than he'd been on recently. It was probably just enough to give his old social life back and assure he remained king of the scene. He wished now that he hadn't asked Danny how much money he would be giving him. It was enough to make him question committing to something really fucking stupid.

I can't date him. He's my fucking brother! But another voice popped into his head that posed a counterargument. *Dating Danny could be an answer to a lot of my problems.*

Levi liked his life here in the Candy mansion but he knew his time here was on borrowed time thanks to his mother's womb. For the past seven years he hadn't just been living the life of some stuck-up privileged twat, he'd been living the life of a rich-lister's son. There was a difference. And Levi wasn't ready to part ways with that level of privilege just yet.

Demon Dave's offer of thirty grand was generous but one lump sum wasn't how you stayed a somebody. You needed a constant flow of income to keep up to date with all the right fashions and to be able to jet set to all the best places. As totally fucked up as it was, perhaps the answer was sitting naked right in front of him.

But Levi had to know the answer to one thing before he made any sort of decision. "If we were to date, right? And you agree to take care of me…"

"Yes?" Danny's eyes lit up.

"I need to know that the money you give me isn't you thinking you're paying me for sex because if it is I can't do this. I need to know you don't think of me as a whore."

"Why are you so concerned about that word? I've told you that's not how I think of you."

"But are you sure? I need to know what you honestly think."

"Yes, Levi. I'm sure." Danny sounded exasperated but he was still smiling. "Honestly, baby, this is just how the men in my family are. We take care of the people we love. You should know that. Look how well Dad takes care of your mum."

Levi stared up at the ceiling for a long moment, thinking over his options. Whatever he chose to do right now would have major ramifications. His indecision eventually ended with a nod and the most dangerous of fake confessions. "I do love you, Danny, and I guess if you are sure we can have a future together then I would love to make things between us a little more official."

"You mean, I can be your boyfriend?"

"Yes." Levi forced his voice to ooze seductive charm. "I

want you to be my boyfriend."

Danny's mouth dangled open before he let rip one of his walrus-like laughs, pure joy tumbling out of his skinny body. He stopped the laugh by latching his lips onto Levi's, kissing him deeply.

Knowing that this was supposed to be a kiss of romance, Levi played the part and pushed his hands up Danny's back to take handfuls of his glossy black hair, their tongues tangling together. He sucked languidly on Danny's lower lip, chewing and licking at it, tasting him deliberately like he was looking for something delicious under the plump skin. He needed Danny to believe this love was real. He needed to trick himself that love was possible.

Danny gave a grunt in the back of his throat, his mouth smouldering against Levi's as they swapped spit in the form of slow, wet, hungry kisses that went on and on.

"You won't regret this, baby," Danny said fervently when their lips finally parted. "I am gonna take such good care of you."

"I know you will, *babe*."

"We should talk about what it means to be boyfriends," Danny said, abruptly changing the subject. "I want to make sure we're on the same page about what being in a relationship means."

"Sure. We can do that."

"First off. No cheating." Danny looked as serious as he sounded. "I won't tolerate a partner who cheats."

Levi nodded, playing along. "Me neither. If we do this, we do this properly."

"I'm so glad you agree. I can't stand cheaters."

The demands kept coming thick and fast as Danny rattled off his list of expectations: dates to the movies, romantic dinners, trips away, nights at home cuddling on the couch. He also expected Levi to start sleeping in his bed with him every night because "that's what boyfriends do." Levi wasn't sure how practical that sleeping arrangement would be while they lived in the family home but he agreed, not wanting to upset his new boyfriend.

Danny was a sweet kid and usually quite agreeable but with matters of the heart he was proving to be quite the little dictator. *Mind you I may have some blame in that.* Levi's stepbrother had gone from a nerdy virgin to having unrestricted access to fucking Levi's arse whenever and however he wanted. That sort of power could change a person. Especially someone who wasn't used to it.

"Will I still be the boss of sex?" Danny asked. "Or do you think it's best we start being a bit normal with that?"

"What would you like us to do?"

"If it were okay with you then I'd like it to stay the same. I've really enjoyed the arrangement so far."

"In that case why don't we keep it that way," Levi returned with a smile.

"Really?" Danny's face was a map of excitement. "You are the best boyfriend in the world!"

Levi knew he probably should have asked for some changes in the sex department, and Lord knows he wanted to, but he was still under some invisible spell that demanded he submit. However, he decided his submissive streak wasn't necessarily a bad thing in this instance.

Right now Danny was smitten because everything about their sex life was so new and exciting to him, but there would come a time when the boy's hetero side would rear its head and Levi knew he couldn't compete for a straight man's heart against a woman. This meant he had to offer Danny something no potential future Candy wife would—complete submission and a willingness to play the role of convenient fuck-hole. It wouldn't permanently starve off the threat of a girl one day winning Danny's heart but it would buy Levi some time.

"I'm glad you're letting me stay the boss when it comes to sex," Danny said. "Because there is something I've been wanting to try."

Levi's ears picked up. "What is it?"

"I'd rather not say just yet. Maybe tomorrow?"

"Why tomorrow?"

"Because I'll need to buy some stuff first."

"Interesting." Levi lifted his eyebrows. "Can you at least give me a hint?"

"You'll find out tomorrow when I've bought what we need." Before Levi could press for any more details, Danny swiftly changed the subject. "When do you want to tell our parents about us?"

"Maybe when we're not both living under the same roof as them."

"You're right," Danny agreed. "It's probably best we tell them after we move to Sydney."

"Sydney?"

"When I move away for uni." Danny looked at him strangely. "You'll be coming with me, won't you?"

Levi paused before nodding profusely. "Of course."

"If Sydney's a problem and you'd rather live somewhere else then I don't mind. My grades are good enough to get me into pretty much any university I want."

"You'd let me choose where we live?" Levi was totally gobsmacked to be given the power over such an important decision.

"I want you to be happy, baby, so you just say where and I can look into it." Danny stroked Levi's face and tickled his chin. "I could always take a gap year and we could travel the world to see what places we like and then decide."

Levi liked the sound of that. He also liked the sound of

living far, far away before breaking the news to Mark that they were a couple. His stepfather's reaction would be nothing short of catastrophic—especially after the knife to his heart from Levi's mother.

Levi studied his stepbrother's features more than he ever had before, knowing that Danny's slender body could be loving and fucking him for many years to come. That's how lifechanging the decision was he'd just made.

To be perfectly honest, Danny was a bit scrawny for Levi's tastes but he wouldn't be scrawny forever. Mark was the finished product while Danny was still finding his way there. In a few short years Danny's body would fill out like his father's and he too would probably end up sporting a chest furred with dark manly hair—a trait that for some reason Levi found oh so fucking hot. And maybe with age Danny's natural scent would smell even more like the mouthwatering sweat found in his father's briefs.

Danny suddenly rolled over and collected the bottle of fuck-grease and squirted some lube into his hand which he then started slathering onto Levi's cock.

"What are you doing?" Levi asked. "That's supposed to go on your cock."

"I'm letting you fuck me." Danny leaned in and pressed a soft, lingering kiss to Levi's lips. "If we're going to date then I should probably let you have a turn fucking me now and then."

"Oh…"

"Don't worry, baby, I still intend to be the one doing most of the fucking." Danny reached behind to apply some lube to his entrance as he stared down at Levi's twitching prick. "Last time you fucked me you used a condom but this time I want you to put your love inside me. Just like I do to you." He straddled Levi's waist, dangling his wet little arsehole above Levi's dick. "Just go easy to start with, okay?"

"Okay," Levi replied, still slightly dumbstruck.

The softest, almost surprised-sounding sigh escaped Danny as he nudged the head of Levi's cock inside his arse. "Oh my golly," he gasped. "I forgot how much this hurts."

"Do you want me to pull out?"

"No. I-I I want you to fuck me." Danny really didn't sound very sure about that but without warning he sank down and took another inch, his passage contracting in a smother-hold on Levi's prick.

Levi's eyes rolled to the back of his head as his dick blissed out on the strangling heat of Danny's sphincter. Clutching Danny's hips with both hands, Levi sank the teen onto his cock with excruciating slowness. As the suction of Danny's ass stretched and clamped around him, Levi released a low, long groan. His cock strained so hard and full inside his teen lover it was agonizing. He wasn't even buried yet. Could Danny take him to the hilt?

The question was answered as Danny slammed downward and ground his arse against Levi's pelvis. Levi grunted, and Danny moaned, clawing at Levi's chest.

Then he fucked him, lifting Danny up and down, pushing into him, and riding the intoxicating waves of bliss.

Danny's face was pained but that did nothing to dissuade Levi from deepening his thrusts. His balls tightened, and his hips flexed as he devoured the view of Danny's dick flopping up and down.

He wasn't a fan of this position, preferred doggy style, but he was still grateful to be given unrestricted access to his stepbrother's body. And he took full advantage, gliding his hands up and down Danny's furry thighs before traversing up his flanks, plucking at his tiny nipples, and caressing the warm smoothness of his hairless chest.

"Oh, baby," Danny moaned. "You feel so big!"

Levi grinned, enjoying the praise.

It was remarkable how well they moved together—the synchronization of their rolling grinds, the give of Danny's young body with the force of Levi's thrusts, and the stretch of Danny's arse as Levi pounded the boy's inner muscles. It felt as though they'd been lovers for years, not just weeks.

Driven by primal instinct and the urge to punish Danny for making him his bitch the past two weeks, Levi fucked him viciously, mercilessly, gasping and plunging, his fingers digging into bone.

The more Danny yielded to him the more Levi remembered how it was in his true nature to take the reins and be in control. It felt amazing to be inside Danny again but the thrill of being the top came at the expense of something else.

His unwavering submission.

CHAPTER 14

"Hey Scott, I just wanted to see if you and Fergus will be home tomorrow. If you think you will be then flick me a text and I'll pop round to catch up." Levi's voice ended the message with a cherry, *"Ciao, bro."*

Scott put his phone back in his pocket and sat down on his bed, his tummy fluttering with sickly butterflies. *Oh God... he wants to do that deal.* Once the dope had worn off that day, it had never crossed Scott's mind for a second that Levi would try and follow through on the scandalous offer. He had assumed it was just another one of Levi's empty gestures. The guy was full of them. And while Scott could do with the money, he wasn't sure if he could go through with something so fucked up. It was one thing to whore himself out to Levi, just one on one with no one around, but it was a completely different story if it meant having sex with Fergus while Levi sat back and watched.

What do I do?

What Scott couldn't do was text Levi back. He hadn't had any credit on his phone for over a week. He was pretty sure Fergus had some credit but to text Levi back from

Fergus's phone would rule out the possibility of convincing Levi to pay Scott for a one man show. As depressing as it was to admit, Scott knew in his heart that Levi was only going to come here if he could pay them both.

It was a safe bet that Fergus could do with the money too but Scott wasn't sure how keen Fergus would be on the idea. There was a high chance Fergus would just get offended and punch a wall or something stupid.

Scott cringed as an image of Fergus fucking him in bed flashed inside his mind. Despite the slimy feeling in his stomach, Scott wasn't entirely opposed to the idea. After all, it was five-hundred dollars. That was a lot of money. Even if he had to split in with Fergus it was still a decent amount. But was it decent enough to warrant him even asking Fergus if he would be keen?

Scott didn't know. Just didn't know.

The thought of having sex with Fergus was a thousand times worse than having sex with Levi. For starters, if a straight guy had to go gay then Levi was the kind of guy you'd wanna do it with. He was the same age, handsome, and always smelled clean. It also helped that despite knowing each other for so many years they weren't particularly close which meant whatever they did together Scott could quite easily pretend it never happened. That wouldn't be the case with Fergus who was his best mate and pretty much lived with him. Also, Fergus wasn't the same sort of guy as Levi; he was older, sort of busted, and usually had a faint whiff of body odour from his aversion to daily showers.

Maybe we could ask Levi to pay extra? Maybe six-hundred? It wasn't like Scott's childhood pal would miss the extra hundred dollars. Levi was so loaded it wasn't funny. He had pretty much won the lottery when his pretty mother had married some rich dude. Overnight Levi and his mother went from being amongst the poorest in the worst neighbourhood to being the richest in the best part of town.

Nearly everyone who knew Levi and his mother out these ways despised them, considered them traitors. But that wasn't surprising. Brixton folk didn't much like seeing other locals succeeding, they preferred you to stay like them—piss poor and addicted.

Scott didn't share the same level of animosity towards Levi as his friends did but he did feel resentful sometimes. While Levi's mother did her bit with the occasional visit and charitable act to the family's former friends, Levi did sweet fuck all to help people out. The only time Scott ever saw Levi was when Levi wanted something. Drugs usually.

However, last year the visit for drugs had been very different with Levi offering him a chance to make extra cash if he did Levi a favour. Scott, being skint at the time, said yes before he'd even heard what the favour was.

"I want you to get naked and jack off," Levi had said.

Scott had laughed at first, assuming it was a bad joke, but when Levi stared at him with a very serious expression Scott realised it hadn't been a joke. He had been dumbfounded at the time, not sure what to do, but when Levi showed him the cash the money spoke to him and Scott convinced himself it wasn't that big of a deal. In a strange way he'd found it quite flattering that someone as attractive as Levi was so keen to see him naked that he'd be willing to pay. No girls had ever done such a thing.

To start with it had been awkward as fuck, laying naked on the bed, grunting and groaning while he tugged his meat. By the time he got erect, the weirdness of the situation dissipated and he just pretended like Levi wasn't even in the room. That had been easy to do since all Levi did was stand to the side in wide-eyed silence. That was until Levi touched him.

"What are you doing?" Scott had asked, more curious than panicked.

"Can I touch?" Levi had asked in a sultry voice.

Scott had hesitated before deciding it was okay. "If you want, I guess."

Levi ran his hands over Scott's legs, his waist and up to his chest. It was as if he wanted to touch Scott everywhere at once. He tweaked Scott's nipples for a while before lowering his hand down to Scott's balls where his hand remained, fondling Scott's nuts like they were the most fascinating thing in the world.

The fondling only stopped when Levi decided to up his offer of cash in exchange for a blowjob. Again, Scott was taken by surprise, but when Levi showed him the extra cash Scott relented and crawled off the bed and sank to his knees in front of his buyer.

After unzipping Levi's pants, Scott probably stared at Levi's dick for nearly a minute until he worked up the courage to stick it in his mouth. It had been beyond strange to have another guy's cock in his mouth but his need for the money got him through and, in all honesty, it hadn't been as bad as he thought.

Levi's dick was clean and his balls had smelled of lime bodywash. The only part he really had a problem with was when Levi had spunked in his mouth without warning. The taste of semen was foreign to Scott's tongue and he'd spat it out all over the floor. Aside from that he hadn't found the experience all that bad. Scott wasn't sure what that said about him but he could honestly say there were worse things in life than sucking a dick.

Afterwards he'd just put it to the back of his mind and figured he could just add it to a crazy life experience, telling himself it was just another one of those dumb things he would never do again.

Yeah right.

The other week when Levi had called him up out of the blue to say he was visiting, Scott had purposely answered the door half-naked, hoping the sight of him in just his boxer shorts would encourage Levi to pay for another round. Unfortunately Fergus's presence had hindered such negotiations but when Fergus had excused himself to take a shower, Scott pounced on the opportunity like a shameless car salesman, exposing and groping himself in front of Levi as he dropped his price lower and lower in hopes of a sale.

It was cringeworthy behaviour and fucking awkward when Levi appeared uninterested to even pay just fifty dollars to fuck him. He was relieved though when Levi had turned around at the last second and handed over some cash without expecting anything in return. Despite being happy to be spared taking a dick up his arse, Scott's ego had taken a beating from Levi's apparent disinterest in him.

He can't be that disinterested because he's obviously keen to do this deal.

Scott wondered if it was himself or Fergus Levi was more interested in. It shouldn't have mattered but for some reason it did. If he could be assured he was the main attraction then maybe it would make doing the unthinkable that much easier.

Scott stood up and walked through the mess of empty beer bottles littered over his bedroom floor and made his way to the bedside mirror. He studied his face which he knew didn't carry the same level of beauty as Levi's but Scott still considered himself a good average. He lifted his shirt and stroked his abs. He was definitely on the runty side but Levi had seemed quite enamoured by his body when he'd seen Scott naked the year before. *Maybe he just wants Fergus to add a point of difference?* Scott settled on that answer and it made him feel better.

He chucked a baggy jumper on overtop of his t-shirt then wandered out to the lounge. As he passed the tiny kitchen his nose crinkled in disgust. The place usually stunk of cigarettes and weed but for the past two days it stunk mostly of whatever was rotting in the dishes left on the kitchen bench. Being unemployed Scott had all the time in the world to clean up but he rarely did, usually only doing the dishes when he'd run out of every clean plate and cup in the cupboards.

As he entered the lounge, he found Fergus dressed in his usual attire of black jeans and a long-sleeved top. The lanky older man was sprawled on the couch watching television, a hand digging around inside his pants as he shamelessly scratched his balls. Fergus swung his dark gaze in Scott's direction, grunted, then focused his attention back to the television.

Scott sat down in one of the ratty arm chairs and gazed at the pile of ripped cigarette butts on the coffee table. The sight of charred tobacco crumbs got him craving a nicotine hit, so he leaned forward and blackened his fingers in the ashtray to roll himself a not-so fresh butt roll.

"Can you roll me one while you're at it?" Fergus asked.

Scott nodded. He had already pulled out two zigzag papers in preparation for the question.

Fergus rolled over and swung his dirty-socked feet onto the floor and sat up. "Are you sure you don't wanna come with me to Blade's party tonight? It should be pretty good."

Blade was one of Fergus's *six* sons. Even though the boy was only turning fourteen, that didn't mean the party wouldn't be filled with booze and drugs. Aside from wayward teens there would be a tonne of adults turning up to Blade's mother's house to celebrate, crashing the party as an excuse for a big piss up. Fergus had been looking forward to the party all week, not because he was excited for his son's birthday but because there was a good chance he would get a root from Blade's mother.

Sex with ex's was the vast majority of Fergus's hook-ups. Having fathered eight kids to six different women—including Scott's mother—it meant Fergus had quite a few options. None of the women seemed keen on the idea of dating him again, preferring to use him as an occasional fling, which according to Fergus was on account of his "huge cock" and "turbo tongue."

"Nar, I'm all good, bro," Scott answered. "I think I will just stay home and have a quiet one."

Fergus shot him a questioning brow. "Have you got a girl coming over?"

"I wish."

"How long has it been since you fed the beast?"

"Too long," Scott muttered as he dropped some black crumbs into the first cigarette paper. He picked the paper up with its ashy contents and rolled it between his fingers before licking the paper to seal it tight. He handed it over to Fergus and proceeded to roll another one.

"So if you haven't got a chick coming over why the fuck would you want to stay at home when you could be out partying?"

"I'm sort of tired, and not to mention skint as fuck. I have no smokes or drinks to take with me."

"Neither do I but that ain't stopping me."

"It ain't gonna be much fun sitting there sober."

"Who said anything about staying sober. We can just drink whatever we find laying around."

That was how they generally operated when he and Fergus went to parties; help themselves to any booze and cigarettes left unattended. They weren't usually busted but even if they were Fergus would just puff his chest out and challenge the person to a fight. They nearly always backed down, and even if they didn't Fergus would gladly swing a punch. He won most his fights but had also lost enough that he wasn't scared of a punch to the face.

Scott finished rolling his own smoke then sparked it alight, taking a deep drag that burned his lungs so much he had to cough. "Fuck I hate butt rolls."

"If you come with me to Blade's party then we can get our hands on proper cigarettes. Maybe even score ourselves some pot."

"I dunno…"

"Come on," Fergus said. "Don't be such a fucking soft cock."

"I'm not being a soft cock."

"Yeah you are, otherwise you'd come with me."

"I told you, I'm just tired."

Fergus blew out a puff of smoke. "Suit yaself."

Scott pointed at the television and asked, "What's this show?"

"Something about rich cunts trying to find a house to buy." Fergus's voice was full of derision. "I usually hate shit like this but the chick who's showing them the houses has nice tits so I decided to watch it."

Scott laughed. "The things we tolerate just for a perve."

"Too right."

Scott settled into the back of the armchair and began watching the show too. Fergus was right. The real estate agent did have nice tits that she liked to show off with lowcut tops. He sat there wishing he had x-ray vision so he could see through her blouse. When the adverts came on, he discreetly turned his head and set his imaginary x-ray vision powers on Fergus, wondering what the hard man looked like naked. It was weird to be looking at Fergus in this was but Scott wondered that if he could conjure up the image then maybe it would make the idea of asking Fergus about Levi's request somehow easier.

"Did you get eyes for Christmas," Fergus blurted, apparently more aware of being stared at than Scott had thought.

"Sorry, I was, um, just thinking about something."

"And what's that?"

Scott chewed the inside of his cheek. "Has anyone ever offered you money for sex?"

To Scott's surprise, Fergus replied with a nod. "Yeah. A couple times."

"Really?"

"Yep. Back in my twenties I knew this chick who paid me a few times to give her a bit." Fergus laughed and bent forward to stub his butt roll out in the ashtray. Smoke kept wafting from its dislodged orange embers so he waved a hand, fanning away the choking fumes. "I'd like to say it was easy money but it wasn't."

"How come? Did you feel bad about it?"

"Nar, bro. I don't care if a bitch pays me to get her mouth on my cock. The only problem with this chick was she was so fucking fat. The type you have to roll around in flour to find the wet spot." He laughed callously. "But I found it alright. Gave it to her so good she paid me an extra twenty."

"How much did she pay all up?"

"Not much. Just seventy bucks. But I was skint at the time so I figured why the fuck not."

"True." Scott nodded, clasping his hands together. "So would you say it's the kind of thing you'd do again?"

"Fuck yeah. But next time I'd charge by the inch. I'd make a fucking fortune." Fergus waggled his eyebrows, grinning.

"What if it was a guy who was paying?"

"Huh?"

"What if it was a guy who was paying?"

"No, I heard you. I just don't know why you'd ask something so dumb."

"But would you?" Scott asked again. "Let a guy pay you for sex?"

"I'm not a fucking shirt lifter so my answer is a big fat no."

"But what if they paid you really good money?"

There was a flicker of discomfort in Fergus's eyes, before it was replaced with cautious curiosity. "Has a homo offered to pay you for sex?"

Scott hesitated then came clean with a slight nod. "Yeah."

"How much?"

"Five hundred dollars."

"Fucking hell." Fergus looked like he was about to jump off the couch. "Get your arse over there and give the fag what he wants."

"But you just said—"

"Forget what I said. It's five hundred fucking dollars, idiot!"

"There's just one catch..."

"And what catch would that be?" When Scott took too long to respond, Fergus hissed, "Spit it out."

"The guy is only willing to pay 500 if he can watch me and you have sex."

Fergus blinked, his face looking like it might crack. "As in you and me? Together? Fucking? Each other?"

Scott's voice was low and controlled; his face felt scorched. "Yeah. That's what he wants."

"Who the fuck is this faggot?"

"Just some guy I know. He's pretty downlow about it."

There was a taut silence.

"I think I might have an idea who you're talking about," Fergus said like a detective about to crack an unsolved murder case. "A very fucking good idea actually."

"Who do you think it is?"

"Levi," Fergus said breezily.

"What makes you think it's him?" Scott replied, doing his best impression of sounding surprised.

"Because he is the only person we both know with that sort of money and because I have heard a couple stories."

Scott gulped. "What sort of stories?"

"Last year there were rumours going around about some young guy who owned a flash red car driving around Brixton offering guys money for special jobs. No one said what the jobs were but I'm guessing they meant sex. I didn't think much of it at the time, but now with this I'm pretty fucking sure they were talking about Levi."

Scott wasn't sure how he felt about discovering Levi was paying others for sex. A little bit offended perhaps.

"So am I right?" Fergus asked. "Is it Levi?"

"It's Levi," Scott confirmed.

"So old Richie Rich is a queer, aye." Fergus laughed callously. "Why the hell does he want to watch us two get it on?"

Scott shrugged. "I dunno. He just does."

Fergus began eyeing Scott head to toe, his mind probably filled with similar images to the ones Scott had earlier of the pair together. "What did you tell him when he asked you?"

"I said I'd ask you about it."

"Right," Fergus said, his tone difficult to read, before falling silent.

The silence stretched, becoming awkward.

Scott chewed on his lip, feeling uncomfortable by the strange tension. His and Fergus's friendship had always been easy. It had no place for weird silences. But that's probably because it had no place for entertaining the thought of fucking one another.

At last, Fergus said tersely, "What do you want us to do?"

Scott didn't want to give an opinion before Fergus had given one but he felt like he didn't have a choice. "It's not something I particularly want to do but for that kind of money I guess I'd be willing to give it a go." He braced himself for a fiery "fuck off" which never came.

Fergus raised an eyebrow, looking more cautious than disgusted. "I see."

"What about you, bro?" Scott asked edgily. "Would you do it?"

Fergus made him wait for a response before finally nodding slowly. "Yeah. It's good money. I'd say it would be worth it."

"Yeah. It is good money."

"If we were to do it though, then we'd have to have an assurance from Richie Rich that he keeps his mouth shut. We don't want Brixton finding out you and me have dined out on smoked sausage."

Scott snorted.

"I'm not joking," Fergus said staunchly. "We need to know the homo can keep his mouth shut."

"Levi can keep a secret."

"What makes you so sure?"

Scott winced as he made his next confession. "Because he's paid me to do stuff with him before and he's never told anyone."

Fergus's mouth dangled open. "Are you telling me you've already taken it up the arse?"

"Nar, man. We didn't go that far. I-I just wanked in front of him and then I sucked him off." Scott forced his face to look more revolted by the memory than he truly was. "It was fucking gross but I just kept thinking about the money."

To Scott's relief, Fergus nodded calmly. "That's all you can do. Think of the coin, brother."

"Does that mean we're doing this?"

Fergus rubbed a hand over his shiny head like he was still weighing up his options. "Yeah… but there would have to be some rules."

"What sort of rules?"

"For starters, I'm not sucking your dick and you're not going anywhere near my arsehole." Fergus followed his comment up with a scowl. "You will suck me, and if the faggot wants some butt action then you're the one who's getting fucked. Not me."

Scott's arsehole twitched. He didn't like these rules. Not at all. But he also had an addiction to feed.

"What are you waiting for," Fergus hissed. "Text the man. Tell him to come tonight."

"I've got no credit."

Fergus rolled his eyes. "For fuck's sake." He dug his hand into his pocket and dug out his phone. "Text him from mine. And when you've done that go take a shit and make sure your arse is clean. I don't care if you're my best mate. No bitch gets my dick dirty."

Scott hid his resentment with a laugh. Nothing had even happened yet but already he felt like something had changed between them. Fergus had cast him in a role he hadn't even wanted. A role that felt more permanent than it should.

But money was money and that's all there was to it.

CHAPTER 15

It was just after ten at night when they arrived at Josh's house and Dwight was utterly fucking knackered. With the two stop offs at Jakarta and Sydney the flight had taken over sixteen hours to get back to New Zealand before they then had to drive the three hours journey back to Fitzroy.

While he waited for Josh to bring in the last of their luggage, Dwight meandered through to the lounge and sat down on the couch. He kicked off his shoes and removed his socks, his nostrils immediately whacked by the stench of sour foot sweat. The toes of his socks were so caked with old sweat the material was as stiff as cardboard. *They're a bit rank on it.* A shower was definitely in order.

As he glanced around the lounge, he noticed it was every bit as tidy as the kitchen he'd just walked through. It certainly didn't look like the sort of place lived in by a twenty-one-year-old man.

He must take after his mother when it comes to cleaning. Linda was always a house-proud bitch.

Dwight decided that the other thing Josh must have got from his mother was most of the furniture. None of it was cheap. The lad worked hard at his supermarket job but it wouldn't have paid him enough to afford such a nice lounge suite and the china cabinet filled with expensive ornaments lining its shelves. Most young men wouldn't suit a pristine home with such nice belongings but it suited Josh. Josh was naturally neat and tidy, and was organised to the point of having OCD. It was part of what would help make Josh a roaring success as he studied towards becoming an accountant.

Dwight wished he could take some credit for his son's academic ability but that honour fell to Linda. She might have been a frumpy barely-pretty know-it-all but she had certainly passed her brains on to their son. Dwight though liked to think he was responsible for gifting Josh an even better gift—good looks. Handsome men ran in the Stephenson family and Josh was no exception.

His son looked so much like him that family and friends used to joke and tell Dwight that Josh was his mini-me. Other than Josh having dark-blonde hair and Dwight dark-brown, they did look incredibly alike—five eleven, fit physiques, tanned skin and killer smiles with perfectly straight teeth. For years Dwight foolishly thought their physical likeness would mean their personalities would be the same too. Wrong! Josh was his own person and viewed the world very differently.

Linda had gone out of her way to raise their son to be the perfect little social justice warrior, teaching Josh to look for injustice in every situation and respond with moral outrage. Her lefty friends all thought it was fucking wonderful she was raising such a "principled young man" but for the most part Dwight found his son's moral compass more annoying than anything else.

However, he was now grateful for his son being a bleeding-heart liberal because it had helped make the last five days less awkward than it might have otherwise been.

Since doing the unthinkable and coming out to Josh with a totally fabricated story about having his heart broken by an unfaithful Levi, Josh had been nothing but supportive. It didn't make it any less embarrassing but Dwight was confident that the made-up scandal hadn't made him any less of a man in Josh's eyes. If anything it had sort of brought them closer. Which is exactly what Dwight had been counting on.

Accompanying Josh's strong sense of social justice was a fierce loyalty to family. It was this loyalty Dwight knew would gift him sweet revenge against Levi Candy for being a spiteful little prick and burning down his house.

You certainly outdid yourself this time, Soggy.

Dwight knew his son's best friend was trouble but he'd never dreamed for a second that Levi would have the balls to do something crazy like burn his fucking house down. What sort of psycho cunt does that? Levi Candy apparently.

Cocky little cunt probably knows he's too rich to get in any real trouble.

As satisfying as it would be to see Levi in court charged with arson, Dwight knew that wasn't an option. Not just because Levi's stepfather was the richest man in town but because the moment Dwight pressed charges then Levi could turn around and dob him in for spending up large on his credit card. Dwight couldn't afford to get in any shit, the last time he'd been in court he was told by the judge that if he ever saw him again in his courtroom then Dwight could expect a very long stay in prison. Fuck that.

As of right now Levi probably thought he had won the war but that's because the dumb little cunt didn't realise there was more than one sort of flame that could burn things to the ground. Dwight's choice of flame was Josh and his target was Levi's heart. With a performance Meryl Streep would be envious of, Dwight had filled his son in on the fictitious heartache he'd endured at the hands of a supposedly unfaithful Levi and—just like Dwight had suspected—Josh's sweet, gullible heart had bought the sob story hook, line and motherfucking sinker.

Levi didn't know it yet but his friendship with Josh was done and dusted. Dwight had made sure of that.

Aside from paying Levi back for the fire, Dwight was also making sure Josh would avoid being sucked into Levi's twisted plans of sex. It was clear as fucking day to Dwight that Levi had no intention of not trying to fuck Josh, and there was no way on this earth he would stand by and let his son get turned into a faggot and have the story flashed all over the internet courtesy of Levi's Candy Boy blog. No fucking way!

No son of mine will ever take it up the arse or suck a dick.

Dwight knew his outlook on gay sex might have appeared delusional or hypocritical to some but the truth was hemdidn't consider himself gay or bisexual or any other colour under the rainbow. Put simply; he was a man who enjoyed fucking and lived life by the philosophy *any hole's a goal.* Sure, he might have liked the look of some blokes now and then but at the end of the day the guys he fucked were nothing more than a hole to use. It wasn't romantic. It wasn't lovemaking. It was all about dark corners, grunting, sweaty hands over mouths, rough thrusts, and deep breeding. It was about power. Authority. The hierarchy amongst men.

Dwight considered himself to be at the top of that hierarchy as an apex alpha. He had been born with potent virility and elite physical characteristics. Financially he might have been near the bottom of the heap but sexually speaking he was a leader amongst men. And so was Josh.

But what Josh didn't know was that if he were ever stupid enough to be led astray by Levi then he would lose the blessings of sexual power he'd inherited. The moment Levi had his way with him then Josh would lose everything he didn't even know he had.

Dwight's savage outlook on sex between men hadn't been born out of his imagination, it had been forged during his late-twenties when he'd entered the swingers scene in Auckland and by chance stumbled upon an underground sect that preached the importance of a man knowing his place on what they referred to as "the sexual hierarchy amongst men."

It was dark, twisted and brutal but the words preached by the men in these seedy clubs made sense to him. It helped explain those niggly feelings of wondering why he found some men attractive. He wasn't queer. He was an alpha male with a natural desire to fuck and claim what was rightfully his—male or female.

It was clear by reading Levi's blog that he too thought of himself as one of the big boys at the top of the food chain, which perhaps he had been for a time, but unfortunately for Levi he lost his alpha status the second Dwight's dick pierced his tight little hole. Just thinking about that night brought a smile to Dwight's face. *I did you good and proper, Soggy. Good and fucking proper.*

Not only had Dwight stopped Levi's devious plan to seduce Josh and turn him into the latest Candy Boy victim but he'd also robbed Levi of his male pride, assigning Levi to a lifetime of knowing he was not the big man he thought he was. Levi didn't need to attend the same grimy sex clubs to know what he was, Dwight had made it very clear to him.

Levi Candy was used goods.

Dwight glanced up when he heard Josh lugging the two

heavy suitcases into the lounge. The first thing he noticed was how Josh's jeans were riding particularly low, flashing plenty of elastic waistband and a few inches of dark cotton underwear. Dwight's gaze lingered down there longer than it should before he brought his eyes back up to his son's flustered face.

With dark-blond stubble covering his cheeks and chin, Josh was looking particularly scruffy. Dwight thought the rugged look suited him but it was a pretty safe bet those whiskers would be gone by tomorrow morning. Josh liked to keep his face like he did his house—tidy and smooth.

"Thanks for bringing those in," Dwight said. "It's muchly appreciated."

"No worries." Josh flashed him a vivid white smile before dropping the suitcases clunkily to the floor. He sighed dramatically, wiping his brow. "I reckon if I walked around with those every day I could probably cancel my gym membership."

"I've told you before you don't need the gym. You take after me. We look good naturally."

"Maybe but I'd still like to build my muscle mass up a bit more. Bigger biceps. Bigger calf muscles."

Dwight eyed his son head to toe. "Trust me, Joshy. You look perfect as you are."

"Thanks, Dad." Josh nodded then looked in the direction of the kitchen. "Did you want a hot drink?"

"Not for me, ta. I'm thinking I'll just have a shower and then hit the sack." Dwight quickly added, "That's if it's okay to use the bathroom, of course."

"You don't have to ask. Consider this your home while you're here."

"Thanks, Joshy. I really appreciate you doing this for me. I don't know what I would do if you weren't letting me stay with you."

"You don't have to worry about that because you can stay as long as you need."

"I appreciate that but I'll try to get out of your hair as soon as I can. No young lad wants their old man living with them and cramping their style."

Josh laughed. "I think you might be the one exception to that rule, Dad. You party more than I do."

That was true. Josh wasn't a huge party animal.

"So where can I find some blankets for this new bed of mine," Dwight said, patting the couch.

"You can sleep in Ethan's room. I don't think he's back for at least another week."

"Are you sure he won't mind?"

"Ethan won't care." Josh sat down in one of the arm chairs and stretched his legs out in front of him. "When he does coms back though, I thought we could go shopping for a bed to put in the lounge because I am guessing it could be a while before you get the house rebuilt."

"It could be never if the insurance don't pay out," Dwight grumbled.

"They'll pay you, surely."

"Let's hope so. It'd be a cunt having to be a renter again at my age."

"To be fair, Dad, you're not actually that old," Josh said, rubbing the stubble lining his jaw. "Lots of men your age still rent."

"That doesn't mean I want to be one of them."

Josh leaned back and crossed his feet at the ankles, the innocent change of position making the bulge in his shorts appear more prominent. Like a seagull after a piece of bread, Dwight's gaze swooped in on the erotic image as he tried to size up of his son's plump lumps. *My bulge would look about the same size if I sat back like that.* Just before Josh noticed him looking, Dwight flicked his gaze away, angry with himself for still being affected by Levi's comment about Josh being the bigger man in the family. Something so trivial shouldn't have bothered him but for some reason it was driving him crazy.

"Where's the bathroom?" Dwight asked, running a frustrated hand through his hair.

Josh pointed towards the hallway door. "Second on the left."

Dwight got to his feet, brushed the seat of his tan cords, and looked over at Josh smiling back at him. "I hate to be a pain, son, but I don't suppose I could borrow some clothes from you? Everything I took with me on holiday needs washing."

"Have a look in my wardrobe." Josh appeared to scrutinize Dwight's appearance. "I'm guessing we wear the same size."

"I'd say you and I are the same size everywhere," Dwight joked, sounding more salacious than he'd intended. Thankfully the sexual innuendo flew over Josh's head and he simply nodded and told Dwight where his bedroom was.

Making his way down the hallway, Dwight sighed in exasperation, telling himself he would have to get over his cock envy if he wanted to avoid an awkward moment while staying here. What did it matter if Josh had an inch on him? It wasn't a competition. *But it sort of is*, said his pesky inner voice.

The first thing he saw as he entered Josh's bedroom was a blur of hissing fur rush past him that nearly tripped him over. "Stupid fucking cat," he muttered under his breath. The second thing he saw was what was on Josh's bed. A pair of underwear and a piece of paper. Against his better judgement, Dwight went to take a closer look and realised the paper was actually a note.

He picked it up and felt his heart squeeze when he read what was written on it.

Thank you for leaving your undies here for me to play with ;) They smell so fucking sexy! I can't wait for you to get back so I can lick and suck what made them smell so good. I still wank thinking about how good your dick tasted the first time.

Yours faithfully,

Cum Bucket.

SOGGY! Dwight's hands trembled with rage as he fought the urge to howl into the night like a wronged werewolf. *That dirty, sick, conniving critter is still up to his faggot tricks.* What made it worse was knowing that Josh had been dumb enough to encourage him. Dwight already knew something was up after reading the text messages on Josh's phone but seeing this filthy fucking note made it clear to him how important it was to put a stop to their friendship.

I'm pretty sure I have achieved that already though.

Dwight tried to process the idea of what would have happened had he not seen those incriminating texts. How far would have Levi been able to take things with Josh had he not intervened? The answer to that worried him. He'd fucking die if he ever logged onto the Candy Boy blogsite for a wank and found pictures of his own son being shafted. He felt possessive rage rising in his throat until he was about to growl. He gritted his teeth to keep the savage sound inside him and stood very still.

I have to be sure their friendship is dead. I can't risk Josh giving

Soggy a second chance.

Taking the note with him, Dwight marched back to the lounge. He felt bad for the embarrassment he was about to put Josh through but it was for the boy's own good.

"Hey, son." Dwight held out the note. "I don't mean to be a prick but I just found this in your room and thought you might have something to tell me."

"What is it?" Josh's brows furrowed together in confusion.

Dwight handed over the note and watched as Josh's face went from confused, shocked and finally red-faced shame.

"Dad, it's not what you think." Josh swallowed heavily.

"I wasn't born yesterday, Josh."

Josh clawed at his scalp, tugging his hair. "Dad, I'm so sorry. It only happened once and had I known you two were dating I would never have done it. I'm so, so sorry." He began breathing heavily, looking like he might cry.

"Calm down. I'm not mad at you. I'm mad at Levi."

"Me too, Dad. I'm bloody furious with the arsehole." Josh looked up at him, pleading with his eyes for Dwight to believe him. "And I want you to know it won't happen again."

Dwight nodded thoughtfully then delivered a guilt-trip in a condescending tone only a parent could. "Levi and I aren't together now, son, so if it's something you want to do then I can't stop you. You're both grown men and are free to make your own decisions."

"It's not something I want to do. It's really not." Josh looked panicky. "I-I'm not even gay. I don't even know why I agreed to let him do that to me."

"Do you mind if I ask what exactly you did together?"

"Only what the note says… he sucked me off. It was only once. I wanted to tell you sooner but I was just too embarrassed and felt so guilty."

"If you didn't know we were dating then you have nothing to feel guilty about."

"I honestly didn't. I had no idea. Levi never said a word to me about it."

"Then you and me are fine, Joshy. Even if you did know I wouldn't be mad at you. You're my boy and I'd love you regardless." Dwight cringed internally, wondering if he was laying the forgiving father role on a bit thick.

"I am telling you the truth, Dad. I didn't know. I haven't even texted Levi since you told me about you two." Josh sat there in despair. "I can't believe what a prick he is. He's supposed to be my best fucking mate but he uses me while he's supposed to be in a committed relationship with my own father! It's disgusting." The mix of outrage and anguish on Josh's face was absolutely potent, but Dwight wasn't done with the guilt-trip just yet.

"Do you think it's best for everyone if I stay somewhere else?"

"No." Josh shook his head. "I don't want you to leave."

"It was always going to be awkward staying here knowing Levi would be visiting you at some point but now that I know he and you have done stuff together it just feels like it takes it to a whole new level of awkward. And I can't expect you not to see your best mate."

"You don't have to worry about that," Josh said adamantly. "Levi isn't my best mate anymore. He isn't a mate at all."

"Are you sure though? Mates have fallings out all the time and then five minutes later they patch it up and move on."

"Don't you think this is a bit different, Dad?"

"Personally, I would say what Levi has done is unforgivable but that's not my call to make."

"I totally agree with you. It is unforgivable." Josh nodded, his eyes brewing with anger. "That's why he isn't welcome here and why me and him will never be friends again."

Mission accomplished.

CHAPTER 16

The heated touch of a morning wood prodding his butt and a clingy arm wrapped around his waist was what Levi woke to the following morning. He cracked his eyes open to see sunlight peeking through the gaps in the curtains and could hear armies of birds outside singing their noisy little heads off.

He was not used to sharing a bed which had made falling asleep difficult. Thankfully Danny wasn't a snorer but he was clingy as fuck, cuddling Levi from behind all night with one leg swung atop both of Levi's, locking them in place for a sweaty sleep. It was like sharing a bed with a needy baby koala. As Levi registered his newly conscious state, he could feel that beneath the sheets was a furnace of heat, their sticky limbs wet with perspiration.

Fucking Danny last night had been amazing and the boy had been a trooper, letting Levi long-dick him for ages. But what hadn't been amazing were the two fucks that had followed, both of which had seen Danny assume his usual role as the top. Previously, Levi had been getting off on being bitched out by his younger lover but not last night, and he suspected maybe never again.

As fucked up as it was, Danny's generous offer to take one for the team had flipped Levi's submissive switch right off. He could no longer view the boy as his sexual superior. Levi knew it was messed up but it was how he felt. The past two weeks that he'd been submitting to Danny had been infuriating but in a strange way his submissive mindset had acted like some sort of invisible forcefield between himself and the reality of the situation. But now that forcefield was gone and Levi was back to seeing things for how they really were: he was the dominant popular male while Danny was the nerdy social pariah. *I'm letting myself get scuttled by a bloody school boy. And the most unpopular one at that!*

Levi's overdue return to reality didn't change anything though. He'd agreed to a relationship with a boy fizzing with hormones and if he wanted to make it work to ensure he stayed in the comfort of privilege then he had best get used to remaining the submissive partner.

"Good morning, sexy." Danny's voice was soft as it drifted over Levi's shoulder.

Levi reached for Danny's hand resting on his stomach, returning some affection. "Morning."

"How'd you sleep?"

"Not too bad," Levi replied as he rolled over so he was face to face with his new boyfriend. "I haven't shared a bed in a long time though so that was a bit weird."

"You better get used to it because you are going to be sleeping beside me every night from now on."

Despite Danny's comment making him feel like a cat stuck in a broom closet, Levi switched on his charm. "You and me, babe—" He paused to kiss Danny on the shoulder. "We're bed buddies for life."

Danny's cheeks dimpled with a smile. "I love it when

you call me babe."

"I'll have to make sure I keep calling you it then... *babe*."

"You better." Danny swept his thumb over Levi's lips, staring into his eyes adoringly. "What are your plans for tonight?"

There was only one correct answer to Danny's question. "Spending it with you, of course."

"So you'll let me take you out for dinner?"

"I think I will allow it," Levi answered flirtatiously.

"I can't wait. It'll be our first date!"

"The first of many."

"It will be my first date with anyone," Danny mused as his hand found Levi's morning wood beneath the sheets. "So I hope you know how to be romantic."

Levi sighed as Danny tugged him gently. "Does that mean someone would like me to bring him flowers?"

"No. That's my job." Danny grinned as he started sliding his hand up and down Levi's erection. "I'm the man, remember?"

Levi didn't argue. Danny could be whatever the fuck he wanted. He closed his eyes and gave into the pleasure of the morning handjob he was receiving. It was short-lived though. Danny's hand let go and when Levi opened his eyes he found his young lover staring at him very seriously. "What's wrong?"

"You still think I'm the man, right?"

"Yeah, babe. You're the man."

"I don't want you to think that after last night I'm not anymore."

Danny's insistence on clinging to his role as "the man" was pathetic and infuriating. *You're almost as bad as Dwight*, Levi thought to himself. Josh's father had spouted similar nonsense but Levi suspected Dwight's outlook on sex was from delusion while Danny's stemmed from insecurity. If they did manage to make this relationship of convenience work then Levi knew at some point he'd have a responsibility to teach Danny that being a man had fuck all to do with where you stuck your cock, but for now it was easier to go along with the boy's fantasy.

With a waggle of his eyebrows, Levi said, "Would someone like me to make him feel like a man right now?"

"Yes, please." The polite response was totally at odds with the depraved smile that slowly morphed Danny's lips. "If you do a good job then I'll make you breakfast in bed."

Sounds a fair deal.

Levi pulled the blanket down slightly and licked Danny's smooth chest, gently biting one of his nipples. He skimmed his tongue across to the other nipple, nipping there too, then licked his way south over Danny's stomach and wetting the thin strip of hair beneath the boy's bellybutton. Slipping beneath the bedsheets, Levi wedged himself between Danny's skinny legs, running his hands up and down the masculine terrain of the boy's thighs.

The air beneath the blanket was stuffy and ball-scented, the smell sharpened by the lingering scent of sex they'd created the night before. Opening his mouth, Levi slid his parted lips over Danny's pole, savouring the tangy taste of unshowered cock. Unlike yesterday, Levi wasn't shying away from the taste of something that had ruthlessly pummelled his shitter. Diligently, he licked clean the flavour of his own arse and the dried perspiration he'd caused Danny to sweat.

Exerting some authority, Danny pushed the back of Levi's head, impaling his face with five solid inches of stepbrother cock. "Suck that dick, baby. Suck it good."

Levi ground his nose into Danny's wiry black pubes, ripe with pent-up hormonal musk. He massaged the underside of Danny's shaft with his tongue, eliciting shivers and moans from the boy's trembling body. Liquid warmth exploded across Levi's tongue, salty and slightly sweet. He swallowed it down. The hot male stink beneath the blanket intensified.

"Oh, baby. Oh, baby. Oh, baby." Danny's delirious words ran on repeat as Levi bobbed up and down, greedily slurping and sucking the sweaty dick, ramming Danny's leaking slit against his tonsils again and again.

Pulling his mouth free, Levi kissed his way down Danny's sexy fuck-flesh, lapping at the free-flowing precum the youngster released in an almost constant stream. Levi's tongue delved lower and he began slathering Danny's ripe nuts with his tongue, bathing them in a mouthful of accumulated saliva and pre-cum.

Danny unleashed a stream of high-pitched babbles punctuated by curse words.

Levi's lips closed around one of his balls and he slurped it in, encasing Danny's scrotum in his warm, wet mouth. He licked every inch of inch of both balls, suckling on each in turn, as his hand slowly jerked Danny's hard cock.

"My dick," Danny pleaded. "Suck my dick some more."

Levi granted the boy's wish, releasing his spit-soaked nuts and enslaving Danny's dick once again. While he sucked Danny's leaking pipe, Levi's free hand roamed up and down Danny's taught stomach, stroking the soft hairs below his bellybutton. He wondered how long it would be before that strip of hair began to spread higher and cover Danny's midriff and chest.

One, two, five years?

Danny's primal half-grunts, half-sighs let Levi know he was on the right track to making the boy cough up the goods.

Mm, mm, mm he urged as he bobbed on his boyfriend's

knob. His neck was starting to hurt from all the thrusting but he wasn't about to slow down. He could feel Danny's testicles pull up in their sac, readying to fulfil their biological function. And he wasn't going to miss it.

"Baby! You're gonna make me blow." Danny panted wildly. "You better slow down if you want it in your arse instead?"

Levi didn't. This load was destined for his stomach.

Slurp, suck, slurp, stroke.

He squeezed Danny's tightening nuts and shoved his nose into his pubes. The head of Danny's cock tickled his throat and a generous spray of pre-jizz coated his tonsils.

"I'm close..." Danny squeaked. "I'm gonna... Levi... Oh fuck, I'm about to…"

Danny's cum exploded from his piss slit into Levi's mouth in one long, continuous shot. There was no spurt, no drip, no ropes— just one long emission, as though the valve to his nuts just opened wide.

Above the blanket, Danny was gulping in loud gasps of air, his body shaking from such an intense release. "Fudge. Fudge. Fudge."

Levi smiled around the boy's prick, finding his stepbrother's sudden aversion to swearing now that he'd cum rather comical. When Danny's dick finally stopped pissing jizz, Levi licked at his piss slit, collecting all the leftover dribbles of spunk before kissing and licking from the tip down to his balls.

"I believe my work here is done," Levi joked when he finally came up for air.

"That was amazing, baby. Thank you." Danny gave him a peck on the lips. "I definitely owe you breakfast in bed after that."

"I think I just had it." Levi winked. "What you just gave me could feed an army."

Danny erupted into one of his walrus-like laughing fits. When he'd finally got a grip of himself he asked Levi once more if he would like some breakfast.

"I'm all good. Thanks though."

"How about a shower? Would you like to come get clean with me?"

"I'd rather stay in bed a little longer if that's okay with you?"

To Levi's surprise Danny didn't respond sulkily. "Aw, you can stay in bed baby. You can stay in my bed all day if you want. It would be pretty sexy to come home and find you here naked waiting for some hubba hubba."

Hubba hubba? Seriously? Danny may have only been eighteen but apparently he was fluent in historical cringe.

"I'll keep that in mind."

Danny rolled out of bed and walked over to his dresser, rifling through the drawers for some clean clothes. While he had his back turned, Levi admired the boy's backside. His arse was quite tiny but not entirely flat. *It's actually quite a cute arse,* Levi thought. His cock twitched as he thought about how he had fucked it the night before, stretching the boy's anal lips to accommodate his girth.

With a bundle of clothes under his arm, Danny flashed him a goofy smile then sauntered into the en suite. The sound of the shower running sounded almost immediately and Levi contemplated going and joining him.

I probably should. This is day one of our future together... however long that may be.

He thought better of it though. He didn't want to give Danny the impression they had to be joined at the hip. The kid was already clingy enough. Besides, that wasn't how relationships worked. Not long-lasting ones anyway and long-lasting was what Levi was after.

Pieces of guilt stabbed at his heart like shards of glass

for committing the ultimate trickery—fooling someone they had found love when they hadn't.

It's not a complete lie, Levi tried to tell himself. *I do love him... just not in that way.*

That was true.

Despite his constant remarks about the boy not being his brother, Levi did love Danny like he was family. *And maybe I will learn to love him a little extra?* It wasn't impossible. Danny was attractive enough for Levi to get hard for and as the boy got older, and looked more like his father, then the lust he felt for him would only increase. *Too bad that until that day comes I'd rather suck Mark off.*

"Get a grip, Levi," he whispered to himself. "You can't be attracted to the biggest pain in your arse."

His dick disagreed; demanding Levi explore his dirty daddy fantasy. Closing his eyes, Levi began masturbating as visions of Mark's naked body added to the throbbing arousal in his cock. He'd never seen Mark naked so it was pure guesswork as to what he'd find beneath the older man's clothes. He pictured Mark's cock to be a genetic replica of Danny's—slight, curved and a masterful brewer of copious amounts of spunk.

Before long Levi was panting and spurting ball juice all over his stomach. He used the bed sheets to clean himself up then rolled over to try and go back to sleep. It was to little avail though; Danny woke him coming out of the en suite just ten minutes later.

Levi was shocked when he opened his eyes to discover that Danny had got changed into his school uniform—a terribly uncool move when you were a year thirteen and not obliged to wear it.

For Christ's sake. I really am dating a school boy.

Danny with his baby face had a tendency to look young for his age regardless of what he was wearing but seeing him in a tight-fitting grey shirt, school socks sagging down at his ankles and his knobbly knees on display in a pair of grey shorts… well, it really did make him look like jail bait.

"You're wearing your uniform," Levi said in a bland tone.

Danny patted his chest and did a little twirl. "It looks good don't you think?"

"If you say so."

Danny chuckled as he knelt down to pull his socks up. "I only have a few weeks left of school so I want to wear it a bit more before I have no reason to."

"You haven't had any reason to wear it for the past two years. Seniors get to wear mufti, remember?"

"I know."

"Why don't you wear some of the clothes I bought you for your birthday? You look really hot in those jeans I got you."

Danny shrugged away Levi's suggestion. "I guess I just feel like showing some school spirit today."

In an odd way, Levi admired Danny for being proud of Verco High considering he'd been bullied mercilessly throughout his time there. Personally, Levi had never given a toss about stuff like school pride. He had certainly enjoyed his time at Verco High but chances were he would have enjoyed his time at most schools. Rich, hot guys tended to find their way to the top of the social hierarchy wherever they went—rich dorky ones like Danny not so much.

"What are your plans for today?" Danny asked as he approached the bed.

"I have a class later this morning and then I thought I might go visit Peach."

"Cool." Danny nodded. "Will you tell her about us?"

Levi blinked. Once. Twice. Three times. "Er…"

"Are you ashamed of me?" Danny said accusingly.

"No, baby. Not at all. I will tell her. I just wanna do it at the right time. That's all."

Danny's gaze went from suspicious to its usual trusting nature. "That makes sense. Maybe if Peach has a boyfriend we could go out on a double date together?"

Over my dead fucking body! Is what Levi wanted to say but he went with a more agreeable, "Yeah, babe. That would be nice."

"I was thinking I might tell Kaleb today."

Levi's heartrate spiked. "Are you sure that's a good idea? What if he reacts badly?"

"Kaleb won't care." Danny chuckled. "Besides, you always said you thought he was secretly gay."

Funny story there, Danny… As much as Levi would have loved to out the young jock, he knew Kaleb had too much dirt on him. The last thing he needed right now was to explain to his new boyfriend why he'd been tied up and fucked by Kaleb *and* Josh's father.

"I don't think Kaleb's gay," Levi finally replied. "I think he is just a regular straight guy."

"And now Kaleb has a regular gay friend," Danny said, all too happy to embrace his supposed homosexuality.

Levi quickly weighed up his options. Did he try and persuade Danny to keep his mouth shut? Or was it better to let him have his moment? It was only one person… and even if Kaleb did open his mouth, it wasn't like it was going to spread into the flyers social group right away. By the time that happened they'd most likely be out of the country.

"If you feel happy telling Kaleb then I don't mind." Levi smiled. "But just be sure to tell him to keep it on the downlow for a while. We don't want too many people finding out before we've moved away just in case it gets back to our parents."

"Don't worry, baby, I will make Kaleb promise not to tell anyone." Danny let out an excited squeak. "I can't wait to tell him. I just want someone to know how in love I am. How hot my boyfriend is and how much sex we have!"

Levi hid his unease behind a forced smile.

"Kaleb's been teasing me for ages about being a virgin," Danny continued, "and even though I told him last week I wasn't a virgin anymore he didn't believe me. He'll believe me now though. Or at least he will after I've invited him here to hang out with us both."

Levi would rather shove his dick in an exhaust pipe than be forced to socialise with that maggot but again he hid his unease with a smile.

Danny stared at him intently, a voracious glint in his blue eyes. Levi knew what Danny wanted to say so he said it for him. "Bongo drums?"

"You read my mind." Danny's dark brows wiggled like caterpillars. "But I don't have time. I think I'm already going to be late."

"Aw, that's a shame."

"Don't worry baby. Me and my doodle you like so much will be home by 4 o'clock."

"I can't wait," Levi said without an ounce of enthusiasm.

"If you get a chance, would you be able to change the sheets?" Danny asked as he squeezed his feet into his school shoes.

"You want me to change the sheets?"

"You did help make them dirty, didn't you?"

"The housekeeper comes tomorrow," Levi replied in a blasé tone. "That's what Mark pays her for."

"Lynn doesn't want to be cleaning our semen-stained sheets." Danny grimaced. "That's just rude. It's better if you wash and change them."

"Is it though?"

Danny chuckled and walked over to the bed to give Levi a kiss. "Consider it practise for when we're living together. That will be your job."

"My job will be cleaning?"

"It will be until I can afford a cleaner of our own." Danny stroked a finger lazily down Levi's chest. When his hand reached Levi's lap, he squeezed Levi's cock through the sheets. "I'd do the cleaning myself but I will be too busy working to give you the life you deserve."

"In that case..." Levi smirked. "I suppose I better get some practise in."

Danny pulled the bed sheet away to expose Levi's naked body, staring down at Levi's dick as if he were inspecting a personal asset he owned. He grabbed hold of Levi's sweaty nuts, plumping them in his hand. "I like playing with your balls," he said matter-of-factly. "They're so smooth and pretty."

Levi blushed. It sounded like a polite way of saying small.

Then Danny said just that. "Such pretty, delicate little balls."

"They're not that small," Levi croaked.

"Sorry, baby. That came out wrong." Danny leaned down and gave his offended balls a kiss. "They're just very nice to play with."

"Thank you," Levi whispered. When Danny's hand gave his nuts another squeeze, Levi half-expected to be given the order to throw his ankles behind his ears for a fuck. "I thought you didn't have time for another round?"

"I don't. I just wanted to remind you to shave this." Danny reached between Levi's legs and slipped a finger inside his moist butt crack. "We talked last night about you shaving it, remember?"

"You really want me to do that?"

"Very much so." Danny nodded, retrieving his hand. "I like your bum a lot, baby, but I think I'd like it more if it was smooth like your balls are."

Levi wasn't impressed. "Will you be shaving yours too?"

"No." Danny snorted like Levi had just told a joke. "I'm the man."

That was worthy of an eyeroll but Levi resisted the urge.

"Make sure it's shaved before I get home from school," Danny added like a bossy parent. "I want it tidy for our date tonight."

"Are we planning on eating off my arse or something?"

If Danny picked up on the thread of resentment in Levi's joke, he didn't comment on it. He laughed fondly then gave Levi a kiss goodbye.

CHAPTER 17

Seven years earlier

If the rumours about Tina sucking guys off at the swimming hole in Wairua Valley were true then Levi was the unluckiest year nine alive. Other than a hint of nipple prodding the material of her bikini top, Levi hadn't got much out of the swim. In fact, Tina barely said a word to him, just waded around in the water until an older boy called Wade from their school had turned up and Tina quite rudely told Levi he should go home.

Fuck you too he'd thought and climbed up and towelled himself dry before walking home with a resentful stiffy.

The first thing he'd done when he got home was get changed before going next door to tell Shay all about it. The rebel with a heart of gold had laughed and told Levi not too worry about the stuck up bitch.

"But I really wanted her to give me a blowjob," Levi whined as he sat on Shay's bed watching the older boy sift through a pile of shirts on his dresser.

Shay chuckled, holding a black t-shirt up to inspect it.

"Be patient, LP. You're still a bit young to be expecting that sort of thing from girls."

Levi wasn't sure how he felt about that, especially since Shay had once told him he had lost his virginity by Levi's age. He knew it wasn't a competition but try telling his dick that. He'd only been masturbating for about a year but already his cock craved more than just the touch of his own sweaty palm.

"If this girl invites you to the watering hole again make sure you go with a friend." Shay dropped the black t-shirt he'd been holding and rummaged through his clothes some more. "I don't like the idea of you walking around town on your own at the moment."

"Why?"

"I don't think any boys your age should be walking around on their own at the moment." Shay bit his lower lip, hesitating to say anymore. "Rhys Broadhurst went missing last week. And after Jackson going missing it's got me worried."

"Young people run away from Brixton all the time."

"They do but I don't think Jackson and Rhys were the types to just run away without telling their families."

"Are you saying someone did something bad to them?"

Shay shrugged. "I dunno but I think it's best to be careful." His deep blue eyes gazed at Levi. "I'd lose my shit if something bad happened to you."

"If anyone tried to kidnap me I'd knock their teeth out." Levi raised an arm, flexing his bicep. "I've got muscles now."

Shay shot him a fond smile. "I'm sure you would, bro, but I still want you to be careful."

"If someone was kidnapping boys wouldn't the police do something?"

"The pol pol wouldn't do shit," Shay snarled. "They

don't give a fuck about us."

Levi had heard Shay say that before. Actually, he'd heard lots of grownups say that sort of thing, usually while complaining that the police needed to spend more time in Brixton to keep an eye on things.

"What are you actually doing?" Levi asked when Shay grizzled loudly at his pile of clothes.

"I'm trying to decide what to wear for my date tonight."

"But I thought you were picking Mum up from work tonight? She's working the late shift, remember?"

Shay's jaw ticked. "Er, yeah. I'm gonna pick her up after my date."

"Should I tell Mum to catch the bus home?"

"Nar, bro, I'll pick her up after my date."

Levi nodded then asked. "Who's the date with?"

Shay paused. "Mandy."

"Who's Mandy?"

"Shit, bro. You sure do like to ask a lot of questions."

"Sorry."

"That's okay." Shay's lip curled and he patted the crotch of his pants. "Mandy is another girl who has decided she wants to join the Shay Jacobs fan club."

Levi laughed. "Your fan club must be huge by now."

"It sure is." Shay waggled his eyebrows. "But don't get too jealous. The Levi Buttwell fan club will be just as big one day soon."

Shay arched his back and pulled the white shirt he had on free of his brown skin, tossing it toward a pair of sneakers on the floor. His bronze nipples were tiny and hard, and he pinched them as he stared at himself in the mirror above his dresser.

Levi discreetly eyed the older boy's muscles, particularly fascinated by the dark hair growing in the centre of his chest. Something about it made his tummy squirm, a lot like how he'd felt when looking at Tina in her bathing suit.

Shay's grinning reflection caught him staring. "Did someone get eyes for Christmas?"

"Sorry." Levi blushed.

"I'm just kidding, LP. I don't care if you look." Shay ran one hand from a nipple across the sprinkling of crisp, black chest hair then down to his six-pack abs. "I know you're not a homo." He then casually added, "Not that I'd care if you were."

"I like girls," Levi said swiftly. "Not boys."

Shay nodded then went back to fussing over what he was going to wear. He eventually picked out a clean shirt he seemed happy with and put it on—black with white trim around the collar. "How do I look?" he asked, turning around.

"Like a boss." Levi gave him the thumbs up.

A knock sounded at the open door behind them. They both spun around. It was Shay's mother Connie. She leaned against the doorframe, noticeably drunk, nursing a smoke between her pursed lips. Her eyes were every bit as brilliantly blue as her son's but the rest of her was just a scraggly mess of bones and sinew. She took a drag on her cigarette and exhaled heavily. "What are you boys up to?"

"Me and LP were just talking about how we plan to take over Brixton with an army of sex robots," Shay replied.

Levi snorted.

"That's nice," Connie said like she hadn't even been listening. She hacked out a pack-a-day cough before training her gaze on Levi. "Your father just called to say that if you want McDonalds for dinner then you better go home now." Before Levi could respond, Connie staggered her way back into the hallway.

"McDonalds for dinner?" Shay mused aloud. "If he's pissed, which I am assuming he must be, then tell him I will drive youse there."

"I don't think he's started drinking yet today."

"Are you sure?" Shay raised an inquisitive eyebrow. "When has he ever shouted you Maccas for dinner?"

That was a good question. Levi didn't know. "I think he's just in a good mood."

"Wonders never cease," Shay muttered. "Let's just hope whatever's put him in a good mood keeps putting him in a good mood."

∞

After going through the McDonalds drive thru, Levi's father drove them down to the beachfront to eat their meals. Brixton Beach wasn't as nice as the beaches hugging the Fitzroy coastline but it was popular with surfers who'd drive out here to catch the better waves. They parked up in a secluded spot under the shade of a Pohutukawa tree, their vehicle instantly surrounded by greedy seagulls after a feed.

"Here ya go ya fucking beggars." Levi's father threw the birds a handful of his chips. Loud squawks erupted as they swooped down and fought over the chips.

Levi laughed, enjoying the show. "They love McDonalds almost as much as I do."

A couple of the birds flew up onto the bonnet, squawking for more. Levi's father threw them one more handful. "That's all ya getting from me shitheads."

Levi unwrapped one of his cheeseburgers, devouring it almost as quickly as the seagulls necked the thrown fries. This was a rare treat. He could count on one hand the amount of times his father had shouted him McDonalds for dinner.

"I used to bring you and your mum down to the beach here all the time when you were little," his father said. "Do you remember?"

"No," Levi replied with his mouth full, slurping the burger down with some of his strawberry shake. "I must have been really young."

"You were. This is back when you were about four or five. Just a little fella." His father chuckled happily. "You were such a cute little dude."

Levi found his father's trip down memory lane a bit cringe but he was too busy ramming more burger in his gob to be that bothered by it.

"Ya mother would sunbathe while you and me would make sand castles and throw rocks in the river. I'd try to take you swimming but you hated the water. You'd start bawling your eyes out the moment ya head went under water." His father sniggered. "Not like me. I always loved the water."

"I don't mind swimming now-ow." Levi's voice cracked and soared, going from high to low quickly.

His father chuckled. "Those balls of yours sure are dropping, aren't they?"

Levi blushed.

"Don't be embarrassed," his father said. "It's all part of growing up."

"I know that," Levi said defensively.

His father went quiet for a moment before chuckling. "I remember what it was like being your age. A pain in the arse when the voice goes like that… and then there's all the stiffys. I bet you get loads of those now."

Rather than respond to the painfully shameful sentence, Levi took another bite of his burger.

"Yep. Stiffys and wanks," his father declared loudly, his tone playful. "That's what I remember fourteen being all about."

"I'm thirteen."

"Oh…" His father looked surprised. "Are you sure?"

"Yes, Dad. I think I'd know my own age."

"You're fourteen soon though, right?"

"In six months."

His father shrugged. "Thirteen, fourteen. Same thing It's all about stiffys and wanks at your age." He turned and flashed Levi an unnerving grin. "I bet that right hand of yours gets a good work out every day, aye son?" A waggle of furry eyebrows. "Does it?"

The tingling heat of embarrassment crawled up the back of Levi's neck and across his face. He couldn't believe his father had just asked him that.

"If you're anything like I was then you probably do it three or four times a day." His father's tone had lost the playfulness and was somehow darker, more serious and heavy. "Me and my buddies used to have a great time playing soggy biscuit. You ever play it with your mates?"

"What's soggy biscuit?" Levi asked cautiously.

"It's a game where a group of lads stand around a biscuit having a wank until they ejaculate. Whoever loses their lollies last has to eat the biscuit."

Levi grimaced.

His father laughed. "I take it by the look on your face you ain't played that game?"

"Eww no. It sounds gross."

"It's only gross for the poor sucker who loses." His father shovelled a handful of chips into his gob, chewing noisily. "You should ask Scott to play with ya sometime."

Levi clutched his midsection, silently willing his father to put an end to this humiliating conversation.

The chubby prick must have got the hint because he turned to look towards the ocean and sighed before taking them for another trip down memory lane again as he reminisced about the "good old days" of coming down to the beach as a family. Then, out of the blue, his father said, "I'm really sorry for being such a shitty father the past few years. I know I've really let you down."

Levi turned to look at his father, surprised to hear the man acknowledge his shitty parenting.

"I hope you know how sorry I am." His father reached over and rubbed Levi's knee. "I know I've been too hard on you and I feel terrible for that."

Levi started at his father's pudgy, calloused hand resting on his knee, not enjoying the clammy heat touching his skin. He knew his father was only trying to be nice but he would rather they just eat in silence. Their relationship didn't have room for this sort of bonding. It just felt too fucking weird.

Sensing that his father was waiting for him to say something, Levi replied with, "That's okay, Dad. I know you try your best."

"Thanks, son." His father finally removed his sweaty mitt and not a moment too soon. "I want you to know I am gonna start making a real effort. It's time I treat you right. You're becoming a fine young man and deserve to be treated like one."

"Does that mean more McDonalds?" Levi joked.

"It certainly does."

"I was only joking."

"I know but you really can have more McDonalds. You can have more of everything if you're willing to play the game."

"What game?" Levi asked.

"It's not so much a game as it is a case of if you be nice to me then I'll be nice to you."

"Aren't I nice to you already?" If nice meant keeping his

hateful opinions to himself then Levi was downright lovely.

His father appeared to think that over before answering. "Most of the time but there's some little things you could do that would help."

"What sort of things?"

"This will sound silly but I really miss you calling me daddy."

Levi snorted. "I seriously don't think I have ever called you that in my life."

"You used to. When you were little. I miss that. It'd be nice if you called me that again."

"No offense but aren't I a little old to be calling you that?"

"Obviously you wouldn't call me it while other people are around. Just when it's the two of us… like right now."

Levi turned his attention back to his burger, wondering if his father had already had a few sips from the bottle today without him knowing. It seemed highly likely considering their entire conversation since parking up had been one giant cringe-fest.

"Try it now," his father suggested. "Call me daddy."

"Do I have to?"

"Go on…"

"But it's weird."

"The more you say it the less weird it will be, won't it?"

Levi wasn't liking this but he did like the idea of having more McDonalds in the future so he gave the pathetic bastard what he wanted. "Okay… *Daddy*."

His father's face lit up with a smile. "That wasn't so hard, was it?"

Levi shook his head. "I guess not."

"I guess not, *who*?"

"I guess not, Daddy."

His father chuckled happily, touching Levi's knee again.

"Good boy. I expect to hear that word a lot more from now on and I promise you you'll get rewarded for it."

Levi forced a smile, deciding it was in his best interest to play the game. "That sounds really good, Daddy."

He had just missed the second sign.

CHAPTER 18

Waking up at the crack of dawn was not ideal but Dwight needed an early start today. He'd text Lucas last night with orders that he pick him up from Josh's house at seven a.m. sharp. It was imperative they get out to Rapanui Beach so Dwight could check on the state of his house and inspect the stock.

If Dwight had had his way he would have spent today catching up on sleep and recovering from jetlag. But rest was not an option when you had to work to pay your bills, insurance claims to make and illegal goods to check on.

Fucking Soggy!

Levi the psycho cunt had certainly caused him a major fucking headache but it wasn't anything Dwight couldn't overcome. The next few months would be a pain in the arse as he waited for a new home to be built but it was better than ending up in jail—which would have been the outcome had anyone who attended the fire wandered too far into the bush at the back of his property.

Dwight grazed a hand down his hairy chest, reaching for his itchy balls. He gave them a good scratch—*scritch-*

scritch—then squeezed his hard-on. Fuck he was horny. He was horny every morning but this morning he was especially so. It was mostly because he hadn't got laid in nearly a week and he wasn't used to go that long without sticking his cock in a hole of some kind.

His last hook-up had been with a young Aussie chick called Anita. She'd been a good time that culminated in a drunken messy blowjob in the hotel room while Josh had been out sightseeing. Since then though, Dwight had been so concerned about his house he hadn't been in the mood to try and seduce any more drunk backpackers. But his need for a root had come back with a vengeance this morning.

Not helping matters was the smell of Ethan's bedroom. Unlike Josh, Ethan wasn't a clean freak. Ethan's bedroom floor was a swamp of unwashed clothes and there was more than one used condom splattered beside the bed. Dwight usually preferred the feminine scent of a woman's lingering perfume but that didn't mean he was immune to becoming aroused from male smells—even unpleasant ones like this room was packed with.

According to Josh, the bedroom had been shut up since Ethan had left for France a month ago, leaving the curtain-pulled room to bake during the height of a hot summer. As a result, the sharp tang of sweaty socks, rank sneakers and dirty undies had been festering all this time.

Gently pulling the sheet down to expose himself, Dwight let his cock breath in the not-so fresh air. He gave it a firm squeeze. It felt so hard, thick, and heavy. It throbbed with a burgeoning torrent of sperm clamouring to be released. Pre-cum flowed from the piss slit in anticipation and glazed the head of his cock with shiny wetness. He squeezed his straining boner again and admired his length and girth, proud to have such a fine specimen of manhood between his legs.

He had no idea what this Ethan lad looked like but it didn't stop Dwight from fantasising about fucking him. He closed his eyes and began to masturbate, imagining himself fucking Ethan in this very bed. In his mind he pictured Ethan to look a lot like Levi; slim, tanned with glossy dark brown hair and a toned body that was hairy in all the right places. He even imagined Ethan as having the exact same cock; a sexy six incher that fit perfectly inside Dwight's hand.

"Fuck yeah," Dwight mumbled, beating faster. "I'll fuck your arse so hard you'll be shitting me out for weeks."

By now imaginary Ethan and Levi had evolved into the same person so Dwight flicked pretend Ethan away and just let himself imagine it was Levi getting fucked in the bed.

"That's right, Soggy… You love dick. You love daddy dicks. You love my dick." Dwight wasn't usually a vocal masturbater but he sure as shit was this morning and it was bringing his balls to a fever pitch.

"Hssss. Ahhh, yeah." He pulled his feet up and bent his knees, milking the full length of his veiny shaft. His breath hissed in his nostrils, his eyes locked on the crown of his erection, watching the beads of precum dribble down his shaft.

"Gonna fuck you. Fuck you so hard, bitch." His mouth was open and sounds poured out of him as he strained toward climax. "Ungh. Ungghh. Aww!"

Just as he was about to pull the trigger on what was set to be an intense ball-draining orgasm, three little knocks sounded at the door. Dwight let go of his cock like it was a hot iron and quickly pulled the sheet up to cover himself. "Yeah…? What is it?"

The door opened and Josh's smirking face popped

inside. "Sorry to interrupt."

"You didn't interrupt anything."

"Are you sure?" Josh's eyes glinted with cheek, giving away that he'd probably been listening on the other side of the door before knocking.

"Okay, Josh. You got me." Dwight rolled his eyes. "Your old man was just saying his morning prayers."

Josh laughed. "I don't think God likes to be spoken to like that."

"I'm sure he's heard worse," Dwight mumbled.

Josh wiped the smile off his face then said, "I just came in to tell you that Lucas is parked outside waiting for you."

"What the fuck is the numbnuts doing here so early? I told him to be here at seven. Not six."

"It is seven. Ten past seven to be exact."

"But?" Dwight rolled over and picked his phone up from the nightstand. Sure enough, it was ten minutes past seven. "I could have sworn I'd set the alarm for six. I must have hit the wrong fucking button."

"You know what they say, Dad. Playing with it too much will make you go blind."

Dwight smirked. "Cheeky shit."

"Did you want me to make you a coffee and..." Josh's voice trailed off when he appeared to spot something in the corner of the room. "I wondered where those got to." He pushed the door open and stepped inside.

Dwight wished he hadn't. Josh had nothing on except a skimpy white towel wrapped around his waist. His son's sun-kissed torso dripped rivulets of water as he trod across the room, the lumps and bumps of his cock and balls clearly outlined with each step he took.

Dwight looked away, not liking the effect his own flesh and blood was having on his still-hard cock.

"I've been looking for these for ages," Josh said.

Dwight reluctantly turned back to find Josh knelt on the floor holding up a pair of red and black trainers. His throat went dry with a sexual hunger that was not only forbidden but disgusting. Against his paternal instincts, he found himself willing the towel to slip. "You two share shoes?"

Josh shook his head. "Knowing Ethan he probably got drunk one night and put them on thinking they were his."

Dwight nodded as he admired one of Josh's hairy, muscled calves that flexed with definition from his crouched position. He felt like the worst kind of pervert, scoping out his own son.

Josh stood up, gripping the side of the towel as it began to come loose. Luckily—or unluckily—it didn't expose anything more than his upper thigh. "Did you want me to make you a coffee?" he asked.

"Yes, please." Dwight bit down on his bottom lip, chewing on it as he studied his son's bare feet and the light hairs on his toe-knuckles. "That'd be great."

Rather than leave the room right away, Josh stood there staring at him with an unreadable expression on his handsome face.

"Something up?" Dwight asked edgily, worried that his son may have been more aware of being ogled than he thought.

Josh smiled. "I was just thinking how nice it is having you stay with me. It's gonna be good spending more time with you."

As if he didn't feel bad enough already, Josh's sweet words and innocent tone made Dwight feel even filthier for his impure thoughts. He returned a smile. "Well, son, I'm glad to be here."

Josh patted his stomach, fingers smacking the bumps and ridges of his abs. Dwight stared at the light trail of hair that went down his son's stomach and disappeared into the towel. He looked away to avoid ogling his bulge again.

"Okay. I'll go tell Lucas you won't be long." Josh went to leave the room but just before he closed the door, he popped his head back in and said, "Or should I tell him fifteen minutes so you can finish your morning prayers?" With a friendly chuckle, Josh finally closed the door behind him.

Dwight let out a troubled sigh and carved a hand through his hair. *What the fuck just happened?* He felt sick. His heart was pounding so intensely he could hear it in his ears, meanwhile his cock was still hard as a fucking rock beneath the sheets.

He knew he'd been scoping Josh out the past few weeks but he was adamant it hadn't been sexually motivated. It had been nothing more than cock envy; a curious need to know just how much bigger his son's dick really was. This though... this was different. He hadn't been staring at Josh's half naked body just now to know the size of his manhood, he'd been staring at him the way he would stare at Levi or Blondie or any other young buck he was contemplating to loosen the anus of.

How could he conjure up such wanton, unnameable desires? Yet, there they were, vandalizing his mind; festering beneath the surface, like a bad wound, aching and throbbing, refusing to heal. He was in a state of hyper arousal. His balls ached, filled with poisonous desire that he needed to get out of his system.

With a shaky breath, Dwight lay back down and closed his eyes. He slid his hand beneath the blanket and finished his "morning prayers" with the most sinful thoughts a father could have.

CHAPTER 19

A pile of ashes in the shape of a square. That's all that remained of Dwight's home. The sleepout was still standing, as was the shed, but aside from tools and a couple old mowers they didn't contain anything of value. He'd told himself to expect the worse but actually seeing the ashy grave of where his house once stood hit him like a kick to the balls.

"Fucking hell," he muttered, staring at the spot he'd called home for twelve years. "It's worse than I expected."

"I'm so sorry, Uncle Dwight." Lucas gave his shoulder a sympathetic rub. "I warned you it was bad."

Dwight knew whose fault this was but that didn't stop him wanting to lay some blame on Lucas. "Had you stayed out here like I suggested then this would never have fucking happened," he said scathingly.

"W-We don't know that," Lucas stuttered. "It might have happened anyway. With me inside!"

"Don't play that card. The smoke detectors would have gone off then you could have got up and put the fire out."

"It still doesn't mean I could have stayed here though. I

don't like the idea of leaving Sophie and Mia at home alone."

"You mean you couldn't go a night without getting your dick wet more like it," Dwight hissed.

Lucas's temple pulsed but he kept his fury to himself.

With a forefinger and thumb, Dwight pinched the bridge between his eyes and dragged in a string of deep inhales. Each one grew slower, calmer, until his shoulders relaxed. "I'm sorry, Lucas. I'm just lashing out because I am angry."

Lucas nodded. "I know."

"Hopefully the insurance company coughs up the goods."

"I'm sure they will. It was just an accident."

"An accidental case of arson, you mean."

Lucas frowned at him. "You don't think someone did this on purpose, do you?"

"Bloody oath, I do. The house didn't catch itself on fucking fire."

"Maybe it was faulty wiring?"

"Faulty wiring my arse." Dwight felt his chest tighten with anger. "It's Brixton scum that did this."

"You reckon you know who did it?"

Dwight wasn't stupid enough to tell Lucas about Levi's role in the fire so he just shrugged. "Nar, but whenever something goes wrong in these parts it's usually some lowlife from Brixton who's responsible."

Levi Candy might have been living in the lap of luxury now but Dwight knew Brixton trash were incapable of climbing out of the gutter. They were born criminals and stayed that way till the day they died.

He was well-aware how some folk might accuse him of hypocrisy considering his own illegal endeavours but unlike the jobless scum from Brixton, he'd always held down a job and worked hard. His crime wasn't for shits and giggles, it was to compensate for the blood sweat and tears of being a working man constantly denied what he was worth.

He liked to think he was the exception to the saying *there's no honour among thieves.* He had plenty of honour. If Dwight Stephenson gave his word, he meant it. The other thing that set him apart from Brixtonites like Levi was that he never fucking ever stole from those poorer than himself, nor would he shit on a mate to get ahead. That went against his principles.

"What will you do until it's rebuilt?" Lucas asked.

"Joshy is letting me stay with him for the time being."

"That's good of Josh."

"Yeah, otherwise I'd be having to stay here in that poxy sleepout with no electricity." Dwight pointed at the small wooden hut he'd just criticised.

"I don't suppose it has a toilet by any chance?" Lucas asked. "I'm busting for a piss."

"It doesn't I'm afraid. But you have my permission to piss all over my house."

Lucas laughed. "I guess I'll go piss in the lounge." He took a few steps to the side then pulled down his zipper. Reaching into the fly of his jeans, Lucas did a kind of semi-squat and pulled out his penis.

Dwight glanced over and took a sly squizz at the pale strip of meat. He wondered how big that fucker would grow to when Lucas was erect. If it was anything like the rest of the strapping young lad's body then it would be sizable to say the least.

Lucas sighed loudly as he let loose a long, steady stream of piss. "It's actually a lovely spot out here," he said, unaware Dwight's eyes were still trained on his gushing cock. "I can see why you liked living out here so much. It's really peaceful."

"It sure is that," Dwight agreed, watching the translucent yellow stream wet the charred ground. He let his eyes drift to the seat of Lucas's scraggly jeans, admiring the shapely mounds of the young man's high, meaty and full rump.

You can bet your bottom dollar that arse ain't ever taken a cock, Dwight thought. He found himself getting turned on at the thought of popping Lucas's cherry and claiming such a burly young man as a sexual conquest. There was always a thrill in claiming another male's anal virginity but it was more of a kick if they were as masculine as Lucas was. And they didn't get much more masculine or alpha-like than the burly six-foot-four Lucas Maxwell.

When it came to fuck-holes of the male variety, Dwight likened it to war. There was little triumph in the scalp of a weak soldier but to get your dick dirtied with the shit of a powerful warrior like Lucas… that's where a man could earn the darkest of honour.

Speaking of honour. Or rather the lack of it. Why the fuck hasn't Blondie text back yet?

The first thing Dwight had done when he'd finished his wank this morning was text his young blond friend, asking him if he'd be keen for some fun later today. Unfortunately the boy had failed to respond yet and Dwight was beginning to get impatient. It wasn't like he'd spontaneously combust without a fuck today but he knew he had to drain his balls so he didn't have a repeat of what had happened this morning. He cringed internally at the memory of how he'd tossed off thinking about his own son.

I was probably just tired. Not thinking straight.

That's what it had to be. Just a case of a tired brain getting its wires crossed. Mind you, he was still disgusted with himself that it had happened at all. What sort of man has impure thoughts about their own son? That's why he needed a distraction. And until he heard back from Blondie the only distraction available to him was taking a piss a few feet to his left.

This wasn't the first time he'd looked at Lucas in a sexual light. Shit. He perved at him most days they worked together, casting sly glances at Lucas's bulging biceps or gazing longingly at the young man's arse. Obviously he would never make a move on the kid out of respect for Lucas's old man but Dwight figured there was no harm in admiring the scenery now and then.

Based just on his face then Lucas was pretty average but he did have nice skin; pale and porcelain-like, perfectly accentuated by the trendy look of his thick auburn hairstyle that tumbled loosely and disorderly on top and faded beneath a severe side part into shaved sides. But his main appeal came from his towering height and menacing muscles. He was a gentle giant at heart but if someone were to cross him then Dwight imagined the lad could look like one scary motherfucker.

Lucas's heavy stream dried up and he shook his dick dry of piss dribbles then put it back in his pants. The free perve was over.

"Right." Dwight drew out a long pause. "Now you've leaked the beast shall we go have a look at the goods?"

Lucas nodded and followed him towards the back fence that sectioned off a dirt track leading into the native bush surrounding the property. The bush wasn't part of Dwight's property but he'd always treated it like he owned it, storing away old rusted-out car parts and bags of rubbish beneath the canopy of nature.

They walked in silence, each of them peering through trees lining the dusty track, making sure they were alone. A couple hundred metres along they veered onto another wide path, this one overgrown with grass and ferns. Eventually they came to a circular clearing where in the centre lay a pile of leafy branches.

Dwight began yanking the branches away, biffing them over his shoulder. "Don't just stand there," he barked at Lucas who stood there with a sick look on his face all of a sudden. "Help me get this shit off of here."

Lucas skulked over to help. With arms like his it should have been easy work but he was pulling limply.

"Put some muscle into it," Dwight huffed. "Ya not pulling out a fucking tampon."

Lucas grunted and applied his real strength, making easy work of the heavy camouflage until eventually they exposed what was beneath: a maroon-coloured Toyota Ute.

"There she is. Betsy the Beast." Dwight walked around the front of the nicknamed vehicle that had once been used for his lawnmowing business before he'd spray-painted Betsy a different colour and removed her number plates so she could take up a life of crime. He frowned at the damage to her bonnet; the metal all scrunched and dented inwards. "I forgot how fucking munted she was. It's a miracle we even managed to drive off the last time."

"I fucking hate this car," Lucas muttered. "I can't even look at it."

"What's Betsy ever done to you?"

"This is what killed Sameer," Lucas screeched. "How could you not hate it?"

"It's not Betsy's fault. She was only going in the direction you were pointing her."

Lucas's lip trembled and tears started to roll down his cheeks.

For fuck's sake. I thought we'd got over the tears. For most of the drive out here Lucas had been an emotional wreck, snotting and snivelling as he spouted on and on about how guilty he felt. Maybe Dwight would have felt bad too if he'd been the one driving that night but luckily for him he hadn't been the one behind the wheel.

Dwight walked over and rubbed Lucas's back, sighing like he was trying to show the lad some empathy but probably sounding more impatient than anything. "Don't cry. It's not like you did it on purpose. The fucking idiot shouldn't have bloody been there at four o'clock in the morning."

"That doesn't make me feel any less guilty." Lucas snivelled. "I've made Asha a widow and left three children without a father."

"Lucas." Dwight grabbed him by the shoulders and shook him. "Lucas. son. I need you to look at me."

Lucas lifted his head, his nose running with snot.

"This was not your fault, okay?" Dwight spoke slowly, clearly. "It was an accident. A horrible accident. Do you understand? Just an accident."

"But we killed a man."

"We did no such thing. This is a case of wrong place, wrong time."

"I don't think Sameer would think so."

"If this Sameer chap was here right now I think he would understand. He would know you're a fine young man who is doing his best to provide for his family. Just like he was."

"You think so?" A sniffle of hope sounded in Lucas's voice.

"I know so." Dwight gave Lucas's shoulders a reassuring squeeze. "Now I need you to pull yourself together because if you don't then people might start getting suspicious and if people get suspicious they start asking questions and questions lead to a whole lotta shit we don't need. We do not want to get busted for this, son, because if we do then we will be going inside for a long fucking holiday. And what good will you be to Sophie and Mia if you're in jail? Hmm?"

"You're right, uncle Dwight. You're right."

Dwight let him go and stepped back. "Good. Now I want you to stop beating yourself up. It's time to focus on your family. You got me?"

Lucas rubbed his tears away, nodding.

"And one more bit of advice." Dwight looked sternly at his accomplice. "You have to keep away from Sameer's family. The fact you went to the funeral is bad a fucking 'nough. Any more contact is dangerous. From now on you need to forget about them and focus on your own family."

"I will, Uncle Dwight. I will."

"Good." Dwight nodded and lowered his gaze to Lucas's stomach. "Now I want you to take your shirt off for me."

"Why?"

"Because I want a free perve at ya tits," Dwight joked, flirting with the truth. "I wanna use it to carry some of the cartons back to the work vehicle."

"Oh… but I didn't think we were going to sell any for a while so we kept a low profile."

"This bundle is for my personal use." Dwight stuck his hand out. "Now give me your shirt."

Lucas hesitated for a moment before grabbing the hem of his t-shirt and pulling it up over his head, revealing the wet tangles of curls in his armpits. He handed his t-shirt over, unaware of Dwight's spiking arousal.

Dwight tied the sleeves into knots, turning it into a pit-stained carry bag. He walked to the back of the Ute and yanked open the boot where piles upon piles of cigarette and tobacco cartons lay. It was the accumulation of all four smash and grabs they'd done. With the soaring cost of cigarette prices in New Zealand it was easily worth tens of thousands. When he'd filled the shirt with just ten cartons, he shut the boot and turned around to find Lucas gawking at his now mishspaed t-shirt.

"What will we do with the rest of the stock?" Lucas asked.

"I'm inclined to leave it here for the time being." Dwight glanced around the clearing that was guarded by the overgrown forest. "If anyone had come snooping while they were putting out the fire then the pigs would have been here already and cleared it away."

Lucas dragged a hand down his sweaty chest and scratched his stomach. "So, uh… when can we start making some money?"

"Soon."

"How soon?" Lucas asked, his brows furrowing.

"Probably a few months."

"That's not soon!"

"It's sooner than it never happening."

"But me and Sophie are really skint. Like *really* skint. We have to keep borrowing money from her family and it's fucking killing me."

Lucas's tone was getting a bit pushy but Dwight let it slide. It was better the boofhead be desperate for cash than revert back to a snivelling mess. "We just have to wait until the heat dies down a bit. The pigs are gonna be all over this for the next wee while but it will die down eventually."

"But what do I do in the meantime?"

Dwight shrugged. "I guess you could try finding another job that pays better than what I'm paying you."

"I've been trying but there's nothing going at the moment." A look of desperation tainted Lucas's face. "The job market is shit."

Dwight did feel bad for his young worker but there was fuck all he could do about it. "If all else fails then I suppose you could try selling your arse." It wasn't a serious suggestion obviously but he was curious to see Lucas's reaction.

"You mean be a rent boy?"

"If your cock's as big as your hands and feet then you'd probably make a fortune." With the arch of an impish brow, Dwight stared at Lucas's groin. "Hell, I'd even consider hiring you for an evening just to see how big it is."

Lucas grimaced, looking like a man who'd just licked a sour minge.

"You could even tie a pretty little ribbon around ya knob for me," Dwight said, pushing the joke even further. "Then I could unwrap it before I bent you over for a good pounding."

Lucas snorted, casting him a derisive glare. "I hope that's a joke."

"What do you think?" Dwight returned an equally serious stare before finally cracking a smile. "Of course it's a fucking joke. Unless that big hairy arse of yours has grown a pussy then I ain't paying to plough it."

Lucas let out a sigh then a deep belly laugh. "That's funny," he said and laughed some more. "For a second though I thought you were actually being serious."

Dwight may have liked the idea of scuttling the lad but he would never pay for it. Paying for a root was for desperate fucks and psycho cunts like Levi.

Lucas began looking at him strangely again, obviously hiding what he was really thinking.

"I told you it was a joke, Lucas, so stop looking at me like I'm after ya family jewels."

"It's not that," Lucas said, voice low, kind of husky. "I was just thinking of another idea that could make us both some money while we wait for the heat to die down."

"I'm listening…"

"What if instead of cigarettes we started hocking off household items like my dad used to."

"Your dad had to actually break into peoples homes to do that."

"Yeah."

"I know how daring the whole smash and grabs were but I only did those because I was confident we could be in and out in less than a minute. If you ain't quick then you get busted. Just like your dad used to get busted."

"But we wouldn't get busted if we do what I'm about to suggest." Lucas's eyes glinted excitedly.

"Spit it out," Dwight snapped.

"What if we used mowing lawns as a cover for breaking into some of the richer clients' homes. There's two of us. One could mow the lawns and keep an eye out while the other goes inside and sees what they can find. That would work, wouldn't it?"

Dwight had thought of this himself a thousand times but he'd always chickened out on account of the damage it would do if he was busted. The person wouldn't even have to contact the police to ruin him. Just one post on Facebook suspecting him of being a thief was all it would take to put him out of business. No fucker was gonna hire a thief to mow their lawns and do their gardens.

"I've considered that before but it's just too risky," Dwight said. "We mow lawns in the daytime so it's not like you'd go unnoticed dragging a sixty-inch television into the Ute."

Lucas thumbed his chin, considering Dwight's response. "What if I just snuck in and went for the jewellery. Anything small that looks like it could make us money."

"Those are just quick fixes that we will struggle to find

buyers for. They ain't gonna solve any long-term money problems."

"Neither are the cigarettes," Lucas snapped.

"I can assure you they will fetch us a damn sight more in the long run." Dwight pointed to the boot of the vehicle. "You've seen how much stock there is."

"I know but I need money sooner than when we can make it from all of that. I've got Sophie's dad constantly at me for being a lousy provider for my family."

"You need to man up and tell the prick to pull his fucking head in," Dwight said passionately. "You treat Sophie fucking wonderfully and you're a damn good dad to Mia."

"I wish Gerald saw it that way," Lucas mumbled before returning to his cockamamie plan of stealing from Dwight's customers. "Could you imagine how much money we would make from a house like Levi's family?"

"As much as I'd love to rip Soggy's family off I ain't going to."

"Why not? It isn't like they can't afford to replace whatever we take." Lucas grinned bitterly. "I'd love to steal that faggot Candy's shit. I'd key his poncy red car while I'm at it."

Dwight certainly shared Lucas's dislike of Levi but he'd already stolen from his son's best mate and couldn't risk having another go. "I fully know what it's like to struggle, Lucas, but you have to promise me you won't steal from my customers. This business is my livelihood and I ain't in a hurry to end up in the unemployment queue with the rest of the dole bludgers if something went wrong. Or worse, jail!"

"But I *really* need to come into some money."

"I know it's hard right now but we just have to be patient. A little bit of struggle now will be worth the wait.

Trust me."

Lucas nodded and Dwight gave a disapproving grunt at his employee's lack of a verbal response. Lucas nodded again and said, "I understand. I won't do anything stupid."

"Good. Now help me cover Betsy back up." Dwight hoped this would be the last of any crazy suggestions about robbing the Candy mansion but there was a glint in Lucas's eyes that made him weary, like the auburn-haired stud wasn't quite done with the harebrained scheme.

After they'd covered the Ute up with its camouflage of branches and leaves, they trudged their way back in the direction of the road. Dwight hung back and let Lucas lead the way. Rather than waste his time worrying about what Lucas might or might not be plotting, Dwight used his position at the rear to check the young man out some more and take advantage of the shirtless show. He loved the way Lucas's back rippled with muscle and strength. His skin was pale and smooth, the only sign of hair was a little patch of sandy fluff peeking over the waistband of his jeans.

I wonder if that hair is on his arse cheeks as well? This guessing game kept Dwight happily occupied as they walked on in silence. But as his mind moved on from the questions to actually visualizing what Lucas's arse might look like, and wondering what noises Lucas would make being breached, he gave his head a shake. *Fuck, I have to get over this real quick, or I'm gonna be mowing lawns all day with a boner.*

When they reached the work vehicle and climbed inside, Dwight started the engine and gunned it back towards Fitzroy. The silence between them came to an end when Lucas started boring Dwight with tales about his daughter Mia, going into mind-numbing detail about how talented she was at drawing. The child could smear shit on the walls and Lucas would probably refer to it as a piece of art.

Lucas was the epitome of an overly proud father, never shutting up about how advanced the three-and-a-bit-year-old was and constantly whipping his phone out to show Dwight pictures of her.

I wonder if he'd be as proud if he realised the kid wasn't even his.

While it wasn't unheard of for a pair of pasty pale white tails to have a dark-haired child with olive skin, it did seem a fucking stretch in this particular case. The girl had Levi's attractive face and his alluring hazel eyes, and Dwight was willing to bet his left nut that Mia's olive complexion came from Levi's Māori ancestry. That wouldn't have been apparent to a lot of people but Dwight was one of the few who'd once known Levi's real father; a large part-Māori man called Barry Buttwell who used to drive Dwight's school bus.

Dwight was willing to bet his other nut that Sophie knew Levi was Mia's father. Dwight didn't blame her for not saying anything though. If Lucas ever found out he'd lose his shit big time. Lucas had sacrificed a lot to help Sophie raise Mia and if he found out the girl was the product of his former high school nemesis then it went without saying that all hell would break lose.

Dwight was unlikely to ever tell Lucas about his suspicion. It would break Lucas's heart to know that the past four years of his life had been a lie. But that didn't mean Dwight would pretend he didn't know the truth. He would keep it in the back of his mind just in case he ever needed it. After all, a secret like that could be the ultimate weapon if he ever needed it.

CHAPTER 20

Rather than stay sleeping in Danny's bed when the boy had left for school, Levi had got up and gone back to sleep in his own bedroom. It was partly because he preferred to sleep in his own bed but it was also because Danny had pissed him off.

He could handle Danny's innocent comment about the size of his balls—it hadn't been said maliciously and Levi knew they weren't huge—but what he hadn't liked was the list of chores he'd given Levi to do. That had bothered him. Bothered him a lot. Not just because it was rude, presumptuous and bossy but because it made him feel like the one thing he refused to be—a whore.

His skin crawled at the thought of becoming anything remotely similar to the stars of Candy Boy who Levi would pay for sex. Those boys were cheap and damaged, forever assigned a dollar value. Not all of them walked away affected but some certainly had. It was the broken ones, the wide-eyed guilt-riddled ones, who Levi enjoyed the most. It was cruel and vicious but Levi had always got strength from stealing their innocence. It was the only way he knew how to make up for the loss of his own.

When he finally dragged his groggy arse out of bed it was closer to lunchtime than breakfast. He started his day off with a shower, washing away the smell of Danny and the sex they'd had this morning and last night. As he rinsed the bodywash off his cock and balls, he naturally found himself slipping from cleaning to masturbating but just before he got fully erect, he stopped. With his unwavering submission now gone, Levi knew he'd need as much sperm in his balls as possible to give his sexually demanding boyfriend the sex the boy wanted.

After getting changed into a clean pair of shorts and a lemon-coloured t-shirt, Levi made his way downstairs in search of strong cup of coffee and some breakfast. He could tell by the absolute stillness no one else was home. Danny was at school, Mark at work and he assumed his mother had probably gone to see Johan.

I wonder if she will tell him about being pregnant?

Levi was still in shock about the news he'd have a baby brother or sister in a few months time. In one sense he felt sorry for the kid that they wouldn't experience the luxury of the Candy home but then they were lucky to be spared the upbringing he'd had in Brixton. Maybe his future sibling would grow up in a much healthier home: not too rich to become a stuck-up prick, not too poor to give up on dreams.

He poured himself a hot cup of coffee and made some toast then went and sat down at the kitchen table. As he gazed outside the glass panel walls that encased the kitchen, he admired his mother's rose garden and its bright array of colours. She'd never actually expressed any interest in having a rose garden but it was one of the many things Mark had set up for her; like the guy just assumed every woman naturally wanted one.

As he munched on his toast, staring out at the roses, Levi began daydreaming about what his and Danny's house might look like. It wouldn't be as grand as this one but one day, if they stayed together long enough, then they could live in something not too dissimilar. He wondered if Danny would insist on putting a rose garden in the yard for Levi. He bloody hoped not. For a brief moment, Levi understood perhaps why his mother was willing to give all this up. She wanted what she wanted, not what some man wanted for her. But that's where Levi and his mother were different. He was prepared to tolerate what Danny wanted for him if it meant he got his own wants as well.

Why can't she see it's just about compromise? That's all. Give and take. But mostly take.

He figured she probably didn't see it that way and would probably give him a lecture about the importance of love and following your heart. *Fuck my heart and fuck love.* Giving into love and following his heart had never done Levi any favours. The last time he'd been stupid enough to let his emotions get the better of him it ended with the humiliation of Sophie dumping him for Lucas. After that he had sworn to himself he'd never suffer that kind of pain again. That's why he'd embraced the single life the past four years. At least with casual sex you knew what you were getting—an orgasm.

Dating Danny, of course, was putting an end to his being single but Levi was confident he would avoid heartbreak with this relationship. With any luck when he and Danny would finally part ways—which Levi knew one day they would—it would be amicable and he'd be in a position to lead his own good life with whatever money he would get in the separation.

The pesky emotion of guilt nibbled at his conscience. *I'm doing what I have to do,* he told himself. *That's all this is. It's survival.*

Levi knew referring to it as survival was a big fucking stretch but his life as he knew it was at risk of dying and he didn't want to join the graveyard of has-beens just yet. He knew a couple people his age who'd lost access to the inner circle of the Fitzroy Flyers after their mothers divorced their rich stepfathers and had had to go back to living within modest means. It wasn't as bad as becoming a Benson Banger but it wasn't far off.

Levi knew he probably wouldn't fall from social grace to quite the same extent as others before him had; his good-looks and close friendship with Peach did count for something, but that wouldn't change the dreary fact he'd wind up being a povo bitch attending parties awash with cashed-up snobs.

A deep voice grumbled "Good morning" behind him.

Levi whipped his head around and saw Mark stumbling barefoot into the kitchen. He was dressed in tartan pattern boxer shorts and an oversized blue t-shirt. "Where the hell did you come from."

"My mancave," Mark replied in a surprisingly rough, sexy voice. "I've been down there reading all morning."

"It's nearly eleven o'clock? Aren't you supposed to be at work?"

"And aren't you supposed to be at class," Mark quipped as he made his way to the kettle to make himself a hot drink. It was rare for Mark to be dressed like a slob but he still carried himself with a stern sort of reserve and control, exuding a natural air of authority.

Levi contemplated getting up and finishing his breakfast elsewhere. He had been avoiding Mark like the plague since discovering his attraction towards the man and his stinky briefs.

Fuck it, Levi decided. He may as well stay where he was.

What was the point of running? He'd have to get used to being around Mark at some stage. Especially now with the prospect of Mark going from being his stepfather to one day being his father-in-law.

While Mark's back was turned, Levi took a moment to admire the older man's hairy calves. They were hairier than Danny's and much thicker. He let his gaze climb higher to the seat of Mark's tartan boxer shorts, wishing he had x-ray vision. He held his breath, half aroused and half ashamed.

Mark finished making his drink then came and joined Levi at the table. Slumping down on his chair, he spread his thighs wide, totally unaware Levi's peepers were trying to catch a glimpse up the leghole of his boxers. The angle wasn't quite right to give away the forbidden sight of his stepfather's dick and balls but the pale flesh of Mark's inner thighs was enough to make Levi's dick throb.

Then it went quiet. Really quiet.

The moment stretched awkwardly like they were both waiting for the other to say something, do something.

"So, uh, how come you're not at work?" Levi finally asked, trying not to look at the wispy chest hairs sticking out the top of Mark's shirt.

"I decided to take a mental health day." Mark rubbed the dark stubble lining his jaw as he focused his gaze on Levi. Before Levi could ask why, Mark hit him with a question of his own. "Why weren't you in your room this morning?" Suspicion crept through his voice.

"Huh?"

"I got up early to email my PA to let her know I wouldn't be coming in today and when I walked past your bedroom I noticed it was empty. For a moment I thought the impossible had happened and you'd actually gone to a morning class for once." Mark's gaze narrowed. "But evidently that wasn't the case."

"I, uh, I went for a walk in the garden."

"Then how come you look like you just woke up?"

"It was a very relaxing walk."

Mark rolled his eyes. "The only thing rested about you is your bitch face."

Levi coughed on a laugh. That was actually quite funny. A rarity for Mark. "Who let sassy Mark out to play today?"

"Danny," Mark replied grumpily.

"What did Danny do?"

"Nothing," Mark mumbled and went back to sipping his coffee.

It went quiet between them again but this time it wasn't awkward. It just felt like any other morning the pair of them would sit around the table. Most mornings there was usually some sort of animosity between them—mostly coming from Levi—but this morning Levi didn't feel any animosity. He just felt content—and more than a little horny as he stared at the inky hairs lining Mark's forearms.

"Has Danny told you anything about having a special friend?" Mark asked, breaking the quiet.

It was obvious where this was going. Levi wondered if he should tread carefully or behave how he normally would: like a cheeky shit. He chose the latter option.

"And by 'special friend' do you mean a partner or a priest fiddling with him?"

"Don't be a dick, Levi." Mark scowled, his brown brows furrowed as he looked at Levi disapprovingly "I'm not in the mood for your crap today."

"Sheesh. I was just trying to lighten the mood with a joke. You look like you need cheering up."

"If I needed someone to cheer me up with a joke then I can assure you you'd be the last person I go to."

"Sassy and pissy… you really are in a good mood this morning."

"I'm sorry," Mark said with a tilt of his head. "It's just that Danny told me he's started seeing someone and I'm not sure how I feel about it."

"Oh…" Levi frowned. "Why's that?"

He watched Mark pull his bottom lip behind his top teeth as if he were holding back his words. Then he released it and said, "I am sure you are going to love this but apparently Danny has grown feelings for a young man he knows. And those feelings also happen to be sexual."

"So he came out to you is what you're saying."

"Levi. No jokes."

"It's not a joke. That's what it's called when someone tells you they're queer… coming out."

Mark made a throaty noise. "I know they use that word positively these days but I still don't like it. In my day it was an insult and for many people it still is."

"Would you rather I just call him gay?"

"No I wouldn't because Danny is not gay."

"Bisexual?" Levi grinned, enjoying seeing Mark get annoyed.

"I think what you'll find my son is, is confused."

Secretly Levi agreed with his stepfather but he wasn't about to say so. He was also secretly sporting some major wood beneath the table, his dick hard and hot against the inside of his thigh. After spending days mad at himself for the hideous attraction, Levi decided it was time to accept it. What was the harm in sprouting an unwanted erection now and then? It wasn't like he'd ever give his cock what it wanted.

Mark sighed, staring into his coffee mug. "So Danny hasn't mentioned to you anything about this boy?"

"I may have heard a thing or two…"

"So you do know!" Mark looked at him, eyes wide. "Do you know who the boy is?"

"No, but Danny told me he makes him very happy."

Mark shook his head. "I don't trust him whoever it is," he said scathingly.

"Why not? You don't even know who it is."

"Because I was Danny's age once and I know from experience that sometimes when you come from money you have people target you for the wrong reasons."

"Not everyone's a gold digger," Levi snapped defensively.

"I know that but that doesn't mean everyone is interested in people for the right reasons either." Mark raked a hand through his mussed black hair. "I would just feel a lot better if I knew who the boy was and if I could speak with his parents."

You're married to one and the other's dead.

"If he's from a good home then I'd probably feel a bit more at ease," Mark added.

"Whoever it is must be really sexy for Danny to want to take it up the—"

"I would strongly advise you against finishing that sentence." Mark scolded him with an expression so heated that Levi was surprised it didn't leave burns on him where it held him in place. "I know to you this is one big laugh but Danny is my son and I am genuinely worried about him."

"The only thing you have to be worried about is how bloody clingy Danny is being. And weirdly fucking controlling."

"So you do know this boy?" Mark said accusingly. "What's his name?"

"I only know *of* him. I don't know him, know him. But I have heard Danny has been a bit full-on."

"He gets that from his mother," Mark muttered under his breath.

Levi scoffed. "Bullshit. Danny is you through and through."

"While I do acknowledge my son and I are very similar, I can assure you I am neither clingy or possessive."

"Yes you are."

"If I was clingy and possessive would I let your mother spend as much time at The Community as she does?" Levi worried he was about to hear Mark voice suspicions of adultery but then he added, "And I encourage it. I believe it is healthy for a husband and wife to have their own interests and hobbies. I think that is important. If you are constantly living in each other's pockets like Danny's mother tried to do with me, a relationship doesn't last very long."

"Maybe you should have a talk with him about that then?" Levi suggested.

"What? And try and encourage the relationship to last?" Mark grimaced. "Get off the grass. If I have my way this boy and Danny will be over by the end of next week."

"Bloody hell, Mark." Levi sighed. "How homophobic are you?"

"I'm not homophobic at all, thank you very much."

"You sure as shit sound like it."

"I've become good friends with Ameesh and he's gay."

"The whole 'I have a gay friend' card doesn't mean you're not acting like a bigot."

"This might surprise you Levi but I honestly don't care if Danny grows up to marry a man or a woman. All I want for him, for both of you, is to be happy. If Danny is happy being in love with a member of the same sex then so be it but what I have a problem with is my son talking about moving overseas with a partner I have not even met."

"He told you that?"

"Danny said he had plans to ask his friend to move to

Sydney with him, yes."

"He really plans ahead," Levi said into his mug.

"What did you say?"

"Nothing." Levi shook his head. "So you're genuinely okay with Danny being gay?"

"Yes, Levi. I am genuinely okay with my son being gay." Mark then quickly added, "That's assuming he is gay. I'm still not convinced."

Levi was tempted to take the piss some more but he decided against it. Any shit he gave Mark now would only bite him in the arse when the truth came out who it was Danny was dating.

"I suppose I should go have a shower and get out of the house and do something productive with my day," Mark said, slipping a hand under his shirt and scratching lazily at the fuzz around his navel.

"What sort of productive?" Levi asked dazedly, his eyes zeroing in on Mark's belly.

"I was thinking I'd go visit my parents before they leave." Mark stopped scratching his stomach, the shirt falling down again and ending Levi's joyous perve. "They're flying out late tonight to go spend a few weeks at their villa in Fiji."

Mark's parents were a pair of frosty baby boomers who had passed their conservative outlook on life to their son. Levi wasn't hugely fond of them and he knew the feeling was mutual.

"I would have driven them to the airport tonight but your mother and I have reservations for Dawson Lodge." Mark's voice carried the hope of a man looking to get laid. Dawson Lodge was a swanky bed and breakfast popular with newlyweds, and apparently with men over forty trying to get some nookie from wives who stop putting out. Too bad for Mark he probably wouldn't get what he wanted.

"Did you want to come with me?" Mark asked.

"As much as I'd love to I think it might be a bit weird watching you and Mum get it on after dinner," Levi teased.

Mark blushed. Even though he was a grown arse man it looked fucking adorable. "I wasn't talking about that," he said with the icy precision of an archaic governor. "I was talking about coming with me to visit my parents. We could grab a bite to eat in town afterwards if you like. Your mother is too busy to meet for lunch today so the privilege of my wonderful company is yours for the taking if you want it?"

It's more than your company I'd like to take....

"What do you say?" Mark stared across the table at him.

"I would but I've got to stay home and do my washing." *And shave my arse.*

"Washing?" Mark's mouth dangled open. "You are staying home to do your washing?"

"Yeah. I've got dirty clothes and sheets I need to clean."

Mark's blue eyes glimmered cheekily. "Who are you and what have you done with Levi?"

"Very funny, dork."

Mark chuckled. "I don't think I have seen you do your own laundry in the entire time I have known you. You usually leave it for Lynn or your mum to do."

"I'm not as useless as you might think."

"I know that. You're very capable. I'm just insinuating that you're lazy."

The slow slide of Mark's smile and the twitch of his eyebrows were so arrogant that Levi wanted to make a snide remark in response but he could tell Mark was only joking—mostly.

"Well, if you're putting a load on then perhaps you could wash this for me," Mark said.

Levi went to respond but instead his eyes became glued

to the path of Mark's hands as they reached for the hem of his t-shirt. He followed its trajectory over Mark's belly and thickly-furred chest. Mark bundled the shirt in his hand and passed it to Levi then went and put his mug in the sink. While Mark's back was turned, Levi sniffed the shirt, his dick throbbing when his nostrils became invaded by the smell of musky body odour.

"I'm going to go have a shower and then get going," Mark said, scratching at the hairs on his chest. "If you see your mother before I get back remind her that we are booked in for Dawson Lodge."

Levi nodded, too dickmatized by the sight of his shirtless stepfather to respond verbally. As soon as Mark left the room, Levi reached under the table and squeezed his cock. The stiffness filled his fingers, pulsing with his heartbeat. He hadn't realized how hard he'd gotten. He groaned, tempted to whip it out and beat off right then and there and cum into Mark's grubby t-shirt. But he decided to wait until he had something more fragrant to smell.

CHAPTER 21

Levi made his way upstairs like a midnight prowler, his bare feet gripping the carpet. He knew he was alone in the house again, but his heart was hammering, his hands jittered, and the idea of someone catching him made him want to vomit. Each step he took elicited a tremble in his body as he headed in a direction there was no coming back from.

He'd withheld the urge to do what he was about to do all week, telling himself he didn't want to start a habit he could not stop, but Mark's innocent display of shirtless masculinity had tipped Levi over the edge and there was no stopping him from coming upstairs to get what he wanted.

Creeping into the master bedroom, he crossed the floor and slipped inside the en suite like a soldier crossing enemy lines. The air inside the bathroom was still misted and warm from Mark's shower. He could smell the body wash Mark had used and saw the damp footprints on the bath mat where the older man had stood. There was something incredibly sexual about knowing Mark had been standing naked here only ten minutes before.

His hands shaking and sweaty, Levi reached into the laundry hamper, sifting through the tangle of garments until he found a pair of Mark's briefs. He lifted them gently like a rare and revered artifact, inspecting every inch of the dingy white cotton, turning it slowly in his hands. Levi's pulse was thunder in his ears, his breathing deep and ragged. He pressed the material to his mouth and nose, inhaling deeply.

Man. Pure man. That's what went up his nostrils.

Levi's knees went weak, his stepfather's private scent attacking his senses without mercy. It was a musky nirvana, like happiness and hard-ons rolled into one. No man had the right to smell this good, let alone an uptight prick who constantly rubbed Levi the wrong way.

With Mark's briefs in his hot little hand, Levi walked stiltedly back into the master bedroom where he stripped off his clothes and lay naked on his stepfather's side of the bed. He stared down at his cock that pointed to the heavens, and he wondered if Mark had ever masturbated while lying in this very spot.

He smothered his face with the potent briefs, detecting the stench of dried piss at the front and earthy arse-scent in the back but the most prominent smell was that of sweaty balls. Mark's nuts had leaked their musky scent all through the fabric and it was fucking heavenly. Danny's nuts carried a similar fragrance but they were nowhere near as potent or as sexual as his more masculine father's.

Levi's cock bounced and throbbed as he pictured Mark's meaty genitals encased in this fabric. He imagined his stepfather's cock bunched up on top of his heavy balls, constricted in sweaty, smelly cotton during a eight-hour workday. He wondered how many erections Mark sprung throughout the day, how many times that cock rose up and fought against the fabric that kept it prisoner. Was the dampness in the crotch purely from piss dribbles or was some of it from pre-cum stains, souvenirs from Mark's constantly drooling cockhead? Just in case, Levi sucked the fabric into his mouth, collecting samples of all of Mark's fluids and mixing them with his own saliva.

Overcome with desire, Levi tucked the pillow out from under his head proceeded to smother both sides of it with his cock and balls. He only wished he hadn't showered already to leave a more fragrant scent. He wanted Mark to go to sleep breathing him in.

Once he was satisfied he'd defiled Mark's pillow enough, Levi cast it aside and returned to sniffing the sweaty briefs. Against the strip of brown hair on his stomach, his cock had leaked a strand of precum. He reached under his balls, massaging them gently. Another bead of fluid appeared at the head of his dick. He rubbed his thumb over it and brought it to his mouth, imagining he was tasting Mark's sexual essence.

That made him leak even more and he began swiping the pearly mess with his finger, gathering more and more which he fed into his mouth. "You taste so good, Daddy. So fucking good."

The dirty talk set him off and he furiously tugged his shaft, crying "Daddy" over and over until eventually his cock erupted in the grip of his furled fingers. A salty strand hit him in his open mouth and slid down his cheeks and chin. One shot flew so high it hit his forehead and ran into his tousled hair.

"Daddy!" Levi cried out one last time, his body deflating with boneless pleasure. Slippery puddles covered his torso, his bellybutton a deep pond of semen. His whole body gave a shudder and he smiled and sighed; his soft eyes drifted closed.

Daddy…

He knew there was a faulty wire in his brain somewhere that was connected to his balls. He'd managed to keep it buried it for years until that day Dwight had fucked it out of him, ripping that twisted word right from his soul. It's origin the most shameful part of who he was.

Seven years earlier

The whole calling his father "Daddy" in private had been super strange to begin with but as the weeks went on it eventually lost its weirdness and soon began to feel relatively normal. Not only did it become normal but Levi found he quite enjoyed it. The more he called his father "Daddy" in private the better his father treated him.

One of the things he learned about his father with their new secret daddy and son bond was just how bloody rich the man was. For years Levi assumed his family was dirt poor but whenever he and his father were alone his father would take him out and buy him things; fast food, boardgames, new clothes. It was fucking sweet as. Scott and Hemi had totally drooled over his new skate shoes and Levi had loved seeing how jealous they were. He felt like a total boss.

The treats and daddy talk were restricted mostly to afternoons and evenings when Levi's mother was at work, allowing father and son ample opportunity to enjoy each other's company. In the past his father would usually just go out and drink elsewhere, leaving Levi to look after himself, but now he was choosing to stay at home and drink and watch movies with Levi instead.

They weren't called movies nights though. Levi's father nicknamed them undie parties where they'd both sit around in just their underwear. Levi had found that funny but he didn't mind. He walked around in just a pair of boxers most mornings so it wasn't like he wasn't used to traipsing about shirtless.

What he wasn't used to though was seeing his father's half-naked body. The guy wasn't a human whale but he was a total chubster. Levi had seen pictures of his father as a young man when he'd been quite muscly but he wasn't muscly anymore. The muscle had turned to fat and when he would sit down on the couch his chest would sag with man boobs and his hairy gut would protrude like a brown balloon.

Sometimes Shay's mother, Connie, would join them for their movie nights. She wasn't expected to follow the underwear rule but after a few glasses of vodka her top and skirt would usually find their way to the floor and she'd laze about in her bra and panties.

The boozy, chain-smoking hag visited a lot when Levi's mother was out and Levi knew his father and Connie were more than just friends. He'd heard them making weird noises more than once when his father would say he had something to show her in the bedroom. Their affair was one of those secrets that wasn't all that secret, if that made sense. Like, everyone in the neighbourhood probably knew what the pair were up to but no one ever seemed to talk about it. Not even Shay or Levi's mother.

During these movie nights Connie would sit next to Levi's father on the couch while Levi would lay on the floor. Levi was usually so engrossed in the film and eating all the candy his father would buy that he didn't pay the pair that much attention but sometimes he would catch them holding hands or kissing out the corner of his eye.

Connie's presence at these undie parties didn't stop how well his father treated him though. The man would still tell

Levi how handsome and smart and special he was, not at all embarrassed to play the role of being an overly proud parent. His father also said it was okay for Levi to call him Daddy in front of Connie, said Connie was aware of their secret "boys club."

Sure enough, Connie didn't blink an eye when Levi uttered the d word. She just sat there, seemingly content to be included. She did blink an eye though the night Levi's father kicked her off the couch and told her to go sit in one of the armchairs so that Levi could sit next to him instead.

"Piss off, Barry," Connie fired back. "I'm the fucking lady here. He's just ya kid."

Levi's father laughed but then very seriously said, "Sit in the chair over there, bitch, or fuck off home."

Connie mumbled something under her breath then moved her bony arse to the armchair.

"Get up, son." Levi's father patted the vacated spot beside him. "Come sit by your daddy."

Levi hesitated when he saw the evil look Connie gave him. "I'm okay down here, daddy."

"Don't be stupid. I want my handsome boy to sit with me." His father smiled. "I want you to have the best seat in the house."

The flattery worked. Flattery always did with Levi. He'd gone so many years not hearing his father say anything nice about him that he had become a moth to the flame whenever his father praised him. And the man praised him a lot these days. Levi climbed up off the floor and sat beside his daddy and enjoyed the rest of the evening sat in the best seat in the house.

Levi ended up keeping the best seat in the house and Connie was permanently relegated to the armchair. After several weeks though something happened that made Levi unsure if it really was the best seat in the house. It started with his father's hand finding its way to his knee. Then the next night it rubbed the inside of his thigh; not high enough to touch places it shouldn't but it was high enough to make Levi feel uncomfortable. They had never been a physically affectionate family. He didn't even hug his mum so feeling his father's hand rubbing his leg like this was pretty fucking out there. He didn't say anything though. Just assumed it was a new part of their daddy and son relationship.

After three more nights of his father's hand rubbing the inside of his leg the man's sweaty palm went to a place it most certainly shouldn't; up the inside leg of Levi's boxer shorts.

"What are you doing?" Levi squawked when he felt his father grab his nuts.

Connie's beady eyes flung over like daggers; her gaze widened at the sight of Levi being groped. Levi expected her to say something.

She didn't.

His father chuckled nervously, slowly retrieving his wandering hand. "I'm just being nice to my boy. I thought you liked Daddy being nice to you?"

"But you just touched my balls!" Levi shrieked. "It was a real homo touch too."

A flash of anger darkened his father's brown eyes and Levi half-expected a whack. Instead of hitting him though, his father looked over at Connie. "Tell my boy here there's nothing 'homo' about a father being nice to his son. Tell him it's perfectly fucking normal behaviour."

Connie's jaw twitched.

"Tell him, bitch," Levi's father snapped. "Tell Levi this is what men do with their sons."

Connie took a breath and smiled. "It is, Levi. It's perfectly normal."

Levi frowned. "I'm pretty sure it's fucking not."

His father clipped him behind the head. "Oi, ya little prick. Don't swear at Connie."

"I wasn't swearing at Connie," Levi replied. "I was just saying I don't think it's normal."

"If you don't think it's normal then you can fuck off to bed."

"But the movie hasn't finished yet."

"I don't give a shit. I ain't having my own son accuse me of doing something wrong when he ain't got a fucking clue what he's even talking about." Fat fingers clicked at Levi's ear then pointed in the direction of the hallway. "Off to bed."

"But Daddy…"

"Nope. You've been told. Get ya arse to bed."

Levi slumped his shoulders, silently stewing about being sent to bed so friggin' early. He wasn't even out of the room before Connie's bony backside was up and sat on his seat, smiling like she'd won the lottery. "It's completely normal," she called out after him. Then she laughed a wicked little laugh.

His father went back to ignoring him after that. No more treats. No more compliments. No more undie party movie nights. Levi wondered if he should tell Shay about what had happened but he ultimately decided against it. It was sort of embarrassing and he didn't want Shay to make a bigger deal out of it than what it really was. It was just one slip of a hand. Nothing to make a huge fuss about.

There was also the chance Levi was wrong about it being something sinister. It wasn't just his father who'd said that touching him in that way was normal. Connie had too. There was no way a woman with kids of her own would allow something bad to happen to a young person. The whole thing was confusing and Levi found himself very quickly missing the treats and affection his father had been showing him.

After a week of being ignored by his father, Levi approached him in the kitchen one morning while his mother was outside putting washing on the line.

"Daddy," Levi said in the sweetest voice he could muster. "Can we have a movie night tonight when Mum goes to work?"

"I don't think so," his father grumbled. "You really hurt my feelings the other night."

"I'm sorry, Daddy."

"It's a bit late for sorry, Levi. You accused me of doing something bad to you and I would never hurt a hair on your head."

What about all the fucking beatings you've given me? was Levi's first thought but he wasn't about to bring all that up. "I'm really sorry, Daddy, the other night just felt…"

"It felt what?" His father glared at him. "Wrong? Disgusting? What?"

Levi hesitated. "It just felt different."

"And is different bad?"

It felt like a trick question. "Not always."

"Exactly. Sometimes different things can be good."

Levi rubbed his heels together, unsure what to say next.

His father glanced out the window and watched Levi's mother still busy at the washing line. He returned his gaze to Levi and said in a throaty whisper. "So you want us to go back to having movie nights and me buying you treats?"

"Yes, Daddy." Levi grinned, hoping his father was about to change his mind. "I was really liking how well we were getting along."

"Me too."

"So can we go back to that? The movie nights and all the presents?"

His father slowly eyed him up and down. "That depends."

"On what?"

"Are you going to let Daddy be nice to you the way he wants?"

Levi's tummy squirmed. "Um…"

"I just want to show you how much I love you and how amazing I think you are. You're a special kid, Levi, and deserve to be treated in special ways."

Levi gulped.

"If you don't want me to be nice to you, son, just say so but this is your last chance. I won't offer again."

With a very unsure nod, Levi agreed to whatever it was his father deemed being treated special.

The undie party movie nights resumed that very night and his father shouted Pizza for dinner as a celebration. Connie wasn't invited this time, Levi's father said he would rather it just be the two of them. Together they sat side by side on the couch sharing a bag of pineapple lumps, laughing their way through the movie We're the Millers.

The evening was perfectly fine to begin with, nothing out of their new ordinary, but about halfway through the movie his father's hand found its way to Levi's knee and like the slowest moving snake in the world it wriggled its way up the inside of his legs until it was inside his boxer shorts. All the while a voice in his head kept telling him *This is wrong.* But he didn't dare say anything, scared of upsetting his father and worried that he was misreading the situation.

What he did do though was flinch when he felt his father grab his dick.

"Just keep watching the movie," his father said without even looking at him, "and let Daddy show you how much he cares."

∞

Even now Levi couldn't think about that evening without his cheeks blushing and his stomach tightening. Not because of how horrendous it had been but because beneath the memory of gross discomfort and heart pounding fear was the ugly truth a part of himself had enjoyed it. It was the first time a hand other than his own had touched him down there and being the hormonal teenager that he was at the time his dick had responded excitedly to the inappropriate situation.

And that was how it began. Every night while Levi's mother was at work—or out fucking Shay as it later turned out—Levi would sit with his father on the couch and let the man sexually abuse him under the guise of it being his father's way to show how much he cared.

The abuse didn't even stop when Connie eventually returned to join them for movie nights. She would sit on the armchair in the corner of the lounge and pretend like she couldn't see what was happening only ten feet away; that a thirteen-year-old boy was being jacked off by his own father.

It was about a month after Barry wanked him off for the first time that the dirty photographs started being taken. Levi had been reluctant to be caught on film but when he finally agreed to let his father photograph every inch of his naked body, Barry rewarded Levi by buying him a television for his bedroom. He was even told that if he kept being a good boy then Daddy would buy him an Xbox to go with it.

By this stage full body massages and oral sex had

slipped into their nightly routine. More stuff Barry passed off as being how a father showed his appreciation. This was also when Connie stopped coming over anymore for movie nights. It turned out even evil bitches who liked to fuck married men had their limits.

In hindsight, Levi couldn't believe what a fucking moron he'd been to be sucked in by his father's bullshit but his younger self had been impressed with all the presents and wooed by the affection. Every time his father had given him a compliment it would sift through him and caress vulnerable places. It made him feel nice and wanted and special but what it did most of all was made him feel loved.

Of all the things Barry Buttwell did that was probably the cruellest—making Levi fall in love.

Barry would spout off all sorts of rubbish about how much he loved Levi. "I love you the same way I used to love your mother" and the classic "I would die for you. No one's ever made me feel this way before." Lines like that were what had planted seeds of romance in Levi's impressionable mind that eventually sprouted and grew very real feelings for someone who didn't deserve them. It even got rid of the voice in his head that had been constantly whispering *this is wrong!*

In the space of about eight weeks he'd gone from finding the word Daddy cringeworthy at best to having the word forever etched into his soul. It was connected to his heart, his brain and his cock. The moment Levi started thinking of his father as being more than just his father he began swallowing his pride in ways he shouldn't. At the time he thought he was doing it all willingly, completely unaware he was being manipulated by a kiddy-fucking monster.

The voice telling him their love was wrong did come

back eventually though. It came back in a big fucking way the night Barry Buttwell showed his true colours. They burned so bright that they sparked a chain of events that would end with a handless corpse and Levi owning a white shirt covered in blood.

CHAPTER 22

Shay sat in Doctor Harten's office listening to the curly-haired twat go over Dave's updated plan for Brayden's leaving ceremony. The Doctor's faux toffee-nosed British accent annoyed him at the best of times but today it was grating him a whole lot more because of the words coming out of his mouth.

The more Dr Harten spoke the more Shay found himself wanting to pick something up and throw it. "That's not fucking fair!" he yelled when the doctor had finished reading out Dave's note. "Not. Fucking Fair."

"I'm sorry, Pinky, but those are Dave's orders."

Shay pounded his fist on the table. "As far as I'm concerned you and Dave can both get fucked."

"Oi, don't shoot the messenger, pal. I'm simply reading to you what the note says."

"You can both still get fucked." Shay huffed and folded his arms.

Dr Harten sighed like he was dealing with a stroppy toddler. "If you have an issue with what is in the note then I suggest you take it up with Dave when he gets back. In the meantime, I'd appreciate it if you spoke to me with a little bit of respect."

"Fucking hell," Shay muttered under his breath before giving Dr Harten the hairy eyeball. "You can't tell me you agree with this?"

"It's not my place to say whether I agree or disagree."

"Which basically means you agree with me that this total cocksucking bullshit but you're too fucking chickenshit to say anything."

"Or maybe I'm wise enough not to bite the hand that feeds me." Dr Harten smiled softly, and falsely. "I may not be a pet but Dave pays my bills, just like he pays yours."

"He hasn't paid all of mine yet."

"But he will be paying you a very handsome sum when you leave here so if I were you I would take it like a man and quietly eat this slice of humble pie."

"Do you how many fucking slices of that pie I have had to eat since I arrived here?" Shay glowered. "Tonnes. Fucking tonnes of that patu shit! And despite what you fucks keep saying it doesn't taste better after the first bite."

"At least this time you'll have something to wash it down with." Dr Harten chuckled.

Shay was tempted to crawl over the desk and throttle the doctor but he knew that was a one-way ticket to losing his contract. He balled his hands into fists and shook his head. "I am gonna fucking kill Brayden when I see him."

Dr Harten briefly stiffened, and his eyes seemed almost pleading, but, just as quickly, he appeared to make a conscious effort to relax. "Please try not to kill anyone on my watch. I would quite like to earn my Christmas bonus this year."

Shay wouldn't kill Brayden but he was very fucking tempted to punch the little prick's lights out for what he'd done. While spending the night with Dave, the blond brat had somehow managed to convince Dave to break with tradition and change the rules of the leaving ceremony. No longer would both the leaver and the newest arrival to The Castle drink each other's piss, it would just be the new arrival drinking the leaver's piss.

But that wasn't the worst part.

Dave had decided that in an attempt to make the leaving ceremony "*extra special*" Brayden and Shay would "*fornicate for the enjoyment of the crowd*" which according to the notes he'd left meant "*Pinky will present his pussy to Twitch and surrender his body.*" The note had then gone on to describe some bullshit about there being a hierarchy amongst men and how it was important for "*lesser males like Pinky to honour alpha males such as Twitch.*"

"Pinky..." Dr Harten's voice hung in the air. "I want you to promise me you won't do anything stupid."

"Don't worry, Doc," Shay said. "I won't kill him if that's what you're worried about."

"Or attack him."

"Or attack him," Shay echoed. "I figure Brayden must have been through enough already to get Dave to make changes to the ceremony."

"What do you mean by that?" Dr Harten looked confused.

"I'm saying a certain big-dicked twink up there would have woken up today with a burning arsehole and a bad case of lockjaw from sucking Dave's dick all night." Shay waited for the uptight doctor to scold him for being so crass but instead what he got was laughter.

"Good God." Dr Harten chuckled some more. "Is that what you really think?"

"It's not what I think it's what I know."

Doctor Harten shook his head, smiling. "I can assure you, Pinky, you have got that all wrong."

"Bullshit. Dave fucks the pets all the time."

More laughter. "I know on occasion he is known to invite pets to his apartment for intimate encounters—"

"Never me," Shay interjected. "I always say no to his invites."

"And also never a resident top. Which is Brayden's role here."

"Brayden stays overnight with Dave all the bloody time."

"Not to have sex though."

"Yeah right." Shay scoffed. "How else does Brayden always get what he wants? He's clearly Dave's favourite because he puts out so fucking easily."

"The truth of the matter is something quite different entirely."

"Are you trying to tell me there's another reason why Brayden is so spoilt by Dave?"

"I believe that is what I am saying," Dr Harten replied coyly.

"What is it?"

"It's not my place to say," Doctor Harten said with smug superiority. "But I must say it is *very* interesting."

"If it's so fucking interesting why don't you just tell me?"

A tense silence crept into the room as their gazes held firm, stretching from pronounced to downright awkward.

"How badly do you want to know?" Dr Harten finally said. His horny predictability was laughable.

"Is this the part where you ask me to 'present my pussy and surrender my body?'" Shay replied with mockful air quotes, comfortable in the knowledge he was under no obligation to put out.

A one-corner smile played on Dr Harten's lips. "It might very well be."

"I don't think so, doc." Shay leaned back and laced his hands behind his head. "No offense but I was looking forward to taking a day off from being buggered by dirty perves."

The doctor's eyes flickered with anger but he didn't lash out. "I could make it worth your while, Pinky."

"And how would you do that?"

"I understand that beautiful penis of yours I get to swab each month is under lock and key for a whole week. I've also been told that you have already spent five days in chastity."

"So?"

"So I happen to have the key that could let you relieve your needs… but I'd only be willing to do that if you agree to help take care of mine."

That took the wind out of Shay's cocky sails. He lowered his hands from behind his head and leaned forward. "You would unlock me?"

"I would." Dr Harten smiled gently. "But only if you do as you're told."

Shay nibbled on a thumbnail while deliberating. He wasn't that fussed in finding out why Brayden got special treatment but he was very keen on the chance to be freed from his chastity cage. Not only would it be glorious to ejaculate but it would be nice to take a piss standing up.

"If I agree to this do I get to have a wank now or after?" Shay asked.

"After," Dr Harten said sharply. "I'm not risking you backing out after you've got what you wanted. I'm not an idiot."

Shay nodded. "Fair enough."

"Do we have ourselves a deal?" Dr Harten asked.

Shay tilted his head, pretending to think it over when his mind was already made up. It was a no-brainer really. Of course he'd take the fucking deal. His balls were so blue they could have starred in Avatar. That's how badly he needed to cum. Besides, compared to many of the crusty clients he'd serviced Dr Harten was quite attractive in comparison. The man was slim, under forty, and didn't look like the kind of guy to have a stinky, unwashed cock. "We have a deal," Shay finally said.

"Brilliant." Dr Harten smiled. "I have been wanting to have some fun with you ever since you arrived at The Castle."

"I hadn't noticed," Shay said sarcastically, thinking about the doctor's wandering hands during his monthly physicals.

Dr Harten chuckled. "Have I made my affections a little obvious, have I?"

"That's one way of putting it."

"You should feel privileged. I don't normally have sex with pets. But I am willing to make an exception for you."

"Cool." Shay nodded nonchalantly. "So where did you wanna do it?" He stood up and started undoing his belt. "I can bend over your desk if you want?"

"Let me stop you right there, Pinky."

"Huh?" Shay's pants fell to his knees as he glanced over at Dr Harten. "Is something wrong. I thought you wanted to fuck me?"

"Nothing's wrong. It's just that I would prefer to wait until this evening so we can take our time." Dr Harten smiled. "I was rather hoping we could have dinner together in my room and share a bottle of pinot noir before we get down to business."

"Are you sure, doc?" Shay lowered his voice to a flirty whisper. "I could really do with a nice hard dicking right about now."

Dr Harten deadpanned with an eyeroll. "I'm afraid you

will have to wait a few hours to get that *nice hard dicking* you so badly want."

Shay sighed and bent over and dragged his pants back up. "Bloody hell." Feeling slightly embarrassed for jumping the gun, he made his way towards the office door to leave.

"Don't worry, Pinky," Dr Harten said just before Shay left the room. "Now that I know you like it rough I'll be sure to fuck you so hard your skull will explode."

Shay's arsehole twitched and he walked away wondering if he'd just agreed to a mistake.

CHAPTER 23

Dwight watched Lucas's beefy arms lift the push mower onto the back of the Ute and place it behind the ride-on. Lucas's chest was sculpted, massive, glimmering with sweat; it was as if testosterone was oozing from every pore of his half-naked body.

A soft breeze blew past them and carried the stench from under Lucas's arms right past Dwight's nose. Rather than be grossed out by the manly stench, Dwight found it appealing, like the scent of some overpowering feral aroma. It smelled like Lucas times a hundred, the pheromones of a sex god mixed with the musk of sweat. He knew it was silly to label Lucas a sex god considering they'd never done anything more physical together than shake hands and exchange one arm hugs but that's what the smell translated to—a young man in his prime who could probably fuck a whole cheerleading squad and not get tired.

Unlike Dwight, Lucas's chest was mostly smooth aside from a little blond hair around his nipples and over his sternum, though there was a decent strip of honey-blond fur below his bellybutton. It took all of Dwight's strength not to reach out and touch the temptation of Lucas's perspiring flesh. He could only imagine how sexually slick the wet skin would feel beneath his hands.

When Lucas was done positioning the mower in place, he knelt down to retie his bootlaces, the waistband of his shorts slipping low enough to expose the top of his moist buttocks. Wide and muscled; Lucas's arse appeared beefy, smooth, curvaceous and very pale. There was no doubt in Dwight's mind the pale mounds would be every bit as firm as the rest of Lucas's ridiculously fit body.

He decided he'd try and make Lucas work shirtless in the future more often. That Adonis of a body was the perfect view to work alongside and Dwight wondered why he hadn't taken advantage of it sooner.

Yep. You're definitely what the dick doctor ordered.

The only problem though with working alongside such a sexy sight was how fucking horny it made him. He'd been sporting a boner all morning and was gagging for a shag. If there were a mirror around, Dwight was convinced he would see on his face the look of a starving man.

Unfortunately he still hadn't heard back from Blondie who he had been counting on for a fuck. As the hours had passed with no word from the usually reliable fuck-hole, Dwight began to wonder if the boy's lack of a response was because of how brutal their last fuck had been.

Fucking the kid hard and dirty was nothing new but the night before Dwight had flown out to Bali he'd forced Blondie to do a bit of roleplay that Dwight knew had wrecked the young buck's ego. It was embarrassing even for Dwight just to think about so he could only imagine how mortified Blondie was.

It was definitely not my finest hour that's for sure.

Fuelled by lust and alcohol, Dwight had forced Blondie to pretend he was Levi and answer to the name Soggy while he fucked the young jock like a two-dollar whore. At one point he thought he'd heard the snivelling of tears but he'd been too focussed on pummelling the kid's anal cavity to take much notice. With the blessing of hindsight, Dwight was aware it had been a bloody stupid thing to do but being horny and doing stupid shit seemed to go hand in hand. Especially when he was drunk.

Lucas finished tying his laces and rose to his full height, stretching well over six feet of gorgeous masculinity. "That's all you need me for today, isn't it?" He patted his sweaty chest, waiting for a slack-jawed Dwight to respond.

"Uh, yeah. That's all I need you for."

"Cool." Lucas nodded, surprising Dwight by not asking if he could stay on and work extra hours.

Dwight fished the Ute's keys out of his pocket. "I'll let you drive, young fella," he said, chucking Lucas the keys. Usually Dwight was the one to drive but he figured that if he was in the passenger's seat it would allow him to drool over Lucas a little while longer.

They climbed inside the vehicle and Lucas started the engine. Predictably, Lucas wasted no time to in firing up a conversation, chewing Dwight's ear off about his selection predictions for the All Blacks squad. The passion in Lucas's voice gave away how much he loved the game of rugby and Dwight wondered how often Lucas was plagued with thoughts of *it could have been me*. To Lucas's credit though, Dwight had never once heard the boy whinge about his sporting career that never was. The only one who did that was Shifty who would get drunk and almost teary-eyed whenever he would bring up how close his son was to being a sporting superstar.

While Lucas continued to yak away, Dwight let his thoughts drift to dark and dirty places. Places that involved Lucas taking his grass-stained jeans off to let Dwight have his wicked way with him.

He does actually have very nice lips. They'd look damn nice wrapped around my dick.

The thought made Dwight's tummy squirm and his balls clench. He knew that if he'd heard from Blondie already he wouldn't even be having such lewd thoughts about his best mate's son, but the longer he kept sneaking glances at Lucas's ripped torso and lightly-fuzzed navel the filthier Dwight's thoughts became. By the time they were on the outskirts of the suburb Lucas and Sophie lived in, Dwight's cock had leaked a sticky mess in his briefs and he was seriously considering doing something stupid.

Shifty would fucking kill me though if I tried dicking his son.

But would Shifty ever find out? If Lucas was like most guys he'd keep such a thing to himself. Young straight men who made drunken mistakes, like letting someone fuck them in the arse, didn't tend to go around telling people. Certainly not their redneck fathers.

The fact Lucas was straight was merely an inconvenience, not a deal breaker. The boy was too dumb and trusting for his own good. Hell, he probably wouldn't know he'd been taken advantage of until he was shitting out semen.

"What are your plans for tonight?" Dwight asked, interrupting Lucas who was still yabbering on about his picks for the All Blacks.

"Nuffin," Lucas replied. "Probably stay in and watch some tele. Five Gold Rings is on tonight. Me and Sophie love that show. Do you watch it? It's the one where they have to place a gold ring down on the floor to try and find a hidden part of a picture."

Sounds fucking riveting Dwight thought to himself sarcastically. "Rather than sit at home and do that how would you feel about joining me for a few beersies? My treat."

"That'd be awesome!"

The enthusiasm in Lucas's voice was tragic. Anyone would have thought he was a ten-year-old who'd just won a trip to Disney World. Dwight knew Lucas was starved of a decent social life so being invited for beers with a man old enough to be his father was probably the highlight of Lucas's week.

"Will Sophie mind if you're out late?" Dwight asked.

"What if Sophie asked her parents to babysit Mia so she could join us?"

"I was rather thinking along the lines of this being a boys' night. Just us men having a few drinks."

Lucas nodded, eyes on the road ahead. "Where is it you want to go for drinks?"

"I was thinking I could buy us a dozen and take them back to Josh's place." Dwight flicked a disarming smile Lucas's way. "He's going straight to work after uni this afternoon so I've got the place to myself until late tonight."

"Did you want me to ring Dad and invite him too?"

"Nar. I'll catch up with ya old man another night." Dwight gave Lucas's knee a friendly pat. "Tonight is just some fun for you and me."

Lucas squinted and smiled, blissfully unaware that he'd be going home tonight with a deflowered arsehole.

Dwight knew what he was planning was every shade of wrong there was but sometimes a man had to misbehave to have himself a little fun. And after the hellish week he'd had he figured he deserved a little fun—even if it was at Lucas's expense.

The guys up in Auckland will be jealous as all hell if I show them a picture of him.

If anyone was to look at Lucas they would naturally assume he was an alpha male, and Dwight didn't doubt that the lad was. But Dwight also knew that alphas could be turned into submissive bitches by other alphas. *Survival of the strongest… or most devious as the case may be.* Like a vampire draining blood from its victims to grow its own power, Dwight's dick would siphon the masculinity out of Lucas via a dubious fuck and claim it as his own.

Blokes who had no interest in cock didn't tend to make the most enthusiastic lays for obvious reasons but that didn't mean they couldn't be forced to their knees to offer up their mouth like a substitute pussy. Once Dwight had Lucas where he wanted him it would be easy to make the boy show Dwight's cock some appreciation.

When Lucas pulled up outside his house, Dwight's phone chirped three times in quick succession, indicating a text message.. He quickly plucked his phone from his pocket, checking to see who had messaged. Lucas's arsehole must have had a guardian angel because it was a text from Blondie.

When can we meet? Missed u so much sir.

Dwight grinned, pleased to see the boy was still besotted. Obviously the whole Levi roleplay hadn't scared Blondie off like he thought it had. He cast a look at Lucas then back at his phone. As appealing as it was to see if he could seduce the hunky Lucas, Dwight opted for the reliable Blondie.

"I'm real sorry, mate, but I think I will have to postpone those work drinks," Dwight said.

Lucas's brows spiked up. "How come?"

"I've just had something come up I'd totally forgotten about." Dwight smiled apologetically, hoping Lucas wouldn't press for details. "But we'll definitely have a lads night soon, aye?"

"That'll be good," Lucas said as he hopped out of the vehicle.

"Take care, fella. I'll pick you up tomorrow morning."

Lucas waved goodbye, strolling away with an air of disappointment in his wake.

Dwight slid over to the driver's seat, started the engine again, and drove off. He only drove a few blocks before pulling over and dialling Blondie's number.

The piece of teen meat answered almost immediately. "Hello sir," he purred down the line.

"What time tonight can you meet?" Dwight asked gruffly. "The earlier the better. I need to drop a load in your arse pronto."

Blondie chuckled. "I can't tonight. I've got a family thig I have to go to."

"Can't you skip it?"

"I wish but Mum would have a fucking fit."

"For fuck sake," Dwight cursed. "I just turned away a potential root for you."

"Aw, really?"

"Don't go getting big headed. I only did it because I thought you'd be down for more fun than they were."

If Blondie was offended then he hid it perfectly with a soft laugh. "If you're that keen to tap my arse then I guess you could meet me now while I'm on my lunch break. There's a public toilet near my school we could use."

Dwight squeezed his swollen cock. That could work. He had to be at his next job soon but he figured he could squeeze in enough time for a quick fuck. "Where would we go?"

"There's some public toilets just down the road from Vercoe High. Across the road from the KFC. Do you know the ones?"

"I know the ones." Dwight wasn't remotely keen on the idea of fucking in the bogs but desperate times called for desperate measures. "Be there in fifteen minutes."

"Yes, sir." Blondie's voice then dropped to an excited whisper. "I'll be able to tell you the gossip I just heard."

"I don't give a fuck about ya gossip."

"You'll like this gossip though, sir. I promise."

"Trust me, bitch, I have no interest in any little school boy gossip. All I need from you is that faggot arse of yours bent over waiting for me to fuck it in fifteen minutes. You got it?"

A slight pause. "Yes, sir."

Hearing the teen's resentful obedience made Dwight push for more. "And I expect to find you waiting for me naked in one of the cubicles."

Another pause. "Yes, sir."

Dwight laughed down the line, a scathing mockful laugh, then he hung up.

Eighteen minutes later he strutted his way into the public toilets they'd agreed to meet at and found exactly what he'd requested: Blondie, without a stich of clothing on, hunched with his hands clutching his arse cheeks, eagerly awaiting Dwight's prick. What followed was ten minutes of selfish and brutal sodomy as he fucked Blondie against a graffiti-smeared toilet stall wall.

No words were exchanged. There didn't need to be. When a man fucked a faggot it wasn't supposed to be romantic. It wasn't lovemaking. It was grunting, sweaty, hands over mouths, rough thrusts, and deep breeding. It was about a man at his most primal. His essence. When a *real* man embraces the animal within. And that's exactly what happened in the cramped bathroom stall.

Dwight owned Blondie's boy pussy just like the tattoo said so on the boy's back, leaving the teenager with a gaping shit slit and cum dribbling down the insides of his thighs. For all intents and purposes the teen was little more than a cum urinal. When he pulled his dick out of the boy's wrecked shitter, Dwight wiped his dick clean with Blondie's briefs then casually put his dick back in his pants. Without so much as a "thanks for the nut, cunt" he gave Blondie a dismissive pat on the rump then walked away, confident he would not have any more dirty thoughts about the wrong sorts of boys ever again.

CHAPTER 24

Lucas waved goodbye to Uncle Dwight and went and let himself inside the tiny two-bedroom unit he and his young family called home. He was disappointed to not be going out for drinks with his boss this evening but that was alright. Uncle Dwight did say they could do it another time. Besides, he actually had Brad coming for a visit this afternoon and there was always the possibility that maybe Brad would be keen to go out.

As he wandered past the kitchen and into the lounge he quickly realised Sophie and Mia weren't home. Sophie did say she would take Mia out this afternoon so Lucas could hang out with Brad in peace.

"You know what Mia's like," Sophie had said. "She will be demanding your attention the whole time because she hates sharing you."

That had made Lucas smile. Mia really was a daddy's girl and was quite demanding of his attention. He never minded though. He found it more adorable than anything else. He'd said that to Sophie too.

"Trust me, babe," Sophie had replied. "Brad won't find

her whining adorable."

Lucas was beyond grateful to be back in contact with his old school friend and it had been a blast to have a night out with him the other weekend. It had been Lucas and Sophie's first night out in a very long time and he'd really enjoyed himself—other than running into Peach and Levi.

That part hadn't been so fun.

To begin with he had taken great delight in mocking Levi with a fake apology for punching the smug prick's face but that fun was short-lived when Peach started talking shit about Brad being queer. She didn't just say he was gay but that he was a Benson Banger. The one thing no one in Fitzroy wanted to be known as.

Lucas only knew what that term meant from following the Fitzroy Flyer social media pages. Benson Bangers were mocked endlessly. He hadn't yet had a chance to scroll through the pages to see Brad's name attached to the local slur but he figured he didn't have to. Peach had probably been talking shit. It's what she was best at according to Sophie.

Lucas had never really had a problem with Peach. He considered her an alright chick. She wasn't Sophie pretty but she was a cute girl with a wicked sense of humour. Half the stuff she used to say back at high school would fly over the top of his head but he would always know by the sniggers from others around him that whatever Peach's acid tongue had dished out was funny.

Sophie hated her guts though and insisted she was fake and not to be fooled by Peach's politeness. Through the years he'd run into Peach a few times while walking about in town and each time he would stop and talk. When he would come home and tell Sophie about it Sophie would always get annoyed. "You need to stop being friendly to her, Lucas. Peach isn't as nice as you think," Sophie would say. "I can guarantee you she makes fun of you behind your back."

That just seemed silly. There wasn't anything to make fun of him for. Yeah, he was poor but he still looked hot and from what he could tell looks mattered an awful lot to the Fitzroy Flyers, so surely that was enough to get him into their good books. Yet oddly he still had never received an invite to one of their parties. He was desperate to attend one too because they looked like a fucking blast.

After dropping his t-shirt in the laundry, he made his way to the bathroom and turned the shower onto cold. The room instantly echoed with the metallic ping of water hitting the shower floor. The cramped shower box really was a hunk of old shit, at least a decade older than he was.

Walking over to the mirror above the sink, Lucas turned around to inspect his back. He hissed at the sight of how sunburned he was. *Thanks a lot Uncle Dwight.* Rather than give him his t-shirt back after using it to carry the smokes, Uncle Dwight had suggested Lucas keep the shirt off to see if a show of his muscles would encourage any of their customers to give him a tip.

He had figured it was a worth a shot but sadly all flexing his muscles had earned him was the reddening skin screaming back at him in the mirror.

Fuck it all.

He pulled off his shoes and stripped out of his pants then turned to admire his face in the mirror. A minute later his sweat-sodden briefs joined the rest of his clothing in a haphazard pile on the floor so he could step inside the coffin-like shower. Being so tall, to stand "under" the spill of cool water, Lucas had to bend his knees, and when he turned, his elbows knocked all three slick walls and the door. Still, the water felt great on his sun-cooked skin.

He released a deep groan, drawing it out as he rotated

his head to stretch the tense muscles of his neck. Fetching the bar of soap, he lathered his body, getting rid of the smell of half a day's worth of hard work. He let his eyes close, lolled his head back to soak his hair.

Straightening, Lucas opened his eyes and glanced down at the beads of water trapped in the tangle of his pubes, his eyes followed the path of one stray drip snaking its way through the forest of hair before rolling its way down his soft dick. He suddenly remembered Uncle Dwight's joke about paying to look at his cock. He really hadn't appreciated that joke. It hadn't been that funny and the way it had been said was as if Uncle Dwight had sort of meant it.

But he does have a weird sense of humour, Lucas reminded himself.

Mind you, the joke about his cock didn't win the award for being the most annoying part of his day. That honour went to Dwight shooting down his idea to rob customers' homes. Lucas knew robbing people was wrong. He wasn't an idiot. But that didn't change the fact it was a good idea. There were plenty of times they mowed lawns when the owners were out and there was nearly always a window left open he could probably climb through.

It would be so easy. And no one would have to die.

A flood of misery crumpled Lucas's face. He held back the tears threatening to spill out as he thought about Sameer. Fuck he felt guilty. So fucking guilty. He knew there wasn't anything he could do to bring Sameer back but he just wished Sameer knew how bad he felt. *Honestly, man. I never meant for you to get hurt.*

Just before he was about to lose his battle against the tears, he heard loud knocking and Brad's voice calling out to him from the front door. He quickly turned the shower off and wrapped a towel around his waist to go let his friend inside.

∞

After letting Brad inside, Lucas had raced to his bedroom to chuck on a pair of shorts. He hadn't bothered with a t-shirt, preferring to let his burned back get some fresh air. Brad had surprised him by bringing a box of beer and together they sat outside on the small patio, warmed by the afternoon sun.

Lucas had considered asking Brad to help rub some sunscreen on his back for him but he figured that might be too intimate a request. Especially when he wasn't sure if Brad was into guys or not. He kept telling himself it didn't matter who Brad slept with, and that it was none of his business, but that didn't stop him from wanting to ask Brad if he was queer or not.

Catching up with Brad was like medicine for Lucas's soul. The talking of random shit really did help take his mind off things he'd rather not think about. It also had him forgetting about the whole Banger Benson drama until after an hour the conversation veered towards sex the way it usually did when young guys hung out.

"What do you think?" Brad said, showing Lucas a picture of the girl he'd been talking to on Tinder.

"She's hot, bro." Lucas took a gulp on his beer. "Not as hot as Sophie but definitely doable."

Brad grinned then turned his phone around to look at his prospective date. "Yep. Definitely doable. With any luck she'll be doing my dick this time tomorrow."

"Is that when you're meeting up?"

"Yeah. She's suggested we drive to Egmont Village for a

coffee at a café there."

"Maybe it's best to not try and sleep with her and see if she's keen for something a bit more long-term."

"Pfft." Brad rolled his eyes. "No way. I'm just on this app for fun."

"Do you meet many girls on it?" Lucas asked, as he finished his second beer and reached into the box for another.

"I've met a few." Brad put his phone back in his pocket. "It's never as many as I'd like but I get enough action to get by."

Brad wasn't a bad-looking guy, some might say he was very good-looking, so he was probably telling the truth. He'd certainly been one of the more popular guys at school when it came to having luck with girls.

"Do you just meet girls off there?" Lucas asked, his voice glitchy.

Brad laughed. "I'm hardly going on there looking for dudes, am I?"

"I don't know… that's why I asked."

Brad looked like he was torn between laughing the comment off and telling Lucas to go fuck himself. "If you've heard any rumours about me then I'd suggest you ignore them. It'll just be people talking shit."

"So you know that there is a rumour out there about you?"

Brad's eyes clouded, darkening with understanding. "I think I may have heard the rumour you are referring to."

"The one about you being a Benson banger?"

Brad guzzled down the last of his beer. "Maybe it's best I head off."

"Don't go, bro," Lucas said, unable to hide his desperation to keep his one and only friend. "I'm sorry if I've offended you. That wasn't my intention."

"Then what is your intention?"

"I'm just curious to know if it's true or not."

"I see." Brad's voice broke into a flat, dead sound. "Would it bother you if was true?" He raised a brow, opening his palm and gesturing, and Lucas realized that Brad was waiting for him to answer the question.

"I don't think so."

"You mean that?"

"Yeah, bro. I don't care about that sort of stuff." The truth was Lucas sort of did care but he was in no position to be fussy about who his mates were.

Brad's sigh of relief was so strong it actually blew his long dangling fringe. "Consider yourself in for a treat," he said. "I'm about to tell you what I haven't told anyone."

"Which is?"

"That it's true." Brad let out a humourless laugh. "You are sat here right now having a beer with a Benson Banger."

Lucas stared at Brad dazedly. "Okay," he finally managed.

"I bet you're thinking twice now about letting me stay and drink with you." Brad let out a sad little sigh. "No one seems to want me near them these days."

"Fuck them. I for one like hanging out with you."

Brad smiled. "Cheers, Lucas. I enjoy hanging out with you too."

"Seriously, bro, they're all dicks if they're not hanging out with you just because of a hook-up."

"It's my own fault. I broke one of the commandments." Brad rolled his eyes. "A flyer must never ever fool around with Wade Benson."

"It sounds like a load of crap to me," Lucas huffed.

"The truth is I used to be one the arseholes who thought the Banger Benson thing was hella funny but now

I know it isn't funny at all. It's just fucking cruel the way they cut you off like you have leprosy or some shit." Lucas had a tonne of questions but before he could ask any, Brad added, "And just so you know, I'm not actually gay."

"You're bi?"

"Not even bi."

"But why else would you do stuff with Wade?"

"It's called being pissed off your face at three in the morning."

"Really? No offense but I don't think there's enough alcohol in the world to make me suck another man's dick."

"I didn't suck his dick," Brad spat back. "And he didn't fuck me either in case you were wondering."

Lucas had been wondering that. "Then what did you actually do to become a Benson Banger?"

"He sucked me off. That's all that happened. Just dick on mouth." Brad dragged a hand through his blond locks and smirked. "I have to give the guy some credit though, he's actually pretty fucking good at it. You can tell he's sucked a lot of dick."

Lucas's gaze flicked towards Brad's crotch and he couldn't help but imagine Wade's face down there slurping all over Brad's cock.

"I was actually about to bust my nut right in his mouth when Hanna Johansen walked in on us in the bathroom," Brad continued. "I was so drunk I tried to deny it even though my pants were at my fucking ankles and Wade still had my dick in his mouth."

Lucas snorted. "Sorry. I shouldn't laugh."

"Feel free. Even I can see how funny it is now."

"What happened next?"

"That's when all hell broke loose." Brad put his hands to the side of his head and slowly pulled them away as he made the sound of something blowing up. "I was kicked out of the party and everyone started chanting *'Benson banger. Benson Banger. Benson Banger'* . Thankfully I was so hammered at the time I didn't care that much but when I woke up the next morning I thought I'd die from embarrassment. I've tried my best to tell everyone that Hanna was lying but no one believes me."

"That sucks, bro."

"Tell me about it. Even if it wasn't true no wone would believe me anyway because once Peach deems something to have happened then no one questions it."

"Peach?" Lucas furrowed his brow. "What's Peach got to do with anything?"

"She has all the power, bro. She's the one who writes the stories and covers all the events for the paper. Her word is fucking gospel in this town amongst the under thirties."

"I knew she was popular but I had no idea she had that much sway."

"Believe it. Her and Levi rule this town with a Gucci fist or whatever the fuck it is they're buying."

"I hate that faggot," Lucas muttered before realising what he had said. "No offense."

Brad laughed. "I told you. I'm not gay. I don't care if you use that word. You can call him a faggot as much as you like. I know I do."

Lucas felt so fucking good hearing Brad talk about Levi like this. They'd shared nasty stories about the rich prick the last time they'd hung out. Badmouthing Levi never failed to grow tiring.

"I hope you call him a faggot to his face when you next see him," Lucas said.

"I wish but no can do."

"Why not?"

"Even though I hate the fake fuck I have to be nice to

him if I want any shot of being let back into the flyers group. I know it's a long shot but if I can get on Levi's good side then he might be able to convince Peach to let me back in."

"But why do you want back in with a group of people you said yourself cast you out so fucking brutally?"

Brad shrugged with a lazy smile. "I dunno."

"Yeah you do otherwise you wouldn't be being nice to the dick."

After a heavy pause, Brad relented with the truth. "This is gonna sound lame as fuck but I miss feeling like a somebody, and when you're at one those Flyer parties you feel like the biggest somebody there is. I miss that. I miss that a lot."

Lucas had never been to a Flyer party but he knew what Brad meant. He missed his own days of being a somebody, days spent strutting around high school basking in the knowledge of being the best young rugby player in the region. That sort of power and adulation was addictive and he missed it terribly.

"Assuming you do get on Levi's good side what do you think the chances are of him being able to convince Peach to let you back in?" Lucas asked.

"I don't know," Brad answered. "She's never let a Benson Banger back in before but I'm hoping that because it wasn't full-on sex that she might be lenient… and there's always a first time for everything."

"I just hope that if you get back in then you don't stop coming here to hang out."

"I'll always be back, bro. You and Sophie are cool sorts." Brad's pale blue eyes lit up. "If I do manage to get back in then I'd invite you both to the parties."

"Really?" Lucas nearly squealed like a teenage girl watching Harry Styles on stage. "You could get us invites."

"Easy peasy. If you're in, you're in. A Flyer can invite whoever they like to the events. Just as long as they aren't Benson Bangers. And I think it's safe to say neither of you two have been stupid enough to hook-up with Wade."

"Fuck no. I'd rather kick a sleeping bear than let Wade near my junk."

Brad laughed. "I'll drink to that." He reached into the box of beer and cracked open another can.

"So how is it going this mission of yours to help Levi get you back in with the rest of the Flyers?"

"Hard to tell. I don't think it's worked yet but he's still a lot less cold towards me than what Peach is. She just won't listen to a word I say."

"Do you think you'll win him over?"

"I don't know. He's so hard to read. I kept wishing I had dirt on him I could use to blackmail him with. Threaten to out some of his secrets in exchange for being let back in."

"You think he has secrets?"

"For sure. We all have secrets, don't we?" Brad quirked an eyebrow. "Things we wished no one else knew. And something about Levi makes me think he's got a tonne of skeletons in his closet. He's just got that sort of vibe about him."

I doubt they'd be worse than mine, Lucas thought.

His biggest skeleton would send him to jail if anyone found out. But Brad was right; Levi probably did have a tonne of shit he wouldn't want people finding out about, and if Brad could use it to get back in with the Flyers then Lucas and Sophie could finally be welcomed into the scene they'd always been meant for.

"I might be able to help you find some of those skeletons in his closet," Lucas said.

"How?" Brad raised his eyebrows a little.

"By going through his actual closet."

Brad laughed. "Now you're talking shit, bro. How many beers have you had?"

"I'm being serious. My boss has the lawnmowing contract for the Candy family home. The next I'm there to mow the lawns I could easily have a snoop around for you."

"Would you really do that for me?"

"Fuck yeah." Lucas grinned wickedly. "I won't just go through the cunt's closet. I'll go through the entire fucking house!"

CHAPTER 25

Balancing on the rim of the bathtub in Danny's en suite, Levi hunched over and spread his butt cheeks. He scraped a finger down his crack then glanced over his shoulder, inspecting his newly smooth rear end in the bathroom mirror. He focused on the centre of his clean-shaven pucker. The skin was pink and tender, darker and rosier as it neared his hole. As he breathed, the tiny slit fluttered open and closed.

Looks pretty good.

He'd shaved his balls a number of times but this was the first time he'd ever attacked the hair lining his crack. He'd used some hair removal cream to start with before scraping away the final stubborn hairs with a razor. He wasn't looking forward to the regrowth and sporting spiky five o'clock shadow somewhere with as much friction as an arse crack. If maintaining a smooth arsehole was to become a permanent request of Danny's then Levi had already decided that he would probably have to start making appointments to get it waxed. It was an eye-watering thought.

Satisfied with his smooth crack, Levi climbed down from his perch and went downstairs to go check on the washing he'd already washed and chucked in the dryer earlier. Strolling through the house naked was nothing new but he did feel a little more rebellious today with a freshly shaved body part. He almost wished Mark would come home early from his parents and bust him walking around in the nude. Levi didn't have the body parts a straight man was interested in but that didn't make him want any less for Mark to see them.

Fetching the clean sheets from the tumble dryer, he pressed the sheets to his cheeks and inhaled the lingering scent of fabric softener. They smelled great and felt dry. He lugged them back upstairs with him, stopping off in the master bedroom to deliver Mark's t-shirt, then went and made Danny's bed.

Changing bedsheets wasn't something Levi had done since he had lived in Brixton but he wanted to show Danny he was willing to be a houseproud little bitch. He even went and stole a chocolate from his mother's box of sweets in her bedroom which he then went and put on Danny's pillow, wanting to show his stepbrother that he could be a kind and thoughtful boyfriend. The fact he was feeling guilty about spoofing into Mark's underwear may have also had something to do with it. He didn't consider what he'd done with Mark's underwear to be cheating but at the same time it didn't make for the finest start to a relationship.

Mind you, it was going to be hard to be faithful when Levi had unfinished business with Josh. They'd made plans to push their friendship into a sexual zone upon Josh's return from Bali and Levi was adamant to still let that happen. It was under the guise of letting Josh have a little control, allow him to explore a little kink with a willing cum bucket. Levi didn't care how freaky Josh wanted to get (chances were someone that vanilla wouldn't go far) just as long as he got a chance to suck the guy's beautiful dick one more time.

After the past couple weeks with Danny, Levi couldn't wait to show Josh how good he'd got at sucking cock. He knew he'd be able to gift his best mate a blowjob worth remembering. He'd flick his tongue in Josh's piss slit, suck the fucker's balls, lick his taint and lick his arsehole if Josh wanted him to. Levi's tongue wasn't afraid to go anywhere anymore.

The guilt of cheating cramped his stomach again.

Once we've moved overseas then I will commit, Levi promised himself, treating fidelity like it was something that could be timetabled.

It would be easier though once he and Danny had moved away from all the distractions and temptations. Once they were set up in an apartment in Sydney, London, or wherever the fuck it was they chose to move to, Levi knew that would be when his new life would officially begin. He wouldn't be the man about town anymore. He would be one half of an openly gay couple. *Danny and Levi.* It had a nice ring to it, he thought.

He doubted if Mark would ever feel the same way. The planets must have been aligned or something because Levi actually sympathised with his stepfather who was having kittens about his son's secret relationship. Levi still wasn't convinced Mark wasn't homophobic but he could understand why Mark would be concerned. In the blink of an eye Danny had gone from squeaky-clean, lemony-fresh virgin to a sexually active adult saying he was planning on financially supporting the *man* he loved.

And that's the part Levi had to keep focusing on. The financial support. Danny was his lifeline and only chance at staying in the lap of luxury. The alternative was too bleak to even contemplate. His mother may have been fine with sliding down the ladder a few rungs but not Levi. Fuck-to-the-no on that one. Obviously life as Danny's boyfriend would take some getting used to but no relationship was perfect, right?

Lost in a daydream about his future with Danny, Levi nearly didn't even notice that his phone was ringing. He raced into Danny's en suite where he'd left it and answered the call.

"Hello," he huffed.

"You sound out of breath, Poppet," said Peach's friendly voice. "I hope it's from doing something naughty."

Levi laughed. "If you can call changing bedsheets naughty then sure."

"I guess that depends on why you're changing the sheets," Peach teased, unaware just how close to the truth her innuendo was.

"Speaking of naughty things," Levi said, "how is the planning for the annual Flyer Ball coming along?"

"It's been exhausting. I've been here all day trying to get things organised."

"You're at the sauna right now?"

"Aha. This place is creepy as when you're on your own." She paused. "I keep worrying I'm gonna see the spirit of dead cum rise up from the drains."

Levi snickered. "I guess you are in one of the biggest sperm graveyards in the city."

"That's not the worst part. No matter how much air freshener I use the place still stinks of sex and dirty ballbags."

"I wouldn't worry about it. It'll just add to the ambience."

"Let's hope so," peach chuckled. "I was actually calling you to see if you'd like to come down and help me set up for a couple hours? I have wine…"

Levi looked from the en suite through to Danny's bedroom and stared at the bed, knowing that's where his arse was expected to be when Danny got home from school. "I would but I've actually got to run some errands. Sorry."

Peach sighed down the phone but quickly hid her annoyance with a sunny tone. "That's okay, poppet. But you better come and help me tomorrow. There is still so much to do and you know I don't want to bring in too many others in case they ruin the surprise for the guests."

"I promise I'll be there tomorrow."

"You're a doll," Peach said. She made a kissy noise like she was about to say goodbye then suddenly blurted, "Ooo. Guess who I just saw?"

"Who?"

"Josh. I was at the supermarket buying some extra wine and he was just arriving to start work."

"Josh is back?"

"Mmhmm. He said they arrived back last night. He looked tired. I told him he was silly to go straight to work like that."

"You know how much he loves work though."

"Has his dad tried calling you again?" Peach asked, sounding like the gossip columnist that she was.

"Er, no. I haven't heard from him."

"What will you do if he calls you?"

"Tell him to fuck off."

"Are you sure? He is a very handsome man, isn't he?"

"A handsome man who's an absolute creep. Not to mention the whole house fire thing."

"Of course," Peach said slowly, knowing it probably wasn't the sort of thing they should be talking about on the phone.

"Sorry, Peach, but I have to go. There's someone at the door." It was a total lie but Levi was too damn keen to go see Josh right away.

"Okay, Poppet. I'll see you tomorrow."

∞

Levi was fully dressed and out of the house in less than a minute, zooming his way to the supermarket where Josh worked. He may have got dressed faster than a dog licking clean a bowl but that didn't mean he looked sloppy. Far from it. He'd slipped into a pair of fitted jeans with the knees ripped out, a white Henley shirt with pushed-up sleeves and had styled his hair to perfection. Once again he was wilfully ignoring the fact he was in a relationship, too excited about the prospect of finally making his Josh fantasy come true.

Just thinking about Josh treating him like a cum bucket made his heart race and the backs of his knees sweat. Levi was more than fine with the idea of spreading his legs for his best mate. Fuck, he'd probably scream like he'd never screamed for any man before, including Josh's father.

The only thing that dampened his excited mood was wondering why Josh hadn't called to say he was back from his holiday. *Maybe he was tired?* Levi thought. *Then why is he at work?* That didn't make a lot of sense but Levi was sure his best mate must have had a good reason.

A distant police siren curved toward him, then away again, interrupting his thoughts. When the distraction was gone he let his mind wander back to Josh, thinking how amazing it would be to finally see him naked. Even when he'd sucked Josh off that day at Dwight's house, Josh had never taken all his clothes off so the full beauty of what lay beneath Josh's clothes was a bit of a mystery to him. Levi patted his hardening crotch as he pictured the glorious sight of a naked Josh Stephenson.

If Levi had his way then they'd fuck behind the supermarket. That's how keen he was for them to take advantage of Josh's newfound single status. Josh had text him last week from Bali to tell him he'd broken up with Jessica over the phone. To say Levi was ecstatic was an understatement. Sure, he felt a bit bad for Jessica—emphasis on *a bit*—but that paled in comparison to how flattered he had felt. He knew Josh hadn't just dumped the girl because he was tired of her, he'd broken things off so he could explore forbidden fantasies with Levi. Of that Levi was sure. Josh was old school and he had said himself he would never cheat on a partner but now that he was single there was nothing to stop him from putting his cock where he wanted.

Suck on that Dwight.

Dwight's vindictive plan of having Josh find Levi tied to the bed with Mark's underwear over his head had backfired. Dwight clearly thought that his son would freak the fuck out but that hadn't been the case at all. It turned out that father and son had more in common than just handsome faces and gorgeous seven-inch dicks. They both got off on the sight of submission. And Dwight had left Levi looking like the poster child of submission that day.

Although Levi hadn't heard from Josh for the past five days, the last few texts they'd exchanged had been pretty hot and heavy, with Josh making it quite obvious he intended to let Levi suck him off again when he returned to New Zealand. It was also safe to say that Josh probably had a lot more in mind than just oral sex. Josh seemed fascinated by the term *cum bucket*—the words Dwight had left scribbled on Levi's back—and every text he sent contained the derogatory term. Levi was confident that by the end of the week he'd be the proud recipient of Josh's bare cock in his arse.

Despite how hot the thought of Josh fucking him was, Levi knew it wouldn't be entirely easy. Whether Josh knew it or not, he wasn't asking Levi for a bit of slap and tickle role play. He was asking for Levi's complete sexual surrender. He wanted Levi to be an object that he could fuck and humiliate. And no matter how hard Levi would try to distance himself from it, the taint of allowing himself to become his best mate's *cum bucket* would always follow him. Once he'd done this there would be no changing the dynamic in their friendship. Josh would remain the king and Levi would always feel lesser than.

Yet submitting for Josh was still going to be worth it. Not only because the guy was sex on legs but because it would be the perfect *fuck you* to Dwight. Josh's father would have fucking kittens when he found out his son went queer, and he would most definitely find out at some point. Levi would make damn sure of that.

Just as he pulled into the carpark of the supermarket, Levi's phone blurted to life in his pocket. He expected to see Peach's name flash up on the screen, assuming she had forgotten to tell him something earlier, but instead it was Danny's.

What's he calling about? School isn't out for another hour.

"Hi, babe." Levi answered, trying to sound like an excited boyfriend and not the cheating scumbag he was about to become. His chest tightened with worry when he heard Danny crying on the other end. "What's wrong? Why are you crying?"

"I-I just found out that Nana Candy isn't well." Danny's voice broke into more tears.

"What's wrong with her? Has something happened?"

"She has cancer. A-And they don't know yet if it's treatable."

Levi hesitated, taken aback. "Did she just find out?"

"I think so." Danny sniffled. "Dad just come and picked me up from school."

Levi's heart squeezed. "Is he with you now? Can he hear us?"

Danny sniffed loudly, his voice calming down. "No, baby. It's safe to talk. We're actually downtown at the moment so I can grab a few things for the trip. Dad's in the car waiting."

"What trip?'

"My grandparents want me to go with them to Fiji so we can spend some time together just in case… you know."

Levi could hear the worry in Danny's voice. The kid adored his grandmother, even though she was a bitter old bitch, and Levi could only imagine how sick with worry Danny must have been. "I'm so sorry, babe. I really hope your grandmother is okay."

"Thank you, baby." It went quiet for a moment before Danny's voice returned. "My flight leaves at ten o'clock tonight so it looks like we won't be able to have our date night."

"That's a shame," Levi said, not feeling like it was at all.

"I promise to take you out as soon as I get back though. We can go to any restaurant you like. I'll make sure it's super duper romantic for you."

"That'll be… nice."

Danny barrelled right onto another topic. "I was also calling to ask for your measurements."

Levi hesitated. "Are we talking clothes and shoes or how big my dick is?"

Danny laughed. "Clothes and shoes, of course." The boy's voice dropped to a whisper. "I know exactly how big your sexy diddle is."

"Why do you want to know my shoe size and measurements?"

"Because I'm buying you some presents."

"You don't have to do that. I'd rather you save your money." Words Levi never thought he'd utter.

"But I want to get you something nice so you have something to think of me while I'm away."

"Aren't you sweet," Levi replied before rattling off his measurements.

"And baby…" Danny dropped his voice to a whisper again. "Can you be waiting naked for me on my bed? It would really cheer me up to see your sexy bottom on display so I can walk right in and start playing the *bongo drums*."

"I would love to, babe, but I'm actually at the supermarket at the moment." Levi smiled in relief. "Sorry."

"That's okay. I won't be home for at least another hour so you have plenty of time."

Levi rolled his eyes. "Okay. I'll be naked on the bed waiting for you, babe."

"You're the best, baby. See you later."

Levi felt bad for Danny about his grandmother having cancer but he wasn't impressed that he'd have to be back home within an hour, potentially cutting short a chance to reconnect with Josh in ways he wanted.

Armed with a smile, Levi walked into the supermarket unable to contain his excitement to see his best friend for the first time in over two weeks. After wandering along several of the aisles, Levi eventually found Josh working in the delicatessen. His work uniform was ghastly but he still managed to look desirable.

Approaching the counter, he flashed Josh a smile while Josh served a young mother with two noisy children in tow. Other than giving Levi the most subtle of nods, Josh kept his attention on serving his customer. He really did go above and beyond, Levi thought, going as far to give each of the woman's kids a free cocktail sausage. When the woman had finally finished getting an assortment of meats and salads, she dragged her noisy angels away, leaving Josh free to talk.

"When did you get home?" Levi asked. "You never text."

Josh gave him the side-eye and a frustrated sound escaped his lips. "We need to talk," he said ultra-seriously then walked over to one of his co-workers and told them he was going for a break.

Levi wondered if something was wrong but he decided maybe it was nerves. *He wants us to talk about having sex!* That kept the smile on Levi's face and the threat of an erection in his pants.

Rounding the corner of the delicatessen, Josh then led them outside to the carpark and down to the side of the supermarket where they could speak alone. Judging by the piles of cigarette butts scattered on the ground this must have been where the smokers came on their breaks.

"If you're wanting me to give you the blowjob right here then I have to say I think that might be being a little too ballsy," Levi said, only half-joking.

"I didn't bring you around here for a blowjob," Josh snapped. "Don't be disgusting."

Levi was taken aback. "I was only joking."

"Yeah well, I'd suggest you keep those sorts of jokes to yourself."

"What's wrong?" Levi stepped closer and touched Josh's arm. "You sound angry with me?"

Josh flicked Levi's hand away. His usually warm brown eyes turned hard and cold. "Dad told me what you did."

Dread hardened Levi's stomach, and a chill tingled across his scalp. "What exactly did he tell you?" he croaked.

"Everything, Levi. Everything."

Levi stood there like a stunned mime, waiting for Josh to blast him about Candy Boy. But what Josh said next had nothing to do with Candy Boy.

"He told me how you two were dating and how you've been cheating on him the whole time."

"He what?" Levi frowned. "Why the hell would he say that?"

"Maybe because it's true."

"But it's not. I didn't cheat on your father because we never dated. That's all crap. Utter crap."

"My dad might be many things but he isn't a liar."

"I can assure you he's lying about this."

"Why would he make something like that up?"

"Maybe because he's fucked in the head," Levi grumbled.

"The only one who is fucked in the head is you, Levi. What sort of sick individual tries to seduce someone while he's actually dating that person's father. That is seriously fucked up and gross, man. So gross." Josh visibly shivered.

Warning bells sounded off inside Levi's head, his instinct screaming at him to run away. But he couldn't run away from Josh. Not now. Not ever. They were best mates and as embarrassing as it was he knew he owed Josh the truth. "It is true that me and your dad have slept together. Twice. But it isn't true that we dated. He's making that part up and I honestly don't know why."

"If he's making that part up why then did he spend most of the holiday crying in the hotel room and telling me how much he had loved you and that you'd broken his heart."

Levi coughed out a nervous laugh.

"It's not funny, Levi. You really hurt him. He's in fucking pieces over the way you let so many men fuck you behind his back."

"Excuse me?"

"Hello? The day I found you tied to your bed. That was you cheating. And from what Dad has said it wasn't the first time."

Holy fuck! Levi didn't know whether to laugh or cry. He was being ambushed by a lie so fucking crazy it was making his head spin.

"It's no secret I've never been a fan of how you sleep around but I always told myself it was none of my business," Josh said, "but it is my busines when your promiscuity hurts someone I love."

"I'm a guy. It's normal to sleep around."

"It doesn't matter what gender you are, it doesn't make you any less of a slut." Josh glowered. "And you, Levi, are a slut. Just a dirty slut."

"Oi, don't talk to me like that."

"I can talk to you however the hell I want. You have lied to me, hurt a member of my family, and tried to drag me into some sort of twisted sexual fantasy of yours."

"No I haven't."

"You sucked my dick, bro. After sucking my dad's. You let Dad fuck you and were planning on letting me fuck you too!" Josh's Adam's apple bobbed up and down. "I-I feel like I've been raped."

"Good God, Josh. That's a bit of a fucking stretch."

"But that's how I feel. I feel like I have committed incest against my will. You wouldn't understand because you probably just get off on it."

Levi took a calming breath. "Look, I am very sorry if

you feel that way. I fully admit that I have not been a saint and I should never have tried sleeping with both of you but—"

"Damn fucking right," Josh cut him off.

"But I only ever wanted you," Levi said earnestly. "What happened with your dad was never meant to happen. It was one of those spur of the moment things. It didn't mean anything and I hope it doesn't stop you wanting us to explore things together."

"You are un-fucking-believable. You know that?" Josh dragged both hands through his hair. "Do you really think that I would consider doing anything with you after all the shit you've done? That is never fucking happening. The fact I was stupid enough to let you trick me into trying it once is bad enough."

Levi cringed. He quickly realised that trying to make sure their sex deal was still on probably wasn't the smartest move. "I'm sorry. I'm just really struggling to understand why your dad has lied to you about me."

"Dad hasn't lied," Josh snapped. "He told the truth. He's been telling the truth about you for years."

"What's that supposed to mean?"

"Dad always said you were trouble. That you couldn't be trusted and that I should stop being friends with you."

"Doesn't that tell you he's lying?" Levi pleaded. "How can he say he was in love with me when all this time he's been saying what a horrible person I am."

That tripped Josh up and made him stop and think for a moment. "Dad doesn't have to explain his heart to you," he eventually snapped, not making any fucking sense. "Just because he could see the type of person you are doesn't mean he was immune from falling for your bullshit charm."

Levi didn't want to argue but he could feel himself

getting angry. "I think you'll find that it has a lot more to do with how good I look naked rather than my bullshit charm that got your dad's dick so worked up." As soon as he saw the horrified look on Josh's face he wished he could kill the words he'd just said.

"You really have a lot of growing up to do, Levi, if you don't want to be a nasty cocksucker all your life." A sudden venom coloured the phrase, as if it had originated with someone else and Josh hoped to sicken it with repetition. "Sorry," he quickly apologised. "I shouldn't have said that. But you do need to grow up and stop using people for fun."

"I don't use people for fun."

"Yes you do. It's what you've always have. And maybe I should have said something sooner but I guess I never thought you'd pull a stunt like this on me or my family."

"Can we please just put this aside for now and maybe talk about it another time when your father is around so I can make him admit this is all nonsense?"

"No, Levi. It's done. We're done."

"What do you mean *we're done*?"

The air thinned, and the tension in Josh's lethal glare grew taut. "You and me… our friendship… it's done."

"You don't mean that." Desperation clawed its way up Levi's throat. "Say you don't mean that."

Josh's shoulders lowered, and the anger drained from his face, replaced with a look of sadness. "This isn't easy for me. You've been my best mate since we were eleven but I don't know if I can get past this sort of betrayal."

"Yes you can. I said I'm sorry."

"So you admit it now that you cheated on Dad?"

"I will say whatever it is you need me to. Whatever will keep our friendship alive. I need you, man. I've always needed you."

A thousand words clashed between them, none of them voiced. In the hideous silence that followed, Levi realised that Dwight had outsmarted him by taking a risk even ballsier than burning down a house.

Josh finally broke the quiet. "I think the best thing for now is that we stay out of each other's way. I honestly don't know if this is the end of our friendship or not but I do know I don't want you contacting me or coming to my house. If I decide we can patch things up then I will contact you but I'm telling you now, Levi, that it won't be anytime soon."

"You've got this all wrong, Josh." Levi swallowed the heartache shredding his voice. "I would never do anything to hurt you."

"Yes you would. You already have."

"But I—"

"But nothing!" Josh thundered. "I've told you I need time to think things over and I expect you to respect my wishes. Got it?"

Levi nodded, biting the inside of his cheek. He wanted to keep pushing for Josh to change his mind but he didn't want to push their friendship over the cliff of no return.

"I have to get back to work," Josh said abruptly and walked off.

Levi staggered to his car like he was spaced out, collapsing into the driver's seat. He closed his eyes and tried to compose himself but once the sobbing began, he couldn't stop. He fell into the black abyss and didn't try to climb out. Curling up in the darkness, he cried the whole way home.

CHAPTER 26

Levi sat in his car for five minutes when he arrived home, making sure his tears were dry before making his way inside. As he climbed the stairs to go to Danny's bedroom, he found himself grateful for his young boyfriend dishing out such a degrading order. He didn't want to think or feel right now and what better way to zone out than be laid naked on a bed waiting to be used.

Once inside Danny's room, he locked the door and proceeded to undress. He climbed onto the bed and waited on his hands and knees, head down and arse pointing towards the end of the bed. He lost track of how many minutes he waited but it was long enough for his knees to start to ache.

Finally, the sound of excited footfall echoed in the distance and the next thing Levi knew Danny was unlocking the bedroom door. The rustling of shopping bags accompanied his excited steps to the end of the bed where he blurted loudly, "You did it!" There was a soft thud as he dropped the bags on the floor. "You shaved your bum for me."

"I sure did." Levi wriggled his arse "Do you like it?"

"Like it? I love it." Danny stroked the smooth trench of Levi's crack. "It looks so much nicer like this."

Levi glanced over his shoulder, flashing a beguiling smile at Danny looking terribly young in his school uniform. "It will look even better with your cock in there."

"That's exactly what I was thinking," Danny replied dreamily. His eyes were heavily-lidded, mere slits, the blue depths glittering with lust.

"Go grab the lube, babe. I need you in me so fucking bad."

It took a moment for Danny to move, his gaze reluctant to leave the bald sight of Levi's hole. "Okay. I-I'll go get it," he said like a jittery robot.

While Danny went to fetch the lube, Levi gripped his arse cheeks and kept himself spread open wide for the impending invasion. Seconds later Danny was once again stood behind Levi's awaiting orifice, his breathing heavy with anticipation. The zipper of Danny's school shorts made an audible *zzzzzip* before the sound of discarded clothes hit the floor with quiet thuds. Without even looking back, Levi could sense his young boyfriend's nudity, like some sort of primal connection. Dribbles of cold and gooey lube slid down the cleft of Levi's arse and he sighed when he felt Danny rub it over his smooth entrance.

Danny slid his wet fingers inside Levi's hairless hole, slicing them in and out. Levi groaned gratefully, accepting the boy's skinny fingers. He didn't feel the usual pain. Not even a pinch. Just a tingling swirl of desire and warmth. He was so determined to get lost to pleasure that he didn't even tense.

"Wow… you're really horny." Danny's breathing was tight, bursting sharp gasps past his lips. "You're opening right up for me. So relaxed."

"Of course, babe. This arse belongs to you. It will always open up for you."

"That's right. I'm your man now," Danny said, thrusting his fingers in and out of Levi's arse.

Danny referring to himself as a man was a bit of a stretch but Levi went with it. Not to keep Danny happy but because he needed Danny to be a man right now. He needed to be fucked and loved by a controlling body that could hold onto him and protect him from the emotional storm waiting for him outside.

Danny's touch vanished. He leaned down and spit on Levi's clenching ring of muscle. Then he pressed the blunt helmet of his cock against the moisture. "I want you so much right now," he said.

"Yeah, babe." Levi breathed deeply. "I'm yours for the taking."

Danny grabbed Levi's waist with both hands and kicked his hips, tunnelling his pulsing teen cock straight in.

Levi choked on the sudden burn, but it only lasted a second. His sphincter quickly adjusted to its repeat visitor as he welcomed the dark thrilling feel of Danny's raw dick inside him.

Danny trailed a shaky hand up his spine and rubbed his back. If he was trying to be soothing, he didn't need to be. Levi was all for this. Needed it. Danny's hands roamed and teased every exposed inch of Levi's back before clutching a fistful of his hair. Using that grip, he yanked Levi up until Levi's back hit his chest.

Levi groaned in delight to feel Danny exude some alpha energy for once.

Danny wrapped a hand around Levi's chest while the other slid up the inside of Levi's thigh and grabbed hold of Levi's shaft, squeezing hard.

"Fuck me," Levi whispered hoarsely, bucking into the

cave of Danny's curled fingers. "Fuck me as hard as you can."

Danny slowly pulled his cock back then rammed forward, plunging and retreating with the speed and stamina of a machine. He held Levi tight to his body as his cock drove viciously, greedily into Levi's anus. He was fucking like a beast, untamed and wild, as he shoved himself deeper and deeper. Levi felt every ridge and bump of Danny's cock, its curved length hitting his p-spot again and again.

"Fuck yeah," Levi cried out. "Take that arse, baby."

As Danny slammed into him tirelessly, Levi reached back and palmed the flexing muscle of Danny's butt. The boy continued to thrust, seriously owning Levi's arsehole in a way he never had before. The masculine display of dominance was as appreciated as it was needed and Levi moaned, panted, and milked exquisite pleasure from the rough ride.

Levi could feel Danny's heavy balls swinging and slapping against his own. His joints soon turned to jelly and his face collapsed into the mattress, but Danny continued to hold Levi's arse in the air and thrust himself into it.

"I love you, Danny," Levi cried out of his own volition. He knew it was wrong to say but he had a desperate need to share. It wasn't the love of a lover but it was the love of someone he considered a brother. And as wrong as it was to mix the two types of love, Levi needed this right now to fight off the dark lonely feeling stabbing his bones.

Hearing such raw passion pushed Danny's sex drive into orbit. He appeared to let go of what little restraint he'd held back, thrusting harder, deeper, faster, as if trying to fuck his way into Levi's heart. "I love you too, baby," he panted. "So, so much."

Abandoning his male pride, Levi rewarded his teen

lover with a long string of high-pitched squeals and girly whimpers; the ones Danny craved so much. "Ooo Danny. Yeah…. Oooo baby."

Danny suddenly rolled to the side, taking Levi with him, and raised one of Levi's thighs. This new position allowed Danny to fuck much deeper, the side angle penetration forcing Levi's sphincter to widen and slacken even more. Half-twisted but mostly on his back, Levi was able to reach down to jerk himself off while their mouths sealed together and Danny drilled into him.

Usually it was Danny who exuded soppy passion but this time it was Levi, his mouth desperate for Danny's tongue as he mumbled "I love you" over and over into the boy's wet mouth. Danny was more than just a convenient boyfriend and lover in this moment. He was a cure. A way for Levi to find something real to hold onto when it felt like so much of his world was crumbling down around him.

Unwittingly, Danny had become entangled in a web of lies, greed, and secret desires that weaved as deeply as his young cock was buried inside Levi's churning shitter. Levi knew it wasn't fair to be using someone so young and naive as some sort of emotional anchor but right and wrong had no place in this bed. Not when he needed saving from himself.

The sensations—both physical and mental—became more and more powerful as Danny continued to fuck him in the butt. Levi's sensitive nerve endings reverberated with greater intensity at each mighty thrust until the pounding became a single, continuous thrum. The pleasure was a raging whirlwind, tossing aside his fears and biases until there was nothing but the cock filling his behind.

Levi came first, chest heaving, eyes watering, and sobbing against the crush of Danny's lips. He was still clutching his prick when Danny flooded his arse with a hot rush of semen.

After several long moments of breathless gasping, Danny pulled out with a sigh and flopped onto his back. Levi missed the stretch of him instantly. He rolled over and kissed Danny again even though the youth was breathing too hard to reciprocate properly.

"I love you," Levi whispered.

Danny nodded, too breathless to respond.

With a grin, Levi slithered his way down the bed towards Danny's softening meat. The last vestiges of the teen's load dribbled out of him in one long, tight string of white. Levi touched it with his tongue, and then—his gaze locking with Danny's—he swirled his tongue over his cockhead and closed his moist lips over Danny's dripping slit. With a slurp, he sucked the last drops of load directly out of Danny's cock and swallowed them with a smile.

Levi wriggled his way back up the bed and draped a needy arm over his exhausted young lover. "You were amazing," he said.

"So were you, baby."

"You did all the work. I just rolled with the fuck-punches."

Danny snorted. "Fuck-punches. I like that."

"I wish you didn't have to go so you could stay and give me some more."

"We still have over four hours, baby." Danny nuzzled his neck. "I think I can give you a few more fuck-punches before I have to leave."

Just as Danny said that, a knock sounded at the bedroom door. Levi's heart somersaulted. It then nearly burst through his chest when whoever was on the other side tried opening the door. *No!* Visions of Mark walking in and finding them together left Levi paralyzed in fear.

Thankfully the lock did what it was supposed to do and the door remained closed.

"Who is it?" Danny asked panickily, hurriedly jumping out of bed and tugging his briefs up his skinny legs.

"It's Kaleb."

Danny sighed like he was relieved. "Just one minute," he called back.

"Tell him to fuck off," Levi whispered hoarsely at Danny.

"It's fine. Kaleb knows about us," Danny said casually. "I told him at school today about how you and I are dating." Levi's disapproving frown did not go unnoticed. "I told you I was going to, remember?"

That was true but Levi hadn't for a second expected his blond rapist to turn up right after they'd finished fucking.

"Just slip under the covers." Danny waggled his eyebrows. "I want you to stay naked for those fuck-punches I'm gonna give you when he leaves."

Levi groaned internally but did as Danny asked, slipping his nude body under the blankets. He winced as he watched Danny stroll over to open the door in just a pair of tight black briefs. *You could try putting a little more on before letting him*, Levi grumbled to himself.

Danny unlocked the door and welcomed his one and only friend into the bedroom. Kaleb's gaze went to Levi immediately and he began to smirk. "Have I interrupted something?"

Danny sniggered. "No. We'd actually just finished."

"And by finished I'm assuming you mean sex." Kaleb sniffed loudly. "Cause that's what it smells like."

Danny burst out laughing, sounding like he had the hiccups gone wrong.

"You know, Danny, I honestly didn't believe you at first," Kaleb said, his gaze flicking between Levi and

Danny. "But I am guessing it's true. You're really dating?"

"We sure are," Danny said as he walked back to the bed and slipped in under the covers beside Levi. "I've been wanting to tell someone about us for ages but we only made it official last night."

"Congratulations." Kaleb went and sat at the foot of the bed. "I think it's really cool. You must be really happy to finally come out." He directed the last sentence to Levi.

"It's wonderful," Levi replied through a clenched jaw. He was dying of shame on the inside but he remained outwardly calm, refusing to give Kaleb the satisfaction of seeing him sweat.

"Technically we're not out yet," Danny clarified. "You're the only person we've told."

"I feel honoured." Kaleb grinned smugly. "I'm glad you two trust me enough with your secret."

Levi sat there in silence while the two boys chatted about Danny's sick grandmother and how he was flying out to Fiji tonight. He considered making an effort to get involved in the conversation but just the sight of Kaleb made his skin crawl. Every time he looked at him Levi just kept thinking about the day Dwight and Kaleb had fucked him while he was tied to his bed, taking him against his will. *Sort of.*

Levi knew it wasn't quite as simple as that but it was true that he had been duped and never intended for Danny's jock pal to put his dick inside him raw. That's what made him so ropable. That Kaleb Ladbrook had earned himself a monumental first in Levi's sex life: the first man to fill his arsehole with semen. It didn't matter how many times Danny flooded Levi's arse; Kaleb was always going to be the Neil Armstrong of Levi's anal canal.

"So when will you break the news to your parents that you're a couple?" Kaleb asked Danny.

"Levi and I have decided we will tell them after we've moved away." Danny rubbed his foot along Levi's shin beneath the blanket. "We think it would be best for everyone if there's a little distance before breaking the news. Haven't we, baby?"

Levi nodded.

"So… you're moving to Sydney together?" Kaleb asked with a frown.

"I don't know if it will be Sydney," Danny answered. "I am letting Levi choose where we move to and I'll just enrol in an institution wherever that may be."

There was a flash of filthy anger on Kaleb's dumb face that made Levi want to smile. It was almost worth being sat naked under the sheets just to see it. *That's right fucker. Danny's my gravy train now!*

"But I thought you were moving to Sydney," Kaleb said. "That you and I would head over there together?"

Danny paused, like he had only just realised his relationship had put a dampener to someone else's plans. "Oh… yeah, uh, I don't know if that will be happening now, sorry."

Kaleb's jaw twitched. "That sucks, bro. I thought you wanted to live with your best mate so we could have the time of our lives in Oz together."

"I guess Sydney is still an option," Danny said weaselly. He turned to Levi like he was asking for a safety exit from the conversation. "I don't think we have ruled it out yet, have we babe?"

Levi didn't come to his boyfriend's rescue. "I *think* it's pretty safe to say we will be ruling it out," he replied smugly. "I was thinking London or Edinburgh might be more our style. That way we can be close to Europe for some weekend trips to different countries. It's going to be so nice living somewhere it is just the two of us."

Kaleb chuckled humourlessly and said, "I've gotta say I was so surprised when Danny told me about you two. I couldn't believe you were both into guys. Especially Danny." He focused his slimy attention on Levi's boyfriend. "You always seemed so straight the way you pined after half the girls in our year."

"Not anymore. I am more than happy to have a sexy *boyfriend*." Danny said the word with pride as he not-so-discreetly slipped a hand under the sheets and groped Levi's dick. "We're the perfect couple."

"Good for you, brah. It's so cool to see you happy." Kaleb's plastic smile turned to Levi. "What about you?"

"I couldn't be happier." Levi grinned. "Obviously."

"Yeah?" Kaleb raised an eyebrow. "So Danny fucks you the way you like it does he?"

Danny laughed. "Kaleb."

"What?" Kaleb smirked back at his friend. "It's a legitimate question. I wanna know if you're fucking Levi the way he likes it?"

"Danny fucks me just fine," Levi said.

"I fuck you better than fine, don't I, baby?" Danny's hand groped him again under the covers.

"Of course, babe." Levi knew what was coming next. A kiss. A big, sloppy kiss. He turned his head to meet Danny's approaching mouth. Danny's tongue slipped past his lips and kissed him deeply. It wasn't a quick kiss either, it went on and on as Danny's frisky hand started fondling Levi's balls. It only ended when Kaleb started clapping, cheering them on.

"Sorry," Danny said with a blush. "We just can't keep our hands off each other."

"No need to apologise, brah. I'm just the same when I'm with a new girl."

"I bet you are," Levi said snidely.

"Tell me something, Levi." Kaleb's voice hung dangerously in the air like a knife about to slice. "I know you're Danny's first guy but I was just wondering who was your first?"

"Kaleb!" Danny gasped. "That's a bit rude."

"Sorry, brah. I'm just curious to know who gave Levi his first load."

Levi wanted to jump across the bed and throttle the young jock but he thought better of it.

"Kaleb!" Danny gasped again, laughing nervously. "Stop it."

"I'm not meaning to be rude it's just that someone once told me that when a gay guy gets fucked raw the first time he's always indebted to the guy who spunked inside him. That they'll always bend over for them no matter what. Even if they're dating someone else."

While Levi willed God to strike Kaleb with lightening, Danny actually made a decent joke. "I can't say I read that in the manual."

Kaleb chuckled. "No shit, brah. Someone actually told me that."

You mean Dwight told you that. Prick.

"I think you'll find whoever told you that was just teasing you, Kaleb," Danny said, falling for his friend's clueless straight boy act. "On the bright side if it is true then that means I'll always come back to you, baby," Danny added sweetly, pecking Levi on the cheek.

If Levi wasn't so furious with the company they had then he would have been smitten by how loving and affectionate Danny was being. Sure, it was quite awkward laying there naked with Danny's hand still playing with his balls but it showed him that Danny had no shame about their love.

"Levi still hasn't said who gave him his first load,"

Kaleb said, pushing his luck.

"Kaleb!" Danny gasped yet again. "Let it go already. You're being very rude."

"It's okay," Levi said, patting Danny's arm. "I don't mind answering."

"So who was it?" Kaleb raised a brow, grinning. "Who gave you that first load?"

"It wasn't anyone special," Levi replied blankly, locking gazes with his tormentor. "I can say with 100% assurance that there is no way I'd ever let them fuck me again. They had this weird bendy dick that couldn't fuck properly. Not to mention he was a total one minute man."

Danny laughed while Kaleb gave Levi a death stare.

"This guy was probably the worst fuck I have ever had," Levi continued. "If you looked up dud root in the dictionary it would probably have his photo under it. That's why I am so glad I'm with Danny. It makes such a difference to be fucked by a real man with a big, beautiful dick who knows what they're doing."

Danny's hand gripped Levi's cock, silently thanking him for the fib-filled praise.

"Maybe you weren't giving the guy much to work with," Kaleb sassed back. "You know what they say. It takes two to tango."

"That wasn't the problem," Levi said. "The guy just didn't know how to fuck. And I don't think he ever will. I think when it comes to sex you're either born with it or you're not."

Kaleb harrumphed before delivering a low blow of his own. "He still made you his *cum bucket.* That must suck knowing you can't change that."

"I'd appreciate it if you didn't talk like that to my boyfriend," Danny said sternly.

"Sorry, brah." Kaleb smiled apologetically. "I was just

joking."

Kaleb's use of the hideous name *cum bucket* hurt Levi's pride more than anything else the young jock had said and showed just how cunty the boy could be. It reminded Levi of everything that happened that wretched day and how he'd fallen from grace at the hands of a man he kept underestimating. Rather than let Kaleb feel like he'd got the final blow, Levi cast his shame aside and slipped his head under the blanket, tugging Danny's underwear down so he could suck his cock.

Danny gasped. "Oh my golly!"

"What the fuck!" Kaleb blurted. "Is he giving you a blowie?"

Danny replied with a sighing mumble. "Aha…"

Levi sucked Danny's soft meat while he breathed in the familiar, nutty scent of Danny's scrotum.

"Baby…" Danny said shakily. "We have company baby."

Levi didn't give a fuck. He kept sucking Danny's dick for all he was worth, and like the pent-up hormonal trooper Danny was his dick began to twitch and come to life again. "I love your big dick so much, babe," Levi said loudly, making sure Kaleb heard.

"What a fucking nympho," Kaleb muttered.

"I-I think you better go," Danny murmured to his friend. "I'll call you when I get back from Fiji."

CHAPTER 27

Not long after Kaleb had left they had yet another interruption. It had been Mark coming to say he and Levi's mother were leaving to Dawson Lodge. This time Levi ran and hid in the en suite while Danny spoke to his father and assured him he would be ready by eight o'clock for his grandparents to come and pick him up.

With their parents out and the house to themselves, Danny made good on his promise to give Levi some more fuck-punches. He gave him a quickie downstairs over the kitchen bench, fucked him outside against a tree in the backyard, and once more back on the bed. By the time they were finished, collapsed together in a sweaty pile of limbs on the bed, Danny was joking that his dick was broken.

"If you think that broke your dick then spare a thought for my arse," Levi joked. "You have fucked it into oblivion today."

Danny slipped a hand between Levi's legs, pushing a finger inside Levi's fucked wide-open hole. "Don't worry, baby, it isn't broken. Just very, very wet." He pressed his face into the crook of Levi's neck and quietly added, "I should probably start packing."

When he lifted to move away, Levi hugged him to stay. "Do we have time for one more round?"

"I don't think so." Danny pouted. "Sorry." He kissed Levi's lips and left the bed to go take a piss.

Levi lay on the bed, listening to the distant echo of Danny's piss splashing into the bowl. He couldn't believe how much of a yo-yo his emotions had been today. This afternoon when Danny had first called to say he was going on holiday with his grandparents Levi had been quite ecstatic, secretly looking forward to not having to fake affection with his new boyfriend. But now he was dreading Danny's departure, not wanting to be left alone with the mess Josh had made of his heart.

The loud splash of Danny's stream slowly began to fade to a trickle followed by the flush of the toilet. He strode back into the bedroom, unabashed with his nudity.

Levi looked his boyfriend up and down, examining not only the pale flesh of his dick and the low hang of his hairy balls but also tracing upwards from the bushy tangle of his pubes to his smooth belly to his chest and the sprinkles of hair sprouting around the hard tips of his nipples. Further up, he studied Danny's face, then back down, examining the whole of him, top to bottom.

"I am going to miss your dick so much, babe," Levi said, sounding like the needy bitch he was.

Danny stood above him and tugged his dick, glancing at it. "I can assure you it will miss you too."

Levi lifted onto his knees and gently kissed along the soft, warm skin of Danny's shaft.

Danny released a happy breath and twitched against his lips. "That's nice." His hand went to Levi's hair, sliding through the strands from the roots to the tips. His cock rose again, but only to a semi stiffy.

"One more round?" Levi pleaded, looking up with a slutty glance. "Please?"

Danny sniggered smugly. "What's gotten into you?"

"What do you mean?"

"You're just so horny."

"I'm always horny for you," Levi replied then gave Danny's dick a quick suck. "You know that."

Danny looked down at him, unconvinced. "I don't know… you just seem extra into me today."

"It's because we're dating," Levi lied.

"Really?" Danny sounded surprised. "Because I was worried that maybe I liked you more than you like me."

"No, babe. I can't get enough of you."

Levi went to start sucking him again but Danny used his grip on Levi's hair to pull him away from his dick. "Sorry, baby. We really don't have time." He stroked Levi's face, flickers of affection in his icy blue eyes. "Danny's dick will be back in a few weeks and it will give you as much sperm as your hungry bum wants."

No matter how hard Levi wanted to hold onto the illusion of Danny being the strong man he needed, unsexy talk like that just killed it for him. He quite gladly gave up his pursuit of one more round.

"Gosh," Danny exclaimed. "I almost forgot."

"What did you forget?"

Danny walked to the end of the bed and picked up one the shopping bags he'd brought into the room with him nearly four hours ago. "The clothes I bought for you." His cheeks pinked and he giggled. "I hope you like them."

Levi sat up, curious to see what his boyfriend had bought for him. Danny wasn't renowned for his fashion sense so whatever he'd bought was probably gonna be tragic but Levi reminded himself to be smiley and grateful regardless of whatever the lame outfit was.

"You will wear what I've bought, right?" Danny said, snapping the bag away just before Levi could grab hold.

"Of course."

"Good because I think you will look so sexy in what I chose for you."

I look sexy in whatever I put on, Levi arrogantly thought.

Danny finally handed over the bag and Levi dug inside, pulling out lacy red material. Confusion warped his face until he realised what he was holding. *You have got to be fucking kidding me!* "Why did you buy me women's underwear?" he demanded, incredulous.

"You asked me last night if I had any fantasies I wanted to try and well… this is it."

The lovey dovey vibe Levi had been feeling quickly evaporated. "Your fantasy is to make me a tranny?"

"I just want to see how sexy you look dressed up."

"As a woman?"

Danny hesitated. "Yes?"

"I'm sorry but I think you're asking a bit much." Levi stared at the red bra. "I can't put this shit on."

"But you said you'd do whatever I want," Danny hissed. "And this is what I want."

"Yeah but I never thought you'd ask me to compete in Ru Paul's fucking Drag Race."

"And I didn't want to sneak into our parents room and steal a pair of Dad's dirty undies for you to sniff but I did."

Levi gaped, taken aback by Danny's venomous comeback.

"I thought that was really gross and super weird," Danny continued, "but I never said anything. I did it because I wanted to please you and I thought you wanted to please me too. But apparently you'd rather I just fuck you while you sniff Dad's piss stains."

"There's no need to get nasty."

"Why not? It's not fair that you expect me to do dirty things you like but wont do the same for me."

Levi didn't want to put the bra on but he didn't want a fight either. Not when he so badly needed Danny's love to replace the loss of Josh's. He looked at Danny's sour gaze then at the lacy garment dangling from his fingers. "I guess it won't hurt to try it on."

"Forget it," Danny huffed. "I know you don't want to."

"No, babe. I-I want to." Levi smiled. "I wanna make you happy."

There was a tense silence before Danny finally smiled and said, "It would make me happy… very happy. You don't have to put it all on right now… just what you feel comfortable with."

Levi studied the bra a bit more closely. "A 36c." He waggled his eyebrows. "My favourite size."

Danny snorted. "I'll turn around and let you get changed."

"I don't care if you watch me."

"I'm trying to be a gentleman," Danny said teasingly before turning around.

Levi climbed down off the bed and emptied the contents of the bag onto the mattress, shocked to see there was more to the gender illusion than just a bra and panties. Aside from more panties and bras, there were thigh-high stockings with a matching garter belt, a makeup kit *and* a blond wig!

Fucking hell, Danny. You really went all out on this.

He'd taken plenty of bras off in his time but this would only be Levi's second time wearing one; the one and only other time was when he'd been goofing about in front of Sophie one morning and had put her underwear on. That hadn't been so bad because it had just been for a laugh. But this time wasn't a joke. Not to Danny at least.

He strapped the bra across his chest and hooked the metal clasps together in front and spun them to his back. When he strung his arms through the straps, the bra cups enveloped his flesh like friendly hands. Levi then slid the matching red panties up his legs, adjusting the lacey material so that it contained his cock and balls.

He decided against going all the way and donning the stockings and garter belt but he did swallow his pride and put on the wig. "I'm ready," he reluctantly mumbled.

Danny turned around slowly, his face erupting with a smile. "Wowza!"

"Is that a good wowza or a bad wowza?"

"It's definitely a good wowza. A *really* good wowza."

Personally, Levi thought he looked like a rough Britney Spears impersonator in desperate need of a leg wax, but Danny must have liked it because his cock inflated to its full size quicker than an emergency life raft. He stepped towards Levi and began groping Levi's non-existent tits and the crotch of his panties.

"You look so sexy like this," Danny whispered, stroking the shoulder-length wig. "And you really suit being a blonde, baby."

"Maybe I'll have to dye my hair for you," Levi said flirtatiously, not really being serious though.

"You don't have to do that. Just wear the wig." The way Danny said that made Levi worry that the wig might be making numerous appearances. "I would have liked you to put the stockings on too but that can wait till I get back."

For someone who had insisted they didn't have enough time for one more round, Danny sure as shit took his time touching and ogling Levi's pantie-clad body. "Bend over the bed," he ordered. "Hurry."

"But I didn't think you had time for—"

Levi's voice trailed off when Danny suddenly pushed

him towards the bed and bent him over the mattress, ripping the panties down until they snagged at Levi's knees. The impatient teen wasted no time ramming his cock inside Levi's arse, using one savage thrust to fully embed himself in Levi's arsehole. The lack of lube or spit meant it should have hurt more but the copious amounts of ball juice already in his channel seemed to double as lubricant.

While Danny fucked and puffed, he reached around groping Levi's cleavage. "I love your titties, baby" he said. "Such nice little titties."

Levi's mouth dangled open in silent horror. He was fucking mortified. He wasn't just being fucked; he was being taken as a girl!

"Make those noises I like." Danny's voice was choked and urgent. "Quick. I need to hear those noises."

An almighty slap suddenly stung Levi's backside. He flinched, clenching his fists from the hurt as tendrils of heat spread to his groin. *Oh my God!* He couldn't believe how hard Danny had just spanked him.

"Hurry up. I need the noises." Danny punctuated his command with another two stinging smacks to Levi's arse cheek. "Do it."

"Oooh," Levi cried out, wailing in the feminine tone Danny desired.

"Yeah. That's it." Another smack. "Louder. More. More. More."

"Oooh. Oooh. Danny. Oooh."

"Yeah, baby. Show me how much you like being my girl." This time Danny followed up his breathy command by spitting on Levi's back and rubbing the saliva into his skin. "Your Danny's dirty little girl, aren't you?"

Levi tried focusing on the ruthless streak Danny was exhibiting, wishing his kid brother had been like this before wigs and panties had come into the picture. "Fuck me.

Ooh. Yeah… Danny."

"Shit," Danny suddenly gasped, his hips jerked violently and he let out a deep groan as his cock ejaculated a fresh batch of swimmers to soak into Levi's pummelled anal tissue.

They groaned in unison as he retrieved his spent dick. "Thank you," Danny whispered. "Thank you. Thank you. Thank you." He kissed Levi on the shoulder then slowly dragged his tongue down Levi's spine, going lower and lower until he stuck his tongue where it had never gone before; Levi's butt crack. He parted the flesh of Levi's buttocks and licked up and down his crack, dabbing the wet opening he'd just filled with his spunk. The rimming was very brief, barely a tongue flick, but it was still a big deal, Levi thought.

"I've never done that before," Danny said matter-of-factly. "Licked a pussy."

"You know I don't have a pussy, right?" Levi whispered shakily.

"You do when you're dressed like this." Danny kissed him on the bum then very caringly pulled the panties back up. "You have a sexy little shaved pussy."

Despite the rough kink and unforgiving humiliation Levi had endured with Dwight, he found Danny's use of the word pussy much more emasculating. It was the way he said it, like he almost believed he'd just licked a vagina.

"Stay like that," Danny said. He walked to the other side of the bed and picked up his phone. "I want to get some pictures to take with me for my holiday."

"Are you sure that's a good—"

"Stay still," Danny ordered rudely, startling Levi into squinting silence. His phone began *clicking* as it took close-ups of Levi's fucked orifice. "Squeeze some out," he whispered excitedly, his breath ghosting over Levi's hole.

Levi found the request a particularly humiliating one but he gave Danny what he wanted, pushing like he was going for a shit to release a flood of trapped sperm.

Click. Click. Click. Danny snapped away, capturing his swimmers exiting the hole he'd pounded so thoroughly for the past four hours.

"You can turn around now," Danny said. Levi slowly unfurled his body and turned around to find Danny smirking at him. "I can't wait to get back so we can do that again." He brushed a strand of blond hair away from Levi's face. "You liked it too, didn't you?"

Levi nodded brokenly.

"I knew you would." Danny placed his hands to Levi's hips then stroked one of his thighs, scratching the hair. "You should shave your legs while I'm away. And your armpits."

"Why do you want me to shave my legs and pits?"

"So they're as girly and sexy as your bottom is," Danny said. "This is how we will work best. Me as the man. And you as the girl."

"But I'm not a girl, Danny. I'm also a man."

"I know, baby. And I'm okay with that, I really am, but I think if we want to last the distance then I am going to need you to do this for me." Danny's voice had an edge of nervousness to it, like he was worried Levi might say no but that didn't change the fact he had the audacity to say what he'd just said. "I love you, baby, and I know you love me too." He chuckled softly as one of his hands snaked between them and palmed Levi's pantie-clad crotch, kneading his dick. "You haven't been able to stop telling me all day how in love you are and how amazing I am."

Levi couldn't think of a response because he was too embarrassed.

Danny's hand climbed its way to Levi's bra, squeezing

his non-existent breasts. "When people love each other they way we do then they make sacrifices for the other person. Don't you think?" He sounded so much like his know-it-all father right now that it drove Levi insane but Levi didn't have the strength to disagree. "I will always look after you, baby. Always. But I need you to look after me too."

Despite his overwhelming hesitance to rid himself of body hair, Levi was wooed by Danny's promise to look after him. "I'll look after you, Danny."

"So does that mean when I get back from this trip I can expect these hairy drumsticks of yours nice and smooth?"

"Yeah, babe." Levi forced out a begrudging smile. "And my armpits."

"You're such a good boyfriend, baby." Danny latched his mouth to Levi's neck, sucking his thanks into the skin. "And a very sexy girlfriend in private."

In private. A phrase that made Levi shudder. The last time he'd been asked to express love "in private" set off a chain of events that had nearly cost him his life. It was a large part of the reason he was the way he was today, and it pained him to think he had gone full circle and was once again on the edge of becoming the one thing he hated most—another man's whore.

CHAPTER 28

Levi didn't often think back to the dark days. What was the point? They were done with now. He considered himself one of the lucky ones really. There were other boys and young men who weren't around to share their experiences with Barry Buttwell.

He knew those days had shaped who he was a person but he was okay with that. There was always good with the bad. It had taught him to be strong and to not run away from fear. It was probably the only reason he was able to even function right now when so much wasn't going his way. *Thanks, Dad. You evil fat fuck.*

What Levi wasn't thankful for though was how he sometimes wondered if he had inherited his father's darkness. That's what Shay had said to him the day Levi had invited him to the house with the intention of paying him for sex. That had hurt like a knife slicing his heart into little pieces. Shay had since apologised but it didn't mean what Shay had originally said wasn't true.

Barry Buttwell had enjoyed the thrill of power and treating his victims like worthless objects. Levi knew he was guilty of very similar things. He had never spilled anyone's blood but he had certainly enjoyed slaughtering the pride of the men he had paid for sex.

What no one realised though was why he did it. Why he felt the need to inflict a price tag on others… it was so he could try and forget his own.

Seven years earlier

Levi lay naked and shivering on his parents' bed. He'd been laying like this for the past three hours, only allowed to leave the room once so he could take a piss. During those three hours he'd had four different men come into the room and have fun with him the way his father did on their undie party movie nights.

He couldn't believe he'd let his father talk him into doing this but his father had insisted it would be a lot of fun. It hadn't been. It had been quite horrible really. But it seemed to make his father happy and that's all Levi wanted.

Each man that entered the bedroom would walk over and stand above him, admiring Levi's naked body like it was an all-you-can-eat buffet. Levi would blush from embarrassment, especially when they made comments about his body to his father who was sat in the corner of the room nursing a bottle of beer in one hand and his iPhone in the other—the one Levi's mother didn't even know her husband owned.

Each of the four men were very different: old, young, fat, thin, rough, wealthy. They were so different to each other Levi wondered how his father knew each of them.

"Remarkable. Just so beautiful," the first man had said, sounding like he was watching the sun set. He must have been in his late thirties or early forties; tall and skinny like an elongated toothpick with a receding hairline and friendly eyes. "Is he really yours?"

"Sure is," Levi's father replied proudly. "That's my boy."

"Had I known you made such good-looking kids, Baz, I would have got you to get my missus up the duff years ago."

Levi's father had laughed before issuing a warning to their guest. "Remember what I told you. Keep the fun external. We don't want no accidents."

"Yeah, Baz," the man had replied, nodding. "All external." He looked down at Levi like a cat eyeing a mouse. "Don't worry, kiddo. You're so fucking pretty that this shouldn't take too long."

And it hadn't. Within a few minutes he'd rubbed himself to climax all over Levi's belly, leaving streaks of sticky white puddles.

The next three men followed a pretty similar formula. Hungry eyes with fast-firing guns that resulted in pools of white dribbles on different parts of Levi's body. While Levi suffered through the sweaty grunts and foul breath of each man, his father had sat quite happily in the corner drinking his beers while he recorded videos of each ordeal. There was about a thirty-minute gap between each man leaving and the next one arriving. Now with number four—an effeminate young man with long fingernails and a ponytail—pulling his pants up and getting ready to leave, Levi was hoping this was it.

Levi's father rose to his wobbly feet and followed number four out of the bedroom, leaving Levi alone to dry up the wetness the man had sprayed all over his privates. About ten minutes later his father let rip a drunken yell telling him to come and join him in the lounge.

Levi pulled his loose boxers on then staggered in a daze towards the lounge where he found his father sat at the couch having another beer. "Did you have fun tonight, son?"

Levi nodded despite not enjoying it at all. It didn't matter that some of the men had made him cum. It just felt gross knowing they were strangers to him.

"That's good. My friends all really liked you."

"They all seemed really nice, Daddy," Levi lied.

His father lifted his butt off the couch and reached into his back pocket before sitting back down again. In his hand was a sizable stack of cash. "I better pay you your share."

Levi looked at him, mute. Confused.

"We had a very good night you and me," his father said as he counted the cash. "Benny said he'd pay more next time if you didn't wriggle so much. He prefers it when the boys are perfectly still." His father glared, scrutinizing Levi up and down with a mild scowl. "It's important to give customers what they want."

Levi furrowed his brow, unsure what was happening as he watched his father count out the notes onto the coffee table.

"Your share." His father extended his hand toward Levi, holding out some notes. Levi hesitated. "Go on, son, take it," he urged. "You certainly earned it." Levi looked at his father, uncomprehending. He blinked. His father nodded toward the money, encouraging him with a smile.

Levi reached out tentatively and accepted it.

"That's a good boy," his father said approvingly.

Levi peeked at his hand. Three $20 bills. That had to put the stack his father still had well into the hundreds. "I don't understand," he said with growing dismay.

"Come on, Levi, you're not that daft," his father said in a placating tone.

The penny finally dropped. "Did your friends pay money to have sex with me?"

"They sure did." His father grinned excitedly. "Congratulations, son, you're a whore. Literally. A prostitute. You just had sex with men in exchange for money." Levi's blood went cold. "Four men," his father added smugly.

Levi didn't know what to say. He looked at his drunk father, dumbfounded, then at the bills in his hand. "But I don't want to be a whore," he finally managed.

"It's too late for that, son. What's done is done."

"But I only let them do stuff to me to make you happy. I thought that's what you wanted."

"It is what I wanted," his father said. "I want to keep buying you nice things but to be able to do that I need you to help me pay for some of it. This is one way to do that."

Minutes passed. Levi counted the number of sips his father had on his beer before either of them spoke. He was up to seven before he decided to be the one to break the silence.

"They weren't your friends were they," Levi whispered. "Those men who came here."

"Not really. I guess they're what you would call associates."

"I feel really gross, Daddy. I-I feel dirty and…" Levi's words nearly got lost to tears.

"Oh, relax," his father said, his tone soothing. "It's not a big deal. Lots of people do this sort of thing. Besides, you'll have to get used to it because each of them have asked to come back for another session."

"You want me to do this again?"

"You made us six hundred dollars tonight, Levi. That's not to be sneezed at. You could make a lot more when you're ready to let them stick it in you." His father saw the horrified look on his face. "Don't worry about that for now though, son. I won't let them fuck you until Daddy's given you a few practise rounds to make sure your arse is up for it." He reached over and rubbed Levi's knee.

This is wrong! This has always been wrong!

A short while later Levi lay in his own bed, thinking about all that had happened to him that night. He thought about the ways each of the men had used his body like he wasn't even there. The way they wiped their dicks clean on him like he was a rag. He'd felt worthless. But he wasn't worthless. He was worth six hundred dollars apparently. But that didn't make it any better. Actually, it just made it worse. Now until the day he died he'd walk around with a price tag attached to his body. No one else would be able to see it but that didn't mean he wouldn't know it was there. Something about knowing that made him feel dirty on the inside, places no soap and water could ever get clean.

Something had been stolen from him but he didn't know what it was. What he did know though was that whatever had taken its place was cold and broken. He rolled over and looked at his wardrobe, blurred by the tears in his eyes. He began thinking of the nights when Lucky and the others would drift out of the shadowy wardrobe, pacing around his bedroom like they were lost. A frightening chill ran down his spine as he remembered all the warnings the sticker-covered fiend had given him. Lucky hadn't been wrong. Levi had been. His *daddy* didn't love him. He was using him.

There was only one person he could talk to and ask for help.

The only true hero he knew.

His rebel with a heart of gold.

CHAPTER 29

"Oh, yeah," Doctor Harten moaned. "You can take the whole fucking thing, can't you, you little slut."

Lying face down, Shay squirmed against the bed as Doctor Harten impaled him on his cock, hammering away at Shay's hole until his dick was sloppy with sweat and juice from Shay's violated arse.

Doctor Harten's cock wasn't the biggest but his sexual stamina was proving legendary. He'd been pummelling Shay's hole for the last forty minutes, practically nonstop. The curly-haired nonce had promised to give it to him rough and that's exactly what he was doing.

Shay had already learned during his time at The Castle that appearances could be deceiving and that saying definitely applied to Dr Harten. The man usually carried himself in a professional manner from his pompous accent, gold wristwatch, right down to his shiny leather shoes. Sure, he had an undercurrent of creep about him but it had never given Shay the slightest inclination that the guy could fuck like a monster once his clothes came off.

"You take it so fucking sweet, Pinky. So sweet." Dr

Harten dragged his cock back so just the tip lay inside Shay's hole. "No wonder you get booked so much."

Shay involuntarily scrambled forward as if to escape, but Dr Harten must've been expecting it because he wrapped his fist into a hank of Shay's hair, holding him still as he sank inside with no mercy, burying himself balls-deep, the rough ends of his sweaty pubes prickling and poking and tormenting Shay's arse cheeks. Shay breathed through the penetration, the dull tug of Dr Harten's hand in his wavy locks, his neck stretched as if for sacrifice.

"On your back, slut," the doctor ordered, pulling his dick out of Shay's arse. "Chop, chop."

Shay rolled over, panting. He raised his legs, feet dangling in the air.

Doctor Harten grabbed Shay by the ankles and licked the sole of his left foot before giving it a bite that made Shay squawk. Part pain, part fright. His tongue then slithered between each of Shay's toes, licking and sucking each one as he made his way from Shay's big toe to his little toe.

The footsy love felt good. Felt real good. It was one of the few things Shay usually always enjoyed with his clients. Most of them found their way to his feet, slobbering over them while they told him how beautiful they were. He'd never thought of himself, or men in general for that matter, as having attractive feet but he'd now learned that some men did have nice feet, including himself.

Dr Harten's mouth moved to Shay's other foot, gifting that one too a kiss, a bite, and each toe a thorough suck. He then dragged Shay back onto his cock, skewering him balls-deep once more.

Shay's eyes rolled back from the almighty thrust, letting out a deep, long moan. "Fuck, you're brutal," he murmured.

"It's what you wanted." Dr Harten sniggered. "Sluts like you love it."

"Oh fuck." Shay winced and closed his eyes as the doctor started long-dicking him.

"You fucking love it. Don't pretend you don't."

Shay didn't love it. But he didn't hate it either. He'd been fucked in the arse enough times by now to handle brutal buggery from a chubby six-inch cock like the one Dr Harten was working with. He opened his eyes and said, "I'll love it more if you take the cage off."

Dr Harten laughed, slowing his fuck down. "Don't worry, Pinky. It will come off. Just as soon as I have cum."

Shay felt his prisoner of a dick twitch in hope. Freedom was coming.

Leaning forward, Dr Harten pressed their foreheads like they were about to kiss. But just as the doctor's lips brushed against Shay's they quickly whipped away again.

Shay gazed up at the man's sweat-covered face. "So we're not kissing then?"

"I want to but I don't kiss whores. Sorry."

Fucker. Shay hadn't even wanted the kiss but to hear that made him feel so tiny and insignificant.

"But you can kiss this," Dr Harten said. He grabbed the back of Shay's head in his hand, pulling Shay's face towards his body and smothering Shay's face in his wet pit.

Shay struggled to breathe, only able to swallow the man's scent, his sweat.

"Lick it," Dr Harten barked. "Lick it clean."

Suppressing his revulsion, Shay stuck his tongue out and licked the damp hair, tasting the funky sweat. He could feel it run down his throat. The damp hairs brushing against his lips, his cheeks, his chin.

Dr Harten finally grabbed him by the hair and pulled his face away from his armpit. Shay ran a finger along his own cheek and sniffed it. His face now smelled like him.

The fuck resumed at full force, Dr Harten giving Shay everything he had, like he was on a personal mission to prove how manly he was in the sack.

To make it more enjoyable for himself, Shay imagined it was Kane who was fucking him. It worked so well that he began to feel his cock struggle to break free of its cage, his balls tingling with very real pleasure at the thought of the tatted-up bad boy ravishing him wickedly. *It's official. I have a crush. A big, stupid old crush.* He got so wrapped up in his Kane fantasy that without thinking he whispered, "Kiss me, bro. Kiss me on the lips."

The fantasy broke into a thousand little pieces when he heard Dr Harten laugh. Shay opened his eyes, blushing.

"I told you, Pinky, I don't kiss whores." Dr Harten smiled and gave Shay a peck on the lips. "Not the kind of kiss you're asking for."

"Sorry I was, um…"

"Don't worry. I know what you're doing. You're trying to make me hurry up."

"Yeah." *Let's go with that.*

"If you want me to cum then I am going to need to you to get up and lean over the end of the bed." Dr Harten lifted up and unglued their sweaty chests as he withdrew his meat from Shay's well-fucked channel.

Shay rolled off the bed, glad to know the end was in sight. He walked around and stood at the end of the bed then leaned forward, presenting his arse for its final round of sodomy.

"It's time for my signature move," Dr Harten said as he pushed the tip of his back in. "Are you ready?"

"What's your signature move?"

"Pissing in a slut's arse."

Shay balked. "You better be fucking joking, bro."

Dr Harten chuckled arrogantly. "No. Consider it my calling card."

Oh fuck, Shay moaned silently. He'd never had this done to him before, or tried it on anyone else, but he knew that if he wanted his dick unlocked then he'd have to take it.

Dr Harten remained stock still, locked in position, clearly concentrating hard. Shay knew it wasn't the easiest trick, pissing with a full hardon, but most men could do it. He soon found out Dr Harten had no problem when the man let out a long gasping sigh.

"Here we go, Pinky. I hope your thirsty."

Shay couldn't feel much at first, except humiliated, which Dr Harten was probably enjoying. Then he felt the pressure growing in his guts, a strange sense of getting filled up from the inside, not unpleasant, but not particular enjoyable, just strange. He soon heard a satisfied grunt as Dr Harten announced he'd satisfactorily emptied his bladder. Shay felt brimming with it, and the man's excess piss was already escaping his arse, which he felt in warm streams down the insides of his legs.

Without warning, Dr Harten buried his cock completely into Shay's brimming rear, sending more of his piss to escape down Shay's thighs. He started fucking as violently as he had all evening, apparently getting off on dicking a hole filled with his own piss.

The ring-stretching lunges brought a new stinging to Shay's arsehole which was stretched wide once again to accommodate Dr Harten's above average girth. But what Shay noticed most was the internal squelching of liquid churning inside him. He could feel it sloshing about up his arse, and leaking out down the insides of his thighs from the fleshy intrusion.

Slap. Slap. Slap. Dr Harten's stomach smacked against Shay's lower back, his piss-drained cock digging deep, swimming in his own mess. He stopped thrusting and started grinding, his hands clawing at Shay's chest.

"Gimme that hot load," Shay whispered, encouraging the fucker to get it over with. "Fill my arse with your cum."

Dr Harten moaned, low in his throat, and at last, at fucking last his chubby cock swelled inside Shay's anus, spewing his poison deep inside. He grunted again, grinding some more, then pulled out of Shay's overflowing hole. He rested his perspiring chest on Shay's back, panting heavily. "Wait right there," he whispered in Shay's ear.

Shay didn't dare move, not because he was frightened of disobeying but because he was worried about dropping his liquid cargo.

Dr Harten went into the lounge adjoining the bedroom, returning with a set of keys. He sank down on one knee like he was about to propose then proceeded to unlock the chastity cage, carefully unhooking Shay's cock and balls from their prison.

"Thank you so much," Shay said feverishly, touching his junk. "Fuck that feels so good. It's like my balls can finally breathe again."

Dr Harten rose to his feet. "Before you get too excited would you mind taking your leaky hole to the toilet, please." He grimaced at the mess on the floor. "I don't need you making any more of a mess than you already have."

It's not like I pissed in my own arse you fucking idiot. Shay kept the bitter thought to himself. He contracted his stomach and stumbled bowlegged towards the bathroom and plonked himself down on the toilet. One push was all it took for a torrent of piss and fuck knows what else to splash out and make the bathroom sound like Niagara Falls.

Seconds later, his hand reached between his legs and

grabbed his neglected cock. He didn't even leave the toilet seat, just sat there and beat off until he howled and his dick blasted milky jizz all over his stomach. His climax was not joyful, though; instead, each spurt of jizz burned like molten magma erupting from a dormant volcano, and his howls were agony, not ecstasy.

"Holy fuck," he sighed, running a hand through the streaks of dampness on his bare torso. "I fucking needed that." Despite the hurt, he could feel the relief in his balls instantly. He inhaled and exhaled, trying to slow his breathing.

He waited a few minutes then started playing with himself again, determined to rub out a couple more loads before Dr Harten locked him back up. Even though he'd only just cum, his dick was keen for another round already and he soon found himself gasping on the toilet seat as his toes curled and his cock shot out more imprisoned sperm.

"That one felt better," he said to himself as he sprawled back—sated and messy—like the toilet was a La-Z-Boy boy armchair. He gave little Shay a few more minutes recovery time before trying his luck for a third load.

Knock. Knock.

"Pinky…"

"Yeah," Shay panted, mindless and horny and chasing his third orgasm with faster strokes. "What do you want?"

"Are you going to come out?"

"Yeah, bro." Shay winced, tugging harder. "Just… Just a minute."

Dr Harten chuckled from behind the door. "I'm not putting you back in chastity right away so you don't have to play with it until it bleeds."

Shay let go of his dick. "You're not?"

The door slowly opened and Dr Harten poked his head inside. "No. I was going to leave you out of it for a couple hours at least."

"Really?"

"Yes. Really." Dr Harten smiled. "I may even let you keep it off all night if you agree to spend the night with me."

"You mean sleep in bed with you?"

"Yes, Pinky. That's what I mean."

"Does that mean you'll fuck me again?"

"It most certainly does." Dr Harten stepped inside, his naked body glistening with sweat. "Several times I imagine."

Shay paused. "And will you piss in my arse again?"

"I think you know the answer to that." Dr Harten walked over to the shower and turned it on. "If I fuck you, I piss in you. That's how it works."

"I was thinking that might be the case."

"So what will it be?" Dr Harten put his hand under the spray of the shower, checking the temperature. "Are you man enough to take some more, or have I scarred you for life with that little kink of mine?"

"Nar, bro." Shay shot Dr Harten a lopsided grin. "I guess it wasn't that bad."

"So is that a yes to staying over?"

"Let's just say you better start drinking some more wine, Doc." Shay reached between his legs, tugging on his balls. "You'll need a full bladder to keep up with me tonight."

Dr Harten laughed. "I'm glad to hear that. Now come join me in the shower so we can get cleaned up before round two."

Flushing away the remnants of Dr Harten's piss and fuck juices, Shay went and joined his arse fucker under the warm spray of the shower. They kept their hands to themselves, saying very little, only touching when exchanging the bar of soap. When they'd washed themselves clean, and drained the shower of all its hot water, they climbed out and Shay was surprised when Dr Harten told him to put his clothes back on so they could go to Dave's apartment.

"Why are we going there?"

"For the other part of our deal, of course."

Shay shrugged. "What was the other part of our deal?"

"You wanted to know why Brayden is Dave's favourite, right?" Dr Harten gave him a somewhat pinched look. "That's what I'm about to show you."

Shay was only mildly curious to know the answer to that but he nodded enthusiastically. "Coolies. This should be interesting."

Dr Harten was staying in the guest room which was on the same floor as Dave and Sione's apartments so it was a short walk down the hallway to Dave's superior suite. Shay had only been in here a couple times before and not past the guest lounge that the door opened into.

Dr Harten used his swipe key to let them in then flicked on the lights. The guest lounge looked just how Shay remembered. Very formal and uninviting. It looked like the sort of place someone would do business more than anything, which may have been close to the truth.

"Follow me," Dr Harten said.

From the guest lounge they walked through to what was like a circular hallway. Shay didn't know what else to call it. Just a large space with different doors that came off of it. Dr Harten turned to the left and flicked on the light in the next room and Shay saw that they were now in a kitchen and living area that was much more homely. There were comfy couches, beanbags, a lime green fridge. On the floor in front of the television set were Xbox games scattered on the ground, no doubt left out from Brayden's visit the night before.

Dr Harten nodded towards a wall where a bookshelf was. "*That* is why Brayden is Dave's favourite. And why I know they don't sleep together."

Shay's gaze followed Dr Harten's nod and he saw that dotted along the shelves of the bookcase were numerous photos of Brayden. Pictures of him at different ages. "Why the fuck does Dave have so many pictures of Brayden?"

Dr Harten snickered. "Take a closer look."

Shay stepped forward and studied the pictures more closely. "What the…" The photos weren't of Brayden but the blond boy in them could have been his doppelganger: cute, slim, cocky smile. "Who is that?"

"That's Dave's son."

"Dave has a son?" Shay couldn't believe it.

"*Had*," Dr Harten corrected. "He passed away quite a long time ago now."

"How did he die?"

Dr Harten shrugged. "Dave has never said but going by the stories I have been told, and judging by the photos on the other shelf, my money is on a drug overdose."

Shay lowered his gaze to the shelf Dr Harten was referring to. In these pictures the boy looked a lot less like Brayden. He also looked like a hardcore addict with a rake thin body, scabby face and rotted yellow teeth. "I think you could be right about him being a druggy."

"I think so."

Shay's breath caught in his throat when he saw the final disturbing picture. Dave's son had his blond hair all spiked up like a punk, oozing a menacing energy that didn't look just for show. He was naked, his hands covering his crotch as he laughed and smiled his jagged teeth at the camera. But that wasn't what made Shay's blood turn colder than a corpse in the morgue. It was the colourful stickers covering the young man's naked body head to toe, a description once told to him by a sad and scared little Levi who had said he had monsters living in his closet. "What was his name?" Shay croaked.

"His name was Jason," Dr Harten said and Shay let out a sigh of relief. "But I gather everyone called him Lucky."

The iciness immediately returned to Shay's veins as a ghostly chill tapped his spine.

He wasn't just staring at a picture of Dave's son; he was looking into the black-hearted eyes of what had once been a young child's boogey man. Quite frankly, it was absolutely terrifying.

Shay's heart bled for his little prince. It also bled for himself.

To be continued…

ABOUT THE AUTHOR

Zane lives in New Zealand in an old seaside cottage with his gaming-obsessed flatmate and a demanding cat. He is a fan of ghost stories, road trips, and nights out that usually lead to his head hanging in a bucket the next morning.

He enjoys creating characters who have flaws, crazy thoughts and a tendency to make bad decisions. His stories are steamy, unpredictable and tend to explore the darker edge of desire.

Printed in Great Britain
by Amazon